"A masterful blend of wonderful writing and black comedy. . . . Thoroughly enjoyable. David Ferrell is a terrific writer."

—MILES CORWIN, AUTHOR OF *THE KILLING SEASON*

"David Ferrell has written a comic tour de force peopled with unforgettable characters—among them a budding superstar whose on-the-field exploits rival Babe Ruth's . . . and whose off-the-field proclivities rival Jeffrey Dahmer's. This is a novel at once grotesque and hilarious, a bizarre tale that simultaneously celebrates the joy of athletic competition and satirizes the greedy, egocentric, win-at-all-cost ethos of contemporary sports."

—DAVID SHAW, PULITZER PRIZE–WINNING MEDIA CRITIC AND COAUTHOR OF *WILT: JUST LIKE ANY OTHER 7-FOOT BLACK MILLIONAIRE WHO LIVES NEXT DOOR*

"David Ferrell's novel is a smash hit! I loved it. The idea of combining the aspirations of a baseball team with the horrors of a serial killer is so unique and American that the concept alone deserves a niche in modern mythology. That Ferrell carries it off with such skill in *Screwball* kept me reading even on a trip to Paris, where reading should not be one's major activity. You can feel the torment of people torn between saving a life and winning a pennant. Witty and insightful!"

—AL MARTINEZ, AUTHOR OF *THE LAST CITY ROOM*

"In the tradition of Christopher Buckley and Carl Hiaasen, David Ferrell offers a hilarious black comedy about baseball, bad luck and bad people. Laugh-out-loud funny and morally provocative, *Screwball* artfully answers this question about the national pastime: What do you do when a serial killer appears on the road to the pennant? You send him out there to win!"

—MARTIN MILLER, *LOS ANGELES TIMES*

"[A] hard-hitting mix of baseball thriller and black comedy. . . . Ferrell captures the dark nature of modern sports." —*BOOKLIST*

"There's enough dark-humor material to carry this project far."

—*LOS ANGELES DAILY NEWS*

Anne McAndrews

DAVID FERRELL has been part of two Pulitzer Prize–winning news teams at the *Los Angeles Times*. His work has also appeared in *The Best American Sports Writing, 1998*. He lives in Long Beach, California.

To receive notice of author events and new books by David Ferrell, sign up at www.authortracker.com.

Screwball

David Ferrell

AN IMPRINT OF HARPERCOLLINSPUBLISHERS

FOR SCOTT AND ALINA,

two young champions

and in memory of

LINDA

A hardcover edition of this book was published in 2003 by William Morrow, an imprint of HarperCollins Publishers.

First Dark Alley edition published 2004.

Dark Alley is a federally registered trademark of HarperCollins Publishers Inc.

Designed by Renato Stanisic

The Library of Congress has cataloged the hardcover edition as follows:

Ferrell, David, 1956–
Screwball / David Ferrell.
p. cm.
ISBN 0-06-008741-2
1. Baseball players—Fiction. 2. Serial murderers—Fiction. I. Title.

PS3606.E54 S38 2003
813'.6—dc21 2002071941

ISBN 0-06-072600-8 (pbk.)

04 05 06 07 08 WBC/RRD 10 9 8 7 6 5 4 3 2 1

Fenway Park, in Boston, is a lyric little bandbox of a ball park. Everything is painted green and seems in curiously sharp focus, like the inside of an old-fashioned peeping-type Easter egg. It was built in 1912 and rebuilt in 1934, and offers, as do most Boston artifacts, a compromise between Man's Euclidean determinations and Nature's beguiling irregularities.

<div align="right">—JOHN UPDIKE</div>

And sunny down snuff I'm alright by the heroes and villains.

<div align="right">—THE BEACH BOYS</div>

The Boston Red Sox represent one of the finest professional organizations in America. To write a novel about big-league baseball, in my mind, requires the use of real towns and team nicknames. So I will simply make this clear: What follows is wholly a work of fiction. Not a single principal character or event in this book is based on any real people or events associated with the Red Sox or the city of Boston. Should any similarities exist between the names here and those of any real managers, players, city officials, or other individuals, it is by accident and not the intent of the author.

He could see the old man in the porch light, stooped and hairless, his head glinting like hard steel, like the polished gray shine of a ball peen hammer. For a moment the old man froze there on the threshold, motionless, and he had to duck back, waiting and listening, seeing that steel pate like a ghost image in his mind. It made him angry, made him seethe with rage.

The whispery jingle of keys ended with the sound of the door coming ajar, and he knew that the old man was going in. It was time to move. He bounded swiftly up the steps, quick and silent and deadly as a panther. He caught the old man a foot inside, forcing him backward, shoving the door closed behind them. The old man had turned and started to yell, but he was too quick, and his hand came up and cupped the old man's mouth. With his other hand he reached into his satchel, got out the duct tape, and spun it in several rapid revolutions around the old man's head.

His mind was fully boiling now, so hot with the fever that he

could just about feel the bubbles rippling at the folds of his brain, warping every thought, cooking the logic until it was all soft and squishy and it seemed as natural as could be to throw the old man to the floor and cut his head off.

So that's what he did.

Prologue

Near Odessa, Texas

Stu Domato's car was a trash heap rolling through a desert wasteland. Under blackening skies, it was about the only vehicle on the road—a big Lincoln, cobalt blue, missing not only the hood ornament but also two hubcaps and the right rear taillight, busted out during a wreck in Altoona. The paint was pitted, caked with the dust and dead insects of untold thousands of unwashed miles.

Inside was worse: a stinking pit littered with scuffed baseballs, paper cups, newspapers, three-ring notebooks, and empty bags stained with the grease of onion rings and chili dogs. The only things of any value were a Boston Red Sox warm-up jacket, two fungo bats, a battered catcher's mitt with new black leather stitching, a Carl Yastrzemski fielder's glove—a castoff from Yaz himself, back in '71—and a portable radar gun.

Domato's heavy face twisted in a frown. He was lost. On the map

spread across the steering wheel he could see the west Texas hellholes of Midland and Odessa, now behind him, and Pecos, which lay ahead. But, damn it, the map did not seem to show the latticework of tiny back roads that would deliver him to Lyndon B. Johnson High School and its evening ball game with archrival Alamo Academy.

The game itself meant nothing to Domato. He had seen close to ninety thousand of them, seemed like, in forty-six states and U.S. territories. He was a scout, out combing the godforsaken hinterland for talent. That had been his sole purpose in life for forty years, a span in which his wife had left him and his two children had grown to adulthood without him. He had sold his three-bedroom home in Brookline and cut the tethers that normally tie a man to the mainstream, becoming an aimless toad with watery gray eyes, close-cropped black hair, and a single consuming mission: to find that one transcendent ballplayer who would justify all the lonely years of struggle and heartache.

Domato kept going because he could never know when fate might intervene, when he might discover that young kid with the fire of Cobb, the arm of Clemente, the speed and power of Mantle. At the moment his slender hopes—the odds were always astronomical against him—were pinned on a reed-thin prospect named Troy Gregson, an eighteen-year-old who played right field for Johnson. If Gregson were like most of them, he would amount to nothing, bouncing around a few years in the obscurity of the minor leagues, if he got a contract at all. But right now, in high school, he was batting .459, and so the grapevine was abuzz with the word of what the kid might do someday, how he had all the tools to become the next Kent "The Raven" Ravinovich or the next Ted Williams. That was all the incentive a Red Sox scout needed to come have a look.

Domato crumpled the map in disgust. Forks of distant lightning had begun to tear through the blackness. Dreading the possibility of a

rain-out, which might condemn him to these parts for days, he pulled into a ramshackle Shell station a few miles from Pecos and asked for directions. The attendant, a slight Cuban, told him there was a school up the road; he had no idea if it was Johnson.

A dozen more miles and Domato at last found the tall arc lights of a ball diamond. Quite a few cars filled the lot. That was sometimes the case when a team boasted a great star; it bolstered his flagging spirits.

Parking on the edge of the dirty asphalt, Domato walked to the bleachers and saw that the game was already in progress. The blue-trimmed uniforms of the home team shone brilliantly in the lights. A batter in green waggled his bat under the expectant gaze of a few hundred spectators, then unleashed a mighty rip. A roar rose up as the catcher coolly flipped the ball back to the pitcher.

"How's Gregson doing tonight?" Domato asked, sidling up to an elderly booster watching from behind the backstop.

"Who?"

"Troy Gregson. Johnson's right fielder."

"Johnson?" The old man's eyes pinched in surprise behind thick glasses. "This is St. Jude. St. Jude High School. We're whupping St. Ignatius. No Johnson in this league."

Domato cursed. "Jesus Christ, I'm looking for Lyndon Johnson High School. Where is Johnson High?"

"Can't say I know," the old man said, turning his gaze back to the field. "But if you got some time to watch some baseball, this here's a real treat."

The pop of the catcher's mitt, followed by the umpire's cry—"Thaaa-reeeeeeee!"—formed an exclamation point to the old man's comment. The crowd roared, and several spectators hollered exhortations to the pitcher.

"That's eight in a row," the old man said.

"Eight?"

"Eight strikeouts. He's got a streak this year of sixteen. Might break it tonight, the way he's a-throwin'."

Domato looked again at the field. The kid on the mound was tall, at least six feet four, with long arms and legs and a blacksmith's powerful shoulders. He lurched into a windup, the left leg kicking high overhead, as high and smooth as the great Juan Marichal, and he let go a curveball that hissed like a Texas rattler.

Arching backward, the batter let his lumber drop as the pitch bit the air and snapped over the inside corner.

"Steeeeee-riiiiiike one!"

"Je-SUS!" Domato stared out with sudden interest. "Who is that kid?"

"Kane. Ron Kane." The old man turned and flashed a gap-toothed grin. "Not a bad arm, eh? And he bats cleanup, got some power—Christ, you can't hardly believe it."

Domato watched the rangy youth kick the leg skyward and come over the top with a fastball. It sizzled and struck the catcher's mitt with a sound like a cherry bomb.

"Steeeeee-riiiiiike two!"

"A *pheee*nom—no other word for him. Just turned seventeen."

"A junior?" Domato stared as if the old man were crazy.

"Yeah—and didn't play last year. Broken leg. He's just a baby."

Domato watched the next pitch in flabbergasted silence. The crowd cheered the ninth strikeout in a row.

"How's his record, this Kane?" Domato asked.

"So far, twelve wins and no one's beat him yet. Games he don't pitch, he's out there in right. Got range, oh man, and I told you he can hit—how's the sound of .682 and nineteen home runs?"

Domato's mind spun. Podunk baseball was his life—hell, he knew it better than anyone—and he'd heard not a peep about this kid.

"What league'd you say this is?"

"Lady of the Light. All Catholic schools."

For a split second that became his answer: inferior competition. But Domato knew many places where Catholic schools were power-houses; more important, it was clear this Kane could put some *stuff* on the ball. Not even Koufax in his prime—and Domato remembered him vividly—had achieved quite the degree of power and torque dis-played by this strapping teen.

"I've gotta get the gun," Domato said. He turned and hustled to the Lincoln, dug the contraption out of the junk in the back, and checked the battery. By the time he returned to his spot behind the chain-link, St. Jude was batting, ahead 3–0. A stocky left-hander punched a single to center, and Kane came up, settling into the box with an ease that was both graceful and menacing, long, fluid strokes as he primed his swing. He let two pitches go by before drilling an outside fastball toward the gap in right-center field. It climbed into the night under the black sky, as tiny and distant as a star, before falling out of view beyond a light stanchion.

St. Jude put up three more runs before the inning ended and Kane moved back to the mound. Domato's pulse quickened as he lev-eled the Jugs gun. Fastballs came in as blurs—96, 97, 94, 99 miles per hour. He knew that no one on the Sox's major-league roster was capable of such speeds.

"This kid can throw!" Domato gushed to the old man, who grinned back at him.

"You working for someone?"

"Boston. The Red Sox. I'm a scout."

The old man introduced himself as Conway—just a fan, a life-long baseball fan, he said. "Been coming to games 'round here sixty years. You know, we've had scouts down this way before. It weren't too many miles from here that old Haywood Rayburn discovered another pretty fair pitcher by the name of Nolan Ryan. Maybe you heard of him."

"Yeah, I heard of him," Domato said. His grin vanished and his mood quickly soured; he did not want to hear about Rayburn, the strutting ass who had not only gotten Ryan but also stolen Domato's wife. The emotional wound had been festering for twenty-nine years.

The two men were silent as they watched Kane ring up his eleventh strikeout in a row. The crowd cheered lustily at the batter's late swing.

"Tell you this," Conway said. "This here Kane would be the find of a lifetime, if he were fit for that type of thing—playing pro ball."

"What do you mean, *if*?"

Conway clucked his tongue just as a boom of thunder cracked across the heavens. "What I'm sayin', hell, Kane's not exactly hero material. As a person, I mean. Strange duck."

"Strange?" Domato laughed. "Christ, I seen Bo Belinski. I seen Jimmy Piersall, Kent Ravinovich, Darryl Strawberry. Mike Marshall—*both* Mike Marshalls. My God, I seen 'em all, and believe me, this day and age you get lots of strange ducks. Part of the biz."

"Maybe, I guess so," Conway said. "But this Kane—he's got an attitude. Been in some trouble. Slipped a snake in Chase Mallory's den window last August."

"Rattlesnake?"

"Rumor was. But no one seen it, and Chase, he don't talk about it."

Domato watched Kane rack up another strikeout—twelve or thirteen, he'd lost count. He thought about the shock Chase Mallory must have experienced finding that snake, maybe in his kitchen or slithering out from beneath the bed. Still, what was that compared to some of the Raven's antics? Spray-painting Luis Tiant's Porsche? Rigging up a set of mountaineering ropes to slip into Farrah Fawcett's hotel suite at three in the morning? Ravinovich had gone to jail over that one, an incident that inspired some of the most scathing columns in the history of the Boston sports pages.

"Let me tell you somethin' about the major leagues," Domato

said brusquely. "These kids, some got rough edges. We work with 'em, guide 'em. Part of our job, seeing they learn some discipline. Lot of times a kid's better off if he's got a bit of a mean streak. Last thing you want is a bunch of pansies."

"I guess—but Kane—"

"I'm serious. Think Roger Clemens ain't got that edge? I can name you a dozen guys—hell, Don Drysdale, Bob Gibson—guys that got themselves in the Hall of Fame based on having some good ol' hard-assed meanness."

Domato watched another fastball scorch the outside corner at 98 mph. "Kane ever got himself in any real trouble? Anything serious? Jail or anything?"

"Not that I know of." Conway scowled, thinking.

Lightning raked the sky. Kane's next blistering bullet sent the red digital gauge on the gun to a gaudy 101.

"No, believe me," Domato said assuredly. "A lot of these kids nowadays, they need guidance. We give it to 'em. They help us, and we help them."

BOSTON: FOUR YEARS LATER

Two pink neon nipples pulsated above the tall figure of a cat—the brazen sign of the Topless Kitty strip club two miles south of Fenway Park. Augie Sharkey parked his big maroon Oldsmobile in the gravel lot out front and lumbered inside, squinting through a haze of cigarette smoke tinted red by moonlike ceiling globes. Up on twin stages above him were two young dancers, writhing to the beat of Pearl Jam; the taller one, a supple honey blonde, had just completed a pirouette and slipped off her brassiere, twirling it overhead with a rouged expression of pouty arrogance.

Sharkey watched her for a moment and searched the room. His face was made more rugged by the lurid light. After nine years of managing the Sox, "Big Fish" remained an imposing presence, tall and rawboned, although age and frustration were beginning to give him a tattered look at fifty-seven. His hair, still mostly black and ragged over the ears, was thinning on top; his jowls had broadened; his skin had grown leathery like an old mitt. He retained the air of a warrior, a leader who could

endure the brutal vicissitudes of baseball, but there was often an aspect of pain in the hard lines of his mouth—a scowling, carplike mouth— and in his eyes, jet-black eyes wedged deep in their sockets.

A scowl creased his face even now, for Sharkey had come to associate strip clubs not with thrills and gorgeous women, but with the drunken improprieties and oh-so-many disciplinary problems of his athletes. That was perhaps one more sign, he thought, of his own inner warping.

Still, he was eager to be here, eager to talk to Domato at greater length, alone. They had just left Wulfmeyer's office, Sharkey's first meeting with the wunderkind. He wasn't sure what to believe. He could scarcely grasp the magnitude of what was unfolding.

"Right here, Fish." Domato hailed him from a corner booth affording the best view of the sinuous dancers. His meaty hand was already wrapped around a shot of Johnnie Walker. Domato's grin was like a kid's at Christmas. "Well, what'd you think? Exudes confidence, don't he?"

"Got plenty of that." Sharkey sat down; he hunched forward as if fearful of being overheard. "You serious about those speeds? Clock him yourself?"

"Swear to God, Fish, he's the fastest pitcher who's ever lived. Hits a hundred and eight miles an hour consistently, and I got him as high as one-eleven. Just twenty-one years old."

Sharkey had heard the stories, the rumors that had swirled within the organization like dust in a whirlwind. That the club had drafted the pitching talent of the ages and secreted him away in the Dominican Republic. It sounded too fantastic to be true, particularly when Kane failed to materialize at spring training. It was like urban legend, talk Sharkey pushed out of his mind, not realizing the hand-wringing that was going on in the front office. Only the depth of the preseason pitching roster had kept Kane from debuting earlier. That had since

changed with the trade of Shaun Lee to Minnesota and the rotator-cuff injury to Brian Cooley. Suddenly Kane was here, and Sharkey couldn't hear enough about him.

"It was four years ago? When we drafted him?"

"A total unknown," Domato said. "Wolf, he assigns him to Sarasota, lets him pitch a game at Pawtucket, and, Christ, I'm ready to see this kid in the bigs, but Wolf wants to give him some seasoning, wants to keep the pressure off him, and sends him down to the Dominican. We actually created a league for him down there, just kept him there and worked him. Jesus, you never seen the likes of what he can do."

"Haaah—" Sharkey made a sound that was half laugh, half disbelief. A waitress arrived, wearing nothing but lingerie, and he ordered a Stoli.

Domato was yakking again, saying the years of grooming had more than prepared Kane to pitch in the majors. The kid was going to be the biggest fucking sensation of all time.

"I'll tell you, what a *relief* he's finally in town." Domato shook his head and grinned. "You heard we were expecting him a month ago. I go to Logan, wait there nine fucking hours, and he never shows up. I really thought Wolf would have an embolism. Kid just vanishes. This whole last month—well, you saw how stressed he looked. Wulfmeyer, I'm talking about. So goddamn paranoid he imagined the Yankees had kidnapped him right off the fuckin' airplane."

They laughed. Sharkey had noticed Wulfmeyer's edginess, his hands moving constantly, his laugh too quick and giddy.

"So finally he calls last night," Domato went on. "Kane calls, says, 'I'm here at the airport.' Just like that. Turns out he'd gotten sick. Some viral thing. Never phoned. Couldn't even reach him. He was staying with some woman."

"Looks healthy now," Sharkey said.

"Healthy, tough, and mean." Domato chuckled. He belted down the whiskey.

Sharkey thought back to the meeting, Kane's demeanor. It was hard to read a kid in an hour, but Kane was clearly intense, outspoken, one of those high-spirited redheads. No fear of the major leagues, no apparent cracks in his bullish confidence. There were instants when Kane's flat copper eyes had fixed on him and Sharkey imagined he saw the same flinty defiance exhibited by so many young athletes, rule-breakers and rabble-rousers with egos the size of New Hampshire. Why couldn't more of them be cut in the mold of a Kyle Levitt? Levitt, the nicest young man Sharkey had ever managed, was a joy every minute of the three seasons he sat the bench for Boston. Too bad he hit like an overmedicated arthritic; he was selling mortgage insurance now, if Sharkey remembered right.

"Let's hope our phenom doesn't turn out to be a handful," Sharkey said. "Last thing we need is more of that." His tone was a pointed reminder to Domato about the character issue. Sharkey's biggest beef with Wulfmeyer was the continuing parade of prima donnas who'd been signed as free agents in recent years, on the theory they could carry the Sox to a title.

"Let me warn you, Fish: Kane's got some rough edges."

"How rough?"

"Loud, exuberant." Domato shrugged. "That so bad? Jaime Diaz—you know Jaime? Ran the Dominican league? Says Kane mouthed off a few times, but, Christ, off the field? No problems. The guy just disappeared; you'd never know he was around."

"Not like Davenport?"

"Hell, no. So maybe once a year he slugs a bar bouncer—I'm guessing. Thing is, Fish, we're talking a hundred and ten miles an hour! It'll be in all the papers tomorrow—Wolf's leaking it this afternoon. Believe me, this is going to be the thrill ride of your life. You're talking about the greatest raw talent that's ever come down the pike.

Wulfmeyer thinks—and I hate to even bring this up—but he thinks Kane might be the next Ruth. Thinks Kane might be a gift from God in some weird-assed karma way; that Kane might be our messiah that finally ends that motherfuckin' curse."

"Oh, come on, Stu, Jesus! Can we not—"

"Hey—I didn't bring it up," Domato interrupted. "Wolf brought it up. I'm just telling ya."

Sharkey grimaced and looked for the waitress; his Stoli had yet to arrive. He could see, up on stage, the honey blonde bent backward, limbo style, with her hands pressed flat against the stage floor. In an amazing feat of contortionism, her pelvis rose like the crest of the Gateway Arch.

"Face it, Fish—" Domato was still talking. "—people think about that curse crap."

"Yeah, but—Jesus." Sharkey looked back at the ex-scout who had been catapulted, because of Kane, into a front-office position, a nebulous role that amounted to assisting Wulfmeyer. Domato's girth had ballooned in the past couple months; he was living well, and also dressing well—Armani suits, designer ties. They looked ridiculous on him, like trousers on a rhinoceros, but he managed to project an air of importance, a smug intelligence, until he shattered it by opening his mouth and blathering about the damn curse.

A taboo subject, as Sharkey saw it, bad luck even to mention it. Like thumbing your nose at the gods. It was seldom discussed, but somehow everyone—every living soul in Boston—knew the story, a tragic bit of folklore that hung over the franchise like a black veil. The Red Sox had last reached baseball's highest pinnacle, a World Series championship, a lifetime ago—in 1918, to be exact. The man who had carried them up that mountain was Babe Ruth, the Bambino, the greatest player ever to pull on a jockstrap.

So what did the Sox do? The end of the very next season, they sold Ruth to the Yankees. Sold him for a pittance—the way the

papers made it sound, enough cash to stage a theatrical production of *No, No, Nanette,* of all things. A whim of the club's owner at the time, Harry Frazee, who was obviously an eccentric, and that was it, the Red Sox never won again. Never.

Not a single World Series title in over eighty years.

To say that Ron Kane would change all that, it was just . . . well, it was the same kind of talk that had started in '87, when the Sox had handed the keys to Fort Knox to big Junebug Jurvets.

That story was well known, too: how "The Bugger" had dropped the soft liner that ignited Baltimore's five-run rally, knocking Boston out of the playoffs. A lot could happen during the course of a year, as Sharkey knew all too well. Any freak error, slump, bloop single, hailstorm, heat wave, domestic disturbance, sore arm, mental block, drunk-driving arrest, broken toe, hamstring pull, bad burrito, tainted shellfish, or attack of hemorrhoids at the wrong time, in the wrong set of circumstances, was enough to tip a potential championship season into the Dumpster.

Still, it was nice to have hope, exciting to contemplate the possibilities of a fastball that could mow down opposing batters like summer wheat. Far better to manage a kid like Kane than to stand in against him at the plate, trying to get wood on a laser pulse.

"So what's the time frame?" Sharkey said. "For using him?"

Blue strobe lights began flashing, turning the bodies of the dancers into surreal, flickering forms. Domato answered without taking his eyes off them.

"Already been activated. You can use him tomorrow night, if you want to."

Gazing out under the lights of Fenway Park, his right foot anchored as it always was, atop the dugout steps, Sharkey dared to imagine he was

on the threshold of history, a triumphant turning point, and it caused him a moment of reverie.

He had managed a long time, twenty-nine years, seven clubs, majors and minors, all over America. He had suffered for it. He had watched the bitter seasons run together one after another until losing seemed to have left its brand in red ink across his forehead—LOSER— and he could rub until his skin bled, rub until his brain rattled around like a marble in a tomato can, and still he couldn't get it off.

The Sox's agonizing downward slide in the American League East—second to fourth to dead last a year ago—had brought a swell of public outcry for his dismissal. During the hellish final days last fall, there had actually been times when Sharkey could see a bright side to being fired: It might save his marriage—Bernice, God love her, was sick of the long road trips that kept them apart—and his migraines and colitis attacks would cease, once and for all. He'd be free of the clubhouse turmoil and he could get on with trying to forget that he was the man who, as the papers always said, could never win the Big One.

But he had come back. Kornblume had wanted him back. For some reason Kornblume held a deep belief in Sharkey, a trust that went far beyond what most owners felt about a manager. Kornblume's wishes, and Sharkey's own unrealized dreams, had been enough to keep him on the job and propel him toward this moment: the top of seventh inning, a balmy, cusp-of-summer night, the Sox out in front of the Tigers, 4–3.

How many of these nights had come and gone? Thousands. Too many to remember. But this one was different, the unveiling of a prodigy. June 3. A date that might go down in history. The story had been splashed all over the morning sports pages; a sellout crowd, more than thirty-four thousand fans, filled Fenway's battle-green grandstands.

Sharkey watched a pitch hurtle toward the plate and get ripped foul down the right-field line.

"Keep it down! Keep the ball down, Fro!" Sharkey hollered to the mound.

The Red Sox's starting pitcher, Frank Frolicky, gave no acknowledgment. The bespectacled left-hander stared for the sign and his next pitch, a fastball, took off like a skeet pigeon, sailing over catcher Ray Tarver's head and hitting the backstop screen. The tying run scampered to second base.

"Jesus!" Sharkey said.

Frolicky winced and spun his arm like an airplane propeller, as if late-inning stiffness had caused the wild pitch, rather than the less excusable misfiring of vital cerebral circuits.

Sharkey turned to Ted Uziak, the pitching coach. "Is he ready?"

Uziak was already on the bullpen phone. He hung it up and said hoarsely, "Just about. Had to go take a piss."

Sharkey scowled and turned back toward the field. He felt oddly nervous. A win would keep the Sox only four games back of the Yankees in the East. That in itself was a minor miracle. A month ago, when the Sox were already nine games out, falling in the standings like Wile E. Coyote off some desert cliff, Sharkey had gone so far as to begin drafting his resignation, a rambling, maudlin farewell that he scrawled on Hilton stationery after a particularly disastrous doubleheader in Texas—losses by identical scores of 11–10, the nightcap going seventeen innings, with Andre Jenkins, his best defensive right fielder, blowing out his Achilles on the dying-quail fly ball that won it for the Rangers.

Only fatigue and the fact that Sharkey was too weepy-eyed to focus on the page had kept him from finishing the damn thing. It was at that terrible nadir that the Sox had started to win.

Frolicky's next pitch was a looping curve that hit the dirt six feet outside. Tarver scrambled to block it. Up went a chorus of boos. One

heckler with the lungs of a moose hollered, "Yank him, Fish! He's a piece of shit!"

The guy was right, Sharkey thought. Glancing back for an instant, into the crowd behind the dugout, Sharkey tried to make eye contact, hoping to shut him up. He'd been bellowing since the national anthem. He was nearly as bad as that other blowhard—Marconi, Marzoli, whoever the hell he was—who usually occupied the third row, shrill as a Roman trumpet. Thank God that idiot had stopped showing up; he'd missed the last three games, the only games he'd missed in two years.

Sharkey turned again to Uziak.

"Two more minutes," Uzi said.

Sharkey's stomach tightened. He reached into his back pocket to finger his lucky tobacco tin, a battered talisman once owned by the great Honus Wagner himself, and resumed watching the field. If only the Sox could play to their potential. The team possessed formidable talent, but its focus was never constant, forever impaired by off-the-field problems and distractions.

Davenport in left was a case in point, a solid ballplayer batting .290 and capable of playing the high outfield wall, the "Green Monster," with a flair reminiscent of the great Yaz. But Jeremy was out on bail and awaiting a court hearing after a humiliating incident in Cleveland, where he had heaved a tear-gas grenade into a Greyhound bus crammed full of nuns from the Sisters of Divine Mercy Convent. A practical joke gone too far.

Jim Weeks and Carl Caruby were not in the lineup at all, one having been arrested for beating his wife with a standing lamp, the other now newly enrolled—for the third time—in a cocaine-rehab clinic.

Sharkey watched Frolicky's next pitch get hammered foul into the seats in the left-field corner. More catcalls cascaded down from the grandstands. It was almost time. Another minute.

He looked around the infield. At third, playing near the bag, was

Trinidad Villalobos—"Cool Daddy"—the slickest fielder in either league. He was another one: the greatest athlete ever produced by the nation of Guatemala, a man hauling down $6 million a year, yet so preoccupied with a personal bankruptcy case that he hadn't driven in a run in two weeks. Villalobos had lost fortunes investing in an Indy racing team, a borax mine, sixteen Thoroughbred racehorses, a biogenetics firm and a chain of take-out meat-loaf restaurants. If he could concentrate on baseball, there was little doubt he could be the greatest third baseman of his era. If.

And then, of course, there was Benito Castillo, the former starting shortstop. Castillo was there on the bench—exactly where Sharkey had learned to keep him—exuding raw malice the way a hog gives off odor. The inactivity was costing him twenty thousand dollars a day—or so Castillo had screamed one afternoon in Sharkey's office—because of his inability to capitalize on all of the lucrative performance bonuses in his multimillion-dollar contract. Sharkey had been begging Wulfmeyer to trade him, please, please, *please* trade him, but nobody wanted to touch the little bastard. Now his behavior was becoming more erratic; the last argument they'd had, on the team bus in Oakland, Sharkey had just about grabbed a fungo bat and brained him.

Frolicky's next pitch struck the batter in the helmet and ricocheted in a high parabola directly toward the Red Sox dugout, causing a lusty roar from the crowd. The runner raced to third. The Tigers' manager, Lon Hauser, leaped out of the visitors' dugout like some mad prairie dog, and the likelihood of a bench-clearing brawl appeared for an instant all but unavoidable.

Enough, enough already. Sharkey lurched forward and bounded up the dugout steps. He raised a mollifying hand toward the Tigers' bench and ambled slowly toward the mound. A swell of noise began to build—cheering. Sharkey, who had been booed in forty-nine consecutive field appearances, kept his eyes straight ahead, no expression

at all. He could see that Frolicky was going to pout and resist handing over the ball.

No matter. Sharkey made an emphatic gesture with the right arm, a signal to the distant bullpen. He was bringing in the right-hander.

The public-address announcer made it sound as if the name were thirty syllables long: "Now pitching for the Red Sox, number eeee-leven, RRRRonnn KAAA-AAA-AAA-aaaa-aaaaa-aaannnee!"

Up on the mound, ramrod straight, Kane tugged twice at the bill of his cap while the Tigers' batter, Grant Thurman, dug a foothold in the batter's box. With runners now on first and third, Kane worked from the stretch, a low leg kick and a fluid, rapid lunge toward the plate. The first pitch was a curve that broke in the dirt; the second, a slider, came up high and inside, forcing the batter to flop to his back like a pancake on a griddle.

"Good God," Sharkey said. He could just see it: This might be one of those knuckleheads that couldn't pitch in front of a crowd. What god-awful luck.

"It's the mound—he's not used to it," Uzi said, cupping his hands to his lips to holler, "Take it easy out there, Ron! Come on, big guy!"

Kane's next pitch was a fastball. It cut across the outer third of the plate and ripped into Tarver's glove with a sound like a pipe bomb exploding. That quickly he seemed to find his rhythm. He came back with two more fastballs for his first strikeout, and got the next batter on a swinging curve to end the Tigers' threat. Up in the press box a Red Sox assistant coach timed one of the deliveries at 108 mph.

Boston scored another run in the seventh, and Kane, using a full windup, struck out the side in the eighth. In the ninth, with the crowd now standing and roaring, he gave up a weak tap to the mound before gunning down the final two Detroit batters as if they weren't even there.

Sharkey clattered down the tunnel behind his players and watched the tumultuous clubhouse scene. Writers and TV crews soon began pouring in, more of them than Sharkey had seen in years. Mitch Harkwood, the runty writer from the *Herald,* came right at Sharkey, his bird's nest of frizzy gray hair bobbing under Sharkey's chin.

"Fish," he croaked in his scratchy, foghorn voice, "how's about a manager's ass-ess-ment?"

The cameras and lights all swung their way. Sharkey tried to offer no more than a sound bite.

"Naturally, we're very impressed," he said, squinting into the glare. "That kind of velocity is astounding, really. We'll take things one step at a time and see if, at some point, we can use him as a starter."

"When, Fish? Do you think—"

The reporters began hollering questions. Sharkey gave short, noncommittal answers.

Kane emerged from the showers, his red hair hanging in wet arcs on his forehead. His freckled torso rose up from gray boxer shorts like a genie from a lamp, a V-shaped fuselage of sinew and steel, lean but hard. Listed at six feet four, he appeared even taller. On each shoulder Kane sported a tattoo: on the left an eye, wide and mysterious; on the right the long-eared head of a donkey smoking a monstrous billowing joint, and below it: WHO'S THE JACKASS?

Questions flew at him. Kane grinned. His enamel-white teeth looked wide and strong as a bear trap. He listened to a man from WCBS ask about the experience of making a major-league debut before such a big, zealous crowd.

Kane's tarnished-copper eyes took on a glow, like a heating coil getting hot, and he said hell yes it was a thrill.

"That many people, all that noise, right here in Fenway Park— God, I can't even describe it. It was unreal, just *waves* of sound. Every strikeout, man, those roars came down, just *vibrated* right through me.

All those screams, for me! For me and my teammates! I could see all those people up there, dots of color, little faces, and I knew they were behind me. God, I knew they wanted me to dominate—and I did."

The words rushed out in his rough baritone, a voice like coarse sandpaper. The writers questioned him about his past—the years in the Dominican, growing up in Texas, his hobbies, his personal life. The Sox had chosen not to hold an earlier press conference—a formal introduction that might have put undue pressure on the rookie—so this was Kane's first encounter with the media. He answered only what questions he chose to hear: He rambled about workouts in the desert heat, an old rattlensake bite, his favorite car, a black Trans Am, and a woman named Marta who took him to Cancún. He talked about a few movies he liked—*Rollerball* and *La Femme Nikita*—and attributed his great speed, in part, to throwing rocks at jackrabbits.

"This club, it's had a tough early start," one writer hollered. "Can you get some momentum going? Make a run at the Yankees?"

Kane flashed a hard grin. "The Yankees? They're a great club. We'll do our best. Off the record? Don't quote me? The Yankees are like any other team in the East, barely above mediocre. You'd better believe we'll make a run. If I got anything to do with it, we'll tear this league apart."

The writers scribbled madly.

Sharkey felt his stomach tighten again. He looked at his watch, eager to clear the room. He'd promised Wolf that he'd give the writers no more than ten minutes with Kane this first night. He found it mesmerizing, though. Kane skated on a razor edge, outrageous but somehow in control, a reckless kid completely in his element.

The room seemed bathed in an extraordinary glow; at first Sharkey thought it was the incandescence of the TV lights, but it struck him that it was more, that it was the ethereal light of stardom, Kane's charisma filling the room as if some big switch had been thrown.

2

Those rare moments of joy, when nothing hindered the flow of excitement, caused Sharkey's grin to flash like sheet lightning. His mouth seemed to take over his face, displaying a startling number of tiny, even teeth. His eyes shrank to little more than dark slits camouflaged by deep lines and crow's-feet.

"Awesome," he said, looking across the desk at Wulfmeyer. "It was beyond awesome. Half those guys, they could barely *see* the ball. Hauser comes over later, into our clubhouse, and he says to me, 'Where in the hell—where in the *hell*—did you find that guy?' "

"You saw this, didn't you?" Wulfmeyer held up the sports page of the *Globe,* a headline stripped across the top: HURRI-KANE! SOX HURLER THE FASTEST EVER!

"It's true," Sharkey said.

"Damn right it's true," Wolf said. "For once they got it right. Kane's another Einstein, a fuckin' genius. Oh, and he'll keep those turnstiles humming. They'll be humming like a goddamn turbine."

Wulfmeyer's crisp green eyes sparkled. It had been a long time since Sharkey had seen him so pleased, despite Wolf's generally high

regard for himself. After six years as general manager of the Red Sox, he remained one of baseball's younger executives, only forty-four, a lean, aristocratic type with fine, pale skin, an angular jaw, and sandy hair combed back in a style that took on a roosterish look in a caricature fashioned by one *Herald* cartoonist. Neville Wulfmeyer was a GQ model come to life: tasseled Gucci loafers, Battaglia silk ties, an air of commanding self-assurance. Every gesture, every statement, even every burst of laughter was quick and purposeful, as if honed to hold to some time-cost efficiency standard.

A Wharton grad, he had risen meteorically in the organization; Wolf's duties involved player trades, contracts and draft picks, and he was the principal vice president assisting the elderly owner, Gordon Malcolm Kornblume III, in running the club's parent corporation, Amalgamated Ball Cocks, the world's largest producer of toilet valves, floats and rubberized accessories. He was, like most modern GMs, keenly attuned to the bottom-line imperatives of major-league baseball, a fierce multibillion-dollar industry; however, Wulfmeyer also managed to maintain an enthusiastic interest in the game itself, as evidenced by the decor of his spacious office: burled walnut walls festooned with autographed bats, gloves and photographs. One corner contained four life-size wax statues of the greatest sluggers in Sox history: Foxx, Williams, Yastrzemski, Ravinovich.

"The media's going to go crazy," Wulfmeyer said. "Don't forget that. Let's watch Kane carefully, help him through it."

"I've talked to him about the press," Sharkey said.

"Good. Let's also keep an eye on the veterans, try to keep morale up."

Sharkey nodded; he remembered Domato mentioning Kane's effect on teammates, the way he could stir up resentment. Sharkey could understand that now, having seen Kane in action, the arrogance rising off him like steam. Sharkey had been pleased with the jubilant atmosphere after the win, and yet he had noticed some signs of jealousy—

subtle displays of body language, a few wisecracking catcalls while the cameras were on. Nothing too alarming, but enough to cause him to reflect on how difficult it was to handle the fragile egos of big-time athletes. It could be a nightmare; a couple of years ago, for example, when Villalobos had gone on a tear and hit .438 for the first three months, Moses, the supposed clubhouse leader, had plunged into such a disconsolate slump that he had to be sent down to Pawtucket.

And, of course, before that, the situation with Ravinovich, during the Raven's final season. Mired in a 2-for-46 skid and riding the pine while the new hotshot, Mark Saxon, played right field, a bitter Ravinovich had taken the rookie out one night, got him shit-faced drunk on mai-tais, and left him sprawled at dawn in the azalea garden of the dean of the Harvard University Medical School. It was one of the most despicable acts against a teammate that Sharkey had ever seen, but the gambit had worked, at least for a day: While Saxon was still being processed out of jail, the Raven was forced into action and slammed his 498th home run, the last of his storied career.

For whatever reasons, the personalities on the club had become noticeably more tempestuous in recent years, a trend that Sharkey attributed to market pressures and indifference on the part of the front office. Boston was not a high-revenue franchise; to be competitive the Sox had to pursue the very best young, affordable talent available and sign free agents unwanted by other clubs. At times those acquisitions proved productive on the field but poisonous to clubhouse morale. Oh, sure, there were good guys on the roster—a core of decent, hardworking athletes—but a disturbing number of personality clashes and extracurricular high jinks had become the subject of at least four shouting matches between Sharkey and Wulfmeyer; the last had involved the Davenport tear-gas fiasco, and they had agreed, not three weeks ago, to work more closely to keep the players in line.

"As often as I can spare him, I'm going to have Domato peeking in on things," Wulfmeyer went on. "Just to see how Kane handles

himself. You'll be watching him, too, of course. He's a very spirited kid. We've got to keep the cockiness in check, got to enforce the cur-few—no running wild."

"Right." Sharkey felt his stomach clench. As well as he liked Domato, or tolerated him, the idea of another set of eyes over his shoulder was about as welcome as a dog bite on the ass.

"You must have your own plans," Wulfmeyer said, "about how to use him."

The statement was, in fact, a question—Wolf testing him, gaug-ing his own feelings about keeping Sharkey on the job. It was a ceaseless process that would end only when some significant event—Kornblume's death, or a prolonged slump, or some terrible incident—finally justified Sharkey's dismissal. Sharkey had adapted to the cognitive demands of the probing: While one cerebral pathway arrived at the correct answer, another pathway had to divine the answer that Wulfmeyer expected, and then, assuming they did not match, which half the time they did not, a central processing unit had to kick in, weighing myriad factors, from Wolf's general mood to the relative strength of various possible arguments and the long-range repercussions on all involved, to determine whether it was worth the risk of disagreeing with him. It occurred to Sharkey, as these assorted calculations were unfolding, that the upcoming schedule—three more home games against the Blue Jays, then a lengthy road trip—offered the chance to ease Kane into the rotation far from Fenway and Wulfmeyer's scrutiny.

"I'll give him a day off and use him in at least one of the games against the Jays," he said. "If he shows any stamina, hell, I'll put him in the starting rotation, give him Diller's spot."

Wolf nodded. "What about a roommate?"

That had been another point of discussion: They had agreed, because of the pressures Kane was sure to face, to experiment with having him room with a veteran during the first few games on the

road. It was a departure from the norm, but the extra supervision, at least during the initial trip, would help Kane to adjust.

"Probably Langley."

"What's your thinking?"

"Langley's easygoing, popular. He handles the media pretty well. Plus, he agreed to do it."

Wulfmeyer nodded. "All right. You're in charge out there." He tilted back his chair back, a movement that seemed to say they were finished, and Sharkey stood up, his heart pounding. He tried to close with the bold dash of positive thinking that Wolf seemed to expect.

"We're on our way, you just watch. It'll be something."

"Ain't no stopping this juggernaut!" Wolf slapped his hands together.

An instant later his secretary, Samantha, called out from the anteroom, "Neville, someone here from the police department."

Sharkey's instant reaction was a sharp gulp of breath, an icy surge of alarm through his fingers and toes, but Wulfmeyer gave him a wink. "Probably wanting tickets. Those guys, they're as bad as the Boys Club." Then, aloud, "Send him in."

Sharkey turned to go; he encountered the man at Samantha's desk, a craggy, white-haired character in a gray herringbone sport coat and blue slacks too wide in the legs. A palm flashed open, displaying a badge—Boston PD. He said his name was Schachter, Barney Schachter, a homicide investigator.

"No, no, Mr. Wulfmeyer's inside," Samantha said quickly, indicating Wolf's desk.

"Oh, sorry," the stranger said. "You are . . . ?"

"I'm Augie Sharkey. The manager."

"Right. Recognized you. How ya doing?" Schachter smiled thinly and stuck out a hand. "Can you— Actually, I need to talk to you as well. You going to be around?"

"What's this about? You looking for me?" Wulfmeyer said. He approached and motioned Schachter into his office. "Fish can hear this, too, right? You need us both, might as well get us both at once. No secrets here. I hope you'll be quick." He glanced at his Breitling watch.

Schachter shuffled inside. He promised he'd be only a minute and ran his cool blue eyes up and down each of them, like a carnival machine that would now spit out a printed card analyzing their personality types. They took seats at Wolf's desk, and Sharkey's mind raced along twin tracks, trying to imagine why in Christ's name a homicide investigator would be stopping by while also struggling to process Schachter's appearance. He looked jarringly familiar, though Sharkey was almost certain their paths had never crossed.

Wulfmeyer asked what was on his mind, and Schachter, lowering his voice, said unfortunately there'd been the death of a fan, a sixty-seven-year-old Red Sox Booster named Angelo Marzoli. "We found him last night. Figure he's been dead three days."

"Heart attack? Stroke?" Wulfmeyer's eyes conveyed the appearance of immense concern. "Guess it must be unclear, if you're poking into it."

"No, no, it's very clear," Schachter said. "Regrettably, he was beheaded."

The word sent a 220-volt spike of current through Sharkey's system, numbing his arms and fingers and triggering an aerosol blast of sweat from his armpits. He watched Wulfmeyer try to form words that took a long time to reach his lips.

"Beheaded? Like partially removed or . . . cut somehow? An accident of some sort?"

"No, it was—again, regrettably—" Schachter wrapped a hand around his throat. "Severed at the neck. Chopped off. Willful malice. Your basic heinous atrocity."

"Jeee-SUS. Well, our fans—" Wulfmeyer made a helpless shrug. "Those people have their own lives. Who knows what the hell—bad loans? Drug dealing? But if we can help . . ."

Schachter reached into his coat and withdrew a sheaf of papers, which he carefully unfolded. "We found these in his home. He kept a scrapbook." He placed on Wolf's desk a series of photocopied letters—some apparently penned by Marzoli, vitriolic missives directed to various members of the Red Sox, including Sharkey. The letters to Sharkey were especially harsh, second-guessing tactical moves, lambasting his lineup decisions. A number of pages were replies to Marzoli's letters. Sharkey had written three such responses; the shortest, dated last August, was also the most hostile: "You're an asshole, mister. Go croak!"

Recognizing his own handwriting, Sharkey went pale.

"If you're trying to read something into that—" He spoke uncertainly, but Wulfmeyer waved an arm and interrupted him.

"Wait a sec, Fish. This thing—if this is headed where I think we're headed, maybe we should get Lacy in here." A reference to the club's attorney, Roberta Lacy, but Schachter amiably raised his hands, touching the fingertips together like a meditative preacher, and said no, no, this wasn't a formal interrogation. Nor was he accusing anyone.

"You're not a suspect, don't see yourself that way," he said carefully. "Mr. Sharkey, we're all very well aware you're one of the best-known men in Boston. A public figure, a reputable guy—unless I'm sadly mistaken. What I want here is mainly to collect your thoughts. You can see, several of these letters—some of the worst ones—are completely anonymous."

That was true: A number were unsigned, one handwritten, others printed out by computer. One expressly threatened Marzoli's life.

Sharkey exhaled sharply. He did not want to seem defensive or reluctant, unwilling to speak without a lawyer. He had nothing to hide, after all.

"You want to know what I thought of him? Of Marzoli? Let me say this first: I hate to see anybody getting murdered, I really do." Sharkey knotted his fingers and went on, "He was a pain in the ass, I'll tell you that. You could hear him from center field, Uggams told me. Sat right in back of our dugout for years, screaming his goddamn lungs out. Riding us, cursing at us. But that doesn't mean I'd actually *do* anything to him. Murder—Christ, that's horrible, just horrible."

Schachter removed a small notebook from his jacket and made a notation. Wulfmeyer's eyes widened; he leaped in.

"Look at that date on there." Wolf pointed at the letter. "I know that time frame. When Fish—when Augie—wrote that—Jesus, check it yourself, we'd dropped fourteen in a row and were falling right out of the pennant race. Second place all the way to last, if I remember. Right, Fish?"

Sharkey nodded.

"The point being what, exactly?" Schachter said.

The anguish of that memory somehow kicked loose the answer in Sharkey's mind: why Schachter looked so familiar. He was a spitting image of Stengel—the late, legendary manager of the New York Yankees, Casey Stengel. Oh, God, what did that mean? It had to mean something. Sharkey had long ago come to believe that the universe was crammed full of chutes, trapdoors and conveyor belts, invisible machinery that moved a staggering load of omens, karma and luck of all kinds, good and bad. And now, in a sudden flash of awareness, he was sure that one of those trapdoors had just popped open and deposited a huge, steaming mound of cosmic elephant dung in his lap.

Wulfmeyer was trying to answer, his speech accelerating to mach-one cadences: "What I'm saying is, that *particular* letter was written at a time when Fish—Augie—might have taken his *own* life, for chrissakes, not that he's the suicidal type. I'm sure he was angry, frustrated. He didn't mean one goddamn word of what he wrote—am I right?" He glanced at Sharkey. "Not a word. Keep in mind we're running a

ball club here; we've got a hell of a lot of things to worry about besides some lousy heckler."

Sharkey nodded; he tried to show by his expression that he was as docile as a baby deer.

Schachter asked about the guys on the team: Were there any who especially hated Marzoli, who complained about his antics? Not a one, Wulfmeyer answered, looking at Sharkey.

Sharkey tried to be more emphatic. "Nothing was ever said. Not a single threat. I'm sure we all hated him, but it wasn't our focus."

Schachter started to rise, but he seemed to think of something else. He asked about the frustration of losing. Did Sharkey feel that now? Were others on the club equally fed up?

Again Wulfmeyer leaped in. "You're off on the wrong track here, frankly. Frustration? Yeah, you'll find it. You'll also find it's a constant. Every goddamn player we got, going back as far as you want to go. See there, our owner? Gordon Malcolm Kornblume, the finest man in baseball." Wolf pointed toward the far wall, a big oil painting, and his hand froze in the air as if Christ himself had just materialized before them. "You want to hear something about that man? He was eighty when that portrait was done, fourteen years ago, and he'd already had that heart of his broken maybe twelve, fifteen times."

Wulfmeyer watched Schachter study the picture. "You under-stand, I'm only talking about times when this team was close—close enough that we could have won. Only we didn't. Never. It's as if . . . well, like God doesn't like this team, and I can't think of one fucking reason why not, but that's how it seems. Kornblume knows it: We get our hopes up and fate takes a goddamn sledgehammer to us, just smashes us to smithereens. Not literally, of course."

Schachter stared at him. "So Kornblume is frustrated?"

"He's beyond frustrated." Wulfmeyer waved his arms. "I started to say he's not been in the best of health. Liver problems, kidney problems, he's had a lung removed. The man is ninety-four years old.

If he lasts the season, it's only because he thinks we've got a chance to win this year. Believe me, we're all in this together—this club, the fans. We understand their pain. We *sympathize* with their pain. We *empathize.* Whatever word you apply to this Marzoli, we're going through the same goddamn thing!"

"Right. Gotcha."

Schachter stood. He said thanks for the time, but Wulfmeyer wasn't quite through.

"You've got to understand, Augie's an emotional guy—he's a motivator. You should hear him in the locker room; he sounds like Knute Rockne, for chrissakes. But he's preaching winning, winning— not crime, not killing people. Intense? You bet. He'd give his right arm, and probably his penis, too, if we could win this year. He might write a nasty letter, but hell, so what? That emotion is all he's got going for him sometimes."

"I understand," Schachter said. "Listen, don't worry about this. We're just tracking leads."

He apologized for intruding and finally left. Sharkey returned to the chair and felt a nervous flush he could only liken to posttraumatic stress. Wulfmeyer sat and glared hard over the desk.

"Tell me you have an IQ. Tell me you're not a moron."

"What?"

" 'He was a pain in the ass . . . we all hated him. . . .' Are you try-ing to launch an investigation? Get yourself some headlines?"

"There's *already* an investigation."

"So you're hoping to be a target? Jesus, you come right out and say you hated the guy."

"He had the letter!" Sharkey said.

"That means you've got to be so goddamned honest? Try to play Diogenes? Damn it, we don't need that; we need somebody to manage the fucking ball club."

"You heard him: I'm not a suspect."

"All right. All right." Wulfmeyer began to cool down. "We're not going to let this thing bother us. We won't let this ruin our promising season."

"Right. He was just asking questions." Sharkey stood again. He realized his knees were shaking.

"So just forget this," Wulfmeyer said. "Forget this and go manage the club and keep all those numskulls in line. Tell Davenport no more tear-gas bombs. Make sure Kane learns to handle the media."

"I will."

"And don't screw up. For godsakes, don't screw up."

Paranoia, the undetectable poison that flows through the veins of every major-league manager, was accumulating again in Sharkey's bloodstream, reddening his eyes, quickening his pulse, causing strands of his hair to fall out. The fears had nothing to do with the dead fan; rather, they centered on the club: the rising expectations, the enormous media interest in Kane, all the personalities involved. Sharkey was afraid the club wouldn't jell; animosities would foster negativity and defeat. He dreaded Wulfmeyer's meddling, the vitriol of the columnists. Most of all he was afraid he'd blow out Kane's incomparable right arm, pitch him too much, or not enough, somehow disrupt the peerless mechanism that allowed him to sling a nine-ounce sphere of leather and yarn faster than any human being that ever lived.

It had happened before, to many a manager. Fans in Los Angeles still blamed the late Walter Alston for shortening the career of Sandy Koufax. Talk about a pitcher—Jesus, what talent. Koufax soared to stardom in the early sixties and just about put the lights out with the standard of greatness he set. A fastball in the high nineties, a curve that came at you head high and took a nosedive toward the inside corner.

The damn thing would end up below your knees. Nobody had that type of stuff, and naturally Alston kept him out there firing—over twelve hundred innings in four years. Four of the most brilliant seasons anyone had ever seen, but by the end of them Koufax was through. He could scarcely lift his arm to shave.

Dizzy Dean was another—hurt his arm pitching with an injured toe. *Kaput.* His manager, Frankie Frisch, "The Fordham Flash," apparently made the not–so–Phi Beta Kappa decision to keep Dean throwing no matter what. If Sharkey were to do that with Kane, oh, Lord God, they'd skewer him. Ride him out of Boston on a rail. An arm, though, had to be worked, toughened, kept in tip-top condition—and still it could fly apart at any moment. That was the rub. A pitching arm was the most temperamental tool ever created. Baseball's junkyard was piled high with million-dollar arms laid waste by snapped ligaments, blown elbows, shredded rotator cuffs.

The tack with Kane, therefore, was one of caution. Sharkey sat him the first two games against the Jays and called on him in the seventh inning of the finale, the Sox clinging to a 6–5 lead. Kane took the mound firing BBs—fastballs of 110 and 111 mph. Nine batters went down in order, seven on strikeouts. The ancient steel girders of Fenway Park fairly rocked from the crowd roar.

Pandemonium seized the clubhouse: Writers and camera crews had poured in from Toronto, Baltimore, New York and other American League cities, a horde of them, all come to see the incredible sensation. It was astonishing, like watching the media pursuit of Mark McGwire, when he was going after the single-season home-run record. Sharkey stood nearby while they packed the space surrounding Kane's locker, waiting, and he remembered his talk with Wulfmeyer. He was determined to see that Kane adapted well to the hubbub and that his teammates also handled it; no doubt it would only get worse.

Kane stepped out of the showers wearing a white towel around

his waist, another over his head in the manner of an Arab sheik. Shouts went up: "Ron! Ron!"

"Ten minutes!" Sharkey called out. "Ten minutes only!"

"Ron!" They wanted to know about his fastball, his family, his career in the Dominican, his impressions of the major leagues. They wanted to hear him speak, to gauge him, to discern whether he would be another of those one-minute marvels who burst onto the scene bright as a supernova, only to fade and vanish with barely a glimmer, or whether Kane was different—that rare performer who wore the true mantle of greatness.

Sharkey shared their curiosity. He listened to every question, every answer. There was something odd, vexing, about the way Kane responded to them. He seemed to hold both a disdain for the media and also a fascination with his power to command their attention. His arrogance was boyishly charming some moments and insufferable, even hostile, at others; it crested like sea waves, reaching points where it became almost a lampoon of itself, Kane seeing how far he could go, acting outrageous just for the sheer hell of it.

Three nights later, in Chicago, after Kane had struck out six of seven batters to clinch a 4–2 win over the White Sox, the media throng swelled to at least thirty, dominating the room, and Kane met them wearing a towel and a red bandanna. He bellowed a series of war whoops, his eyes gleaming. Strobe lights flashed. Questions flew at him, and Kane indulged the writers with breezy rejoinders, expounding on earlier stories with all manner of extraordinary details. He recounted his early teen years in a succession of one-stop towns in Arkansas, Oklahoma, and finally Texas. His parents had been virtual nomads, living for several years in a VW van. They were dead now, his mom of emphysema, his dad of a rattlesnake bite.

Kane shrugged about it. He spun tales about sneaking into movie theaters, surviving desert flash floods; he retold his stories about throwing rocks at jackrabbits for food when his dad was out of buckshot.

"That's how I got the arm," Kane said, enthralling the room. "Had to throw the heat or we didn't eat."

The writers laughed—was it all true? No telling. The guy was a character, for sure. Sharkey wanted to think it was an act, just harmless braggadocio. In some ways Kane was not so different from Sharkey's own brother Aaron, an ex-athlete who had played quarterback at North Carolina before going on to become, of all things, an elephant poacher near the west border of Ethiopia. Wild stories were always spilling out of him, his favorite being the time when cannibals seized him and ran screaming to a cauldron at the edge of a mangrove thicket. A man with saucer lips then drenched him with something that could only be likened to A.1. sauce.

How Aaron had gotten out of it defied every law of probability and physics, but it always made great listening, and Kane's tales were like that, full of all of the pompous bluster of a kid who had never been taught one whit of modesty. It would only magnify his stardom, unfortunately, but if his teammates could see the humor in it, grin and bear it, the club might be all right; might start winning regularly.

The prospects of that were difficult to judge. Looking around the locker room, Sharkey tried to read the faces. Langley was grinning; Villalobos and Uggams, too. Moses sat motionless, staring at his shoe tops. Annoyed? Or only frustrated by his 0-for-4 night? No way to know. Davenport and Maynard were huddled in the back of the clubhouse, saying what? Castillo, that acerbic little fruitcake, had bolted from the bench in the eighth and was now dressing as if he'd left his wallet on a park bench somewhere, in a fast-motion fury to get out.

Sharkey considered having another talk with Kane, but there would be time for that. He decided to see how the situation played out, just letting Kane be Kane. Maybe the guys would accept him. These were grown men, after all. Kane might earn their respect, earn it through the sheer magnitude of his talent. It was as plain as the

seams on a baseball, a new order had come to the Red Sox: This was going to become Kane's team now.

That idea contained a germ of hope. Yes, it had been a difficult season so far—the Davenport fiasco in Cleveland, problems in the outfield and at second base, the beheading of a fan—but the Red Sox had finally found a stopper, a pitcher who could be counted on to slam the door on the opposition, slam it with a force that was rapidly capturing the imagination of all of America. The future was looking good, and the Sox were only two games back of the Yankees.

Wulfmeyer called while the team was packing to leave Kansas City. Kane had not pitched at all against the Royals, disappointing sellout crowds, but he had been throwing in the pen and messing around in the batting cage, taking some cuts, displaying remarkable power for a kid not trained as a hitter. Wolf had found out from Domato.

"Think it's worth trying him in a game?" Wolf said. "Let him take a few rips, see if he can turn on one?"

"In a game?" Sharkey had to press the cell phone to his ear.

"See if it works. See if he can turn on a good fastball. He'd be something if he could hit some for us, too."

Sharkey was planning to give Kane his first start in Texas, and he'd been impressed watching Kane take BP. Normally, in the American League, with its designated-hitter rule, you could expect to see cows dancing a chorus line before you'd watch a pitcher come to the plate. The rule permitted any hitter on the bench to bat in the pitcher's spot, a wrinkle added many years ago to keep the game from bogging down, since most pitchers were virtually automatic outs. Invariably *someone* on the bench was a better hitter than the pitcher, and teams usually employed one poor-fielding slugger specifically for the purpose. Kelvin Briscoe had been doing the job for the Sox, but he had a

bum knee—he would need surgery after the season—and he was off to a poor start, with only six home runs.

Sharkey insisted it wouldn't be a problem, but Wulfmeyer wasn't so sure. He dug out the most recent edition of the *Official Baseball Rules* to see it again with his own eyes: Rule 6.10, which stated clearly, "It is not mandatory that a club name a hitter for the pitcher. . . ." Yes, a pitcher could take his hacks. If some superathlete came along, a powerhouse like Kane, a manager could go ahead and send him up there.

"They've got Morris going Friday," Sharkey said, meaning Trent Morris, the Rangers' veteran starter. He was a left-hander with a good fastball and slider, but not too overpowering.

"Hell, why not do it?" Wolf said.

"We'll learn something. Find out what the kid can do."

The anticipation of the experiment made the Friday-night contest with the Rangers doubly exciting. Sharkey's feeling was that Kane might prove himself capable of hitting for himself in at least some of the games he was pitching, and maybe even in pinch-hitting situations where the Sox needed a right-handed bat. Against a junk-throwing lefty, for instance, he might be effective. Whether Kane could catch up with real heat was another issue—his swing was flawed by a hitch—but Sharkey was eager to see him let loose in a real game situation.

A packed crowd of forty-nine thousand filled the Ballpark in Arlington as the Red Sox broke on top in the first, scoring on a hit, a stolen base and Villalobos's double into the gap. Kane struck out four of the first five batters he faced and held a 1–0 lead when he was due up in the third. Hefting one of Cool Daddy's black bats, a big thirty-four-ouncer, he ambled slowly toward home plate with the cool of a gunslinger. Sharkey leaned on the dugout steps.

"Ron!" Sharkey yelled and took a pantomime swing. "A full cut. Take your best rip."

Kane glanced back, nodded without smiling and dug a foothold in the batter's box.

Sharkey snapped the lid off his tobacco tin, poured himself a few sunflower seeds, and tossed them back in his mouth. He watched Kane take a curveball low and dig in again for the next pitch, crouching slightly, wagging the bat two times, three times, four times, long arcs consistent as a metronome.

"Jesus, look at him move," Sharkey said, spitting seed hulls into the dirt. "He's like a cat up there."

It was true: In every gesture Kane seemed to convey grace and power, the perfect amalgam of leverage and timing. There was something about the angles and planes of his limbs, intangible and yet obvious—he saw the game differently, reacted differently. He was superior in some way that defied analysis.

"Uzi," Sharkey said. "Hey, Uzi."

Uziak appeared at Sharkey's elbow.

"You remember the record for the fastest time going from home to first?"

"Not sure, Fish," the almond-eyed coach said. "A little over three seconds, I think. Mantle, wasn't it? Mickey Mantle?"

"I betcha Kane could break it."

Uziak shrugged. "He can run. No doubt about it."

"Fast-twitch muscles. Natural power." Sharkey's long face had the look of a zealot.

"He's a specimen, all right." Uziak spit a chaw of tobacco that seemed the size of a meatball. "I told him, he ever learns to get the bat extended, watch out. Guy could probably hit 'em as far as the Raven."

Sharkey nodded. It was lofty praise. The great Kent Ravinovich was a tragic case because he was dying now, disfigured by no fewer than six different cancer surgeries. But during his tumultuous career, spanning twenty-four seasons, he had racked up huge numbers: 498

home runs and 2,997 hits. It seemed possible that Kane possessed the same kind of incandescent talent.

A fastball came in and Kane attacked it, whipping the bat around with enormous torque. The coaches were right, however: The flaw in the swing, barely perceptible, kept the barrel from connecting solidly with the pitch. Instead of a screaming line drive, or even a soaring blast that might have carried to the distant seats, the ball went far too high, a titanic mortar shot that nearly disappeared into the night sky before dropping into the waiting glove of Juan Montañez near the warning track in center field.

Sharkey shrugged.

"Well, he *is* only a pitcher."

The game ended in another win, 8–0, and Kane, who worked seven innings, allowed just two hits and a walk and struck out fifteen. He was 0 for 4 at the plate, though he slashed a line drive in the fifth that Alex Rodriguez snared at shortstop.

In the cacophony of the locker room, Sharkey was startled to find Domato lurking at the back wall in a dark brandywine suit—a three-hundred-pound mobster, he looked like, watching for hit men. Angling over, Sharkey learned what he had suspected: Domato had been dispatched to look in on the club during the road trip because Wulfmeyer had gotten a complaint from Kansas City—drunken players screaming on the street at three in the morning.

"You'd best rein in the horses," Domato said, grinning, a good-natured barb, but the circumstances ruined the humor of it. Implicit in Domato's presence was Wulfmeyer's concern that Sharkey could not handle the club. He couldn't, of course—no one could—but still the message was chafing. Wolf had signed all these hellions and seemed to hold Sharkey accountable for failing to keep them in line. The fact was, these millionaire athletes were exempt from the rules.

They could throw bowling balls off the Empire State Building if they wanted; it was their world.

Sharkey felt a familiar burning in his stomach. He needed a quick shot of his Pepto-Bismol, that and his beer. He'd left half a Heineken on his desk in the tiny visiting manager's office.

Pushing through the door, Sharkey came upon Castillo hunched over the bottle. Castillo glanced in Sharkey's direction with a look of alarm.

"What the hell are you doing?" Sharkey said. He realized Castillo was doing something to his beer; there was something in the little cretin's hands. Sharkey sprang forward and grabbed him and twisted his fingers until Castillo screamed like a mynah bird.

"I'll break your goddamn thumb," Sharkey shouted. "Let go! Let go!" At last he got it: a packet of Ex-Lax. "Jesus! Are you fuckin' psychotic?"

Castillo stood motionless, his black eyes glinting with hate. "You fulla sheeeet!"

"That'll cost you two grand!" Sharkey said hotly. "*Mucho dinero,* you little faggot."

"Play me or trade me."

Sharkey grabbed him by the collar and nearly lifted him off the ground. "Trade you? I'd give my right eye to trade you, goddamn it! And God knows Wolf is trying. But no one seems to want an insolent little fruitcake with a seventeen-million-dollar contract and three hits in his last seventy-nine at-bats. And I bet you didn't think we were counting. Now, get the hell out of here!"

Castillo took off with one last maniacal stare and Sharkey popped open a new beer and found the bottle of Pepto. With trembling fingers he downed two spoonfuls. He was up to a quarter bottle a day, and it was only June. All because of his nerves, of course, the way they'd been savaged over the years like a delicate electronic circuit beaten with a polo mallet. The solution to the Castillo problem

would be to dump him, either by trade or by sending him down to the minors, but Wulfmeyer made all those personnel decisions, and there was no one at Triple-A capable of stepping up and providing reliable defensive help at shortstop. A fine was the only piss-poor alternative. They'd ding Castillo a couple grand, enough to make him squawk, but in the end it would accomplish nothing.

Angrily, Sharkey returned to the locker area and shooed the writers away from Kane.

"All right, time's up, let's go."

The *Herald* writer came over. Harkwood's frizzy gray hair sprouted like mouse ears. His thick glasses were suddenly tilted right up in Sharkey's face.

"Fish, got a moment?"

"I've got two seconds—and I'm in a bad mood."

"This won't help," Harkwood croaked. "I'm wondering if you know about this incident in Boston? Some players, a young girl?"

Sharkey winced. "Where do you hear this crap?"

"I've got friends."

"*That's* hard to believe." Sharkey stared. "I know nothing about it. Nothing. You got facts, or was this from some drunk you dropped out of school with?"

"My buddy's a cop," Harkwood said. "Boston PD. He told me don't be surprised if four guys get busted on statutory rape. That it happened during the last home stand."

Sharkey's voice rose. "Damn it! You want a quote?" He yanked off his cap and gesticulated wildly. "Here's a quote: We're two friggin' games out of first. Anything else, I don't know. Jesus, how many headaches do I need?"

Harkwood scribbled furiously, saw that other reporters were drifting over, and turned away.

Sharkey intercepted them by screaming, "Out! Out! Out!" and strode to the other end of the clubhouse to change. He began to feel

a horrific loss of equilibrium, the certainty that ominous things were happening in dark, unseen corners of reality. He was determined to stay centered, keep life in perspective. The club was rolling; they'd just picked up a big win. Now he could go to dinner, unwind a bit. And that's what he did: He and Uziak left and had T-bone steaks and stopped afterward for a pitcher of Lone Star at an old-time Texas honky-tonk. They didn't get back to the hotel until shortly after 1:00 A.M., and Sharkey felt a bit more relaxed, almost happy—yet still he couldn't sleep.

He lay in bed until all kinds of pernicious thoughts began filtering back into his mind. Castillo. Ex-Lax. Harkwood's big potato nose, those distorted little reptile eyes, that flyaway bird's-nest hair—a surprise there wasn't some kind of egg inside it. Oh, Lord. Four players. A young girl. Statutory rape. Could it be true? Who? Did Wolf know?

Sharkey stared at the ceiling, that blown acoustic material with glittery flecks, like stars. He saw a pattern that looked like the Big Dipper.

Should he run a bed check? The last time he had tried to enforce curfew by means of a bed check, the Sox had blown four games in a row and eight out of eleven. But, of course, there was big-time pressure now to run a tight ship. Sharkey took a deep breath and rubbed his eyes. In a book he had once read, *Winning Through Psychic Power*, the author described a state in which the mind became an antenna for knowledge that coursed through the universe like radio waves. Sharkey tried to imagine himself like that, aware by intuition of the whereabouts of his players. His head filled with images: strip joints, illegal poker parlors, cockfights, opium dens, bondage clubs, the bedrooms of unsavory women.

"Oh, good God Almighty." Sharkey scowled and stared at the clock on the nightstand. It was 2:04, four minutes after curfew.

Statutory rape. Jesus, if Harkwood had heard it from a cop, it was probably true. Sharkey rolled out of bed and dressed and found his

room roster. He stepped into the hall. One by one he tapped on the doors, checking off the names of the players still out. Castillo. Villalobos. Davenport. Uggams. Tarver. Maynard. Hazzard. It was unbelievable, an outrage. It had the feel of mutiny.

At the last door Sharkey looked at the roster. Room 312. Kane's suite. Sharkey pounded. He had worked himself up into a state of extreme agitation.

"Open it. You got a key." Langley's voice.

Sharkey said nothing, banging as if to knock the door down.

At last it swung open and a lithe young redhead stared at him. She had fetching emerald eyes and was smiling slightly, her hair mussed. She was wearing only a man's white T-shirt.

"Oh, so this is your famous roommate." She giggled toward Langley, who was watching *The Sopranos,* and said to Sharkey, "I thought you were young. For some crazy reason. How are you?"

Sharkey reacted before he could think, grabbing her T-shirt, yanking her out into the hallway, and hefting her onto his shoulder. He set off running, oblivious to her screams. He clambered down the metal stairs near the ice machine and turned toward the sun deck.

Lights flashed on in the security office as he reached the edge of the pool, where he heaved the young woman with every ounce of power in his rawboned frame. Her shrieks rose by a full octave as she half cartwheeled through the air and plunged headfirst into the glassy water.

"And next time," Sharkey shouted, "you keep your hands off the Red Sox when we've got a good streak going! You hear me?"

Sleep was damn near impossible, despite a double dose of Sominex. Sharkey lay in the dark, taking huge breaths and exhaling, feeling the mattress move with every rapid thump of his heart. He rolled over, looked at the clock. It was now 2:46.

Damn. Damn, damn, *damn!* He squeezed his eyes closed, his mind

racing. He would call a team meeting, lay it on the line for those clowns. He would demand that Wulfmeyer do something about Castillo—anything. He could not manage a lunatic who was dumping Ex-Lax in his beer. What would be next? Cyanide? The little bastard had no conscience whatsoever. And Langley: What kind of completely irresponsible—

His thoughts were interrupted by a scream, a terrible-sounding cry. It came right in through the cracked-open window. Sharkey was horrified for an instant and then became so righteously angry that he leaped out of bed. Sharkey knew that it was Langley, Langley out there in the pool with that woman, having an orgasm. The nerve! Sharkey wouldn't stand for it. He'd yank him out of there, haul him out of the pool and throw that hussy over the fuckin' wall if he had to, and get Langley to the vet; yeah, take him to the vet tomorrow and get him *fixed,* get him fuckin' *castrated*.

Sharkey bounded out onto the balcony, ready to yell down at the top of his lungs. But the pool was empty, still as ice now, and Sharkey realized the yell had come from out back, from the alley. He threw on some trousers and hurried down for a look.

At first he saw nothing, just a hooded light throwing shadows beyond the trash bins. A dog trotted by, and that's when he noticed it—a body propped against a cinder-block wall. The head was almost completely cut off, blood slicking one side of the torso. The man looked to be about sixty and was wearing a Texas Rangers T-shirt. On his nearly hairless scalp were two vertical gashes, identical in length, and a sweeping curved gash that crossed the forehead, so that blood trickled into one eye.

Sharkey's saddlebag jowls bellowed out, and he fought the urge to retch. Instead he turned and raced to the lobby on knees that barely carried him.

"Somebody help! Good God, we got a problem!"

4

The coffee was hell on his innards, but Sharkey lifted the foam cup and drained the rest of it. He stood at the front of the bus and stared with bloodshot eyes at the groggy players seated before him.

In a minute or two they would be leaving for the airport and the final destination of this interminable road trip, Cleveland, if he didn't strangle the whole lot of them first. He was in a rotten mood: hadn't slept at all and his nerves were buzzing as if wired to high voltage. The Arlington police had questioned him until six in the morning, and then a noisy coroner's crew had been out there in the alley until 7:20, when they hauled away the corpse. Sharkey thought he could feel the beginnings of an angina attack.

"We're missing somebody."

Rage caused his voice to quiver as he spoke. He ran his eyes once again down the rows of seats. Players stared back, tense and expressionless: Kane, Villalobos, Langley, Briscoe, Maynard, Frolicky. . . .

"Where's Davenport?" Sharkey said suddenly. "Where in the hell is Davenport?"

Just then Jeremy Davenport bounded up the steps.

"Sorry, Fish. This girl's husband—"

"That'll cost you a grand," Sharkey thundered, his eyes boring holes in Davenport's back as the left fielder hurried to a seat. Sharkey stole a glance at the driver; the man looked agitated, with good reason, since the club had been scheduled to leave half an hour ago. Sharkey gestured to him to hold on another moment. "We're still short. Where's Castillo? Benito!"

The charter was still as a tomb.

Sharkey bit his lip. Damn him. That sniping, backbiting, friggin' little psycho bench-warmer malcontent. "If he ain't here in two minutes, he's AWOL. AWOL!" Sharkey shouted. "We're leaving without him! And if you're wondering why I'm a bit edgy today, gentlemen, it's because I'm just a tad concerned about the hours we've been keeping—eh, John?"

Johnny Uggams stared at his knees.

Sharkey was aware of their fear of him. Even these modern, millionaire ballplayers showed an aversion to Fish's wrath. That was his gift, when he could make it work. The joy in managing, if there was any, was the chance to shape the lives of these young men, teach them values as well as baseball—how to pull together, play hard, sacrifice for the common good. To see a young guy respond to that, become a better man and a better ballplayer, gave Sharkey a profound satisfaction, a sense of worth he had never achieved in his own abysmal playing career. He took pride in the art of leadership; he had mastered the gestures, the tone of voice, everything to enable him to come across like Teddy Roosevelt, which is what he did now, hitting them hard, condemning the late-night carousing, the antisocial antics, the me-first, damn-the-team attitude that was apparent far too often, even in the midst of a winning streak.

"None of you saw it, but fate left us a very pointed lesson last night in what can go wrong if you're out on the streets at all hours,

breaking curfew. A man was viciously murdered right outside our hotel—the Hilton, gentlemen; the goddamned Hilton—his head practically hacked off. Think about that. That could have been any one of you. We live in a dangerous society. Isn't it safer, smarter, to be in your room asleep at night, and maybe, as an extra bonus, you get some rest? You get enough rest to rap out a couple of hits for us?"

Sharkey gave another hold-on gesture to the driver and reminded them that generations of fans have come to expect class and character from the Boston Red Sox. "We have an owner, Gordon Malcolm Kornblume, who has been more than generous—generous to a fault—in signing the tremendous talent here, talent that should carry us to the top." Sharkey looked at each of them in turn. "You probably know this: Old Gordo's in the bottom of the ninth. Oxygen tubes snaking out his nose; drool running down his pathetic little chin. A couple nights ago, Wulfmeyer told me, it looked like he was done."

Sharkey raised a fist. "But Old Gordo, he's fightin'. He's fightin' to hang in there until his guys—and I mean *you* guys; he loves you guys—until you guys bring that world championship to Boston. And he's rallied some. So let's not leave him stranded on third. Let's fight like demons and bring him home!" He clapped loudly and the players joined in spontaneous applause. Several let out earsplitting whoops.

"Let's roll," Sharkey said, and the driver accelerated and yanked the wheel; the bus shuddered and moved into traffic with a guttural roar and the sound, from somewhere, of squealing brakes. "Diller's pitching tomorrow, then Hazzard, and then we'll throw Kane at 'em. All right? Let's give those guys some support. Play hard. The Yanks blew a big lead last night—win a few games and we'll have ourselves a shot at first!"

Sharkey said it like it was the Nobel Prize, clapped his hands again and sat down, feeling utterly drained. He watched the flat Texas landscape go by—office buildings, then open prairie—and wondered if

the team had seen how distraught he was, how close he was to crack-ing up. It was a feeling a lot of managers experienced without ever letting on. Talk was that the late Yankees skipper, Billy Martin, had reached such a point while managing the "Bronx Zoo" in the 1970s that he had bought a handgun and every so often began slipping into the executive garage to fire holes through the fenders and doors of George Steinbrenner's Mercedes, just to release the stress.

No one seemed to know for sure if the story was true, but Sharkey could relate to it. He had flirted with a complete breakdown himself the year after he was fired in Baltimore, during a particularly difficult season managing Humboldt in the California League. His club had dropped sixteen out of nineteen during the stretch drive, prompting Sharkey to slug his so-called relief ace in the eye and earn himself two years in a league-mandated anger-management course. The doctor, Dr. Leeds—how Freudian was that?—had preached for-giveness, letting go: nice ideas, if you didn't have the press and Wulfmeyer chewing on your ass and guys screaming and getting their throats slashed outside your hotel window.

As the team reached the airport, a very disturbing idea occurred to him, an idea that burned like a hot wire through paraffin wax, right down into the core of his brain. It sizzled there, compelling Sharkey to bound off the bus as soon as it lurched to a stop at the Delta termi-nal. He moved away far enough for some privacy and pulled out his cell phone. He dialed the hotel for Castillo.

No answer. Not surprising, but Sharkey could feel his anxiety worsen. His nervous fingers punched the numbers for Wulfmeyer's office in Boston.

Wolf was in a cantankerous mood, upset by what he called another hatchet job in the *Globe,* a new angle on the Villalobos bank-ruptcy. Sharkey had yet to see it.

"I hope you're going to cheer me up," he said.

"Probably not." Sharkey told him in detail about the screams, finding the body, the fact that police had been grilling him half the night.

"You *reported* it?" Wolf's voice grew tight with alarm.

"You think I should have ignored it? Just walked away?"

"*Yes,* frankly. Given the circumstances."

"I couldn't just leave a dead man lying there in the alley! The guy's head was almost cut off!"

"Fish, listen to me—" Wulfmeyer seemed far more stressed than necessary. "First of all, nothing's going to bring the poor guy back to life. Whether you leave him there or not. Secondly, you and I both know you're a good guy, salt of the earth, but do the cops? I don't know why they'd even consider the question, except that you hated Marzoli, and now he's dead—and they're well aware of all that—and now you're screwing around in an alley and there's *another* dead guy. Jesus!"

"I wasn't *screwing around.* I heard a scream and went—"

"Those cops in Texas—have they talked to the cops back here in Boston?"

"I don't know. I don't think so." Sharkey could feel Wolf's panic transmitting itself at near light speed over the phone lines; it fanned out like an aurora borealis in Fish's brain and sent a tingle right down into his bladder, which nearly emptied itself on the sidewalk. "The cops, I think they just wanted to know what I heard, what I saw— which wasn't much. Anyway, what I'm worried about is, Castillo has disappeared. Gone AWOL. He was missing at curfew last night and no one's seen hide nor hair of him since. And we're at the airport, flying out of here."

"AWOL? Owing to *what?*" Wulfmeyer's instinctive paranoid fear did not have to be expressed. It was clear that he understood the extremely grave implications of what Sharkey was telling him.

"He's gotten more erratic lately." Sharkey lowered his voice to a

whisper. He told Wulfmeyer about the attempt to slip the Ex-Lax into his Heineken. "It's not just that he's riding the bench; there's that other thing—that situation with his little brother, Estéban, in Puerto Rico, how we wouldn't sign him. How our scout went down there and looked at him and wouldn't sign him."

"Did you see the *report*?" Wulfmeyer's tone suggested that the horrors expressed in the scouting report made the whole controversy moot.

"Never mind that," Sharkey said. "I'm talking about the fact that 'Nito may be totally losing it. I think we have to seriously consider the possibility that the little pinhead may have murdered somebody last night."

There was an excruciating pause. "Did you tell that to the cops?"

"No. I didn't know he'd disappeared."

"Good. Show some sense for a change and leave it. It's not possible anyway. Highly unlikely. He's an asshole, I'll grant you that, but I don't think he's a killer. Jesus H. Christ in a hot-air balloon." Wolf made the point that professional baseball men should not attempt the work of trained law-enforcement agents. "Which reminds me, that investigator, Schachter, called this morning. He's got a theory that Marzoli was followed home from Fenway."

"Why would that have happened?" Sharkey had a feeling it was going to be another sleepless night. "Anyway, what should we do? About Benito?"

"He'll turn up, trust me. Meanwhile, this is just the kind of potential fiasco we need to keep out of the papers. We're taking too many hits already."

"I know it," Sharkey said.

"It would be a fuckin' tragedy if our most promising season in decades gets ruined by some *incident* that Harkwood gets wind of. You know as well as I do that rotten PR can just knock a club flat, kill any hopes."

Wolf's tone became accusatory. Sharkey thought about Harkwood's recent line of questioning involving statutory rape. He couldn't bring himself to raise that issue; he could only hope to God it would go away before Wulfmeyer ever became aware of it.

"Fish, you've got to *manage* those guys."

"I *am* managing."

"Anything new with Davenport? Maynard? And how's Kane? We don't want those guys influencing Kane."

"Kane's fine. The writers love him." Sharkey stayed mum on the curfew violations.

"Remember: Kane's our ticket to the top."

"I know. He's starting game three in Cleveland."

"*Watch* those guys, for chrissakes."

Sharkey's thinning black hair, molded by a rocklike pillow, stuck straight up, a cresting squall wave pointed right at the hotel ceiling. It was the final day of the grueling road trip, in Cleveland, and he had slept in tormented fits after the previous night's wrenching 4–3 loss in twelve innings—a defeat made worse by injury. Jimmy Tynes, the Sox's starting shortstop, had shattered his collarbone trying to score on a chopper that was ruled foul. Ryan Bauer, a second baseman obtained in an off-season deal with the Angels, had taken Tynes's place at short and failed to turn a double play that might have kept the score tied in the eighth.

Room service brought a newspaper with coffee. Sharkey took a sip, followed it with a teaspoon of Pepto, hoping to immediately counteract the acid, and spread the *Plain Dealer* on the table. Page one was crammed with boring congressional news: A budget battle was threatening to close down the federal government, and the House had rejected a billion-dollar farm-subsidy plan, a big blow to the corn growers. Sharkey skimmed a couple paragraphs and turned the page.

Inside, in the local news, was a three-column story about a murder downtown. He hunched forward, began reading. It had happened near the Lake Erie shorefront. The victim was seventy and had not yet been identified. His neck was slashed and his mouth covered with duct tape. Police were still investigating for clues and a motive. They had found "signs of mutilation" on the body but had declined to give details.

Sharkey sat upright, took a deep breath. Wow. It sounded similar to what he'd seen in Arlington. *Signs of mutilation?* The image flashed again in Sharkey's mind: that poor wretch propped against the wall, those strange gashes on his head. A cop there had thought they were ritualistic symbols. Certainly that would qualify as mutilation. But Sharkey didn't remember seeing any duct tape.

Was there any chance on earth the two cases were connected? The Texas murder and now Cleveland? The distance alone would seem to make the odds against it astronomical, unless somehow— unless it was Castillo. Unless the malicious little shit had whacked the guy in Arlington and somehow made it to Cleveland in spite of missing the team flight.

Jesus. That was possible. If he planned to rejoin the club . . . yeah, he might have traveled on his own. The idea hit like the zap of a stun gun. It meant—good God, it meant maybe he had butchered the guy in Boston, too. Marzoli. It was a possibility far too horrible to contemplate.

Sharkey tried to imagine Wolf's reaction. Wolf would say he was reading into a lot of unconnected facts. If Castillo were here, if he had come to Cleveland, he would have turned up by now, or called.

The phone rang, loud as a firecracker.

Please, God, don't be him. Don't let the moron be here in Cleveland.

"Hello?"

"Hey, Fish, it's Stu." Domato. "Listen, you hear anything about this incident last night?"

"What incident?" He looked at the *Plain Dealer.*

"A couple of the guys, they'd rented a Jag, they were out late and apparently coming back they knocked over the fountain in the courtyard. It's not a very big one—"

"Who?"

"Reeling and Uggams. I told the hotel manager I'd—"

"Fine. That's fine—do what you have to do." Sharkey tried to remember seeing a fountain. "Tell them they're paying for the damage, plus two grand apiece. Yell about it."

"Will do. And I'll tell the hotel guy."

They hung up. Sharkey stared at the floor. The phone rang again. What now?

"Hello?"

"Feeeesh, you muthafucka son-uffa-beeetch."

"Benito!"

"Yooose a sheethead to put me on the bench. Now what you do? Hah! What you do?"

Sharkey took an instant to comprehend Castillo's fractured English. He realized that Castillo was taunting him, making allusions to Tynes's broken collarbone—a tragedy itself, the truth be known. Sharkey felt his blood rise. He spoke through clenched teeth.

"You . . . little . . . *ASSHOLE!*"

"Looozer, Feeesh. Beeeg looozer!"

The L-word. It hit another button, made Sharkey want to rip the phone out of the wall. Oh God, he wished he could wring Castillo's fucking little neck. He started to hang up and caught himself, realizing he should try to pin down Castillo's whereabouts.

"Oh God, I hate you! I hate your fuckin' guts, and I'll tell it to your face," Sharkey said, "but we've got bigger concerns right now—the fact we need a shortstop. Even a lousy hitter like you. You here tonight? Ready to dress?"

"You make me a starter? Start now, every game? I hit good you put me a starter—"

His voice sounded close—or they had a very good connection. He sounded like he might be in the lobby. "Just answer me," Sharkey said. "Where the hell are you?"

"You tell first—promise me to play. All the games. You screw me before. You and Red Sox. You screw me over. And then my brother. I want Estéban get a contract—and no contract. You sign muthafucka Kane and no sign my brother—"

"I didn't sign anybody," Sharkey said, comprehending scarcely half his ramblings. He asked again, point-blank: Was Benito in Cleveland? That triggered another round of ranting. He wasn't going to say. He saw it as leverage somehow, a secret he wasn't going to give up. Fine. "All right, listen, you fucking idiot, I wash my hands of this! You want to come back, you want to play, talk to Wulfmeyer. *Comprendes?* You're suspended as far as I'm concerned! You may never wear a Red Sox uniform again!"

Sharkey hung up. He knew what would happen next. Castillo would dial Wulfmeyer immediately. He was in such a lather he'd call right away and scream and moan and hopefully, *hopefully,* Wolf would manage to discern where he was. Wolf would think to do that, and he'd call Sharkey, and they'd discuss the situation, whatever it was. He'd be pissed off about the phone call, no matter what, but they'd discuss it and go from there.

Nineteen minutes it took. Sure enough, Wolf was on the line, and he had just heard from the shithead. Wolf spoke in the tone he often adopted when he was dealing with a dozen things at once and annoyed with all of them.

"Nothing's settled," he said. "I'll have to talk to Gamboa. Deal with that joker." Oscar Gamboa was Castillo's agent, a shyster known throughout the majors.

"You find out if he's here?"

"No idea where he is."

"You ask him?"

"My first question. Look, Fish, you know yourself the man's practically incomprehensible. The gibberish he's speaking, he might have said he's in Kazakhstan. The important thing is, we work this out and get him back soon. Otherwise we're up shit creek defensively."

Sharkey squeezed the receiver. "Work it out? Christ, let's get rid of that bastard once and for all. You should send him down, trade him—or suspend him. That's what I said we'd do. Bar him from the clubhouse. He's poison. I think there's a real chance he may be involved in all three of these murders—even the guy in Boston, Marzoli. Wasn't there something about that case? Mutilation?"

"His head was cut off. Fish, you're getting too way out with this murder crap. Only thing Castillo kills is maybe too many rallies."

"Wolf, he's a psychopath. He's already tried putting Ex-Lax in my beer. Ex-Lax!"

"That's certainly not murder!" Wulfmeyer seemed to be losing patience. "Get a grip on yourself. Yeah, fuck it, he can't hit, and he's an asshole, but he's not out cutting the *heads* off people, for chrissakes!"

"How do you know? Don't you think it's weird these attacks have happened three different places, and we're there every goddamn time?"

A long silence. "It's not weird—it's America. Weird? All right, it's a little weird, but don't go jumping to all kinds of absurd conclusions. We live in a violent age. You're talking about big urban areas where murders happen all the time." Wulfmeyer cut off the next rebuttal: "Look, we can't solve this now. Let me discuss it with Stu."

"The writers will find out. They'll be asking—"

"They've got it already, Benito's disappearance. It's in today's papers. Harkwood called me yesterday and I just told him the facts. Said we're fining him five thousand dollars a day. Naturally, they played it up big. You'll see it in the faxes."

Sharkey wasn't sure what to say. He felt dismissed as some crack-

pot. Wulfmeyer seemed to sense his disappointment and said, "You can do a couple of things: Keep your mind focused on that ball club. The Yanks looked great last night; they're loaded. Keep everyone pulling the same direction. And you might poke around and ask, see what the guys are saying about Castillo. Don't mention the murders—for godsakes, don't even *think* about that—but maybe you can find out why he went AWOL. Maybe someone knows what's up."

It was a good suggestion, for once. Sharkey sat thinking for a while, wondering whom he might approach. During the course of a day, if he hung around the hotel, he could usually count on running into his players. That would be the best way—catch a few alone, away from the clubhouse gossips.

His own game-day habits would allow for that. He liked to have a good breakfast, take a walk, and slip back to the room to look over stat sheets and analyze the night's opposing pitcher. This being Cleveland, Sharkey started the morning off at Weatherby's, a new grill he liked, where he and Uziak devoured stacks of blueberry pancakes, and then Sharkey walked to a Barnes & Noble.

Later, bucking a strong breeze, he strolled all the way to the lake, where along the promenade he finally saw someone, saw Mad Dog Moses by himself on a shady bench.

Moses was a forty-year-old second baseman who had bounced around with six different teams, playing in more than 2,400 major-league games without ever reaching the World Series. Another season and he figured to set the all-time record for futility, moving past two of the game's legends, Kent Ravinovich and Ernie Banks. The thought of eclipsing Banks's mark, 2,528 games with nary an at-bat in baseball's ultimate showcase, had begun gnawing on Moses's hide like a bad case of psoriasis; but in spite of it he was regarded as a leader, a winner, because of an intensity that burned in him hot as a blowtorch. He and Sharkey often clashed—twice they'd been caught by network

cameras jawing in the dugout—but Sharkey knew they shared the same hunger: They'd shove flaming coals down their own shorts if it meant a chance to finally capture a title.

"Hey, Dog, mind if I join you a minute?"

Moses's glowering stare followed the slow progression of a catamaran. "Nope. Park yourself," he said, his eyes never leaving the lake. "It's about my hitting, ain't it?"

"No, it's not that—"

"I can't help it, Fish, I'm trying, swinging good; nothin's falling in." Moses's heavy face swung toward him. He was a large, intimidating man, with gold inlaid monograms, MD, on his two front teeth, and a thick silver chain bearing a pendant that spelled out ATTACK DAWG. His eyes showed the desperation of a man in a 2-for-39 skid. "Shit, it started when he got here, that arrogant son of a bitch."

"You mean Kane?"

"Damn right I mean Kane. Thinks he's Jesus Christ, so fuckin' special. You seen him, telling his stories, every motherfuckin' writer hangin' on every word. Writing it all down. Goddamn!"

It was just venting, a frustrated athlete blowing steam because he wasn't hitting, but Sharkey was taken aback by the fervor of it. Moses's lead would likely be followed by any number of the younger guys, even a lot of the veterans; the roots of divisiveness might run deeper than Sharkey had realized.

"He'll settle down, Dog. He's a kid. Give him time."

"Damn arrogant kid. Heard he's already talking about a new contract; been in the majors a month. Fuck, he gets some fan-tas-tic deal, gets himself seventy or eighty million, you'll see a lot of us mothafuckas go apeshit."

"He'll help us win, Dog, he really will." Sharkey hadn't heard the contract rumor; it bothered him, too, how much money a young athlete could make, when he himself, who worked and worked and put up with God-knows-how-many problems, barely earned enough to

keep Bernice in pearl earrings. The Red Sox were paying Sharkey $680,000 this season, the third year of a four-year deal, but the figure seemed a pittance considering the tony neighborhood where they had bought and the lifestyle that Bernice had fashioned for herself as patron of the arts and all-around society gadabout. Sharkey sighed and said, "Actually, I came to ask about Castillo—what's been up with him?"

"Fuck if I know."

"There anyone he'd talk to? Or phone?"

"His brother. Wherever the hell *he* is."

Sharkey nodded, studying the proud veteran. Moses had gone through the wringer himself dealing with personal problems. His mistress had tried to attack his wife with a cinder block during spring training, and a security guard had been brain injured in the subsequent melee. It had made all the Florida papers, and now the lawsuit was escalating into an ugly three-way pissing match.

"Listen, Dog, I got a favor to ask you. An important favor."

"Shoot."

"Keep your ears open," Sharkey said. "You hear anything that disturbs you, clue me in, all right? Off the record? Just between you and me?"

Moses almost laughed. "Jesus, Fish, the longer I'm around this game, the more I hear things I wish I never heard before."

Sharkey cuffed him on the shoulder and stood.

"Me too, Mad Dog. Me too."

5

There are times in sports a special magic takes over a place, a glow like St. Elmo's fire that envelops a whole stadium, a crowd, the athletes on the field. It can be felt but not touched; it amplifies sound, makes all things look crisper—the baselines, the scoreboard lights, the specks of dirt on the dugout steps—and it can raise goose bumps on those that fully grasp its invisible presence.

Sharkey became aware of it in the third inning. On a warm, humid evening, under the brilliant lights of jam-packed Jacobs Field, Kane was reaching a level that few other pitchers had ever reached. The crowd, sensing it, grew louder with each pitch, a pro-Indians crowd, but Kane had them screaming. He struck out the side in the fourth and again in the sixth and seventh. He entered the last of the eighth throwing that rarest of baseball masterpieces, a perfect game. He had struck out sixteen batters and allowed no hits, no walks; not a single player had reached base against him.

The Sox led, 3–0, in part because of Kane's first major-league hit and run batted in, a bloop single that scored Langley in the third. Now, as he worked to the dangerous middle third of the Indians'

lineup, the fans were standing. The heart of the Cleveland order was one of the toughest in baseball—a right-handed hitter, Wilford Giles, who had walloped fifty-three home runs the previous year, and two lefties, Rico Mendoza and Jim Thome, who had driven in more than one hundred runs apiece.

Kane appeared to hold them in utter disregard. Sharkey watched him carefully as Giles strolled to the plate. Kane bent for the resin bag, juggled it in his hand, dropped it behind the mound. He climbed the rubber, let Giles dig in, and forced him to wait, peering motionless for Tarver's sign. The entire stadium seemed to be holding its breath by the time Kane finally rocked into his fluid windup and flashed his high leg kick. He came in with a fastball that Giles tried to attack. A vicious swing and miss brought thunderous noise from the stands.

Sharkey fidgeted. This was mano a mano, a classic encounter between a power pitcher and power hitter. Kane kicked again and delivered a hard inside curve that Giles lashed toward the gap at short. Ryan Bauer broke late but lunged to his right, nearly snagging the ball in the webbing; however, it crawled out and rolled into shallow left field. It came to a stop near the foul line as Davenport scrambled in to get it and Giles raced to second base. At Fenway it might have been ruled an error, and Kane would still be working on a no-hitter, but the Jacobs Field scoreboard flashed DOUBLE, and the charge went out of the ball park as if a power plug had been pulled.

The perfect game was spoiled. Kane, momentarily distracted, allowed Giles to take a big lead and steal third. Mendoza yanked a fly ball to right to score the run, and then Kane struck out Thome and got through the eighth. Sharkey brought in Rick Reeling to save the ninth, and the Sox nailed down a 3–1 victory.

What a night. Sharkey was wrung out but happy—elated, actually. A commanding win, and the Sox were now a game off the pace in the East. Too bad about the play—Bauer had the range of a garden

flamingo—but Kane would have other chances. An arm like that, he was bound to have plenty of chances.

Dropping heavily to the bench in front of his locker, Sharkey carefully untied his left shoe, then the right, then placed his tobacco tin in the locker next to a string of boar's teeth. Next, since the Sox had won, he stood and turned three complete circles to the right, knelt for an instant, then reversed it with three circles to the left.

His postgame rituals had become more involved over the years. In the shower he would touch the soap first to his nose, then his left kneecap. He would let the water spray directly into his right ear and later remove it with a douse of rubbing alcohol. Once he had dressed, he would phone home, let it ring twice, and hang up before Bernice could answer.

Sharkey sat for a minute after removing his cleats, wondering if she had gone to see *The Imaginary Cuckold,* that Molière farce, which had just opened in Boston. After twenty-six years of marriage, the last thing she cared to do was stay home and watch the Sox on television, even an important matchup with Kane on the hill. It was always the theater, or a gallery exhibit, followed by dinner at some froufrou restaurant where they charged you nine bucks for three chilled asparagus spears, a few hearts of palm, and a couple chunks of gorgonzola— the salad, naturally, being only a prelude to an entrée that cost as much as a tune-up for the Oldsmobile. The woman seemed to be on a mission to take every dime of Sharkey's income and refunnel it into the economy. Sharkey imagined her in her pearls, trading droll remarks with some Russian impressionist and then snapping open her compact to touch up her lipstick. A reverie that ended with the sound of Kane shouting.

"That's right, any fucking shortstop in the majors could have had that ball! You can't stand out there asleep!"

"Give it a rest, asshole!"

"Make me, why don't you! You move like a fucking turtle!"

Sharkey spun around to see Bauer take a menacing step toward Kane. He was stocky for an infielder, broad in the chest, but no match for Kane's size and power, and the last thing Sharkey wanted to see—the very last thing on earth right now—was a clubhouse fight, this tough veteran attacking Kane, maybe injuring Kane's arm, for godsakes.

"Cool it over there!" Sharkey yelled.

"Come on, punk!" Kane's face had changed, his freckled cheeks glowing hot, like steel out of a forge. His nostrils flared. His bare torso rippled with strength, immense mass gathering up in the chest and arms and shoulders—all the muscle there becoming firmer and harder without really growing, twitching with juices as deadly volatile as nitroglycerin.

Somehow Bauer didn't see it, either didn't see it or was too stupid to care, and he moved forward, his broad face as fixed as a death mask. Kane's right arm drew back, a big pile driver waiting to trip, so dangerous-looking that nobody could ignore it. Somewhere Sharkey had heard—from Stu, probably—that Kane had studied martial arts in the Dominican Republic, but he looked like Jack Dempsey now the way he cocked back that arm for a haymaker. Luckily, it never came. Teammates rushed in ahead of Sharkey to intervene: Tarver and Langley and Maynard. Moses, too. Tarver got up in Kane's face, same as he did to pitchers at the mound, and Mad Dog came from behind. Moses got hold of that right arm of Kane's and held on, hollering in Kane's ear to cool it, go take a shower.

Langley pulled Bauer away, and there was a din of voices, guys yelling at Kane, Kane shouting back. Sharkey moved into the middle of the fracas and screamed for order, overpowering the noise until finally they had to listen, and it all began to break up.

"God*damn,*" Sharkey said under his breath to himself, and then to Kane, the anger still twanging in his voice, "I'll talk to you later." And finally Sharkey turned his wrath on a more natural target, the writers

and cameramen, who had begun streaming into the clubhouse. "Let's go! Out, out, out! Circus is over! Nothing tonight, Harkwood, move along! This ain't some coffeehouse!"

Kane's face had drained of the red-orange; it was cool and dull again. He was in jacket and tie—the Sox's dress code on the road—and was hunched forward on the metal chair in the cramped visiting manager's office, elbows on his knees, looking hard at Sharkey. In a voice absolutely without inflection, Kane said he had just lost his cool.

"It shouldn't have happened," he said. "I'm not apologizing—I just don't know what came over me."

"You *should* apologize," Sharkey said.

"That's not what I'm saying. It was like something snapped inside. Snapped real bad."

Sharkey thought about his own rage at Castillo, the shouting match on the phone. He rubbed his fingers deep into his eyes.

"I understand. Believe me," Sharkey said. "Just try to remember, we're a team. We've got to support each other. The press is going to skewer us on this one . . . oh, God, it'll be a mess . . . and we're going to have to weather the storm, pull together. That clear to you?"

Kane nodded.

"You pitched a hell of a game," Sharkey said. "Are you happy, so far? With the club, how things are going?"

"Oh, yeah—" Kane's eyes brightened; he spoke in a sudden rush. "All these cameras, writers—you know who was here tonight? *Newsweek, Time, Sports Illustrated*. It's fuckin' weird, man; it's like I'm in some other dimension, like I'm big as the whole fuckin' world, 'cause my face is out there in every living room, millions of places all at once, and my voice out there, channel after channel, like it's echoing down through this big electronic tunnel, so many rooms and chambers you can't even see them all."

"You've got quite a way of picturing—"

"Last night, if you're wondering what I mean. Last night I'm on ESPN, this interview, and I'm layin' there in my room, watching it, and I think, 'Shit, this is great. People seeing me coast to coast.' And I turn the channel, another sports show, and I'm on there again! And another one, they're talking about the fact I'm pitching tonight!"

Kane went on; he couldn't seem to slow down. The same shtick he gave the writers, bluster that seemed to gloss over what was really inside, whatever that was. Sharkey could not penetrate it; he did not feel he was coming to know this kid—he was too intense, too invulnerable, a strange sort of caricature. What he knew of this athletic genius he gleaned from seeing him strut before the writers and from tidbits he got from Domato and Kane's teammates.

Besides being mercurial, a man constructed of elaborate hot and cold pipes, Kane possessed a freak-of-nature power plant that seemed never to need recharging. He almost never slept. He was said to spend some of his nights gambling at card clubs—poker, pai gow, Pan 9— often alone, sometimes with Langley. Or they would organize a game at the hotel, dollar-ante poker with Reeling, Hazzard and Frolicky. Like Domato, Kane had quickly acquired a taste for the finer things— nice threads, Davidoff cigars; he was looking forward to the end of the road trip, according to Reeling, so he could buy a Maserati.

"Goals?" Kane said in response to Sharkey's question. "I want to be big. Big as Elvis, big as Michael Jordan, so fucking big these guys here—" Kane made a gesture that seemed to indicate his teammates. "They'll have to get down on their goddamn *knees* when I walk into the room."

"You see, Ron, *that's* the kind of attitude we want to discourage." Sharkey dug in his drawer for the Pepto-Bismol. "You want greatness, fine, that's wonderful—we *want* you to be great! But there's nothing that can rip the heart out of a team faster than resentment, alienating your teammates, especially once it gets into the newspapers."

Sharkey related a story about one of his years managing in Baltimore, when the big rookie Tom Chambord had gone on a tear and belted twenty-six homers by the All-Star break. He immediately bought a local cable-television station and began broadcasting nothing but interviews of himself and highlights of his own games, then started hiring pricey call girls to accompany him on the road. The reaction was so negative that five or six veterans jumped him one night in Chicago and shattered three front teeth—the start of such ugly internal bickering that the club lost forty games in forty-nine. The Orioles dropped out of the race like a rock falling off the Sears Tower, and three years later, because of an Achilles injury, Chambord was running a hardware store in Andover.

"One day you're the toast of the world, and then suddenly things can go south on you," Sharkey said, chuckling to try to show he had recovered from the trauma of that woeful season—when, in fact, he never would. "The point is, you've got to think, Ron, keep some perspective, work on developing leadership and self-control."

Kane ran a hand through his damp hair.

"These guys don't understand me, do they?"

"No. Some of them don't." Sharkey gulped down a swallow of the Pepto. "I don't want to name names, but look at Mad Dog: He's paid his dues in this game a long time, close to twenty years. He's a leader. It probably bothers him to see a young player come in, a guy like you, and start trash-talkin', ragging on his own teammates."

"Mad Dog's worried we've got some kind of curse on the club."

"Forget about that," Sharkey said hastily, clenching his jaw. He slipped his hands beneath the desk and rapped his knuckles seven times. "This curse crap—you can't dwell on it. Don't even think about that. Just do a better job of fitting in, being one of the guys."

"All right. We done?"

"Yes." Sharkey sighed. "Let's get out of here. We've got a plane to catch."

They stood and left through the cavernous clubhouse, nearly empty now except for Davenport and Uggams, still packing. Glass doors and a flight of steps led up to a long concrete walkway that would take them to the charter bus, idling at the edge of the parking lot.

It was a nice night, balmy and clear. As they emerged together at street level, Sharkey was surprised to see several hundred fans still waiting behind yellow cordons, two hours after the final out. They were there for a glimpse of Kane, up close, and upon seeing him they let out a wild cheer. Cameras began flashing. There were people of all ages—grown men, teenagers, younger girls and boys, dozens of beautiful women—straining at the ropes, leaning over to hold out caps, game programs and scraps of paper, hoping Kane might veer their way and stop and sign.

Kane only walked, his eyes straight ahead, his sleek Italian shoes clicking in long, limber strides. He did not see, and might never have noticed, the strange-looking guy in the forest green cap, down near the end of the throng.

Lanky and tall, with broad shoulders and a huge aquiline nose, the man stared mutely with haunting eyes, large and hollow and blue as the sea. He was surgically disfigured: Part of his lower lip and much of his chin were removed, accentuating the nose, which seemed to overhang his face a good four or five inches. No one met his gaze or realized who he was, but he watched with keen interest, because once, long ago, he had walked in the same brilliant limelight, the crowds reaching for him, the women falling at his feet. And even now, back in Boston, there were some who swore they had never seen a more exciting ballplayer than Kenton Randall Ravinovich.

The Raven.

6

He watched them board the gleaming silver bus: Kane first, quick steps, so slick and strong he slipped right through gravity's fingers, and then Sharkey, a slower ascent, his broad, rounded shoulders stooped and weary, his narrow butt tight as a two-thousand-year-old mummy's. It triggered a memory, a moment Ravinovich hadn't thought about for years: the night in New York, just before Labor Day, when he had sneaked a slingshot out of his locker and fired a steel BB into the showers, thwacking Sharkey flush on the right ass cheek. And he let out a cry, a deep, rhinoceroslike cry—"Aaaa-ooooooo-OOOO-GGGHHH!"—that had been so goddamn hilarious that the tears spilled over on Greenwell's cheeks; Mike Greenwell and Jim Rice were bent over for five minutes, laughing so hard, and the whole club took to mimicking that cry for weeks afterward, until Sharkey called a team meeting and threatened fines.

It caused a smile, even now, a tiny cracking open of the Raven's mutilated mouth. The humorous moments of his life now passed quickly, though, and his mood shifted again toward melancholy as he

watched the bus pull away. Inside it a band of young, talented men, Kane the most talented of all, on a wide-open highway to glory.

But not Ravinovich. No more.

Crossing the dark, emptying lot to his rental car, a wine-colored LeBaron, he screeched out into the street, rocketing toward the airport. He would pass them now, but they wouldn't notice him, would never see him; he always took a different airline whenever he followed the club on the road.

The last three years—since his fourth or fifth surgery; he wasn't sure which—he had been tracking the Sox more and more, attending almost every game at Fenway, going out on road trips. He traveled light and was seldom recognized; he looked little like the superstar of yore and hid in broad daylight beneath his assortment of caps and wraparound shades. He read the sports pages and listened to the sports-talk shows on the radio. He taped games on television even when he attended them in person. What he craved, what he loved most of all, was hearing some commentator mention his name, how great Ravinovich had been, pointing out the seats in the upper deck where one of the Raven's blasts had landed. That was a thrill, but it happened too rarely, and it did not fully explain the obsession he felt. He knew he was clinging to the past, but why, when it caused him such pain? He cheered like a madman for these morons, these modern Red Sox, and yet he was bitterly aware of the huge gulf between their lives and his own.

They had the glory now, the cars and women and Nike commercials, while he was only a sorry relic, a man ground up like summer sausage by his years of boozing and debauchery. He had been very public about taking the blame, showing a good side to the fans. At a tearful press conference, two years after his retirement, Ravinovich had answered questions about the newly discovered cancer by telling his admirers, "This didn't have to happen. I did this to me."

But inside he harbored enough anger to launch a ground war. A lot of it was still directed at Sharkey, that asshole, sticking him on the pine that last season, costing him a shot at five hundred home runs, at three thousand hits. A shot at the Hall of Fame. The rest . . . well, he was angry over so much, angry at the despicable circumstances of his life. So fucking angry that his love life, once the envy of every ballplayer and sportswriter in America, was now reduced to porking Henrietta Prichard, the Sox's powerful board president, Kornblume's sixty-two-year-old niece. That fact, and his own mangled mouth, the amputated chin, made it just about impossible to look himself in the mirror.

Ravinovich checked in at the United terminal, carrying only a leather handbag, and boarded the crowded late-night flight to Boston. He had requested the last seat, as always, way in the back, hidden near the corner window. He fell into it and sat there exhausted, staring at the city lights in the blackness, as the jet climbed into the sky.

He was on his way to see her. He hated himself for it, but he would be sleeping with the broad tonight, gazing into her beady blue eyes, trying to ignore the heavy makeup caked over her crow's-feet. Touching her hair, piled up and held in place by God-knows-what means, stiff and steel blue as some space-age fiber.

No one saw the side of Henrietta that he saw. Her public persona, so proper and haughty, was a mask for the private woman, so lonely and lascivious, wantonly craving him even now. He hated it, despised her for it, and yet he needed it, needed her flesh, and those repelling forces were driving the last thin filaments of sanity out of his brain.

Nothing was visible below now, only blackness. Raven peered down into it and let his mind drift back. He thought about Rita, the one woman he had truly loved. Beautiful Rita Kataya. Gone now. He wondered what it had been like for her, dying. Sliding off the cliff, feeling the sudden weightlessness. Slamming around inside the car.

Plunging down, down, down, a full quarter mile, that blasted grocery bag tied over her head.

It must have been frightening, horrifying. In retrospect he realized his luck with women had not been so great as he liked to pretend.

Henrietta had come into his life the way any number of women had, through random chance and alcohol. But she was different. She was the biggest fan of all—always had been, apparently. And rich as an Arab sheikh.

It seemed so long ago, way, way back in the winter after his fifty-five-homer season, the year his contract ran out. Negotiations were bitter. He was holding out for a puny $7 million—it seemed like huge money then—and one day, stopping at Fenway for his golf shoes, Ravinovich had run into her on the concourse level. Henrietta had stopped him: "Hey, Raven, let's talk a minute." She was, of course, younger then, not exactly Britney Spears, but not yet ripe enough to scare the kids on Halloween. So they ended up at Muldooney's, downed enough tequila and bourbon to pickle a healthy elephant, and through an opaque haze ended up entwined on the Raven's king-size waterbed. He had got his $7 million—or close to it, $6.8—and a clandestine lover who stuck to him like roofing tar.

At least a dozen times he banged her that season, and later, even after he tried to extricate himself, he found himself with her at least once a year. She cared. She loved him dearly, that tough, ball-busting bitch, loved him even now. She was behind the big tribute the Sox were planning—"Day of the Raven," sometime in the fall—to honor all his achievements before he was gone. That was reason enough to keep her happy. A tribute like that, an outpouring of love from the fans, might sway some of those son-of-a-bitch writers to finally vote him into the Hall.

The jet touched down at Logan and Ravinovich found his Jag and tooled across the city—under the channel, across the Charles, a zigzag route to Henrietta's imposing brick mansion in Cambridge.

It was way past midnight, but she was up waiting; she met him in a red silk nightie, her toenails dangling like paint droplets on the end of those long, ugly chicken feet. Her hair was bigger than before, stacked high above her diamond earrings. Ravinovich could see the outline of her breasts beneath the sheer silk, two deflated sacks hanging low enough to make a man gag. Except he was starting to get a little horny.

"Got something for me?" she said raspily, moving into his arms.

"Only my big hunk of burnin' love." Ravinovich chuckled as he slid his hairy hands down onto her buttocks.

"You are a dirty old bastard," she teased.

"Mmmmmmm." He clamped his truncated mouth onto her mouth, and they fought in a desperate kiss. Out of breath, Henrietta finally broke free.

"A dirty bird!"

He kissed her again, kissed her with a force that surprised even himself. She pulled away again, only for a moment, breathing hot on his neck.

"Give me your bird, Raven! Give me that dirty bird!"

"It's comin' after you, lucky lady!"

"Ooooooooooooo!"

The typical baseball contract had become an absurd document, more complicated than the blueprints of a skyscraper. Wolf strained to make out the fine print even in his reading glasses. He had spent half the afternoon going through a whole stack of them, focusing specifically on bonus clauses, a devilish invention of the cocksucking agents that could cost the club a fortune if not managed properly.

On a yellow legal pad he compiled brief notations about the contract language and possible preemptive strikes. Frolicky was due an extra $90,000 if he finished the season with twenty starts. "Move to

bullpen?" Wolf jotted tersely. Villalobos, with nineteen homers, was on a pace for a windfall of $150,000 if he could slug just eleven more. "Hit and run with him? Sub out for Bauer/Nieves w/three-run lead? Pretense of gaining them experience?"

Wolf exhaled wearily and began poring over the dense legalese of Davenport's pact, one especially loaded with contingencies and semantic gobbledygook. The multiyear deal contained a provision that sent a shudder through Wulfmeyer as he saw it and remembered: Davenport, who was on a tear now—his average had climbed to .322—was in line to reap a $300,000 bonanza if he made the All-Star team.

Shit! Wolf mouthed the word. *Shit shit SHIT!* Joe Torre, the Yankees' manager, was due to announce the reserves next Tuesday. Wulfmeyer decided to call him; he'd make up something, say Davenport's wife was pregnant, his son was ill, some excuse to make him unavailable. It was dicey business—Davenport might rail about the snub, in which case Wolf might have to smooth enough feathers to fill an ostrich farm—but the Sox were a small-market franchise; it had to be done.

He reached for the phone just as Samantha picked up the other line. She called out, "Neville, it's the White House. Office of the President."

"The president?" That was a shocker; sure, there was a tradition of presidents calling certain teams, or individuals, if they had accomplished some great feat, like winning a title—and a few even got to visit the White House. But the Sox had won nothing, and hadn't since the Woodrow Wilson administration. It was probably about Kane, the ultrasensation.

Wolf punched the line. "Hello. Neville Wulfmeyer."

"Mr. Wulfmeyer. This is the most important call of the season. Believe me." The voice was husky and oddly muffled.

"Great. I'm honored, naturally. I don't always vote in—"

"I sent you something. A videotape. You got it?"

"I don't know. From the president? I'm not sure yet; I'm not always as organized—"

"Find it and watch it."

"I will. Is there a title, or some—"

"It's in a red envelope. Look at it. It's the kind of thing that could easily fall into the hands of the police."

"Police? What are you talking about?"

"Just watch the fucking thing. Then we'll talk."

Wolf raised in his chair. "You're not—this isn't the White House, is it?"

"No."

"Senator Puccini?" He had once met Ray Puccini, the junior delegate from Massachusetts—but no, couldn't be, no senator was that coarse in a formal phone call. Or would make such a joke. "Who the hell is this?"

"Never mind who I am. This tape, look at it and think to yourself, 'My God, this could have been shot by a Tigers fan, or some Yankee zealot.'"

"Look, I'm extremely busy," Wulfmeyer said hotly. "I'll look at the damn thing when I get a break in my schedule."

"Don't wait too long."

The caller hung up. Wolf slammed the phone.

"Is it a dinner?" Samantha called out.

"No. Fuck it! Just some asshole." Wolf dug through a foot-high stack of unopened mail. He found the envelope, saw his name in black block letters, and tossed the packet in his bottom drawer. He had no interest in seeing it, knowing who was on there, or what antisocial act was involved. Any real Sox fan would have just erased the thing, thrown it away.

Wulfmeyer removed his glasses and rubbed his eyes. The day was turning into another succession of annoyances. So many goddamn hassles. Castillo still AWOL, no team in either league willing to deal

for him. The sports pages filled with questions about team chemistry and morale in light of his disappearance and the fight between Kane and Bauer. That one was getting lots of ink. The writers were beginning to understand that Kane was not exactly a stabilizing influence. Though he had apologized to Bauer, and even gone out for a few beers with him, there were still deep fissures in the club.

Moses was threatening to play out his option. Briscoe had been heard grumbling to Tarver about Kane batting for himself. Villalobos wanted more money—didn't they all? Davenport, in spite of his surging average, was showing signs of recidivism: "He feels he no longer has to abide by curfew, rules of conduct, etc., etc., because Kane doesn't," Domato had written in one of his weekly reports. "In KC he got in a bar fight, mirror broken, and in Texas D got rental car, ticketed, almost arrested for going 105 mph, lecture by Fish, lecture by me. Sullen. What is he thinking?"

What, indeed? It was scary. Fish was going to have to be harder on him, take a firmer hand. Now, there was a guy, Davenport, who deserved to be screwed out of an All-Star berth. Physical talent galore, but a head case beyond the powers of modern science. Not three hours ago Wolf had got the latest word from Lacy: The nuns were rejecting the club's tendered settlement offer of enough cash to build a castle on the Rhine, and so now, in addition to facing criminal assault charges, it looked as if Davenport would be hit with a mammoth civil claim, with the ball club, of course, a codefendant.

Wulfmeyer grabbed the Excedrin and downed four tablets; he could feel one of those wrecking-ball headaches coming on. He wished for once, just once, the Sox could get through a season without some horrible legal mess, without all these problems, but it would never happen. They weren't fielding the Vienna Boys' Choir. This was hardball. You were damn lucky if you could find even one or two players who combined top-tier talent with class, a guy like Joe DiMaggio. There just weren't very many DiMaggios around anymore.

A tune began to drift through Wulfmeyer's head, the old Simon & Garfunkel hit: "Where have you gone, Joe DiMaggio? Our nation turns its lonely eyes to you . . . woo woo woo. . . . Joltin' Joe has left and gone away . . . hey hey hey . . . hey hey hey. . . ."

If only he'd played for Boston. Imagine that, Joe DiMaggio in Boston—

The phone rang again.

"Oscar Gamboa," Sam called out. "Says it's very important."

"Oh, I bet," Wolf said with disgust. He shook his head. Gamboa, the worst agent in the Western Hemisphere. He tilted forward and grabbed the line. "Oscar, you're calling at a bad time; I've got a million things going on. But I'm trying like hell. Nobody wants to deal for him."

"This time we're not discussing Castillo," Gamboa said evenly, "although he's ready to play, if you're ready to deal."

"He's *got* a contract!"

"We want the performance bonuses rewritten into his base salary. It'll take your legal people about twenty minutes."

"No fuckin' way. No chance, Oscar."

"All right, we can discuss that later. Right now I'm calling about Kane, Ron Kane."

"What about him?" Wulfmeyer swallowed. He felt the first clammy dampness of a cold sweat.

Gamboa said he was now representing Kane, a man destined to become the greatest athlete of all time. He was no dummy either, and damn concerned that his $2.8 million contract was far under market for a player of his stature. What he wanted was a long-term agreement, eight years, $270 million, plus various options and incentives, a percentage of concessions and parking, television fees. "I've got a list prepared. Soon as you're free, we should go over it."

Wulfmeyer found it difficult to speak. His tongue seemed to be swelling and blocking his throat. A contract that big—Christ, it was

more than the Rangers were paying Alex Rodriguez, a good $20 million more. And the hell of it was, the worst part was, Kane was probably worth it. A deal of that magnitude could sink the whole goddamn ball club.

"Oscar, this is—I have to see if, once I look at—" He swallowed hard. "Let me call you back."

7

The purpose of the breakfast was unclear, and Sharkey dreaded the possibilities. The last time he'd been summoned to a breakfast meeting, nineteen years ago, he'd been fired right in the middle of a Belgian waffle. A psychological kick in the nuts of that magnitude left the indelible feeling that it could happen again—or something else was wrong. Old Gordo was finally dying, or one of the guys had been arrested—another assault charge. Or maybe Wolf just wanted to ruin the start of a perfectly decent summer morning by launching into one of his blasted second-guessing fits, the last of which, when Caruby went into rehab, nearly ended in fisticuffs.

Sharkey slipped into the circular booth, saw with some alarm that Wulfmeyer and Domato were both in a funk, and stared, bleary-eyed, at the grinning circus clown on the cover of a menu labeled HOUSE OF FLAPJACKS.

"See Harkwood's story?" Wolf brandished a copy of the *Herald*. "He openly wonders why Uggams was allowed to steal third with a nine-run lead."

"He ran on his own," Sharkey said.

"I'm wondering the same thing, frankly." Wulfmeyer seemed not to hear him. Wolf's eyes were red. He carped about Langley's error in the sixth, groused about dealing with Henrietta, all the demands she was making for the Raven's year-end tribute, and veered into a complete non sequitur concerning Frolicky's loss of velocity, the fact that Sharkey should try him in long relief. Wolf grimaced and drained his coffee. Sharkey realized he'd kept them waiting.

"Traffic this morning—sorry."

"Forget it," Wolf said. "Anyway, we got problems. Other problems. *Bigger* problems. Oh, shit, what a day I had yesterday, a day like I haven't had in fucking weeks—and I should be able to say *years,* or *decades.* I've been in piss-poor moods, gentlemen, but this is one *really* piss-poor mood."

Sharkey braced himself. Wulfmeyer's use of a word like "gentlemen" was a clear sign he was clinging to his last frayed strands of civility. Wolf's face puckered, as if he were gagging up an old meatball, and the words came hissing out: first a blast at Gamboa, about the bloated snake demanding a huge new deal for Kane—a mammoth deal, and the kid only in his first year in the majors—and the sick state of the game being such that he'd probably get it. They'd have to deal with the bastard. Fuckin' highway robbery.

"Then I'm sitting there, stunned, thinking is this going to be the blow that finally kills Old Gordo, and who should wander in? Just take a guess!"

"Mariah Carey?" Domato couldn't resist the joke.

Wulfmeyer glared at him. "That goddamn cop, what's-his-face. Barney Schachter. 'The Barnacle,' they call him. That's from Lacy, from her friend in the DA's office. 'The Barnacle' because he just latches on to a case and *hangs* on to it." Wolf made a rigid clinging gesture with his hand. In a reflexive response, Sharkey sucked in a breath utterly devoid of oxygen.

"Just visiting—or what?"

"They know about Cleveland." Wulfmeyer let out an exclamatory "haaa!"—an emergency tension release to keep his chest from exploding. Then, under his breath, *"Fuck it!"*

Sharkey felt his stomach start to grind; he feared another colitis attack. Wolf stared, inscrutably, and went on to say that the FBI crime computer had linked the Marzoli murder to the one in Texas, the one in Cleveland *and* one in Kansas City, the stop before Texas. There had been one in KC that nobody on the club even knew about. And there had just been another one, last night, down in Savin Hill, same type of attack.

Five murders, very distinctive crimes characterized by the heads of the victims being cut off, or nearly cut off. Markings of some sort on every victim. And, if it meant anything, Schachter said all the victims were bald. The sickest kind of sick ugly shit imaginable.

"That's as specific as he got, but it was more than I wanted to know, and I bluntly told him so," Wulfmeyer said. "'Good God Almighty,' I said, 'I hope my guys are not in any danger.'"

Wolf's dour expression, the listing of his head, made it clear he was unconscious of his own genius. In spite of the horror of the news, Sharkey felt a flash of admiration for him, that at a moment of such clear crisis he had managed to turn the equation completely around to make it seem as if the Sox were likely victims. Sharkey struggled to formulate the question thrashing in his own head.

"And . . . are they watching anybody *in particular?*"

Wulfmeyer's green eyes locked on him with feral intensity. "Like you, for example?" He laughed without humor. "Fish, I'm telling you—yeah, I'm just going to tell you what they've got. They've got a task force taking shape. A fucking federal task force. Some brilliant cop—and it's probably this Barnacle—had the idea to correlate these crimes with our travel schedule. Imagine! A brainstorm that arose from the fact that they're going over these crimes and they see you found the body in Texas! You! YOU!"

Sharkey was stunned to realize that the rant had been building to an accusation.

"Wolf, the guy screamed right outside my room!"

"This Barnacle," Wolf went on, "he's having an extremely difficult time believing that of all the millions of people living in Texas, *millions* of people, it was *you* who happened to be in that alley. You didn't listen to me, did you? I told you it was a mistake. 'Just leave it,' I said. 'Walk away from it.' Now you're connected to the crime scene there and it's a documented fact you hated the fucking moron Marzopan."

Sharkey stared hard, trying to gauge the slippage in Wulfmeyer's cognitive gears. Marzopan? He felt a strong impulse to point out that Wolf's very dubious advice had come *after* the body in the alley was found, much too late to leave the thing lying there, as if that were truly an option. But he sensed that Wulfmeyer was incapable at the moment of comprehending such a subtlety; instead he forced himself to ask about Castillo. Had Wolf mentioned Castillo going AWOL? The suspicions that Castillo might be the perpetrator?

"No. No, I didn't," Wulfmeyer said flatly. "I don't like the little bastard either, but the fact is, he's presumed to be an innocent man."

"Remember, Wolf: He went AWOL the same night as that Texas thing! The same night!"

"He won't be AWOL for long. Gamboa left a voice mail. He's talked him into coming back while we negotiate—not that I'll budge an inch, frankly."

"Wolf!"

"That could be total coincidence. The guy's never killed anybody his whole career. Why in the hell would he start now?"

Domato had finally caught the eye of a waitress, who took orders and poured more coffee. He swung his heavy face back to the table. "I know this shouldn't matter, but we're really thin right now at short."

"Stu, that is just—"

"He's got twice the range Bauer does."

"Are you following this conversation? We're talking murder—MURDER!" Sharkey's pulse rate had climbed to twice normal. "Say for a moment he *is* a killer—I'm practically *certain* to be one of his next targets."

"Oh, I just can't—"

"This is my *life* here!" Sharkey said. "My God, this mental case should be checked out, or traded—something!"

Wolf said, "I'm *trying* to trade him, goddamn it."

Sharkey mentioned a point that he had been reluctant to bring up: that he had taken home Castillo's personnel file two nights ago. Wulfmeyer immediately demanded to know why he was taking home personnel files. "Because I don't want my head cut off!" Sharkey spoke so emphatically he nearly spilled his coffee. "Right there, in black and white, it says Castillo attacked one of his teammates down in Sioux City four years ago. Hands right on the guy's throat. A third baseman. Six or seven guys had to drag them apart."

"Just a fight. That's just baseball," Domato said, shaking his head. "Tempers flare all the time. Jesus."

Wulfmeyer hunched forward. "Listen to me, Fish, we've been over this before, at least six hundred times: We all have a role here. I have my role, Stu has his role, you have your role. The cops have their role. You're getting damn good money to decide when to change pitchers and play hit-and-run. Don't blow it by conducting psychological analyses with old personnel files. Trying to play homicide dick."

Sharkey understood the implied threat that Wolf might try to fire him. His antenna for that sort of thing was far more acute than anything ever devised by NASA. "You want to blow me out, you're going to need Old Gordo's approval."

"Fish, I am well aware you've got the support of that ninety-four-

year-old fart—" Wulfmeyer punctuated the blasphemy by stabbing his index finger on the tabletop. "He could be dead any day now. He's back in intensive care, you know."

"What?"

"His IV fell off the pole. A couple nights ago."

"Oh, Je-SUS Christ!" Sharkey looked at Domato, who was watching the waitress's sashaying fanny, and felt himself overcome by an enormous sense of despair. He stared a moment at the dirt under his nails—he could never get the damn things clean—and sensed Wolf's eyes on him, sensed the weight of his fierce intensity until he felt obliged to reiterate, as he did every two or three weeks, that winning was of course his primary aim. Nothing mattered more to him than bringing a championship to Boston, but these disciplinary problems . . . well, they just had to be brought under control. "I'm sick of the malcontents, the hoodlums, and I *certainly* don't want a serial killer on my club, if that's what we're dealing with."

"None of us do, Fish. None of us do!"

"Trade him, then! Send him to Pawtucket! Tell the cops about the bastard!"

"We are *not* going to invent murder allegations out of thin air because of some personal animosity *you* happen to hold." Wulfmeyer shook his head in disgust. "You say one word to the cops and it's all over, I swear to God. Am I clear on that?"

Sharkey realized that if he wanted to take a proactive approach, if he wanted to look out for himself by probing these dark possibilities, he would have no support whatsoever from the front office. He'd have to do it entirely on his own, keeping it secret. Even if it involved nothing more than sorting through papers.

"Look, I don't want to fight about this," Sharkey said. "But if you're thinking this kind of thing is going to go unnoticed, you're dead wrong. Someone's going to see something. The cops or the

public—somehow it's going to get out, and if it does, believe me, we're going to face a considerable amount of public criticism and second-guessing."

Wulfmeyer pursed his lips. He keenly understood the financial hit the club might take if a player were arrested for decapitating fans. The impact on attendance, endorsements, cap and pennant sales and other concessions might last for years. It might even wipe out television and radio contracts.

"We need some ideas."

"How about we move up the curfew?" Domato suggested. "Say, midnight after night games, get them right to bed. Keep them—"

"No, won't work," Wolf said. "We tried that one year and the goddamn players' union was all over our asses. Ended up slapping an injunction on us."

Sharkey remembered it; Ravinovich had led the clubhouse revolt. "What about private detectives?" Sharkey mentioned how, during the wife-swap scandal in Baltimore, the club owner had hired a guy, a famous sleuth, who had followed the blonde into a rifle shop south of the harbor, and it had ended up saving the franchise a bundle in liability costs during the civil suit. "If we got ourselves a few good PIs, we could find out who's out late, why, and maybe cut a whole lot of the extracurricular nonsense."

Wolf scowled, thinking. "Maybe. Except the money might be a problem. We'd need six or eight, at least, to watch all these guys, plus travel, lodging. You're talking about a couple hundred thousand bucks between now and October."

It might not sound like that much, he added ruefully, but the club was in a financial pinch like a headlock from the Boston Strangler. Less than a week ago the club had been forced to lay off nineteen maintenance workers in anticipation of trying to re-sign Langley and Villalobos.

"It's better than this thing blowing up in our faces," Sharkey said.

"Right. I know that."

"These cops, how suspicious are they? They talking like we could really be suspects?"

Wolf glared. "Presumption of innocence. Remember that. It's the cornerstone of our democracy."

Steam billowed out of the showers. Sharkey moved through it like a Scottish ghost—congratulating Tarver, Kane, Davenport, making conversation, stealing what tidbits he could—and then angled toward his office.

It had been a great win, a 5–0 victory in the last road game before the All-Star break. The Sox were still hot—two out of three against the Twins and three straight in Baltimore—but, of course, every win was an illusion, just part of a big roulette game where you had to let the money ride. Ride and ride and ride. No payoffs until October.

Knowing that, and dealing with the darker issues at hand, took the edge off even the finest performance. Castillo had returned, strutting into the clubhouse half an hour before game time like Babe Ruth himself, so high-and-mighty he couldn't be bothered to speak to anyone, let alone Sharkey. He had doubled twice and made a diving catch, a fluke display of potential that figured to have negative repercussions for weeks. Now, hunched at his locker, shirtless, he watched the room with those little black demon eyes, fantasizing who-knew-what.

Sharkey tried to ignore him, keep his thoughts on the mental list he had put together, sketchy notes about the guys' plans for the night: Uggams, Tarver and Reeling to the movies, Langley and Kane to a dance club, Frolicky to see his aunt Hedda.

A lot of it was poppycock, pure poppycock, but Wolf wanted a record; Sharkey was only beginning to see how utterly pointless it was. He stepped into his office and fell into the chair.

Domato came in a moment later, closing the door behind him.

"Ready for this?" he said.

"Probably not."

"Just talked to Wolf."

"And?"

"Your old pal Ravinovich—he's, you know, a fan, and very close to Henrietta." Domato smiled luridly. "Anyway, he's going to be hanging around. Wolf's given him clubhouse privileges."

"Lord God Almighty." Sharkey felt a torpedo hit the starboard side of the season.

"He's dying, Fish."

"Yeah, but . . . why take us with him?"

Domato shrugged. "Starting after the break. He'll probably be at the banquet. And there's more news, even worse."

Sharkey was still fixed on the Raven. "Why is Wolf allowing this? He knows how disruptive that idiot can be."

"Orders. From on high. It'll mean the world to him."

"Christ." Sharkey stared between his cleats. "What's the other? What could possibly be worse?"

"That Barnacle came back, wanting records. Left with a big stack of Xeroxes."

"Of what?"

"Records. Various shit." Domato sighed. "Fortunately, the cops want to keep this all hush-hush, keep it out of the papers. They don't want to tip off the killer. That's a big break."

"Halle-fucking-lujah." Sharkey could imagine word leaking to the press. Oh, God, how things would fall apart at that point—like an oatmeal cookie in a driving rainstorm. Domato asked about the efforts to glean a sense of the players' postgame plans, and Sharkey only shook his head. "These guys are just shining me on. It's useless."

"Wolf thinks it's a fan. Might be true." Domato's expression was haunted, fearful. Sharkey realized that Wolf had probably blasted him, his usual ranting and raving. "You grabbing a bite? I'm starved."

"Yeah." Sharkey glanced at his watch; it was just after eleven. The team flight wasn't leaving until nine the next morning. "I told Uzi I'd meet him at the Crab Cooker. He just took off. That place okay?"

"Seafood's great." It seemed as though Domato wanted to talk; there were things on his mind. Together they packed up, left their bags with the equipment man, and went out, hailing a cab. It smelled of cigarette smoke and urine. Sharkey asked the driver, an old Greek with silvery black hair, to turn down the radio, and for a while he and Domato sat in silence, brooding, just watching the late-night traffic.

"Wolf kills me," Sharkey said as they swung within sight of the harbor. "He wishes I'd quit, doesn't he?"

"Yeah, but you're not a quitter. That's one thing you ain't."

"And such a cheapskate. We've got serious trouble here, and he knows it, and he should break down and hire us some detectives. It's stupid not to."

"Interesting choice of words: 'break down.' That's where he's headed, I think. A breakdown."

"Why? Why do you say that?" Sharkey studied Domato's rounded profile, pulsing with every streetlight. He thought about Wolf's mental slip, the alleged instruction to ignore the dead body.

"Stress. Too much going on." Domato folded his arms across his chest. He said there was a crisis brewing at Amalgamated's largest subsidiary, Industrial Tank Ball, a manufacturing plant in South Boston where the Teamsters had been grumbling for two years over salary and benefit issues. "There's that, plus these murders, contract negotiations, and of course Old Gordo's in terrible shape. You heard the rumors? About Wolf's contract?"

"No. What?"

"A million-dollar bonus, if we win while Gordo's still alive. A sure sign of Gordo's senility."

"Amazing." It was more than amazing—it was an outrage. Sharkey's mood had just been ratcheted three levels lower. Gordo was

his biggest supporter, and his own bonuses were nowhere near that lucrative.

"But he ain't going to last another year, Old Gordo. This year's his last chance to see it."

"Wolf will fire me for sure—if we don't win it all." Sharkey stared out the window. A million bucks. "What's the latest? On Gordo?"

"He was out of the coma yesterday for ten minutes, said something, I couldn't understand it, about Raquel Welch's brassiere, and then he goes right back under again."

"Jesus."

"Anyway, Wolf's been falling behind on things, neglecting a lot of important stuff. Like the Raven's tribute. We don't even have a target date, nothing whatsoever."

Sharkey stared at the meter; it was up to $17.50 and seemed to be turning over at a prodigious rate. The radio, still playing very faintly, carried a sports report: The Yankees had scored five in the ninth to beat Cleveland. Damn! Sharkey winced, and he thought about the Raven, the old scars from their one year together.

On the surface the rift had involved playing time, Sharkey's decision to sit him down and go with the young hotshot Saxon. That had touched off the political struggle, Ravinovich lobbying the board behind his back, trying to get Sharkey fired. On a deeper level, though, the issue was one of respect. What Sharkey had wanted, what he hoped for from every player, from Wolf too, was some sign that his leadership was accepted, that he was deserving of confidence. Ravinovich was like so many swaggering athletes; he had never been willing to give that. It meant surrendering too much of himself.

Instead he would sit there on the bench—not unlike Castillo, really—and when Sharkey would look over, the Raven's tongue would come out, just a little at first, like he was wetting his lips, and then a little farther, and Sharkey would notice that his eyes were cross-

ing. The effect started very subtly, growing more pronounced until Sharkey signaled, by some severe expression, that he suspected he was being mocked, and then the tongue would slip back inside and the Raven's steely blue eyes would fix themselves on the playing field.

Domato was still talking; it took a moment for Sharkey to realize he was still discussing Ravinovich. "I know you can't stand him, Fish, but the more I talk to him, the more I feel kind of sorry for the guy."

"Because he's dying—"

"Well, yeah, because of that, but also because he's so screwed up, tormented." Domato turned to Sharkey; in the partial silhouette of lights, his face was half obscured. "Do you know he still roots for the Red Sox? Goes to games and sits all by himself?"

"Doesn't root for me, I bet."

"No, I'm sure he doesn't. But he's been watching Kane and just dying inside, wishing he could be young again, all that glory, and I think he's almost kind of jealous, except he's told me what a big fan he is. They're a lot alike, I think. They might really hit it off."

Sharkey clenched up, hit by a feeling, or premonition. The cab lurched and pulled up in front of the Crab Cooker.

"God, I hope not. I hope he leaves Kane alone."

8

Nights were the worst for most managers, the brutal wee hours when fears and anxieties played themselves out in wide-screen, surround-sound, Looney Tunes nightmares. Over the years Sharkey had learned to control the incubus, repressing all those unruly emotions down into a cold, mangled knot of unresolved trauma, which adhered like a banyan root to the core of his psyche.

Lately, though, the stresses were beginning to percolate up through hidden membranes. He had nightmares about the murders, about Castillo coming at him with a bayonet, about getting fired, about something god-awful happening to Kane. Those were some of the most vivid: One night Kane was out hitchhiking when a section of sewer pipe tumbled off a flatbed and crushed him like a stink bug. Another night he was striding to the mound when he stepped on an old World War II land mine, which blew him clear through the roof of the SkyDome.

During the final week before the All-Star Game, it happened again: Kane was bleeding, Wulfmeyer attacking him with a knife,

because he had walked in a run or somehow cost the club the World Series. Lurching awake, Sharkey lay almost in shock, numb, aware of a soft voice—a news report on the bedside radio; he'd left it on low to hear a late-night talk show.

"—tobacco companies are disputing the report," an announcer was saying, "offering their own evidence that secondhand smoke actually *enhances* some types of immune response. And in local news tonight, another tragedy: Police have discovered the body of a fifty-nine-year-old Chelsea man in a hotel room near Logan Airport, one more in a series of apparent ritual killings—" Sharkey hunched up on one elbow. "Police say at least six known victims have been identified, all with distinctive wounds and markings. The motive is unknown. The attacks have occurred from Boston to—"

Sharkey reached and switched it off—he had to think. Christ, it was unbelievable. He lay in the dark, his skin tingling. He looked over at Bernice, her upturned face only a series of thin lines—thin lips, thin eyes and eyebrows, a tiny straight nose—within a great tumbleweed of hair. She was asleep. He got up, padded to the bathroom, and sat on the toilet, staring at the wall. Was all this really happening? He thought about Castillo and the pattern of the crimes: Boston, Kansas City, Texas, Cleveland, Boston. Now Boston again. With any luck, Wolf was right: Someone out there had blown a head gasket, someone with absolutely no connection to the Red Sox. A fan, like he said. A whacked-out fan, one of those nitwits that had watched *Taxi Driver* four hundred times, or *The Silence of the Lambs*. That was as likely a theory as any, but—

Standing again, Sharkey got the Pepto from the cabinet, took a couple spoonfuls, and washed the sweat off his face, looking hard at the ugly purple vein that was becoming increasingly visible on the tip of his nose. He thought about downing a Sominex, but instead he got an idea, went out, checked the clock. One in the morning. But only

ten out west, not too late for a phone call. He sat down in the den, in the pale moonlight pouring in the front window, and dialed up Sherm McClintock, a good guy, a friend now managing out in San Jose.

"Fish! Hey, long time no hear from. How are ya? Got yourself quite a club this year—quite a young superstar."

"Yeah, I sure do," Sharkey said, and then, after a few minutes of small talk, he got down to it: What was Sherm's read on Benito Castillo? What had happened the night in Sioux City when he had gone after that third baseman?

"Benito Castillo." McClintock repeated the name and laughed. "You ever tried communicating with that guy?"

"All the time," Sharkey said. "Rather have my teeth pulled." They both laughed. McClintock said the attack on the teammate, a guy named Stockman, didn't really amount to much.

"Funny moment, though. Next to last game of the season and Stockman holds up at third after Castillo rips a shot into the gap, cost 'Nito his fiftieth RBI. Never did get it. Lost a ten-thousand-dollar bonus, I believe."

Sharkey smiled. "Hard to imagine he got that close."

"Weak pitching. Say, you got two of my all-time head cases. Jeremy Davenport, too."

"I didn't know you had—"

"Oh, yeah. Davenport, he was with me three years earlier in Charleston. Just my luck. That nun thing, I said, 'Wow, there he goes again.' You know one time in Charleston he tried to knock off a liquor store? For kicks, nothing else. Luckily, it was a first offense, and we got him off with probation."

"Really? I didn't know that." Sharkey frowned. He was about to ask another question when he noticed someone outside the window, a figure hovering beside his car in the driveway. Leaning over the hood.

"Oh, hey, Sherm—I've got to go. I'll call you back. I'll call you

some other time." He hung up and hurried closer, near the couch. His blood pressure rocketed up until his pulse was pounding on his eardrums, banging on them like a monkey on a tom-tom. It figured: If the killer was coming after him, it wouldn't happen at the park, nowhere in public. It would be here at home in the wee hours. A car bomb—maybe he was attaching some kind of bomb to the Olds.

Sharkey wasn't about to take any chances. He turned and went flying through the hall, into his bedroom office, catching his baby toe on the doorjamb.

He knew right away he had ripped the blasted toenail off; the pain shot through him like fork lightning through a black sky. Oh God, God, God, God, but he gritted his teeth, fought it, oh God. And he reached the top shelf, above the desk, and brought down his old Walther nine-millimeter Luger, a black, satin-finished little baby he'd bought ten years ago. Never used it. Got it and ran, hopping through the hall, gritting his teeth until he got to the door, his finger on the trigger, threw it open.

He was there. Standing right next to the car.

"Freeze, sucker!"

"Hey, good evening. Hope you got a license for that." Schachter. Barney Schachter. What a shock.

"Yes, I do," Sharkey said, slowly lowering the gun, fighting the incredible urge to grab hold of his bloody toe.

Schachter strolled toward him, his white hair scattered over his ears. "Not a good practice to blow away anybody that comes sauntering up your drive at night. We frown on that. Although I guess you're probably wondering what the hell I'm doing."

"That thought crossed my mind." Sharkey wasn't sure which was worse—the screaming agony in his toe or the chilling realization that he might have shot the man.

"Just procedure. Routine investigative crap of a sort that bores us cops out of our minds."

"With my car?"

"Those Goodyear tires, they're a popular make. You weren't out at Logan messing around, three or four hours ago? Your engine's—"

"No, no, I was here. Except I picked up a pizza around ten." Sharkey was alarmed by how intensely the Barnacle studied him. The angled streetlight turned one of his eyes a giant luminescent blue, leaving the other one dark.

"Well, anyway, don't mind me," Schachter said. "Just routine. Weird thing is, this case we're working on, so far every victim's been bald."

"Bald?" Sharkey didn't dare let on that he already knew that. Wolf had said it at breakfast.

"Incredible coincidence," Schachter said. "Or a baffling enigma of the human mind. Good night."

Her gaze swept the room, and her smile flashed at Sharkey like the brilliant pulse of a lighthouse. A moment later she broke away from a knot of people at the bar and moved toward him—a gorgeous woman, probably forty, dark-eyed, auburn-haired, voluptuous. For some inexplicable reason she was crossing the ballroom just to introduce herself.

Annie Tusch, she said, reaching out her hand. A lifelong Red Sox fan, but she remembered Sharkey even from his days in Baltimore.

"Seeing you on TV," she said, "that walk out to the mound to change pitchers. Such a *look*—so serious, *severe*."

"I made a lot of those walks," Sharkey said.

"Not that you've stopped. Oh, you wish!"

She laughed, showing perfect teeth. They talked for a while, and she explained she was a member of the Boosters. She knew a few—the real diehards—who traveled the country rooting for the Sox, but

she wasn't quite that zealous. She laughed again. She was actually sitting with a crowd of them—they'd bought three tables. The club's annual fund-raiser, held the first night of the All-Star break, was one of the highlights of their social season.

"You ever have a need for the most beautiful flowers in Boston— roses, lilies, orchids, the most gorgeous bouquets—you give me a call." Annie handed over a card. She owned a floral company: Annie Occasion Gifts.

"That I'll do." He grinned and tucked the card into his wallet.

"Or even if you don't need flowers . . ." Annie smiled and drifted away with her glass of Chianti. Sharkey felt a pang as he watched her go. His love life had gone into a slump in recent years on the order of Mad Dog's batting woes. Bernice had never been much of a baseball fan; lately, in addition to her involvement in the arts and the theater, she had begun collecting nineteenth-century handbags, a diversion that took her up and down the eastern seaboard and seemed to be calculated to further drain the bank account and expand the distance between them. It was clear that she had come to resent Sharkey's road trips, his erratic hours and incessant worrying and colitis attacks. She had long ago stopped attending banquets.

Usually the fund-raiser was a sleepy summer soirée, but Kane's arrival had turned it into a fifty-thousand-watt circus—ticket prices of a thousand dollars, celebrities, exotic decor: a faux-tropical landscape of hanging moons and papier-mâché palms bent over pastel islands of hors d'oeuvres. The game was scheduled for the following afternoon in Detroit. Villalobos was the only Red Sox regular voted into the lineup, though Kane, with his sensational debut, had received an impressive number of write-in votes from the fans and had been added to the pitching roster by manager Joe Torre. The two players had already made their appearance at the fund-raiser, addressed the crowd from the bandstand, and were now on their way to the airport

while the party went on. A number of other Sox regulars—Bryan Hazzard, Johnny Uggams, Larry Langley, Ray Tarver—still mingled in the crowd.

Sharkey wore a midnight blue tux and was glad he had come, even though he had done so out of obligation—and to try to follow Castillo afterward. He had begun a radical secret strategy to tail the likely suspects himself, especially that malevolent little bastard, on the theory that the life he saved might be his own.

He was biting into a crab-stuffed shrimp when Wulfmeyer approached, cradling a martini. Wolf looked as if he'd just eaten a tomato worm.

"Fucking cops. I've just about had it."

"What's going on?" Sharkey noticed in him subtle signs of disarray: Wulfmeyer had shaved the right side of his neck but not the left. There was a ball of cotton in his ear.

"Hassles. Did Domato tell you? They called this afternoon—not the Barnacle, someone else. They found a speeding ticket Davenport got, ninety-seven miles an hour, heading north on I-93 the night the guy from Savin Hill was murdered. North, they figure, means away from the scene, if you assume he was heading home."

"The same time as the murder?"

"Close to it, I guess. Just after midnight."

"How can they assume he was heading home?" Sharkey said. "He could be going anywhere at that hour."

"I know, I know. This is what the cops are figuring." Wulfmeyer gritted his teeth. "They're also checking out the Booster Club. At least that makes sense."

Sharkey thought of Annie. He pictured Davenport robbing that liquor store in Charleston. "What about Benito? Look, he's right over there." Sharkey had just spotted Castillo in line at the bar. His hair was combed back slick as sealskin.

Wulfmeyer frowned, watching him. "According to Stu, he may

have an alibi on the night of the last one, the murder out near the airport. Cool Daddy said they were at a party that night. What time he left isn't clear."

"Imagine inviting that guy to a party."

"I don't think he's a killer."

Sharkey wasn't going to argue it; he knew Wolf's mind was locked tight on that one.

"Damn it, damn it!" Wulfmeyer said abruptly, as if tweaked by some inner demon. "Those assholes are even asking about Kane, questioning what we told them about when he first got to Boston. We know damn well when he arrived, because Stu picked him up at Logan—but now they want the record of it. As if he could have possibly killed Marzipan—Marzo—that fuckin' fan—"

"Marzoli."

"Which he couldn't have. No goddamn way. Except Stu can't find the airline receipt."

"It's got to be somewhere. The airlines have to—"

"Yeah, of course. Just got to check with them." Wolf drained the last of his martini. "Anyway, shit, a thousand things I've got to deal with. Tank Ball on strike. Henrietta with a bug up her ass about getting a woman in the broadcasting booth. Some crackpot keeps calling, leaving messages, saying he's from the White House. Like I've got time for jokes."

"Maybe it's not a joke; maybe it's really—"

"Nah, it's some idiot with too much time on his hands. Christ, I'll be glad when things calm down. Anyway, catch you later; I've got to check on Old Gordo. He's actually here tonight. Talk about miracles."

With that, Wulfmeyer whirled away and was gone, slipping through the crowd. Sharkey felt sorry for him—so driven, so consumed with problems: murders, contract negotiations, that ugly Tank Ball mess. Over a thousand men, the entire Teamsters local, had walked off the job because of salary and benefit cuts and a new mech-

anized tank-ball sealing system. The stresses seemed to be eating Wulfmeyer alive.

Sharkey loaded up a plate with taquitos, shrimp, stuffed mushrooms—the food looked fantastic. He poured a glass of champagne, turned, and bumped right into the Raven.

"Oh—oh, Fish," Ravinovich said awkwardly, and he tried to smile. His amputated chin and partially missing lower lip gave his speech a slightly sputtering effect, despite extensive therapy. His smile had a forced, almost clownlike look, one that failed to mask the animosity lingering inside him.

Sharkey cursed his luck, running into Wulfmeyer and Ravinovich back to back. Still, he wanted to be gracious, aware that the Raven was dying.

"Kent, great seeing you." He shook Ravinovich's hand. Sharkey was amazed at how thin his hand felt, like a bag of sticks, and yet it was strong. Ravinovich still had a good, firm handshake. Sharkey fumbled for words and managed to bring up the tribute the club was planning. "About time, I'll tell you. There will never be another Kent Ravinovich. I really mean that."

"Ah, well, that's nice you'd say, but these fans today, they've got Kane. No need to live in the past when you've got Kane here in town." Ravinovich said it with admiration, and with a sparkle in his fiery blue eyes, but Sharkey knew him well enough to know it was probably chewing on him, tearing away what was left of his insides. Ravinovich began talking about Kane's magnetism, his extraordinary charisma.

Half of Sharkey listened, nodding, while the other half studied him. Ravinovich was only a shell of the swift, powerful slugger who had dominated so many summers in Boston. The chin was gone, and so were those lustrous locks, the long chestnut waves that the women went crazy for; the chemo had left no more than ten hairs on his entire scalp, hairs pointing straight up, miserable little antennas. Ravi-

novich was genial, and yet he made minimal eye contact; his inflections seemed out of sync with his words. Sharkey could almost see the writhing beneath the surface, like the ripples on a sail when the wind is stiff and the rigging's set wrong.

"The tribute, that'll be a tremendous honor," Ravinovich said. "Course, it ain't the Hall of Fame. I'd have been in the Hall if you'd have got me a few more at-bats." He tried to smile, as if he were joking now, and all was forgiven, but it didn't work, and the sting of it came through.

"I should've played you," Sharkey said, trying to be kind.

"You should've. I begged you," Ravinovich said, more pointedly.

"You just weren't hitting, man."

"A slump. I was in a fuckin' slump."

"For a whole year? Look, never mind. It was my fault, I just didn't see—"

"Ah, forget it; Christ, what am I doing, harping on that crap? I'm trying to show a new attitude, appreciate the things I had." As he said it, he looked into Sharkey's eyes for the first time, a long hard look, and Sharkey suddenly remembered a cold April night at Yankee Stadium, a night he'd almost forgotten, when the Raven had belted a slider way up against the grandstand facade in right, up where Mantle used to hit them, a titanic home run that beat New York, and when he got back to the dugout, grinning, he looked straight into Sharkey's face almost the same way and said, "I'm going to hit you fifty like that." But there had been only one more, and they'd fought all season, up until his suspension in the final weeks for that incident, that truly bizarre and regrettable incident, where he'd broken into Farrah Fawcett's hotel room with all that preposterous mountaineering gear. He'd shocked the holy hell out of her, of course, waiting for her under the sheets, naked but for a coating of pineapple ham glaze.

Or so the *Enquirer* had reported.

It was amazing how all that, so vivid then, had slipped away

through the years. "I wish you could've played for me in your prime," Sharkey said.

"I could get it done, couldn't I?"

"You had it. And the fans, they really loved you."

"I despised those bastards, and they loved me anyway. And you know what? That love, it's all in here now." Ravinovich touched a bony hand to his heart. He could feel that emotion start to knock around, like scalding water through a latticework of old pipes. His face twitched. "So much damn love. I love these players today, they're great. I got to meet Kane tonight. Seein' him throw—wow! I go to a lot of games, you know, when I'm feeling up to it. Plan to keep on goin', too, up until the time comes. . . ."

He trailed off, eyes flooding. All the wonderful memories, the regrets—so many of both, so much distance between the highs and lows. To look back now, the what-ifs, knowing he'd never be there again—so hard. He wiped his eyes, allowed as how he'd had quite a ride, quite a fucking great ride, and he again shook Sharkey's hand. A long, heartfelt handshake, and Sharkey heard himself saying, "Stop by. See the guys in the clubhouse some time."

"I will. I've talked to Wulfmeyer—"

"I know."

Ravinovich backed up and then ambled away. Sharkey felt rattled. Somehow it was like the Raven was already dead, the Raven that Sharkey had known, and now this new character had come in, this skeleton from out of the boneyard. A dead Raven from the boneyard.

Sharkey finished off his champagne and got himself a Stoli. He wandered around saying perfunctory hellos, engaging where necessary in obligatory small talk. The rest of the night just about vanished, disappeared but for discrete moments, scenes that flickered before him in between the long periods he spent way down in the hollow of his own mind, walking dark corridors and picking at locks. He was aware

of Wolf returning a while later, far more composed, and seeing Davenport conversing with a willowy young Asian woman. Sharkey spent long moments observing him, a handsome guy, a stocky Cary Grant type, but so often silent, brooding, troubled in ways no one really understood. In a tux Davenport looked like a game-show host. It was hard to imagine him a terrorizer of nuns, a liquor-store bandit, a Lothario who had been nabbed for speeding on the night of a grisly murder. A killer, maybe. Sharkey was beginning to have accusatory thoughts anytime he looked at one of his guys. A killer? A madman?

He drifted on, eyeing the gowns, the chandeliers, the vats of Roquefort, salsa, avocado dip, and then, boom, exploding right before him was a startling drama: Kornblume was on his feet at his wheelchair, supported by a pair of shapely, well-coiffed young women, talking to Meg Ryan; and just as Sharkey was on his way over, about to pay his respects, out of nowhere came Oscar Gamboa, the agent, yapping about his contract demands for Kane, loudly accusing the Sox of dodging him. There were shouts, and Kornblume grew white as a chalk carving, then collapsed. Pandemonium then: Wulfmeyer yelling, people running, Gamboa scurrying away, and Sharkey trying to help get Old Gordo some air, get him outside to the ambulance.

It ended with Wolf and Domato riding off with Kornblume to Harvard Med Center, and Sharkey under orders to stay, keep mingling, and so he stayed, upset, distracted, sipping another Stoli and wishing the night would end.

The dinner itself was boring. Halibut, baby greens. Henrietta spoke. They watched a highlight film of the season's first half. Castillo slipped out during the cappuccino cheesecake. Sharkey followed and managed to fall in behind him as Castillo raced in his black Corvette onto the expressway and into South Boston.

Before reaching the Naval Annex, Castillo hung a right on D Street and took it almost all the way to the railyard. Veering south

again, another mile, he finally stopped at a barren lot containing a small wood structure with a gabled roof, no larger than a boathouse. Sharkey couldn't tell what it was. He drove on past, and he saw two other men standing near it in the deep shadows, as if awaiting Castillo's arrival.

Strange. A rendezvous here in the dark of a gritty industrial zone. Why? A few blocks down, Sharkey turned, pulled over, and waited a bit, then came back from the other direction. There were four men now, including Castillo, huddled near a chain-link fence. Sharkey saw their cars and caught two of the license-plate numbers. Rounding a corner, repeating the numbers out loud, over and over, he kept them in his head until he could grab a ballpoint from the dash and write them on an envelope. With any luck he could find out who the buggers were.

Sharkey switched off his headlights and eased the car around to a spot where he could barely see two of their silhouettes, and waited. In a while it looked like another man was there, a taller one, and somebody came out of the structure. They stood together for a few minutes beside the little building, and then they walked to one of the cars, got in and drove away, heading north.

What to make of it? Sharkey sat puzzled for a moment, knowing they would return at some point for the other cars, unsure whether to risk a closer look. He eased his car forward. He had come this far. He really wanted some idea of what was up, what was inside that gabled hut. In a grim fantasy he imagined a body in there, a corpse mutilated by Castillo and his pals, vile devil worshippers, a sick murder cult.

It rang with enough truth to make his mouth go dry, to make him stop the Olds and get out. He approached on foot. Below the roof were narrow windows. Twenty yards away he could see that the windows were protected by thick-gauge mesh. They were several feet long, but only as tall as a row of cinder blocks.

Then they flashed. A bright light, a tremendous noise, glass flying everywhere. An explosion. A blast so loud Sharkey could not even hear his own scream. The building stood firm, but the door blew off, sailing away like a massive playing card. Sharkey watched the light fade again and stood with his fingers and toes numb, his ears stinging, a warm trickle moving down his leg.

9

His ears were still not right. Four days later and there were a couple of seashells down inside them, rubbing the nerves raw and making roaring ocean sounds.

"I'm sorry," Sharkey said. "Say the name again?"

"Enrico. His older brother. He's from Miami, and he comes up a couple times a year to see Benito here in Boston." The private investigator, a man named Mankewitz, had run the plates and tracked down a few sources, research that was costing Sharkey enough out of his own pocket to set up a trust fund. "So apparently, not too long ago, Enrico found this strongbox—or stole it, who knows?—and brought it with him, thinking they could somehow break it open, or blast it open, which they did. Right in that little building."

"What was in it?" Sharkey pressed the phone to his ear.

"According to my source: ninety dollars in nickels. No great shakes. Nothing nefarious."

"Nickels."

"You get my faxes?"

"Sure did. Wish I had a shortstop of your caliber." Sharkey hung

up, scowling. Nickels. Castillo had just about blown Sharkey into the cardiac unit for loot you couldn't even use in a parking meter. Imbecile. Stupid screwball bastard.

The incident had not caused Castillo one whit of the trouble he deserved. Apparently, after Sharkey had fled, Castillo and his pals had returned and got most of the haul before the cops showed up. The mysterious blast had been ruled out as terrorism and was dismissed with only a few buried paragraphs in the papers. Sharkey had not dared accuse Castillo or fine him for fear of having the mess get back to Wulfmeyer. The bitter reality was, Wolf would have come down twice as hard on Sharkey for disobeying his direct order not to trail his players. He'd have gone apeshit to learn Sharkey was out playing "homicide dick," as he had so caustically put it.

It wasn't fair, but Sharkey resolved to force the matter from his mind and refocus his thoughts on baseball. It was almost five, time for the daily crapshoot known as filling out the lineup card.

The Sox, despite a streaky offense, were still hot. They had opened the second half by slaughtering the Orioles at Camden Yards. Their lead in the East was two games, and Kane was about to crank up the Howitzer. Amazing how hopeful those highly abridged facts could sound. The *Sun* had just run a story going on and on about how the Sox were such a well-oiled machine. Only a handful of people in the entire world—Sharkey and Wolf and Domato and a gang of Boston police and FBI agents—knew the reality of it, how the machine was running hot as a Rambler in the sun-scorched Mojave, about to throw a piston rod.

Surveying the clubhouse, Sharkey saw Villalobos tugging on his spikes, his face dark and unshaven, his strong arms working the laces. Sharkey stepped out of his office for a moment, called him over. He came carrying his battered glove and sat down opposite the desk. Sharkey closed the door and took a moment to ask about the All-Star Game, how Villalobos had enjoyed it. It was his third, and he had dou-

bled and singled. Kane had been the overwhelming sensation, giving up one hit and striking out six of the nine batters he faced.

"Hell of a lot of fun—for both of us," Cool Daddy said. "Never seen so many cameras."

"Super. Just super. You probably know this, but we're proud of you—real proud." Sharkey thanked him for his hard work, for being such a role model. "You're not in any trouble, but I'd like, if you don't mind . . . well, a couple questions, things unrelated to you."

"Just don't ask about Langley's wife."

"Okay. Yeah. What's she got to do with anything?" Sharkey forced a laugh, trying to show no interest in the potential meanings behind the veiled remark. He exhaled hard and brought up the recent party in Boston that Villalobos and Castillo had attended together. "Where exactly was that thing? And what time did 'Nito leave, the best you can remember?"

Villalobos frowned, his long face showing concern. "A couple cops asked me about that and wouldn't say why. Is there some problem? I hope he didn't rob a bank."

A bank robbery would be welcome news, Sharkey wanted to say. Instead he shifted in his chair. "Who the hell knows? The cops, Christ, they tell you less these days than the KGB. I'm just covering bases. For Wolf. So it was . . . ?"

Villalobos bent forward, a gold cross dangling from his neck. "Up on Beacon Hill. Gascon's office suite." Michael Gascon—Miguel— was the only Hispanic on the Sox's board of directors; he was a high-powered attorney and, in fact, had assisted Villalobos with his bankruptcy. "I saw 'Nito leave, just happened to see it out of the corner of my eye, but the time? Wasn't looking. Not sure. I'm thinking it was close to one in the morning."

"What kind of mood was he in?"

"Upset, actually. A woman there—oh God, I'd have done her in a minute—she asked him why he never played. Gorgeous blonde,

and he's pissed. Starts talking about you, actually, and then he just takes off."

Inner valves pumped up Sharkey's blood pressure by ten or twelve points. "All right. Thanks, Cool. Keep this between us, okay?"

Villalobos nodded and went out to warm up, and Sharkey opened his satchel, eager to check this out, this important new information. He had some paperwork: a faxed copy of the police report and a Rand McNally map of downtown Boston. Twice he had been to Gascon's office, and he knew exactly where it was: Revere Street on the west side of the hill, overlooking the Charles. The victim on the night of the party—Paul Gelson Woodson, fifty-nine, of Chelsea—had been found in Room 404 of the Spinnaker Inn, near Prescott Square, northwest of the airport. A hotel guest a floor above Woodson's room had heard muffled screams and phoned the desk at 1:22 A.M. No one actually saw the killer.

The distance from Gascon's party to the murder scene was less than five miles, an easy drive even in Boston, where the streets seemed laid out by some Revolution-era sadist with a neurotic aversion to perpendicular lines. Castillo could have handled it even after half a dozen beers, probably a conservative estimate of his brewski consumption that night.

Sharkey stared at the map. All right. Leave the party at about one, kill at 1:22. Twenty minutes, roughly. Was it possible? Twenty minutes to ride the elevator, find his car, get across the city center, take the tunnel under the inner harbor into East Boston, drive a mile or so, park and slip into Room 404, and all but tear the unsuspecting Mr. Woodson's head off.

The phone rang. Wulfmeyer.

"Who you starting at second tonight?"

"Mad Dog."

"He's hittin' like crap."

"He's batting eighth." Sharkey kept studying the map. Figure

eight or ten minutes to reach the tunnel—twice that during the day, but this was at one in the morning—

"Why not Uggams at second? Put Maynard in center?"

"Rogowski's pitching. Uggams hasn't hit him in two years." Maybe ten more minutes the rest of the way. Figure he might have been speeding; he had a Corvette, for chrissakes—

"Rogowski? What happened to Taylor?"

"He worked last night. We shelled him in the fifth." It was certainly possible. Very possible, especially if he left the party *before* one. What were the cops thinking? How could they claim he had an alibi?

"I'm considering Pawtucket. For Mad Dog. Hate to do it, but we should send him down a few weeks, get his confidence back."

"Let's wait. He's swinging better. He lined out twice last night." But why Woodson? Why this victim? Of all the people in Boston? If Castillo took off from Beacon Hill, drove all the way up there, and went right to the fourth floor to attack somebody, there had to be a reason. Otherwise, hell, why not kill someone downtown, save himself the drive? He must have known who the guy was, seen him before, maybe at Fenway, planned it all out. "Wolf, I'm still worried about Castillo—"

"I don't want to talk about that little creep. Gamboa's still asking for the moon, talk about nerve, after that despicable display—" Wulfmeyer went off about the fund-raiser, Gamboa causing Kornblume's collapse with his demands for a new contract for Kane. "Which reminds me, let's think about letting Kane DH now and then—against lefties anyway. Briscoe's in a tailspin, and his knee's a god-awful mess. He'll be lucky if he finishes the season."

Kane had been showing the ability to handle major-league pitching. He had collected three doubles, a triple, and was batting a solid .294 in limited at-bats. He had also stolen a base despite Sharkey's strict order not to run.

"Let me see how Kelvin takes to it," Sharkey said. "You know what morale's like. He does give us good power."

"Kane wouldn't?"

"I'm not arguing. Let me try it. I'm all for letting Kane get more rips."

"He might hit a ton."

"He might. It's worth trying him." Sharkey hung up. He rubbed his eyes and stared blearily at the police report. The paranoia was beginning to poison everything. The hours spent playing baseball, usually the most stressful for a manager, were a welcome respite. He hid the police report in his satchel, made a note about Castillo in his journal, a repository for all his random thoughts, and delved into the much easier task of dealing with the Orioles.

Bad moods were like storms, to Neville Wulfmeyer's way of thinking. In which case he was now stuck in the middle of a tornado, clinging horizontally to a telephone pole.

The problems of running Kornblume's empire almost completely overshadowed Boston's lead in the East. Even as Old Gordo clung tenaciously to life, the indoor-plumbing industry he so dominated was suffering its worst slump in half a century. Amalgamated Ball Cocks was about to post second-quarter losses of $147 million, and the strike at Industrial Tank Ball was costing $97,000 a day.

Wulfmeyer was skimming over a scathing memo from the head of the Teamsters local when the phone rang. Samantha picked it up.

"Neville, it's that guy from the White House again. Did you see the message from after lunch?"

"Yeah, Christ, what is that guy's problem?" Wolf flung his pen down on the desk and watched it bounce onto the floor. "What is that, about ten calls the last two days?"

"He sounds upset. He's very insistent."

"Fuck it." Wolf grabbed the phone with the patience of a man double-parked. "Hey, I got about fifteen seconds. And no, I haven't seen your goddamn videotape."

"You'd better see it. Ignoring my phone calls is not exactly summa cum laude, my friend."

"I'm a busy man. Busy, busy, busy. Tell me what the hell you want and then you're going to stop bothering me. I haven't got time for this nonsense."

"Listen carefully: You're going to make a drop. One million dollars, cash, nothing over twenty, no marks, the whole drill." The caller's tone had become menacing. He named a place north of the Charles and a time, midnight, in two days. "No cops, no funny business, or that tape goes straight to Boston's finest. I'm sure you're beginning to understand—whether you bothered to watch the goddamn thing or not—the gravity of what you're dealing with."

Wulfmeyer straightened. "You asking for cash?"

"A million dollars. You've got two days. No funny business."

Clack. The line went dead.

Wulfmeyer stared at the phone. He felt his mouth go dry, felt himself starting to sweat. *Jesus Christ Almighty,* what was on that tape? He yanked open the drawer and dug it out, ripped open the envelope, and hurried over to the portable Sony on the wall opposite the desk.

"You going there?" Samantha called out.

"Going where?" he asked. He fed the tape into the VCR.

"The White House! That's so exciting! I tell you, I'm really envious—"

"Maybe. Maybe next spring." He cut her off. "If we win it this year." Wulfmeyer watched an image materialize on the set. He checked to make sure Samantha wasn't looking and leaned close to see the picture more clearly. It was grainy—a darkened alley, a wall dimly lit by a floodlight. A brick wall shot through a fish-eye: a cou-

ple trash barrels set against it, the field of view sweeping across to a narrow loading dock. Obviously recorded by some security camera.

A car suddenly moved into view, a dark Lincoln that rolled to a stop just beyond the barrels. Wolf saw a tall, broad-shouldered figure emerge from the driver's side and move in an exaggerated hunch to the rear. The trunk popped open and the figure reached inside, dragging out, with some apparent difficulty, what looked to be a body, a human body, letting it fall splay-legged to the pavement.

The driver then stooped and gathered the body—it *was* a body, and no head! oh, my God, no head!—in both his arms, gathered it, and took three long strides to the taller of the two barrels, then dumped it inside.

Wulfmeyer swallowed hard. He felt as if his very skin had turned to cellophane, and it was shriveling under a blast of unbearable heat.

Turning, the driver retraced his steps to the trunk, glancing to his right just long enough to reveal a grainy face to the camera. Grainy, but—Kane's face. The strong, angular face of Ron Kane, good God Almighty, holy shit! Kane! Then he turned away just as quickly, his face disappearing from view as he reached once more into the trunk, this time removing an irregular round object—the head. The dead man's motherfucking head!

And, wheeling gracefully, his face not quite visible this time, Kane executed a rapid underhand swooping motion and tossed the head in a perfect arc directly into the shorter trash barrel. Nothing but net.

Seconds later he was back in the Lincoln, roaring away.

Wulfmeyer stared. The image turned to snow.

"Samantha?" He could barely choke out her name.

"Yes."

"Hold my calls, all right? For a while?" He lifted a quivering hand and hit the eject button.

"Sure thing. I was going to ask you, would you mind me taking

off a bit early? There's a lingerie sale at Macy's. I'd like to get my niece—"

"Go."

He looked at the clock. It was 4:20. He held the tape in both hands, like a plastic explosive that would blow if he let it go, and gradually lowered it and stuck it back into the VCR, watching it again—three, four, five times. Watching and trying in vain to comprehend the reality of it.

The possibility of such a catastrophe had never really entered his consciousness; he'd kept it out like a badger defending her cubs. It couldn't happen. It was an impossible paranoid delusion of the type that only Fish could concoct. Fish, that veritable fountain of paranoia, a man who could win first-ballot election into the Paranoid Hall of Fame—he'd been right. Right-o, baby-o. It was a player out there beheading people. Not just any player, not Castillo or some lame-ass benchwarmer who could be thrown right into the Big House with no real loss to the club, but Kane, for godsakes. The greatest talent of all, the one incomparable star who could finally give the Sox a legitimate shot at a championship.

Wulfmeyer drifted back to his desk, leaving the tape running snow. He sat and inhaled sharply. He squeezed his temples between his fingers and lowered his nose to the desktop, low enough to smell the wax and eraser crumbs. Just froze there and tried to run it through his mind—what he had seen, how to deal with it.

For an instant he was back in fourth or fifth grade, a kid with his head on the desk, his ragged mitt there at his feet awaiting recess. A kid of maybe ten who was completely unaware that he was on a track in life to land in this fucked-up spot, a place so unbelievably fucked up he wasn't sure if he could ever stand again, ever move.

Nothing could outlousy this doozy. Those who looked back on the bleak history of the Red Sox and said they were jinxed, star-

crossed, had never imagined so black a day as this. Oh God, oh God, oh God, oh God, the tragedy.

Kane. Kane who, yeah, had been troubled. A kid who was arrogant, temperamental, undisciplined—all those things. Wolf thought he had dealt with the worst of those potential problems. He had taken steps even while Kane was being groomed in the Dominican Republic. Twice a week down there Kane had been in counseling with the French therapist Dr. Jean-Luc Matthieu, one of the tops in the field at dealing with troubled athletes.

Clearly, he hadn't been enough. What an unbelievable, mind-blowing disaster.

It would break hearts all over Boston. That was the worst of it—the heartbreak. So brilliant a career, so new, so filled with promise, *kaput!*

Wulfmeyer lifted his head. He struggled to his feet like a dazed bantamweight rising from an eight count and moved numbly to the wet bar. Grabbing a bottle of Chivas Regal, he poured himself a double shot. His hand trembled as he quaffed it and let it burn in his throat. He stared at the blank TV screen.

The whole season was over. The most promising season in decades was going right down the toilet and there was no way in hell to save it. Kane was a cold-blooded serial killer, and this moron, this sick "White House" extortionist, wanted a million bucks cash to keep it a secret.

Talk about impossible: Wolf was powerless. No way he could free up a friggin' million dollars without going to the board. He'd have to explain it—if not to the entire board, then certainly to Henrietta. Henrietta, the big mama herself, who by virtue of being Old Gordo's niece was running the whole show now.

Henrietta. Oh God, how Wulfmeyer despised her. The cruel part was, Wolf had to tell her anyway, even surrendering Kane to the cops.

She would want a role in managing this fiasco—the circumstances of the arrest, the obligatory press conference—what a nightmare that would be—and, of course, the ensuing media explosion, which would take on a shape of its own, rising and twisting and spreading like that mushroom cloud over Hiroshima.

Wulfmeyer squeezed his eyes a moment and tried to collect himself. He downed another drink and moved dizzily to the VCR, rewinding the tape and ejecting it, grabbing the tape and the envelope, and stepping into the hall. Arms tingling, legs carrying him unevenly through the corridor, he found the escalator and rode it up a level.

At the burled-walnut door of the board of directors suite, Wolf stopped a moment and took three rapid breaths—Ah! Ah! Ah!—to steady himself.

Then he lifted a fist and knocked.

10

Henrietta was alone at her desk in the inner sanctum, a lavishly appointed board office dominated by a nine-foot LeRoy Neiman of Ravinovich in full stride, reaching for a high drive that seemed to balance on the tip of his glove.

Wolf passed it without a glance; he knew the play, the ignominious moment that had inspired the impressive artwork. The Raven, misjudging George Brett's easy fly ball, had knocked what should have been a sure out into the right-field corner, costing the Sox a crucial game during the 1986 pennant race. The club had managed to overcome the setback and reach the World Series that year even without Ravinovich, who fractured his kneecap on the final weekend of the season. The campaign, however, ended in the manner of all Red Sox campaigns—in utter despair—because of a more infamous fielding miscue: Bill Buckner allowing a ground ball to squirt through his legs in game 6, giving the New York Mets an improbable comeback win that all but clinched the championship.

"Henrietta—you're here, thank God. I hate to— Sorry, we've got to talk. We've got a terrible, terrible problem."

She turned, raising her painted eyebrows in that prim way of hers, as if to say she would be the judge of what was a problem. "Neville, don't just come barging in here—"

"It can't wait! It's important! Sorry, but it's far more important than anything you could possibly be doing, and I mean no disrespect."

Her eyes fixed on him. "You obviously haven't seen this disturbing legal memorandum that Roberta Lacy just sent over. And I'm trying— trying!—to sort out this mess with Grillmasters. We've had forty-eight complaints, in just the last homestand, about the hot dogs being cold. Forty-eight!"

"That's terrible," he said flatly, regarding her pointed face, her heavy makeup, her hair coiffed up stiff-looking as carbon fiber. "This is—I'm pretty sure—way worse. It's about Kane, for godsakes."

"Kane? What about him?"

"It's hard— We're in a spot, unfortunately; I don't even know where to—"

"Just spill it, Neville. I've got to wrap up here and get out to the Embassy Club. My time is valuable."

Seeing her severe expression, Wulfmeyer had the sudden aware-ness that this might be the very last minute of his career in Boston. Henrietta never reacted well to bad news, nor would she be prepared for this. Hers was only the fuzziest inkling, carefully spin-doctored by Wulfmeyer himself, that Kane posed the likelihood of disciplinary problems. His mercurial temper, his gambling and curfew problems— none of it had passed Wolf's lips during their conversations. Even allowing for the fact she might have heard rumors, or seen the press coverage of Kane's clubhouse fight in Cleveland, there had been no real cause for alarm. There had been no reason to think he was any worse than Davenport, or any worse than that broken-down egoma-niac, the Raven, whom she worshiped as if he were Jesus H. Christ himself.

Until now. Now there was a reason.

"Brace yourself. We're not talking cold hot dogs here. The financial impact—oh God! Oh God, oh God, oh God, oh God!"

"Gamboa? Neville, we've been over all this. We're standing firm—no sixth year. Tell him everything's our option after five—everything."

"There won't be a sixth year. Or even a second."

"What do you mean? They're demanding a trade?"

"Kane is . . . aah . . . he's been . . ." Wolf's mouth dried up like a sun-baked biscuit. "I've got evidence here—" He shook the videotape. "That he's been killing people. Kane. Committing murder."

"Murder?" Henrietta grew rigid.

"It's on this . . . aah . . . right on here. This guy—who sent it—he's wanting a million bucks or he goes to the cops."

There was no response. Wolf thought for a second she had swallowed her tongue.

"It can't be true," Henrietta finally blurted. "Let's see it. See that thing."

Her television was tuned low to an afternoon game in progress: Kane facing the Orioles at Camden Yards. He had not allowed a base runner through seven innings. Wolf fed the VCR and his shaking finger mashed PLAY. The close-up of Kane, peering in to Ray Tarver for a sign, disappeared and gave way to the tape's grainy image. The body coming out of the trunk. The flash of Kane's face. The deft movement where he wheeled and tossed the head into the trash can.

"Can you really tell if that's . . . ? Back it up," Henrietta ordered. She bent closer, her glasses reflecting the screen. They studied it again. "It's hard to— Dear Lord! It looks like him. Maybe shorter, you think? Let's see one more—"

Wolf started it over. She squinted hard.

"I can't—it's so grainy. When he turns—"

"Oh God, it's Kane! It's Kane!" Wulfmeyer flailed his arms. "Any reasonable person—"

"You don't think . . . ? That he's too short to be . . . ?"

"It's him! For crying out loud, it's right there! They're going to arrest him! Oh, Christ, he's that serial killer! Our whole season's over! This thing, it'll blow us right out of the pennant race. Right out of contention and *ruin* us. Absolutely *ruin* us! Our revenues—" He broke off; he couldn't tell if it was rage or fear in Henrietta's eyes.

"Oh . . . dear . . . Jesus!" She wrung her hands. "How's this going to *look?*"

"The papers, they'll go crazy. Berserk."

Her mind spun. She imagined the reaction down at the club. The looks she'd get. Laura Hollis, her mouth puckering. Judy Blumenthal. Marilyn Seales. Their eyes widening. The remarks.

Oh, how horrible!

Didn't you know?

Oh, you poor thing—how embarrassing!

Embarrassing beyond comprehension. Humiliating! The board would be apoplectic. The people at the Chamber. All of Uncle Kornblume's old cronies. Lester MacLellan. He'd shuffle up with that smug expression, the condescending bastard, and put a hand on her arm, that big gnarled hand, and say, "A shame, a real shame. This running a ball club, it's a tough racket." The implicit message being that it was no place for a woman. Les would make it clear, with that moronic smile of his, that such a scandal would never have happened under Gordon's watch. Which might be true, goddamn it.

Henrietta's ascent to power within the organization had come only in recent years, as Old Gordo's health problems became critical. Prior to that her time had been spent mainly in the upper echelons of Boston society—not just the Embassy Club, but the Falcons of Liberty, the Fleur-de-lis Lamplighters, the Boston College advisory board, the yacht club. Any kind of civic involvement. Her parents, Henry and Lois Prichard, had been activists and big-time political donors in town since arriving from Philadelphia in 1914. Henry, in

fact, had been one of several investors recruited by Harry Frazee, then owner of the Red Sox, to bring *No, No, Nanette* to Boston, the venture that necessitated the sale of Babe Ruth, for $100,000, prior to the start of the 1920 season. The Prichards, both baseball fans, hated to see Ruth go but would have no direct involvement in Red Sox management for another forty years.

When Lois's brother, Gordon, purchased struggling Amalgamated Ball Cocks during the early years of World War II, Lois and Henry became minority partners, a move that would lift all three to the front ranks of America's richest citizens. The wealth enabled Kornblume to purchase his favorite baseball franchise in 1963 and the Prichards to come in with 40-percent equity. Neither Henry nor Lois played a visible role in running the club, though both served for an extended time on the board. Henrietta's precocious mind—she earned her degree in economics from Radcliffe at the age of nineteen—made her a favorite of her uncle. Having no children of his own, he groomed her, kept her at least marginally involved in his own business affairs, until his own health began to fail, at ninety-one.

Kornblume's lung-removal surgery had been the point at which Henrietta stepped to the fore. Her ability to deal with corporate infighting and politics was soon clear as she consolidated the votes to control the Red Sox board, raising herself to a position as the most powerful woman in baseball. She also took over the chairmanship of Amalgamated but continued to place the daily administration of the company and its subsidiaries largely in the hands of Wulfmeyer.

She sensed that, despite her auspicious start, there were still many skeptics in baseball who expected her to fail—gray-haired chauvinists who considered it only a matter of time before she plowed the ship into a reef. The real horror was thinking they were right. Or seeing them think they were right. This new problem might even put some of those ugly thoughts in Kornblume's head. His disappointment in her, and in the club, might be like a bludgeon.

"This will kill Gordon," Henrietta said suddenly. "I just know it will."

"It's going to be—oh God—such a mess," Wulfmeyer agreed. "We've got to think about—you know, the networks, and all that—"

"Damage control."

"Right."

"It's murder. We've got no choice but to turn him in. No choice whatsoever."

"I wish I had an answer," Wulfmeyer said.

"Cutting people's heads off! It's just—ugh, it's *reprehensible*. What is this world coming to?"

Wulfmeyer moved away from her and fell into the chair facing her desk. He looked at the Neiman. "What about this tape? This fucking—excuse my language—this fucking asshole extortionist?"

"He's not getting any money, that's for sure." Henrietta sat and wrung her hands again. "We'll have to plan a press conference. We'll have to make it—I think we can make it—look like we took the lead, like we took the initiative in finding out and giving Kane over to the cops."

"So . . ." Wulfmeyer wasn't sure how to react. "That'll help, I guess. It won't be like—like some fan blew the whistle."

"I know Chief Hardeway. Those cops, they're all Red Sox fans. We can negotiate something, work it so this extortionist will look like a fake, if he tries to publicize that tape. Like he got a copy somehow. Hardeway will vouch for us." She stared moodily at the painting of Ravinovich. "I wonder if I should call him now. Or wait, you know, till morning. Seems like we could allow ourselves a few hours to think. Jesus, such a disaster."

Wolf bit hard on his lip.

Henrietta glared at him again. "Look, we'll meet here tomorrow morning, nine sharp. I'll call Lacy tonight. We'll make sure we deal with Hardeway personally. You think this through, and I'll think this

through, and we'll make damn sure—*damn* sure—we keep the damage to a minimum."

Kane climbed the mound in the ninth and loomed there like a colossus. The late-afternoon sun at Camden Yards seemed to shine on no one else. The crowd noise rose to an expectant pitch. He was Zeus raining down thunderbolts, a wrathful god intent on closing out his first perfect game. Leading, 3–0, and still firing at 110 mph. Unhittable.

Sharkey hunched forward, scanning the Sox defense, his right cleat planted, as always, on the top step. He noticed Davenport back near the track and launched into a spastic array of semaphores to bring him nearer the infield.

Kane whiffed the first batter anyway.

To see such overwhelming dominance was thrilling, of course, but also strange. Unnatural. It reaffirmed for Sharkey the inequities of life, the fact that men are not created equal. His own talents had been scarcely a pale fraction of Kane's, if even that. He loved this game of baseball—its angles and planes, its clean geometry, its deceptive simplicity, which was, in fact, a mirage, because each swing, each throw, introduced new complexities that piled up until the mind could not even grasp them all. It was a hard game of incalculable nuance that favored only the very best.

Sharkey had spent eight years in organized ball, stuck in the minors but for one delirious week in 1969, when the Tigers acquired him and brought him up to the bigs: four games, two official at-bats, a strikeout and a grounder to third. That was it. A big chunk of his life spent in the joyous, bitter, unrequited pursuit of a dream, gone in seven pitches. It was the hardest lesson of all, to learn what you are not.

The final two Orioles were like ghosts facing Kane at this moment, with his extraordinary power and timing and confidence.

The Baltimore fans rose to their feet, cheering Kane's brilliance as the batters swung their phantom bats and seemed to vanish in thin air. Kane bounded off the mound, jubilant at finally achieving the pitching masterpiece that had eluded him in Cleveland, and he and his teammates hurried off the field still two games ahead of the Yankees.

In the clubhouse the circus began anew—the writers, the cameras, the incredible hubbub. Kane stripped off his number eleven uniform and carefully hung it like a sign on the wall of his locker while he answered questions, relishing the attention. He had gone hitless at the plate, but in the fourth, on a two-strike change-up, he had drilled a shot to the wall in left center that the whippet Ken Stacey grabbed with a spectacular leap. Kane told the writers he thought it was gone. He'd hit one out the next game or two, he brashly predicted. He might even throw another perfecto.

As soon as a few of the writers drifted away, Ravinovich pressed his way in, wearing a Sox cap and a black leather jacket. The Raven flashed his half-amputated grin and cuffed Kane on the pitching arm, a typically ill-considered gesture that caused Sharkey to flinch.

"Never seen such a lousy display," Ravinovich said, joshing about the ineptitude of the Orioles. "Those guys—what a bunch of pussies. Couldn't hit a pumpkin ball if my grandmother was pitching!"

Kane grinned, haughtily flexing his biceps.

"Sheeeee-it!" The Raven beamed, playing the room. "Shoulda had me up there, teeing off on ya. I'd a slammed one up against that fuckin' warehouse!"

They went on like that, barbs and braggadocio. It was exactly what Sharkey had hoped not to see, Kane and the Raven establishing a rapport. A young superstar as volatile and impressionable as Kane needed mature guidance, not the influence of a head case like Ravinovich, the original poster child for bad judgment and squandered gifts. A number of people in the organization, including Wulfmeyer

and Domato, seemed to believe that the Raven was finally getting his act together—that his terminal illness was forcing him to grow up—but Sharkey was far from convinced. He saw the Raven as a man infected with losing and he'd spread that infection like a wet cold, be it to Kane or anybody else.

Sharkey tried not to think about it. He was tempted to intervene—to pull Kane aside and broach the idea of his taking Briscoe's spot as designated hitter tomorrow night, against the left-handed Pat Morrison. But he decided to wait. Sharkey restrained himself and drifted back to his locker.

Langley was there with a cracked bat.

"Can you believe it? Last one. Broke that sucker right up the grain—and the new ones aren't in yet."

"When'd you order them?" Sharkey said.

"Four days ago."

"Four days? And they're *still* not here?" Sharkey ripped him with sarcasm. Langley's thick-handled thirty-five-ouncers were custom-lathed by Hillerich & Bradsby, the only ones like them on the club. He'd had weeks to worry about that fact. "Look, you'll have to see if you can use some of Mad Dog's. He's got thirty-fours. He's trying the thicker handles."

"Yeah, I guess. Thanks, Fish. Anyway, just don't know how that happened, running out like that."

"I know how it happened: carelessness." He said it, but Langley was already gone. Sharkey wearily got changed. Langley's lack of accountability was one of the season's many disappointments. Sharkey had been relying on him to provide some guidance to Kane, keep him toeing the line, obeying curfew, but the sad fact was Langley could not even keep himself supplied with bats. The idea that he could show a free-spirited rookie how to behave as a professional now seemed like the height of foolishness.

Sharkey felt himself sliding into melancholy. It came on suddenly sometimes, even after a great win. The end of a victory was the start of the inevitable transition into the nonbaseball part of the season: the hours of travel, hotel rooms, ego clashes, roster issues, and calls from Wulfmeyer filled with second-guessing and meddling. Any triumphant moment was a smoke ring in a wind tunnel.

While awaiting the team bus, he took a moment to update his journal—logging thoughts about Tarver's adroit pitch-calling, how he'd mixed low curves and inside sliders to complement Kane's blistering heat. Sharkey boarded in silence, sealing himself against the raucous mood of the players like a crab slipping under the rocks of a breakwater.

A short charter was due to deliver the Sox home by eight. Sharkey rode in the haze of a tired funk. At Logan he decided, despite the fatigue, to swing out by Harvard Medical Center and see Old Gordo. Visiting hours went until ten. Sharkey made it a point to get there at least once a month during those rare stretches when Gordo was sufficiently in command of his faculties to actually sit up and speak. That was supposedly the case now for the first time since All-Star weekend.

The ward was nearly deserted. Sharkey lumbered off the elevator and into the private room. It was always a reminder of the precarious nature of life to see firsthand what a shriveled wisp of his former self Kornblume had become. Thirty-seven years of declining health, starting with a botched procedure to correct an acid-reflux condition, had shrunk the once great man to a sinewy, liver-spotted rail; and now oxygen tubes and IVs looked to be finishing him off, giving the macabre appearance that they were draining out every last drop of his bodily fluids.

Thin bristles of white hair fringed Kornblume's bony little head. His mouth quivered uncontrollably for a moment before he managed a cheery greeting.

"Auuu-gie Fish, that you? God bless it, comin' here, seein' this old carcass. How's my club?"

"Winnin', for once. See the game today?" Sharkey bent and carefully hugged him before taking a seat at the bedside.

"Glad a that. Yaz hit one out?"

"Yaz didn't play." Nor had he since retiring nearly thirty years ago. "That new kid, Kane? He threw a perfecto. Guy's got blinding speed—unbelievable."

"That's, uh—say it again?"

Sharkey repeated it. "Did you watch? On TV?"

"Is it tonight?"

"No, today. We beat Baltimore. A perfect game!"

"Oh, yeah? Yessiree. Tha's—wow, that's fan-tastic. But what I want—my question—if you'll please tell me—" Kornblume broke off, his jaw working. "You say—you say Yaz didn't play. Whassa matter, he hurt?"

The angst involved in the question caused a spasm in which Kornblume jerked suddenly and dislodged the oxygen tubes; they fell across his chest. He pawed frantically for them, eyes widening. A bedside monitor began to display chaotic spikes.

"Shhhhh—ssss—shhh—sh—shhit!" he sputtered.

"Hold on! Hang on a sec—!" Sharkey grabbed the two tubes and angled them toward Kornblume's nose, but a nurse hurried in and took over, deftly shoving the conduits back up his nostrils and spooling out the white medical tape that would keep them there.

"Oh, oh, *oohhhh,*" Kornblume said, groaning. "Oh, oh, ohhh, Mother a God."

"You all right?" Sharkey said.

"He's fine. Big baby." The nurse ran a strip of tape that looked like a mustache.

"Oh, oh God a God, God, Mother a God—"

"Yaz—he's okay," Sharkey said, feeling helpless. "Just resting."

"Huh?" said Kornblume, gulping for air, groaning again.

"He's resting!"

"Hold still," the nurse ordered, determined to apply more tape.

"Who? My ears—say again?"

"Yaz! He's not hurt! Just resting!"

"Right. Tha's good. Rest him some. Like me, I'm resting some." The monitor was no longer fluttering so rapidly, but Old Gordo's nose had begun bleeding, and he wriggled and moaned like a man undergoing medieval torture. The nurse clucked in dismay and swung her ample backside Sharkey's way as she stripped off the tape and removed the tubes, cleaned him up, and jammed a single tube up one nostril and a wad of cotton up the other. He let out another "Ooohhh! Sh—shhh—shhh—shhhiiit! Ohh, oooh God!"

"*Please* relax, Mr. Kornblume."

"Maybe I should go," Sharkey said.

Kornblume's gaunt hands gripped the bed rails. "And leave me with—ahhh, ahh, this—"

"Just hold still. There."

"—woman. This woman's tryin' a—aaah, God, God! Hurts like a son of a bitch!"

"Where? Let's get your pills."

"My leg! Cramp in my fuckin' leg! This woman, ahhh—"

"Which leg?" the nurse said.

"—tryin' a kill me. Right leg! Right leg!"

"I just wanted to stop by," Sharkey said.

"Oh, ohh, ohhhh—shhhh—shhi—shhhi—shhhhit! Mothafucka, mothafucka, mothafucka!"

The nurse had moved to Kornblume's right calf, kneading it with her thick hands. She lifted her doleful face to Sharkey and mouthed the words, "You can go. Go ahead—he'll be okay."

"You need anything, Gordo?" Sharkey called loudly.

"Need? Yeah, ah, need you to—ahhh, aaahhhh!—get that club goin'. Finally get us a—ahhh, oohhhh! Oh, oh, oh, oh, God a God a God a Mother a God! Oh, oh, oh, Mother a God! Get us—aaah, aahhhh, ahhh—on! On—ahhh, ahhhh, aaaaahhhh—on top this year! Oh God, oh God, oh Mother a God!"

11

*I*t was a loop running through Wolf's head, a chain of thoughts that always circled back to an inescapable conclusion: He was getting fucked, fucked over good by whatever karmic forces reigned on high. Not that he believed in that crap, the way Fish did, but it was damn strange that Boston finally had a chance to win, a legitimate shot, and this horrific little problem had cropped up.

Wolf lifted his coffee and drained it. A glance at his watch—it was 7:20, a rotten time on a rotten morning. Everything was rotten.

He was passing the time at a McDonald's in Charlestown before meeting with Henrietta. He had been up all night, thrashing in bed, watching wee-hour porn on the cable, sitting downstairs in the dark with his glass of Chivas, listening to the plaintive *click-clacking* of the grandfather clock. No sleep at all, the same fucked-up loop running over and over through his mind.

It was tragic, tragic either way. Tragic that Kane was killing people, and tragic they would have to turn him in. Tragic to see the season wasted. Tragic to have to drop such a cataclysmic bombshell.

The papers had been amazing lately—the *Globe,* the *Herald,* the

New York Times, all of them. Even the magazines had been covering the Sox like no one could remember, all because of Kane. There were sellouts every time he pitched. A piece had landed in *Esquire* two days ago that Wulfmeyer had especially enjoyed. It was a profile containing quite a bit of revealing information about Kane and his personal interests—his love of scary movies, the stripper he'd been dating in high school, the fact that he never learned to swim. Just little things, but Wolf had begun to see some redeeming qualities in the guy, a side of him beyond the loudmouthed, arrogant star.

Now what? He'd go to prison. He'd waste away on death row, sure as shit, while once again the Sox went down like the *Hindenburg* in the second half. Déjà vu all over again. The fans were the real losers. They'd be heartbroken beyond belief.

Wolf fingered the empty styrofoam cup. He eyed the last uneaten chunk of his Sausage McMuffin and felt sick to his stomach. It was 7:24 now, time just dragging.

That was the galling part, the anguish of the fans. Excitement turned to tears. So many triumphs, so many capacity crowds, all that revenue, the future titles, that would never be realized. What was that line? That line of poetry? Yes: "For of all sad words of tongue or pen, the saddest are these: 'It might have been.'"

That had been the story of the Red Sox for more than eighty years: Might-have-beens. Frustration.

Wulfmeyer got up, swept the uneaten McMuffin angrily onto the floor, and made his way out to his gold Eldorado. He seemed weighed down by the force of thirty gravities, a man plodding across the surface of Uranus. He fell into the seat and glanced in the mirror at his bloodshot eyes. He looked like hell. No wonder. He felt like a man about to step off a cliff.

The cellular rang. Henrietta.

"Neville, you there yet? On your way?"

"I'm in my car. But it's only—" He looked. "Seven-thirty."

"Right, okay. Anyway, let's discuss this at my place. Forget the office."

"Sure."

"Lacy isn't coming, so make it anytime you want. No point waiting. It's so horrible, just horrible. I have some thoughts about handling this thing. My God, I've been wide awake since five."

"Right-o." He bristled; she had that imperious tone in her voice, a sure sign she would make a conspicuous attempt to demonstrate her leadership. That would only make the torture worse. "On my way, then."

Wulfmeyer cursed under his breath. He had been to Henrietta's only twice, once for Old Gordo's ninetieth birthday, again for some nameless charity pageant where he got sick on tainted crab cakes. He'd been knocked on his ass with three days of vomiting and diarrhea.

The mansion—big enough for the Third Army, though she lived there alone—was the second-oldest in Cambridge, a forbidding palace of mottled brick and majestic Palladian windows furnished with a sufficient number of early French antiques and Eastern rugs to finance a moon shot. A butler met Wolf at the foyer and led him to a cozy upstairs office overlooking the garden.

His mood worsened, if that were possible, as he walked in, seeing her there sipping tea from a coral china cup. A snooty society woman whose idea of a big policy decision was turning up the flames on the Fenway wieners.

"Morning, Neville."

"Yes, you're right, it's morning."

She exhaled sharply. Her face looked strangely drawn and thin, as if she'd slept with her head in a vise.

"I don't want to drag this out," she said raspily. "We've both . . . well, I'm sure you must have had a night like mine. Worst night of my life."

"Tonight will top it, believe me."

"Maybe. Thing is, I've got worries beyond my own. Like I said yesterday, this'll kill Gordon. I'm sure of it."

"He's no spring chicken."

"You know, I saw him last Thursday. He's certainly looked better. I thank God he's still got his mind—most of it—but in terms of reacting to stress, I can't . . . well, you saw what happened at the fund-raiser." Henrietta took a sip of the tea. Wolf noticed the palsylike trembling of her hand; usually she was steady as a glassblower. "So naturally I'm thinking about this, this very *dire* decision that we're about to make."

Wulfmeyer clasped his fingers beneath his chin, trying to effect a thoughtful look. He was sure they had decided this thing last night: They were going to arrange the most favorable circumstances for Kane's arrest and brace themselves for the inevitable storm. But suddenly Henrietta seemed to be wavering—or did he imagine it? He would have to tread very carefully.

"We should be proud of ourselves," he said with as much genteel high-mindedness as he could muster. "Very proud we're willing to do the right thing."

She met his eyes without speaking. He pressed on, more boldly.

"Except, as you know, as I think you very clearly sense, we're expecting too much from it. Acting like it's going to raise the dead. Like it's going to somehow *bring back* those poor dead souls."

"It won't do that," Henrietta said ruefully. "Might put another one in the ground—Gordon, like I say."

"Those murders, they're over and done with. Nothing we can do will change that. Nothing, and I swear to you, I'd cut off this right arm—" Wolf raised it dramatically. "—just to erase *one* of those crimes, but I can't. Can't, can't, can't."

Henrietta remarked on the difficult position she found herself in, concerned about Gordon and yet believing so strongly in the club's moral responsibility. "I can't tell you the deep—the very, *very* deep—

empathy I feel for the families of those poor victims. What's it been, six so far?"

"So do I—a powerful empathy," Wulfmeyer said. "Sympathy, too. Empathy and sympathy both, more than I can even express."

"I was curling my hair this morning and thinking how horrible it must be to get news like that: So-and-so dead, your loved one beheaded. It has to hit you like a ton of bricks. It'd scar you for life, really."

"No doubt. No doubt about it," Wolf said dourly. He stared at her. The silence seemed to consume them.

"Well, I guess we can't—"

"Don't say 'can't,'" Wolf interrupted. "This thing's here in our laps, and we should acknowledge that fact, the power we've got this very minute—the power to deal with this thing. We *can* deal with it. We *have* to deal with it."

"Right. But he's a killer—and so it's pretty much decided. We have to turn him in, tough as that is. Painful. So very painful, but how's it going to look otherwise?"

"If they find out—"

"Right. And they will. It'll come out, eventually; you can bet it will, tape or no tape."

"There you go: our answer. Fuckin' do the right thing." Wolf stared moodily at his shoes. "The rotten shame is—and I just want to say this, get it off my chest—" He looked at her again. "We're talking about murders, grief, those families. Right, I understand that. But what about the suffering of our fans? That pain? How do you compare the grieving of a very few with the collective *agony*—and I don't think that's too strong a word—of all the die-hard Red Sox fans?"

"That's a strange—"

"Is it? Think about it—it's not so easy a question. Our fans, Christ, 'die-hard' says it all. We're talking entire generations. Hundreds of thousands of them. Millions, maybe."

"That's true. I've suffered, certainly."

"Me, too! We all have. Gordon. Fish. Coaches and players and fathers and uncles and schoolkids. Seems so damn shortsighted, callous—whatever you want to call it—wrong to ignore all that hurt. The near misses, the blunders, the times when those athletes, heroes in the eyes of all those people, got so *fucking close,* only to fail. Jesus Christ God Almighty, when is this franchise going to *finally get over the hump?*"

Henrietta straightened; the club's failure to deliver a title during her own tenure as board chairman was never far from her mind.

"Six murders," she said. "Least it's not more."

"Six, when you think about it, it's almost nothing!" Wulfmeyer grew more animated. "Six murders in more than a month? Six in a nation of three hundred *million* people? Not to be crass, but *good God!* That many people get mowed down every year crossing Commonwealth Avenue. You can bet six people a month die in New York City just doing kinky sex acts. Where's the outcry over that?"

Henrietta pressed her fingertips together. "What do you suggest?" She laid it right there for him, a big softball question floating suddenly in front of him. She did not want to be the one to say it.

"I feel for the fans," Wulfmeyer said. "God, those poor suckers."

"No question. We have to consider the people out there."

"I just think, what good would come of turning him in? At this point in time? It would destroy him—not just him, the whole franchise. That's what we're talking about, besides killing Old Gor—besides killing Mr. Kornblume. This franchise just—I mean, can you imagine the media? The *vicious* attacks? Can you just picture what Harkwood will write?"

"If we don't turn him in—right away, I mean—then what do we do?"

"Do?" Wulfmeyer was startled by her passive willingness to yield authority, so uncharacteristic of her. Had this been a less momentous matter, an issue more on the scale of lukewarm wieners, she would

already be dictating orders, telling him how and why and when. This was different, however. Wolf sensed that the power had now shifted to him, at least for the moment, and he plunged ahead. "Seems obvious to me we need closer scrutiny, much closer scrutiny. Watch Kane like a hawk, keep these . . . these *atrocities* from happening."

"In other words—oh, dear God—you're thinking we should cover this whole thing up?" Her face twisted suddenly into a look of disbelief. Wolf wondered where in the hell that had come from.

"Not a cover-up." He laughed, a rat-a-tat release of unbearable tension. "Cover-up sounds like, Jesus, we're actively trying to *hide* something, whereas I think— I mean, look at this, it just *happened* to us. This just gets *dropped* in our laps, out of the blue! It's not so much we're covering it up as just *ignoring* it, just pretending, you know, this blasted tape never arrived. That's the trick, just pretending this damn tape never reached us."

He paused to let that sink in. "Except, quite naturally, we've got to deal with this guy, this sicko, who's trying to extort a million bucks from us."

Henrietta scowled. Her gaze fell on a brass-framed photo of Kornblume, a studio shot taken nearly fifty years ago, when there was still some black in his hair. Finally she looked back at Wulfmeyer and asked about the demand, when and where the money was supposed to be dropped.

Wolf told her it was due tomorrow night, that it was supposed to be left, in cash, in a duffel bag hidden in the shrubs along Shady Hill Lane, north of the river.

"That's near the cemetery," she said. "Not far from here."

"We'd have to get board approval, I guess. Or you would."

"That's manageable." The realization that only she had the power to come up with $1 million in cash seemed to reenergize Henrietta. "Let's be very clear about this, Neville. We're not condoning murder in any way, shape, or form. These crimes, we've got to nip 'em in the

bud. Nip them *right* in the *bud*! I won't have one more innocent man killed, beheaded, or even injured, even tragically disfigured, by that player of yours."

"Ours—"

"And if these crimes continue, God forbid, we'll have to take that tape, as if the damn thing just arrived, and give it directly to Chief Hardeway himself. God forbid."

"God forbid," Wulfmeyer muttered. "There is another problem, though—Sharkey. He's all but convinced one of the players is committing these crimes, and naturally he's on edge. He's been spying on them, following them around, trying to get to the bottom of this whole thing."

"Which he might."

"God forbid. But yes. A delicate situation." Wolf allowed that he was sympathetic with Fish's fears of being on the road with a psychopathic killer, but the energy spent chasing after these young guys, all hours of the night, was bound to erode his effectiveness as a manager. The word from Stu was that Fish was ignoring the directive to cease and desist, which now raised the question: Was Fish really in the right job, given the circumstances?

"Let's say, just for argument's sake, Augie finds out about Kane's, you know, involvement," Henrietta supposed. "Is he any different from us? He does care an awful lot about our prospects this season. Wants very desperately to win."

"He's obsessed," Wulfmeyer agreed. "But he's the type—I'm just afraid he'll blab."

"He told the cops about Castillo?"

"Not yet. No, don't think so."

"We can't exactly fire him. He'll go to the cops for sure. He might go on a vendetta, make it a full-time job to expose this whole thing. And Gordon wouldn't hear of it anyway—firing him. Gordon loves that guy. He wants Augie there in the dugout."

Wulfmeyer bit his lip. He had wanted to suggest kicking Sharkey upstairs, putting him in charge of scouting or something, but he could see that Henrietta was against making any changes. The good thing was, Sharkey would put up with a lot—he'd tolerate this god-awful situation, as long as he couldn't confirm the worst, because this was his one big opportunity to win. Worse came to worst, Wolf would have to deal with Fish his own way—maybe misdirect him, keep him chasing after Castillo, if it came to that.

He brought up another concern: Kane's contract. Henrietta was well aware that Gamboa was threatening to sit him down if the club refused to agree to an exorbitant new deal.

"Oscar. That *creep,*" Henrietta hissed.

"One possibility—we could trade him," Wulfmeyer said. "Get a wealth of talent, seven or eight guys. The Cubs might give up Sosa."

"But what if he's arrested? Later on? They'll say we knew. They'll make a stink to high heaven."

Wolf saw he hadn't thought it through. He felt the stress pressing down on him like barbells.

"Remind me," she said, "our offer's for a hundred and—"

"—forty-five million," Wulfmeyer said. "One forty-five, over five years." He thought of something, a brilliant stroke, an idea that temporarily lifted the hard blue funk that had settled down over him. "We could go higher, give Kane the moon, because we know this is a one-shot season; he won't be back. There's no next year. I guarantee you that. We'll give him the goddamn moon—and nearly all of it deferred."

Henrietta nodded. "Have Lacy be very clear about the 'out' clause—moral acts, heinous whatever."

"Right. Oscar wants to play hardball, we'll play hardball."

Tough loss," Ted Uziak said, patting Sharkey on the butt and slipping quickly into the clubhouse tunnel.

"Tough, all right." Sharkey moved into the tunnel at a slower pace, walking alone. Tough was an understatement. They seldom got tougher—two walks in the ninth, as Rick Reeling's control disappeared, followed by a lazy drive that caromed off a low-flying egret for a double. A play like that, it was just the kind of rotten luck that could trigger a ten- or twelve-game losing streak, which the Sox could ill afford. The Yankees, after losing three of four, had begun to get hot again, sweeping the Royals in Kansas City. New York was now a game back and entering one of the easiest stretches in its schedule.

Sharkey ducked into his office to drop off the stat sheets. Kelvin Briscoe followed him inside.

"Fish, got just a minute for me?"

"Sure, come in, Kelvin. Take a chair."

Briscoe closed the door and sat, looking grim. He was a large man, six feet two and 260, heavy through the chest, who had been one of the American League's top sluggers while playing first base for the

Angels and later the Twins. The Sox had acquired him three years ago for a starting pitcher and two draft choices, but the emergence of Langley and an off-season knee injury—he'd ruptured a ligament while Rollerblading—had cast Briscoe in a designated-hitter role. Sharkey did not have to consult the Amazing Kreskin to guess what was on his mind.

"You're concerned, I bet, about riding the pine. Not getting any at-bats."

"I've always hit McLeish," Briscoe said. "Hit him like a drum. Look it up, it's right there in the box scores." Jared McLeish, the A's starter, had struck out Kane three times and allowed him only a ground-ball run batted in.

Sharkey rubbed the sweat from his cheek. "Yeah, I know, you want to be up there, and who can blame you?" He laid it out plain, his strategy for using Kane against most lefties, saving Briscoe for the right-handers. Sharkey had mentioned it during batting practice, but he felt the need to go through it again, all the pros and cons, Kane's power and potential, what it might mean down the road. "You're still our big left-handed bat in the DH spot, no question," Sharkey said. "No question at all. Just hang in there. Give us what you can. Kane— who knows?—I might be using him some in right. The time comes, we might use him some in right field."

Briscoe nodded. His eyes, always mournful, showed that he had been more hurt than anything. He wasn't going to rage, like Mad Dog, or go into an apathetic drift, as Davenport was apt to do, or turn to drugs, like Carl Caruby. He just wanted to know, just wanted to feel valued.

Sharkey dispensed a requisite amount of ego salve and slapped him on the shoulder as he headed out. What a relief. No demands for more plate time, no rants about being traded. He might grouse to his friends, feel frustrated, but he understood, and he wasn't going to become a problem. Sharkey turned back to the desk, glanced at the

letter tray, and noticed a thin brown parcel with a note attached. He lifted the note: "Sorry, Raven's file is in archives. Might take a week or two. Meantime, here are D'port, Kane. —WH." From Walt Howlett, the board secretary. Bless him. Sharkey had gone to him on the sly to ask about reading certain personnel files, a part of a stepped-up plan to watch out for himself.

Sharkey had decided to learn all he could about the guys who showed tendencies to be disciplinary problems—men who might be capable of the unspeakable. Sharkey was becoming more determined than ever to track them, see where they were going in the wee hours after curfew. He had collared Howlett in the hall at Fenway two days ago, right after the latest attack hit the news: the beheading of a seventy-four-year-old retired taxi driver in Roxbury.

Knifing open the sealed packet, Sharkey found two files, differing greatly in size: Davenport's an inch thick, Kane's only ten or twelve pages. Sharkey decided to tackle the big one first, stripping off two thick rubber bands and opening the crinkled cover.

Inside were notes and evaluations dating back to Jeremy Davenport's minor-league career in Charleston, Rochester and Pawtucket. Many of the incidents Sharkey knew about—the liquor-store robbery showed up with a long memo and a police report—but other items were complete surprises. Prior to spring training of last year there had been an alarming domestic-violence incident: Davenport's wife at the time, now his ex, had rammed their home with a Jeep Cherokee, touching off a melee in which an unidentified Norwegian woman was burned on the buttocks with a butane torch. He had been fined twice in Florida for hunting marlin with a semiautomatic rifle.

Thumbing through it all, page by page, Sharkey began to see Davenport more clearly: He was not just a sullen star, he was a resentful, tormented young man who had spent years skating the razor edge between infantile pranks and wanton criminality. Had it not been for

the guidance of certain fine men in organized baseball, and for a few other breaks, he might well be playing the angles off the high outfield wall at San Quentin.

Kane's file was less instructive. The first entry, two typed pages written by Domato, summarized Ron Kane's troubled childhood—itinerant poverty, an abusive father, expulsions from school, fights—a lot of problems Domato had never bothered to mention. Difficulties Kane blithely glossed over in his showboating to the media. There was a page entitled "Psychiatric Summary," blank but for a notation: "See Matthieu reports." Puzzling. Very puzzling. Sharkey was noting it in his journal when Domato walked in, no knock, no greeting at all.

Sharkey closed the file and quickly pushed it aside, hoping Domato hadn't noticed. He didn't appear to. Stu's thoughts seemed far away. He dropped into a chair and stared blankly at the floor.

"He's losing it. Really losing it," he muttered.

"Who?"

"Wolf." Domato's eyes had locked onto a cockroach near the far wall; he followed its slow progress across the floor.

"Why? What's happening?"

"We went till midnight last night, haggling with that asshole Gamboa. Kane was ready to sit out the rest of the season thanks to that fuckhead. Scary shit, I'm telling you."

"Jesus. They resolve anything?"

Domato glanced up. His face looked brittle and red. "We caved. We're giving away the store. Wolf agreed to a hundred eighty-six million, over six years, and he came out of there, I swear to God, shaking like a wet dog. Only thing is, a contract that big is going to take board approval. Three of them, Lacy says, won't go for it, and if we renege, Gamboa's going to order Kane into street clothes. It's a mess. It's going to take the wisdom of Solomon to sort it out."

Sharkey exhaled sharply. The wisdom of Solomon. That was one ingredient unlikely to surface at Fenway. The player backlash, if and

when Kane's deal was announced, would blow a hole right through the clubhouse roof.

Seeing his expression, Domato asked, "Are you okay?"

"Yeah, I think. Just burned out. That egret—"

"Hell of a way to lose." Domato ran a hand through his bristly hair. "I think he's hiring detectives. Wolf is. Maybe it'll help."

"Really? About time."

"You still, ah, looking yourself? Trailing those guys?"

"Probably. Here and there." Sharkey waited for a reaction, a tacit show of approval or disapproval. He was still unsure how much of their conversations got back to Wulfmeyer.

Domato's eyes were cast aside. Without warning, he bounded out of the chair, crossing the small office in an astounding burst of movement for a man of his girth. Slamming down his foot like a thunderclap, he tried to smash the cockroach.

The black wing tip slowly lifted. Nothing there.

He looked up at Sharkey, his expression still rigid, unchanged, as if he had never left his seat.

"Just don't get yourself hurt."

Kane's midnight blue Maserati glided to a halt outside a stately colonial home in Somerville, and Kane got out and climbed the sloping lawn. Sharkey cut the lights of the Olds. From a quarter mile away he could see the door open and a woman emerge, shapely in a long, cream-colored dress. Kane's hot date, apparently.

She moved down the hill and entered the sports car. Kane came around and drove away.

Following from a distance, Sharkey felt oddly glad for the clandestine mission, a chance to get out and drive and forget about the pressures at Fenway. The Sox had just blown another home game, an interleague contest with the lowly Brewers, and Harkwood, the

Herald's Brillo-haired columnist, had landed a hit piece speculating that the Red Sox would not extend Sharkey's contract beyond the end of next season. "Too 'old school,' too out of step with the front-office brain trust," or so one club official had said. Anonymous, of course, but a child could guess it was Wulfmeyer's comment, leaked despite the Sox's one-game lead in the East, because he wanted to apply leverage, keep Sharkey in line, keep him from mouthing off.

Mind games. Goddamn mind games.

The Maserati rolled several miles and finally disgorged Kane and the woman at the door of the Electric Alligator, a trendy downtown bar built into an aging brick facade—a cavern aglow inside with funky neon artwork, twisted tubes of blue, red, green and yellow. Sharkey parked on a side street. He thought about waiting in the car, except he knew this bar. The Alligator attracted quite a few jocks and entertainers; it was the type of milieu where a superstar such as Kane could hang out and not be harassed by the fans, thanks to bouncers the size of cement trucks.

Approaching the window, peering in, Sharkey saw Kane and the woman at the long brass bar. She looked barely eighteen, if that—a stunner, though, a dark-eyed blonde. It brought to mind that tip Harkwood had confronted him with, about some of the guys and a statutory rape. Thank God that had never hit print. It was sure as the winter snow that Harkwood had turned over every rock in Massachusetts trying to confirm that one.

Kane and the woman drank for an hour, had dinner, then hit the Lion's Den, where they danced until two. Next they arrived at Kane's place—a smoky brick building ornamented with black wrought iron—and the beautiful young woman and the superstar moved together up the walk and through the door.

Sharkey cut the engine and switched off the lights. He could see the house well from his vantage point, high on the sloping street. He planned to wait long enough to be sure Kane was done roaming for

the night. Settling into the seat, Sharkey turned up the radio. An old Cole Porter tune was playing. His mind drifted; he found himself imagining the carnal feast unfolding inside—wet tongues, writhing bodies, swaying nude breasts, this woman who might be barely out of high school, stripping and making love to a near delinquent she barely knew. It set Sharkey's pulse going, heating him up until the windows began to steam.

He had been sitting only ten or twelve minutes when Kane's door burst open. The young woman raced out, waving her arms as she fled in the opposite direction. A lithe, mantislike figure who rounded the corner and disappeared.

Puzzled, Sharkey sat forward, forearms against the steering wheel, waiting to see if Kane would come out. Several moments passed and Kane sprang out the door, wearing only what appeared to be white pajamas.

Kane looked around, yelled for her—"Marcia! It was a joke! It was just a fucking joke!"—and retreated indoors. When he next emerged, Kane was fully dressed. He climbed into the Maserati, sat a moment, then climbed out, striding back into the house. The lights flashed on and went off.

Finally Kane appeared again, moving quickly to the Maserati. He slammed the door and rolled away with a short screech of rubber.

13

That was the rumor, Mike. . . . Right, that's true, I do think he's a shitty little twerp. All the more reason you don't need him." Wulfmeyer laughed and pressed the phone to his ear. "No, it's not some tactic—I don't want Gregson either. No, no, you're reading too much into— No, I'm just not going to trade him . . . He's a magician in the— Right. No, absolutely not. . . . That's right, we're going to keep the little bastard."

Wolf hung up. He felt edgy, rattled, a state of mind that seemed to be gaining a rocklike permanence. To carry out the grand scheme he'd been hatching, a scheme with no defined boundaries, no shape, merely a vague direction he would have to follow by instinct, Wolf had just yanked the plug on a trade that would have sent Castillo to the Dodgers, getting rid of the little hemorrhoid once and for all.

It was probably the last chance; Wolf hated to sabotage it. In a few days the trading deadline would pass and Fish would have a fit, whining, groaning, probably go down with another colitis attack. Poor guy.

Now every night he'd go to bed wondering if Castillo was going to break into his room and hack his head off. Not a situation Wolf relished dealing with, but it was far preferable to have Fish fixated on Castillo than to allow the alternative, Castillo somewhere else and Fish poking after Kane.

The phone rang again. Samantha called out, "Henrietta."

"Thank you." He grabbed it.

"Neville, would you step down here a minute? Something disturbing has just come up."

Disturbing? Considering that Henrietta applied the word to everything from undercooked wieners to grisly beheadings, it was hard to gauge the depth of her unease; even so, he was filled with a sudden sense of foreboding. "Give me ten seconds. Be right there."

He stopped at Sam's desk on the way out. "Would you have Stu come by when he's got a minute?" Wolf checked his watch. "Maybe half an hour? Not any later, though, because I haven't had lunch, and I'm afraid he'll try to tag along."

"He's down in Accounts. I'll call him now."

"Great."

Wulfmeyer followed the empty hall to the board suite, dreading that something had gone wrong with the drop—a passing vagrant had lifted the duffel bag, or Henrietta's ex-Teamster, a goon she called "my security man," had failed to make delivery.

She was staring at one of her rings, a baroque object with a heavy garnet, as he walked in. Seeing him, Henrietta quickly placed her hands primly on the desk. She looked especially gussied up, wearing a smart red Donna Karan jacket, her hair somehow higher and more plastic-looking.

"Any word from Mulgrove?" Wulfmeyer said, sitting down. He and Henrietta, in arranging the cash drop, had enlisted the services of one of Boston's best-known PIs, a former police detective named Jack

Mulgrove. It was Mulgrove's job to track the recovery vehicle and try to ascertain the identity of the asshole who'd demanded the million.

"Bad news there," Henrietta said. "They lost the tail in Charlestown. And that's not our biggest problem."

Wulfmeyer noticed the deepening lines under her heavy makeup; she was taking extra efforts with her appearance because she was becoming a wreck. She rocked convulsively forward.

"As I—as we discussed, or as you know, I'm personally acquainted with Chief Hardeway—who is, incidentally, quite a Red Sox fan. As I said, most of those cops are. We should really be very glad about that."

"Yes, for sure . . ." This didn't sound good.

"So, anyway, with this task force, the FBI involved . . . well, I called him after you and I talked, after this, uh, videotape came to light. Called him, just caught up, sounded him out on the general nature, the direction, of their investigation. He very well remembered our last get-together, when I took him to the Haliburton Club. And, of course, he's extremely concerned about Gordon, who's in a lot of pain, by the way."

Wulfmeyer felt his pulse quicken. He wished to hell she'd get to the point.

"So this morning he calls back. Hardeway, I'm talking about. Keeping me informed, which I asked him to do. And he brings up Ron Kane."

Here it was, the kicker. Wolf's bladder constricted to the size of a golf ball.

"What about him?"

"This question of when he first arrived here. When he showed up for the first game."

"It was early June, right? June first or second?" Wulfmeyer knew that the question had surfaced before. The Barnacle had brought it up, and Stu had been trying to locate a copy of the plane ticket. Wolf was

certain of the date of Kane's debut—June 3—and he was reasonably sure that Kane had flown into Logan two or three days before that; Domato had specifically gone to Logan to pick him up.

"Leyland—Chief Hardeway—expressed to me in utter confidence, as a courtesy, that this task force ran Kane's flight records. Says to me, 'Don't panic yourself, but there's been a suspicion raised.' His exact words. And I'll tell you, Neville, we'd better thank our lucky stars the cops want to keep a tight clamp on the investigation. This thing leaks out—"

"What'd he say?" Wulfmeyer said. "About the flight records?"

"May tenth. Ron flew in May tenth. And, I guess, just hung out for a few weeks. Strangest thing."

They fell silent. The implication was immediately obvious: It clearly put Kane in Boston on the date of the first murder, Marzoli. But of course it did, Wulfmeyer reminded himself. Kane was the god-damned killer.

What made this news so horrific was that the cops now knew he was in town—not that it was illegal to be in Boston in early May. That would be an important point to remember: There was nothing illegal about being in Boston in early May. But the cops knew it, and they had made a deliberate effort to uncover it.

"As to why this came up—" Henrietta lowered her voice. "Evidently there was an anonymous tipster, somebody saying, 'Hey, look into Ron Kane.'"

"A tipster?" It triggered an electrical storm in Wulfmeyer's brain. Sharkey? Or someone else on the club? His first paranoid thought was that the tip had come from inside, though, as far as he knew, not a single Sox player was aware of the murder probe. Unless somebody had seen something.

"The tipster hinted, I guess, that he might have a videotape, and hung up. But I don't think—"

"A videotape! Jesus—it's the same guy!"

"Maybe. It might be. But we don't know that for sure, Neville. That's the real—"

"Sure it is! A videotape? Good God Almighty!"

"Neville, pipe down!"

"That fuck-ing ass-hole!" Wulfmeyer thought the pressure in his head would explode it, send his brain flying like spaghetti against the ceiling and walls. "This guy's screwing us over! Gets his fuckin' million, and now he's dropping tips!"

"Neville, we paid him—he's *agreed* to shut up."

"You got that in writing? My God! He took all that—and I bet he sniffed out the tail. Knew he was being followed. Yeah, outran the tail and now he's upset about it, figuring he can royally fuck us over!"

"Neville, let's *please* stay calm!"

"Jesus!"

"We'll deal with this!" Henrietta flashed the withering glare that had ended debate at so many acrimonious board meetings. "Right now we just don't know."

"Mulgrove. We need him on this full-time."

"Agreed. Meanwhile, that tape you've got. That copy. I certainly hope by now you've destroyed it."

"No, no I haven't, and there's a reason for that." Wulfmeyer tried to will himself into a passable state of composure. He would need her support in the weeks ahead, which, by the looks of things, would be turbulent on the order of a Third-World uprising. He did not want to antagonize her any further. In spite of his own great reluctance to elucidate the truly idiotic-sounding plan he had concocted for that videotape, she had brought it up, and he calculated that it was wise to let her in on his thinking.

Wolf told her that Mike Sanders, the Dodgers GM—they'd just got off the phone—had supplied the name of an outfit in Hollywood that could digitally alter a tape, change one man's face to another.

"Amazing technology. Like in *The Terminator*. You see it just about every movie nowdays. So Sanders, he's in the middle of all that. I told him we're working on our highlight films. Going to do one of the Raven for his big tribute."

Henrietta recoiled. "Why in the *hell* would you want to alter that tape?"

"I don't, that's the thing. Let me be perfectly clear about that: The *last* thing I want to do is alter that tape." Wolf felt himself sweating through his shirt. "It's just that I can foresee a circumstance— All right, picture just hypothetically, and it's quite possible, suspicion falling on someone other than Kane. Some other player, say. Not to pinpoint anybody, but let's imagine the cops find reason to take an interest in Benito Castillo. And incidentally, I just put the kibosh on a trade to the Dodgers. So if there's another murder and his face should happen to show up—"

"On that tape? You've *got* to be joking!"

"I know, I know, it sounds far-fetched."

"Sounds like a felony. Sounds like the most ridiculous—"

"Let me finish! This is only a very last, *last* resort. A way to buy some time." Wulfmeyer had expected this kind of recalcitrance from a woman who balked for ten months at raising ticket prices. "Should we get late in the season—who knows?—the pennant could be on the line; we could get in a situation where one or two more strong out-ings by our number-one pitcher could finally put this franchise over the hump."

"Framing an innocent man."

"They'd see right through it. Eventually. Believe me, I'm not sug-gesting we actually *obstruct* justice in some sense, only that it would be such a shame if the hammer came down too early. The last thing we want—and I know you're with me on this—the *very last thing* we want is to get screwed out of our big chance, have it ripped away from us, because of nothing more than bad timing."

Henrietta rubbed her fingertips together. Her finely drawn eyebrows creased sharply over her steely blue eyes. For an instant she wondered what the sisters would think of the Red Sox up at the Divine Mercy Convent, if this ever got out on top of the Davenport tear-gas fiasco.

"Let's consider your assertion: They'd see through it eventually. You know that for a fact?"

"Listen—" Wolf threw up his hands. "What I know about digitally altered videotapes you could squeeze into a thimble. Christ, I haven't even talked to these people. But I wouldn't be a bit surprised if the cops have some supersophisticated, high-tech way of analyzing all those little tape molecules, seeing which ones have been *shifted around*." His frenetic hand movements betrayed his agitation; he hated her piety, her inflated school-girl desire to keep her hands clean.

"Don't forget, Henrietta, by the end of October all bets are off. Either we win this time, either this city's going through a championship orgasm enough to blow the roof off the Old North Church, or it's another fuckin' wasted year, and I'll give you a hundred to one against Gordon Malcolm Kornblume living to see another stretch drive, frankly."

Henrietta regarded him with the judgmental detachment that had become one of her governing trademarks. Her trembling fingers lifted a silver cigarette case and she lit up a Kool, her fifth in two days. Nine smoke-free years had suddenly gone by the boards owing to this crisis. In a pang of self-loathing, she lifted her eyes to the Neiman, as if that dynamic image of the Raven would offer some solace or even inspire an answer. A hardening of her expression signaled that a decision had been reached.

"How do you plan to pay for this?"

"Concession revenues. It's a drop in the bucket."

"I'm against— As you know, I hate the idea of turning this mess into some type of cover-up."

"Insurance, that's all it is." Wulfmeyer saw that he had prevailed. He stood to leave. "It's just one of, you know, a bunch of things I've got in the hopper to keep the lid on this situation. Chances are, it'll never be important."

Wulfmeyer sat alone in the office coffee room, sipping the battery-acid brew the secretaries somehow tolerated. He wanted to isolate himself, hide somewhere—not just the coffee room but the Galápagos Islands, the North Pole. He could almost smell the smoke from his frying brain. Was he capable of handling this overwhelming burden? Was his thinking as clouded as Henrietta seemed to believe?

Kane's contract was nearly ready; he'd meant to run the final changes past Henrietta, but now was clearly not the time. Oscar was having the usual shit fit, wanting a big press conference; he'd leaked a barrage of inaccurate details to Harkwood, who'd led his column with it this morning. Meanwhile, Lacy needed Wolf's response to the latest development in that Davenport mess.

Davenport was another candidate who might plausibly be linked to serial murder. There'd been that incident where he was caught speeding near a murder scene. Would that be enough? That and the nun bombing? And being in every city on the date of every killing? It might work, yes. Given those facts, and a videotape of Davenport dumping a body, the cops would toss the troubled outfielder in the slammer before you could say "Jack the Ripper."

Pulling it off would be tricky, though. Tricky to time it. Wolf would need to introduce the tape anonymously, and do it before the cops got definitive evidence on Kane. But not too early. The tape might only buy a week, two weeks, who could tell? That Davenport was hitting .318 was another consideration. You didn't yank a bat like that out of the line-up any longer than you had to. It was so much more inviting to nail Castillo.

Or even Fish.

That was one more option on Wolf's mind, a notion straight out of hell that carried huge downside risk. Henrietta would be furious. Kornblume might exact retribution, if he was still alive. Wolf might end up out on his ear, or in jail, or both.

But if it worked, if Henrietta could be appeased, sacrificing Sharkey might be a brilliant, bold stroke. It might keep Kane in the lineup without losing any roster players. Ted Uziak could step in to manage. Or they could bring in somebody; there were rumors Greg Goossell was about to get the ax in San Francisco. The Barnacle's prior interest in Sharkey gave the gambit a considerable chance of succeeding. Fish was directly linked, after all, to the first two corpses.

There was so much to consider. A lot of the game plan would depend on how the events of the season unfolded, what Wolf could learn from Mulgrove, from Stu.

Stu— Oh God, he'd forgotten his meeting with Stu. Wulfmeyer jumped up, tossed out the dregs of his coffee, and hurried back up to his office. Domato's corpulent frame was wedged in the seat across from Samantha, his tie loosened. He was chatting her up about a winning night he'd enjoyed in Atlantic City.

"Stu, sorry, come on in," Wulfmeyer said, brushing past him, trying to shift gears so they could square away some vital details.

The ex-scout shuffled in, an amiable smile playing across his sizable mouth, as if the concerns of a murder investigation were as distant as the Horsehead Nebula.

"Should we hit the Empress Room, Wolf? They got a prime-rib special this month."

"Already ate. Sit down. Let's talk about keeping our boys in check. The board's on my ass, and we've got to prevent any further disciplinary problems. A herculean task, given our track record." Wulfmeyer had not told Domato about the videotape, but Stu was still

one of only four people in the organization, along with Sharkey and Henrietta—five if you counted the PI Mulgrove—who was aware of the police probe.

"I'm going to be blunt, Stu. Looking over this club, the frightening list of off-the-field shenanigans, I can't remember a team so beset with personnel problems, incidents, and reckless disregard for right and wrong. Unless it was the '98 club, with Hauser's assault indictment."

"Fish thinks we'll solve half our problems once we unload Castillo."

"Yeah, well, a trade's looking iffy. And Benito's a hell of a glove." Wulfmeyer shifted uncomfortably. "Anyway, I'm especially concerned about our big guns—Kane, Villalobos, Davenport, Langley. We lose any one of those guys we're on the express train to Shitsville."

Domato sensed Wolf's direction. "I hope to hell they're not implicated in that, ah, murder thing."

"No, no, but I want to get to that in a minute. These big guns, I want to make sure they're happy, well occupied. Idle hands, you know. And we can't seem to enforce a curfew no matter how many fines we hand down, so I've been racking my brain—I'm sure you have, too."

"I got your memo," Domato said. "Far as interests, yeah, those guys all love the ladies."

"Thought so. Red-blooded American boys." Wulfmeyer reached for a folder. He pulled out a typed list of escort services. "It can't hurt if we get these guys a little companionship. Make sure they're not, you know, frustrated." He handed the list to Stu. "See to it, when we get into a town, these guys get pampered. Room service. Arrange it with them, you know, informally."

"Right. Can I—"

"Yes. You, too. Just don't blow the budget." Wulfmeyer hated to have to squander money on escorts for anyone but Kane, for the real purpose was to draw Kane away from his darker habits. But if it sur-

faced later that he got preferential treatment, it might somehow point a finger at him. Wolf watched Domato for a second, the big doofus grinning ear to ear. "Now, this other thing, this serial-murder speculation. I'm just about certain this is going to turn out to be some fan, like I said before—some total nut case out there—and I sure as hell hope it's not one of our Boosters."

"I saw that Barnacle. He was at the game Thursday night."

"A freebie, I bet. Never mind him. We've got to watch our own asses, which brings me to Fish."

"He's the scaredest manager I've ever seen." Domato laughed.

"Yes. Understandably. Anyway, I'm acutely aware—because you're doing your job so very well—that he's continuing, despite my direct order, to act like he's some amateur detective, like he's going to save his own ass, and save this nation, save all these murder victims, by determining just who done it. I can't condone that type of behavior. I think it's detrimental. But as long as he's doing it . . . well, you can see where I'm heading."

Domato stared dumbly. "Where?"

"Well, as long as he's doing it, let's collect the information. See what's there. Let's try a for-instance: Fish finds out some very incriminating information concerning Benito. He's not going to come and tell me, is he?"

"No, because it'll get him in trouble."

"Right. I'd ream him out—and deservedly so. But if he tells you, if you can maintain his confidence, maybe we'll understand the whole situation just a little bit better."

"Sure thing. Gotcha." Domato thought a moment. "You know, last thing he mentioned to me, he's also worried about the Raven. Guess the Raven's one of those fanatics who goes all over, watching us play. And now, of course, he's been hanging around the clubhouse. It's creepy—him dying, and that mouth of his."

Wulfmeyer considered that. "How many games does he get to? All of them?"

"Just about. Says he does."

"Look, all right, you keep a close eye on things. Keep an eye on things, and keep those reports coming in."

14

Sharkey glanced at Johnny Uggams on third and slapped the tobacco tin in his left rear pocket three times. Langley danced off first. The two-out rally, in the ninth, before a screaming Sunday home crowd, required the type of agonizing managerial decisions that made baseball the most intellectual of all sports.

Langley's speed was probably good enough to steal second, what with Hasselman's delivery and Beniquez's poor arm. That would put the Sox in a position to score twice—and win—with only a single. But a steal would open up first. The Twins would likely walk Doug Maynard, setting up the force at any base, and bring in the flamethrower Golic to pitch to Boston's weak-hitting lefty, Ryan Bauer. An inner vein, a sixth sense honed over twenty-nine summers—more than four thousand games—told Sharkey to hold Langley at first, allowing Maynard his chance.

Hacking viciously at the next pitch, Maynard blasted a pop-up that seemed to climb into the ionosphere. It fell into a waiting glove.

Boom. Another Sox defeat. The race was dead even again, the Sox and Yankees tied atop the East Division standings. A hundred games

in the books, sixty-two to go, and it was like the leaders hadn't even started.

In the clubhouse Moses sidled up. "Don't like what I've been seeing, Fish," he hissed through his teeth. Mad Dog had gone hitless again; his average, falling like the temperature on the dark side of Pluto, was now an abysmal .196, worst of any regular in the majors.

"And what's that, Dog?"

"Not here. The Kitty. Midnight." He moved away, and Ravinovich sauntered over, his blue eyes riveting.

"Another tough one, Fish."

"A bitch," Sharkey agreed; he was in no mood to rehash it.

"If you don't mind a quick thought . . ."

Sharkey looked at him. Something called to mind those times when that tongue would start creeping out, ever so slowly. It was an immense act of willpower merely to be civil. "Sure. Anything. Let's hear it."

"Just thought, well, maybe you could have had Tarver bunting in the fifth."

"He tripled home two runs!"

"I know—listen, I'm not trying to second-guess. Just, with a sinker-baller throwing—"

"All right, all right, it was a possibility—thanks for the input." Sharkey moved past him, eager to shower, change, get the hell out. The jerk. Tarver bunting. What an ignoramus.

He sat heavily at his locker, yanking off his spikes. It had been a blistering August afternoon, heat and humidity enough to wilt a camel. The Sox had squandered Kane's first home run by botching a double-play ball in the eighth. Sharkey felt dizzy. He looked up, saw Castillo glaring at him, and decided against the shower, just changed and left. Fought the horrible traffic, brooding over the loss, the ominous tone in Mad Dog's voice, and got home and collapsed in bed.

He fell into the haze of a restless sleep, tossing and turning until

he heard the door slam. Bernice getting home. She'd gone to some exhibit in Brookline, an artist who turned chicken wire and crepe paper into animal heads. He dreaded the inevitable discussion about it; she would sense his lack of interest—again—and leave in a huff—again. Heaven forbid he should fail to appreciate the genius of a wire-sculpting zealot, while she herself seemed to be drifting away, losing all interest in the Red Sox. The club could collapse and finish forty games out and she probably wouldn't bat an eye.

"Augie! You here?"

Her voice drifted up the stairs. He tried to ignore it.

"Auu-GIEE!"

"Whaaat?" he shouted hoarsely.

"Come down and help!"

"I'm tryin' to sleep!"

"I bought a statue for the garden! It's Pegasus, and it weighs a ton!"

A half-naked woman hung upside down on a trapeze, peeling a banana. Moses, his head in his hands, appeared not even to see her. Sharkey dropped his Stoli on the table and joined him, surprised by the depth of his despondency.

"So, Dog, how ya doin', man?" He tried to affect the edgy street rap that was the best way to communicate with Mad Dog. An edge with an undercurrent of cool; Sharkey threw an insouciant glance toward the stage.

"Worst year of my life," Moses said tightly. "This funk I've been in, it's tearing my insides out. Seein' the ball, just ain't hittin'."

"You'll break out. A matter of time."

"Four for fuckin' sixty-eight."

"Sixty-nine. Or sixty-eight, whatever it is. Keep swinging," Sharkey exhorted him. "You had a great rip last night, that foul into the dugout."

"Sheeee-it." Moses's scowl deepened. Sharkey decided to change the subject; he asked what Moses was seeing, what was going on with the guys. Moses's hard black eyes swung toward him.

"Kane. Fuckin' Kane, Kane, Kane. That's all we fuckin' hear about. I think he's a jinx on me. A jinx on my hittin'."

"That ain't true, Dog—no way the man's a jinx." Sharkey knew it was necessary to take a strong stand against that line of thinking. At the same time, carefully avoiding Moses's attention, he slipped his hands beneath the table to execute his standard hex-busting gesture—seven raps of his knuckles. "The last thing you need, or that any of us needs, is to dwell on the negative. Get your confidence back, you'll hit; and meanwhile Kane's going to make all the difference for us. One thing I won't tolerate is you two on a collision course. It could wreck us."

"No one likes him. Freak's settin' a bad example for the other young guys. Runnin' wild, playin' cards all night, or whatever the hell he's doing. Reeling says we've got a PI startin' to tail us—heard it from Stu Domato—and he says Kane's already figuring ways to get out there, slippin' away, so he can keep breakin' the curfew."

"We'll see about that," Sharkey said. He was glad to hear that Wolf was following through with a detective, though he wished Wolf would keep him in the loop on those things, and he wondered if one sleuth was enough. "Appreciate your concern, but let's not go ballistic unless we got a specific problem. Got a specific problem, let's deal with it. Otherwise let's prop up the attitude."

Moses took a swig of his Coors. Sharkey realized it was not his first. "Tell you one thing Kane was doin'. Saw it myself, comin' home one night in Chelsea. Two o'clock in the mornin'."

"What was that?"

"Pissin' in the mail slot. Pissin' right in the mail slot of the International House of Pancakes."

Sharkey hunched forward. He took a long sip of his Stoli.

"Let me tell you somethin', Dog. Tomorrow morning there's

going to be a press conference out at the yacht club. Wulfmeyer's going to announce that Kane's getting a huge new contract. I don't want any resentment, no trouble on my team."

Moses glared moodily through the smoky light. A brunette in a G-string was now crawling across the stage like an inchworm.

"He gets some huge deal—gets eighty or ninety million—we're gonna be hacked off. A lot of us guys, first thing we're gonna do is break down the fuckin' door of Wulfmeyer's office, set him straight on what's up with this team."

"Dog, I'm tellin' ya again: Don't sweat the small stuff, things that aren't really your business." Sharkey felt his stomach tighten. "Just do your job and those hits'll start fallin'."

Wulfmeyer made the announcement: "One HUNDRED and EIGHTY-SIX *MILLION* dollars!"

The multiyear deal, second only to shortstop Alex Rodriguez's $252 million contract with the Texas Rangers in all of professional sports, was by far the biggest bonanza ever accorded a rookie, a player with only seven wins and sixteen hits in the majors. The fantastic, almost incomprehensible size of the agreement underscored the fact that Kane was not only the most sensational talent to burst on the scene in decades, maybe ever, but also a man of unparalleled star power, a figure whose feats had captured the imagination of America.

Strobe lights flashed, murmurs filled the air. A leggy brunette tip-toed onto the dais in heels, presenting to Wulfmeyer an enormous quill with a white plume. Wulfmeyer waved it with a flourish, took a moment to introduce Gamboa and Kane, and then placed the quill in Kane's famous right hand.

He signed, and the questions started: What did he plan to do with the money? Did he think the Sox could win this year? Dozens of personal queries that Kane had answered dozens of times. A press confer-

ence like this was strictly about marketing, scoring the club free column inches and airtime, and once those goals had been achieved, and all the questions answered, it began to break up.

Wulfmeyer headed across the lot toward his gold Eldorado, wedged against a fence by the bay. A stiff offshore breeze was pushing around dozens of bright sails out among the whitecaps.

"Wolf, wait up!"

Sharkey caught him at the car.

"Fish, didn't know you were coming. Nice show of support. How are ya?"

"Not good. Frankly." Sharkey had left him six messages at the office.

Wulfmeyer's squinting face betrayed his own unhappiness. He looked as if he hadn't slept in days, except he was cleanly shaved, marked by a deep razor burn.

"If you're upset about that story in the *Globe*, forget it. It's bull-shit," Wulfmeyer said. "They quoted me completely out of context. I have no complaints whatsoever about your late-inning decisions."

"Let's talk about another detestable subject—murder." Had he heard? Sharkey asked him. There had been another one, number eight—a retired upholsterer from Malden. He'd been found inside a sofa bed. Or his body had; the head's whereabouts remained unknown. The report had just been on the news. Sharkey had been so unfortunate as to hear it during breakfast. "Must've happened last night. A cleaning woman found him. They hospitalized her for shock."

"Appalling," Wulfmeyer said. "No other word for it." He turned his gaze to the horizon.

"I can think of some other words. This thing's getting scary, Wolf. Fucking scary."

"It's some fan—like I said before. Some psychopathic sack of shit, Christ God Almighty."

"It can't go on like this. It goes on like this, it's going to be the biggest murder case in America. Maybe already is. And our guys, they're out running wild, out all night. I can't keep up with them. Stu can't. I heard we got a PI—great—but is one man enough? Is one man up to the task? Ask yourself. These guys, they don't even care about the fines. Kane missed a team meeting, and I nailed him for five grand—and now, my God, he turns around and he's making a hundred and eighty-six million."

Wolf glowered. He didn't want to hear it. His nerves were bad enough just sharing a dais with Kane. Kane and Gamboa, too, a killer and a snake. Plus all the other crap—Henrietta, her nagging, still thinking her Red Sox should be above reproach; her own fears, so goddamn terrified now she was leaving the office early when the club was at home, avoiding the clubhouse, the field, anywhere Kane might show up. Yeah, it would be great having a gang of private eyes, an ensemble cast, to see that these murders stopped, but the hell of it was—what Wolf couldn't say—was the attendant risk involved: A guy might witness something. He might feel an ethical compulsion to report it. Destroy the whole season by catching Kane in the act.

"This guy we got—Jack Mulgrove—he's the best in the business," Wulfmeyer said. Mulgrove was said to be exceptionally discreet; even so, Wulfmeyer had resisted, so far, using him for anything beyond basic security outside the team hotel. His main role had been to try to track the frigging extortionist. But Wolf let Sharkey hold to the illusion that Mulgrove was out cruising the streets, keeping the guys out of trouble. "Whether we get anyone else, that depends, but if Kane's running wild, breaking curfew, you'd better talk to him, goddamn it. Any of those guys, talk to them! You've been a manager half your life—I shouldn't have to tell you what to do."

Sharkey stifled a powerful urge to punch Wolf right in the face. He had talked to Kane more than once, he said hotly.

"And last night—last night I'm talking to Mad Dog, having a

drink, you know, BS-ing about the guys, and he brings up Castillo, how much that little bastard hates me. Know what he said? What Castillo said to Villalobos?"

"Since I'm not a mind reader, no."

"He was telling Villalobos he wants to cut my throat!"

"He'd like to, or he plans to?"

"Yes!"

"Which one?"

"My throat! How many have I got?"

"Slow down, Fish." Wulfmeyer grabbed Sharkey's arm. "*Nobody's* going to cut your throat, I swear to God. You're getting way too overwrought."

"Am I? In this nightmare? We're sitting on a time bomb, Wolf!"

"Fish! Get hold of yourself!" He was about to further dismiss Sharkey's paranoia when he remembered it might be necessary, at some future point, to skewer Castillo with the steely prong of justice. Wolf exhaled sharply, looked out at the boats. "Christ, I don't know. Castillo's so—" He broke off. "How'd he do over the weekend?"

"Oh for fourteen."

"It's possible. I guess it *could* be him."

"I think you should talk to the cops. Immediately."

"I might, but let's— Look, I'll do that, I'll do exactly that and talk to them, if you don't breathe a word. No one can know about this. Ever!" Wulfmeyer dug out his keys and stabbed the door of the Cadillac. "I shouldn't tell you this, but Mulgrove's looking very closely at Castillo's every move. Davenport's, too. We're pouring more resources into this than you know about, so let's keep your cool, all right? And we'll talk tomorrow."

15

HEADLESS BODY FOUND IN TOPLESS BAR, screamed the headline in the *Herald*, about a new attack in West Somerville. Wulfmeyer spread the paper across his desk, reading. The gruesome account—the head had been propped in the dressing room—left no doubt that the crisis was worsening. The last three murders, besides being particularly brazen, had occurred in a span of only a couple of weeks, intensifying media interest in the crimes. The accounts were being splashed across page one, and Boston police had acknowledged a link among incidents in the greater Boston area.

So far, fortunately, the connections ended there. The papers had yet to make the broader leap to include the bodies discovered in Texas, Cleveland, Kansas City—places and dates that would correlate so perfectly with the travels of the club.

How long before that disastrous information leaked out? Surely someone would eventually connect the dots, even if federal authorities maintained their present silence about the investigation. A few bad breaks and the whole situation could go into a meltdown, and Wulfmeyer had the feeling that none of the countermeasures were

working: not the fines, not Fish's lectures, not even the carnal delights of Boston's finest escort services. Nothing was keeping Kane off the streets at night.

It was maddening. Infuriating. It made Wulfmeyer want to hit somebody, take a polo mallet and whack someone just to vent the stress. He thought about calling Fish or Stu, lashing into them, but before he could pick up the phone it rang.

Samantha called out, "Neville, for you. Important."

"Who is it?"

"The White House."

The White House? Wulfmeyer's blood pressure jumped sharply.

"Same guy?"

"Sounded like him."

He punched the phone. "Listen, you fucking shithead! We paid your fucking ransom! Go put a bullet in your brain!" He slammed the receiver, breathing hard, feeling suddenly faint.

Seconds later it rang again. Samantha said, "It's the presidential appointment secretary."

"No, it isn't! That is *not* the presidential appointment secretary!"

A long pause. "He insists on talking to you. Says 'your whole goddamn season may depend on it'—I'm quoting him."

"Fuck! *Fuck fuck fuck!*" Wolf grabbed the line. "I'm in no mood for this! No mood! Just say what you want to say!"

"I need more money. In fact, I need five million dollars."

"Right. Like hell you do!"

"Whether I actually *need* the money is really not your concern, Wulfmeyer. I'm keeping your terrible secret, and it's hard work. My conscience is screaming at me."

"Your conscience swallowed a load of rat poison and died!"

"The same arrangement. Tomorrow night. Try anything funny and that tape goes straight to the cops. Am I clear about that?"

Wolf couldn't speak.

"Later, Wolfie, baby."

The line went dead. Wolf reached down and swept the phone off the desk, a vigorous sidearm throw that sent it crashing into the wall. He yanked open a drawer and fumbled for the Valium.

"You all right in there?" Samantha craned her head in.

"I'm fine! Fucking prank calls!" He took the last pill in the vial, downing it with stale coffee. "I'm going out. I've got to see Henrietta."

He stormed out, up to her office, only to discover she was having lunch at Les Deux with Ravinovich. Racing there in the Eldorado, Wulfmeyer found them in a cozy corner booth of the swank restaurant. Henrietta was punctuating some humorous story by touching a painted nail to the Raven's once mighty arm.

"Henrietta, sorry—don't mean to interrupt. We've got to talk," Wulfmeyer said. Ravinovich looked up and extended a hand. Wolf grasped it and tried to sound calm. "Hi, Kenton."

"Hiya, Wolf. A great thing you guys are doing for me, this wonderful tribute. Which I've said before, but it means so much."

"Well deserved. Long overdue. Henrietta—"

"Sit down, Neville. Join us."

"In private. If you don't mind."

Her tone became petulant. "Honestly! Can't this wait?"

"No, no it can't. We've got a hell of a situation."

"Excuse me, would you, just a moment?" She gave Ravinovich the best smile plastic surgery could construct and slipped out of the booth, following Wulfmeyer outside with icy coldness. They avoided the valets and stopped on the broad sidewalk out front. "If this is about that body this morning—"

"No, that's another disaster, but we got—"

"Your tapes. You're doing those tapes, aren't you?"

"I'm making arrangements. We got another call from—"

"Who's on them?" she interrupted again. "I want to know.

You're talking about framing one of our players, I think I've got a right to know."

"Castillo's one—Benito Castillo." Wolf could see he had riled her. She wasn't going to let him get a word in until she had finished this unsavory tape business. "And Davenport. That's our second option, but he's having a career year."

"And who else?"

"That might be enough."

"I saw the invoice last night on your fax machine. I know there are four."

Wolf swallowed hard. "The other two, there's almost no chance—"

"Tell me, Neville!"

He knew he might as well deal with this. "Fish. Just in case he, you know, tries to finger Kane. Or whatever. It wouldn't cost us a roster player, and he's already on the police radar."

"That is *awful*!" Henrietta let out a woeful moan. "That idea, God! Gordon would terminate your contract so fast—" She raised a bony arm and snapped her fingers. "And I'm really—I'll tell you, I'm starting to think about it myself."

"I'd go right to the cops," Wolf said harshly.

"Don't I know it. This is so *sick*!" She shook her head with a vigorous show of disgust. Wolf hoped she would stop there, not ask about the fourth, but she did, her hard blue eyes demanding an answer.

"Again, this is *really* a long shot," he said. "A long, long, *long* long shot—and I was going to discuss it with you. How you would feel about it. Because, again, we wouldn't have to waste a roster spot. If it could work out, by chance, if the right pieces fell into place, and if we could finger Ravinovich."

Henrietta's face grew rigid, pale, and it took a moment before the heavier rage, the oily black rage from some deep inner well,

climbed to the surface and she lit into him. "You will do no such thing! Never! And I don't care how desperate we are and how much we want to win—and I've made a commitment to winning this year the likes of nothing any board president's ever made!" He could smell the brie on her breath. "Let me make this very clear to you, Neville Wulfmeyer: If anything happens to that poor dying man as a result of this fiasco—anything whatsoever!—I will—personally— see to it that you are—" She stopped and sputtered; Wulfmeyer thought she was having a stroke. "See to it you are *castrated, beheaded,* if that can be arranged with your prodigy, and sent away to prison until you rot!"

Wulfmeyer had never endured such an outburst from her. He made a concerted effort to calm her, assuring her there was no way, no way in hell, he'd use that Ravinovich tape. He'd destroy it immediately. It was just a spur-of-the-moment idea, a thing he was going to run by her—and, well, now he had her opinion.

"I hope that takes care of today's business," she said hotly.

"No, actually, there's one more thing: That jackass called back. He wants another drop—five million this time."

Henrietta seemed to hiccup. She took a lurching breath, wheezed, and tilted violently forward, vomiting onto Wulfmeyer's shoes. She stayed hunched a moment, hacking up brie and crackers.

"I'm as upset as you are by this," Wulfmeyer said. He regarded his $340 Italian loafers with surprising indifference.

"This—this demand—" Henrietta said, straightening, wiping her chin with the gossamer corner of her flowing red scarf. "When?" Her mouth was smeared with lipstick.

"Tomorrow night. Same deal."

"Christ Almighty." Her face hardened. It was clear that she did not welcome the prospect of shelling out millions of dollars a pop to some extortionist. "We'll have to discuss this. We'll discuss this to-

night. My place. I'm going to have Mulgrove come over, and we're going to sit down and see if there's some way to deal with this."

The fourth member of the cabal was Doyle Horgan, Henrietta's Teamster friend, or ex-Teamster, a man who had evidently worked as a foreman at Industrial Tank Ball, long before the current wave of unrest, and who had left some years back to run his own concrete and asphalt company. He was very successful, judging by his hefty gold rings.

Horgan, in his Dockers and yellow sport shirt, and Mulgrove, wearing a brown pin-striped suit, were already sipping cocktails when Wolf arrived. They were meeting in Henrietta's informal dining room, an intimate enclosure she called The Miro Room, for the four vibrant paintings that adorned each wall. She made introductions and got right down to business.

"Jack can only stay a minute, so I'd like him to report. Jack, we engaged your services the last time this—I'll use Neville's word—this asshole tried to blackmail us. Why don't you tell us, at this point, if there's any concrete information we can use."

"Well, not as much as we'd like." Mulgrove shifted uncomfortably. "We tailed him and did manage to get a license on a red Chevy Lumina that was, of course, a rental, on loan from Avis to a Ralph Westerly. We're sure that's an alias, but our man was traveling under that name. He caught a flight later that night to Chicago, with a connection to Kansas City."

Mulgrove went on with some speculations about the fate of the cash, where the man lived, his professional and psychological profile, a bunch of bullshit that Wulfmeyer found useless, though Henrietta listened raptly. When Mulgrove was finished, she asked if he thought, once the second drop was made, the $5 million, the creep would go away or dare to demand even more.

"A gambit of this sort, the risk factor's huge," Mulgrove said, his white teeth flashing against his ebony skin. "It's the rare perpetrator that has the *cojones* to attempt this type of strong-arm more than once. Then again, the return is pretty huge."

"Five million big ones," Wulfmeyer said.

"Right. Minus expenses. Pretty damn close."

"Might he try it again?" Henrietta repeated.

"Abso-fuckin'-lutely!" Wulfmeyer answered, before Mulgrove had a chance. "Pardon my Portuguese, but this is one evil bastard— I've talked to him—and we've got two months left in the season! You think the stakes are going to go down? Down? You'd better wake up and smell the Bromo-Seltzer!"

"Neville's very agitated over this—as we all are," Henrietta said, apologizing for him. "Jack? You agree?"

"Sorry to say, I think Neville's absolutely correct."

"All right, then. Jack, thank you very much for coming. Obviously we'll need you tomorrow night." Henrietta indicated that a few remaining matters would be handled in private, and Mulgrove understood. He rose and shook hands all around, and Henrietta escorted him to the door. The air in the room seemed to grow thicker as soon as she returned. A great weight seemed to settle over them all.

Henrietta took a long sip of her Tom Collins and finally said all right, decisions had to be made. It struck Wulfmeyer that she was at last gaining her footing in this god-awful mess, showing the confidence that she brought to the wiener crisis and the bullpen redesign, no longer inclined to abnegate the decision-making power to others.

"Looks like, if we don't pay this bastard, our season completely blows up," she said, "a situation we faced once before, and frankly we're damn tired of it. Am I right, Neville?"

"Damn right." He braced himself for what might come next.

"So we need ideas. Neville, let's start with you."

He was startled to be called on, like the kid in fifth grade who'd neglected to read the chapter. His brain took an exceedingly long time to engage itself.

"You know, running a major-league club, it's dog eat dog, I'll tell you. You Teamsters—" He looked at Horgan. "You see some tough guys, I'm sure, but I doubt there's quite the pressure we're under in baseball. And, despite that, I consider myself a good guy—honest to some degree, hardworking, a guy who abhors violence or dishonesty—or extortion—in any form. Abhors it!"

They stared at him.

"But I think, considering everything, this guy should be rubbed out."

"Murdered?" Horgan said.

"It's an ugly word," Wulfmeyer said. "I'm just thinking, what kind of choice do we have? My God, this situation? We can't keep coughing up five million bucks every other week! And if we don't, clearly this guy intends to torpedo us. He's got to be stopped!"

"I agree with that last part," Henrietta said. She turned to Horgan. "Do we have to resort to killing him, Doyle?"

"No, not necessarily." Horgan cleared his throat. "Let me say, just for clarity's sake, I have no firsthand knowledge of handling these types of situations. It's stuff I heard about, a friend-of-a-friend type of thing."

"Sure."

"Situations that come up, you know, and get talked about."

"Right. How might we proceed?"

"There's one avenue of thought, you teach the fucker a lesson. He gets his payday, so he's happy, he can leave you alone, but you make the emphatic point that there's no more paydays. You establish his identity, and he knows you can track him down. He knows there are repercussions."

"Interesting," Henrietta said. "You have to pay him?"

"Psychologically, it's best. Because there's usually residual anger."

Wulfmeyer felt clammy. He wished he could get outside.

"Can you be— Well, specifically, what type of lesson are we discussing?" Henrietta said. "Hypothetically?"

Horgan smiled, revealing a gold front tooth. "Heard about a case once, no shit, they hung this guy over a steel furnace, hung him upside down right over all that molten steel, and lowered him just slow, slow, slow, until his hair caught fire. Screamed like a son of a bitch, I heard. Got third-degree burns all over his head and face and shoulders. Course, you'd need access to a steel mill."

"Which we don't have." Henrietta scowled. "That's very dramatic, though. Anything not quite so dramatic?"

"You got a whole gamut," Horgan said. "Cut things off—cut off ears, the guy's nose, cut out his tongue, keep him quiet. Cut off fingers, toes. Get really personal, cut off his wanger. That one makes an impression. Or break things. Put his head in a vise, you can break that, but you might kill him, or break his arms, break his ankles, break his legs."

"I see."

"You can be very creative."

Henrietta nodded. Wulfmeyer wiped his sweating hands, glad for once to just sit there without a word. His heart was racing. Henrietta looked at him, for only an instant, and issued her decision.

"See if you can find me a few guys," she said evenly, "and let's relieve this—again I use Neville's word—relieve this asshole of a few toes."

16

Sharkey opened the desk drawer.

"Oh *God!*"

A fish. A dead barracuda lay right in the drawer, its head chopped off. The head was there, too, a cold eye cast blindly toward the ceiling. A rivulet of half-dried blood pooled in a tangle of paper clips.

Sharkey leaped to his feet, stepping back. The shock of it was bad enough, but he quickly saw the meaning behind it: A dead fish. No head. Oh, that was a bit of symbolism. Yes, yes, that was a message in big-screen surround sound.

How had it got there? When? The Sox had arrived late the previous night for a three-game set in Anaheim, the start of a long road trip. With Uziak out handling batting practice, Sharkey had sat down in the office to update his journal, finish some notes on the pitching staff. The fishy odor had puzzled him at first, until he found the damn thing. Now what to do with it? He looked around, saw a copy of the *Midnight Star,* and used the tabloid to carefully lift the fish and deposit it in a trash can. It hit the bottom with a *thunk,* and immediately the phone rang, as if one sound had caused the other.

It was Wulfmeyer, agitated. "Tell me something. Did you say—or did somebody say—you found a time bomb?"

"No, I said we're *sitting* on a time bomb."

There was a long pause. "No bomb, right? I want to be absolutely clear about that. Because if there's a bomb, if you got some inkling there's a bomb, or somebody's going to plant a bomb, let's deal with it. Let's not ignore it."

"I don't *think* there's a bomb. How would I know?" Sharkey began to imagine there was a bomb somewhere. He could see it—the killer blowing up the whole clubhouse. He thought about Castillo and the blast in the warehouse yard, an incident he was tempted to finally bring up, except Wolf wouldn't want to hear it. He'd do nothing to Castillo and throw a fit about Sharkey tailing him out there. "I did find something else," he said. "A fish, a dead fish. Somebody cut off the head."

"What?"

"A fish. It was here in my desk."

There was another long pause, followed by a flash of anger. "This is not the time or the place for jokes! We are dealing with serious shit!"

"I'm not joking! Can't you see what it means?"

"You said fish, right? Like a sardine? A grouper?"

"It was no sardine!" Sharkey smoldered over having to explain about the symbolism, what any moron could see. "I don't know what to do. This crap, it's driving me out of my mind!"

"Are you afraid to manage? We can always hire Goossell—the Giants canned him today."

"Goossell? You're kidding."

"He'd work for half your salary."

Sharkey took a breath. He wasn't some lily-livered wimp, scared of shadows. There wasn't anything he wanted more than to lead the Red Sox to a championship. But a serial killer in the clubhouse—

there were some things a manager shouldn't be expected to handle. He decided to broach a very delicate subject. "What about Ravinovich? Are the cops checking on *him?* He's been out here, hanging around."

"I don't know what the cops are doing," Wolf said sharply, "but watch what you say concerning Ravinovich. You're talking about a legend. Henrietta worships the very ground he walks on."

"He's not God, I'll tell you that much." Sharkey chafed at the reprimand. "And I've seen sicker people, I swear, water skiing off Martha's Vineyard."

"Forget about the Raven." Wulfmeyer stressed the need to maintain morale. Kane's new contract had resulted in—surprise, surprise—a flurry of calls from player agents. Six of the bastards had voiced an interest in renegotiating deals, including the representatives for Frolicky, Davenport and Villalobos. "Stu tells me some of our guys are really unhappy. We can't let them drag their chins. You've got to work your rhetoric, Fish, coax them, cajole them, get back that sense of esprit de corps."

Esprit de corps. Wolf's gift for preposterous buzzwords was always impressive to experience. Sharkey didn't want to tell him how bad it really was. Moses was about to bolt. He and Villalobos had managed to infect at least a dozen teammates with their resentment of Kane's $186 million deal. Cool Daddy, who had just sold his mansion in Marblehead as part of his bankruptcy liquidation, had organized a players-only team meeting to which Kane was not invited. Signs of it rippled through the clubhouse afterward. Davenport could not look Kane's way without giving him an icy glare. Briscoe came whining to Sharkey again, this time openly bitter about the loss of at-bats in his diminished designated-hitter role.

All in all, it was remarkable that the Sox had won three out of five and were again a game up on the Yanks.

Sharkey mumbled his assent and hung up knowing he was all alone in the mess. Wolf didn't care about the unfolding soap opera, the implied threat of a dead fish in a desk drawer. Wolf was way up in the stratosphere, pulling strings, orchestrating the grand plan. Sharkey hoped to hell he knew what he was doing.

The barracuda was a detail for Sharkey to handle himself. He examined the office and the floor around the lockers. No blood. Not a drop. The trash can: no bloody plastic bags, no large containers. No evidence whatsoever about how the fish had got there.

The tough part was to jam the questions into some remote corner of his mind for a while to focus on baseball. Kane and the Angels' stocky left-hander, Julian Wysocki, hooked up in a classic duel, putting up zeroes for six innings. In the seventh a batter's late swing on a Kane fastball sliced a triple into the right-field corner, and the Angels pushed the run across with a ground ball. That was all the scoring; the 1–0 loss was Kane's first defeat of the season.

Afterward the clubhouse rancor and the tension of the pennant race quickly escalated to shouts, then a fistfight: Kane and Mad Dog going at it. Half the others joined in while half tried to break it up. Racing over, Sharkey watched in horror as Kane tumbled backward under a surge of bodies, Moses, Davenport and Villalobos on top of him. Moses's bloody fist rose and fell like a sledgehammer.

"Break it up! Enough! Off him right now!" Sharkey's shouts were scarcely heard. Hotter heads prevailed for several more minutes, until finally, hoarse and exhausted, Sharkey succeeded in untangling the bodies. Kane and Moses were still locked up on the floor, Kane's face contorted in agony.

"My elbow!" he hissed.

"You all right?" Sharkey crouched over him. Mad Dog at last climbed off. Kane lay stricken, clutching his right elbow, the most valuable elbow ever born. The whole team froze. A high-voltage

charge filled the room, crackling along the floor and ceiling. It held everyone in place, no one even breathing.

"Can you move it?" Sharkey said.

"Don't think so. Something popped, or tore."

Wolf scowled, rewound the tape, and watched it again. The Castillo tape was the only one of the four that troubled him. The technical quality was superb: The graininess of Castillo's face matched perfectly with that of the scene in the alley, the Lincoln pulling up. Castillo's head was seamlessly aligned with the neck all throughout.

The only nagging concern was the incongruity of Benito's little face on that strapping frame, like a chihuahua head on a Saint Bernard. The wizards at VHS Technical Services—who believed they were editing a short scene in a feature film—had tried to improve the match by expanding the dimensions of Castillo's *cabeza,* shrinking the image of Kane's body as it exited the car and performed its grisly tasks at the trunk—but it still seemed out of proportion. Was it just an illusion, because Wulfmeyer knew the two men? Or would the cops also notice the mismatch of those powerful limbs and that pinched, bony face? Was it even feasible to fuse those disparate elements?

Wolf ejected it and rubbed his eyes. He was too tired to think clearly. It was nearly two in the morning, but he felt he had to keep working. He was obsessed, unable to sleep. He grabbed the Ravinovich tape and slipped that one back into the machine. The Raven's tape, and Sharkey's, were close to perfect; both had those big, angular frames. Too bad Henrietta was so righteously opposed to skewering her dear Raven.

The phone rang. It made Wolf jump, the hour was so late. He reached quickly.

"Hello."

"Wolf, it's Stu. Sorry it's— You sleeping?"

"No. Fuck it, I'm talking to you. What in Christ's name is going on?"

"Bad news. Really bad news."

"What? What the hell is it?"

"Kane's arm. He hurt his arm. He got in a fight and—"

"A fight?" Wolf sat upright. He had watched the game; he didn't remember a fight.

"With Moses. Moses and Cool Daddy and— Oh, shit, I couldn't believe it. A total free-for-all. Someone stepped right on Uziak's face. Took three stitches right on the tip of his nose."

"Damn it! DAMN IT! What's wrong with Kane's arm?" Wulfmeyer felt his limbs go numb. Here it was, August now, the play-offs and World Series just two months away, and the club's biggest weapon was down with an injury.

Domato said Kane had wrenched or torn his elbow and was being transported to UCLA Medical Center to be examined first thing in the morning by Dr. Stan Rubens, the famed orthopedist. The team trainer had given the arm a preliminary look and couldn't be sure if the injury was serious. Kane might be out a few weeks, maybe more. Worse case was he'd need surgery.

"Good God," Wulfmeyer said.

"We'll fly back tomorrow. Fly back to Boston as soon as he's examined."

"Yes, yes, get him back here immediately. You stay with him. Call Henrietta in the morning. Let us know soon as you get a report from Rubens." Wulfmeyer hung up. He felt sick to his stomach. He felt overwhelmed by the continued accumulation of problem upon problem. Kane's loss for even a month might cripple the team's chances. Henrietta would be in a state. She was becoming more insufferable by the day, what with the goddamned extortionist and the untenable labor situation at Tank Ball. That whole place was set to close in a

week; the nation's largest producer of heavy-duty toilet flotation devices, an output that exceeded 240,000 units a week, was about to come to a screeching halt unless Wolf could make a heroic last-minute breach of the impasse. A mediation session was scheduled for ten-thirty in the morning.

Wulfmeyer carefully put away the Castillo and Ravinovich tapes, went to bed, slept fitfully, and got up in time to down two cups of coffee in a deep morning funk, knowing that the day was already ruined. The sun was barely over the horizon, and he knew it was shot. He had to shift himself into survival mode, just slog his way through it. He packed up his briefs and drove out to meet Roberta Lacy, who was assisting the Tank Ball legal team; together they proceeded to the plant in his Eldorado.

The union negotiator was late—he'd had a flat—and the session did not start until after eleven. It went on for seven rancorous hours, stale turkey sandwiches for lunch, bad coffee all afternoon, until at last they broke, having dispatched with nine of the remaining fourteen contract issues.

Exhausted, Wulfmeyer fell into the Eldorado and punched up Henrietta on the cellular.

"Stinking Norwich won't budge an inch on the overtime rate," he said dourly. "And vacations—they still want three weeks after seven years. Orthodontics with dental. A bunch of crap, but we're making some headway. We've knocked off for tonight. I'm about to take Lacy home."

"All right," she said. "Stu just called. He and Kane, they got in an hour ago and went straight to see Minkowitz." Dr. Robert Minkowitz was the Red Sox's physician in Boston.

"What did Rubens say?"

"Same thing as Minkowitz: good news. Definitely a strain. Nothing's torn, and Kane's got good range of motion."

"Blessed Almighty God."

"Three to four weeks. That's bad, but it could be worse. He'll just stay here in town, recuperate. I hope you talked to Augie about that *deplorable* clubhouse fight."

"I'm going to ream him out good. I'm thinking I'll start the rumor that we're talking to Goossell."

"One other thing." Henrietta seemed unsure how to say it. "We've got to hope— Well, if his arm's not too bad, I'm just a little wary about Ron getting involved with that awful *hobby* of his."

Wolf squeezed the phone; he saw where she was heading.

"We get another of these headless chickens here in Boston, if you catch my drift, not that I want to say it on the phone, but if we get another, this task force might think hard about that. It might point more of a finger, you know. I wonder if we can somehow confine him to his condo. You know, keep him home."

"I doubt it." Wolf felt a clammy sweat popping out. He roared north onto the expressway. "Let me think about this."

"Those damn tapes of yours won't do a bit of good if something happens now."

"I need to think about that. You got Mulgrove's number?"

She read it off; Wulfmeyer barked it to Lacy and had her write it down. He hung up. He wondered if Lacy noticed his panic.

It was after seven when he dropped her off near Fenway. He was supposed to pick up a lady friend, a woman named Tara Lane, a red-headed flight attendant with legs from here to Wellesley. They'd been dating since April, and they were planning dinner at the Crab Pot, where Wulfmeyer was particularly fond of the oysters, followed by, he hoped, the usual tryst at her luxury apartment suite, city lights below and wrapped up warm and wet in one of the great leg locks of all time.

But now—damn, could he? Could he spare the time? He sat at the curb, Mulgrove's number in front of him, wondering what strategy to broach. He had to think very clearly. He could direct Mulgrove to

camp out at Kane's and tail him, actually try to intervene if he should make an attack, but that would be more than a little risky. Mulgrove was not explicitly aware that Kane was committing these crimes. Even someone who came as highly recommended as Mulgrove might react in the worst way, tipping the authorities, if he should actually witness an attack. Mulgrove was, after all, an ex-cop himself.

The tapes. Henrietta was right—they'd be useless as nipples on a toucan if somebody got murdered while Kane was in Boston and those other idiots were on the road. It so happened, the usual horrendous luck, that the Sox's current trip was the longest of the year, a nightmare of late-summer scheduling that would send them from Anaheim to Oakland, then on to Seattle for four games, and Minnesota before they finally returned home the first of September.

Who could calculate the odds of Kane beheading another victim during that stretch? One lousy murder now could wreck everything the club had been working for. The task force had already singled out Kane, for whatever reasons, pinning down the date of his initial arrival in Boston; God knew what else they were digging up.

There was only one way to keep them guessing: make sure, if something happened, that some of those other bozos were also in Boston at the time—Castillo, the Raven, maybe even Davenport and Sharkey. Then he could still use the tapes, select an appropriate one, and drop it on the task force anonymously. Drop it like a napalm bomb and pray.

Now: Castillo. What possible ruse could bring him back home in the middle of a vital road trip? It was not like Sharkey could arrange to injure him, though Fish would probably brain him with a poleax given half a chance. Wolf's knowledge of his personal life was zilch; no way he could contrive a parental heart attack, that type of thing. No chance of— Oh, but he thought of something. Thought of an idea that had danced in and out of his mind for weeks, though there had been no urgent reason for doing it. Now there was a hell of a

good reason, despite the fact it would cost the club its best infield glove. Wolf would send him down, demote the little bastard to Triple-A Pawtucket. Send Castillo where any backbiting .226 hitter ought to go—*to the minors!*

Pawtucket was close enough to Boston. And the farm club was at home now, just opening a stand with Ottawa, if Wolf remembered right. Perfect.

The Raven was easy. The tribute. Wolf had to see him to start planning the tribute. He fished out a pen and scratched a note to himself: *Castillo to Pawtucket, Raven home—tribute. Call him first thing!*

Too bad Henrietta worshiped that asshole. It could complicate the decision. Tough, tough choices, nothing easy on the path to a World Series title.

What about Davenport? One of the club's top hitters, healthy as a Kentucky mule, all the more valuable now with Kane on the shelf. No way Wolf could really yank him home. It'd draw attention, and Jeremy was already pissed off about the All-Star snub. He'd be barking to the press. He'd be missing a couple games anyway, the last week of August, to give a deposition in the nun-bombing case. The Sox couldn't afford to lose him much longer than that.

Sharkey? Same problem: What excuse to yank a manager home in the middle of a pennant race? It just wasn't done. Nothing Wolf could contrive would get him on a plane. But, shit, the alternative was as white-knuckle scary as water snakes in a bathhouse. Making do with only two likely suspects, that just opened the door to all kinds of god-awful possibilities if something should happen, if, say, there was a murder and both guys happened to have alibis. A party, a poker game, late-night drinks at a crowded bar, and suddenly there would be a noose around Kane's neck.

The paranoia began to accumulate in Wulfmeyer's system. It would keep building in there like steam, pushing on the brittle sheet

metal of his psyche, until he figured out an answer. He lifted the cel-
lular and punched Tara's number.

"Baby, hey, listen, I can't do dinner tonight. This thing, the pen-
nant race, it's been crazy. . . . Yeah, stress up the ying-yang, and I've
got a new problem, a thing that—well, I'll be working late. . . . I
know you wanted to. It's a great place. . . . Well, I could stop by later,
maybe around ten? . . . Oh. How about tomorrow night? Okay, we'll
talk about it. Sorry about dinner. Me, too."

He hung up, frowned. Climbed out of the Eldorado and went
upstairs to his office, dug out Sharkey's file. Maybe there was some-
thing in there. Some idea. He'd feel a hell of a lot better if he could
get Sharkey back, too.

Wulfmeyer spread the file on his desk, a green folder containing a
copy of his contract and a raft of out-of-date papers, including a rep-
rimand from the commissioner for the time, in 1992, that he hurled
an umpire's mask into the box seats behind third. There were PR facts
and family phone numbers on a page stapled to photographs—one of
Augie Jr., who was twenty-two now, attending Wake Forest, and one
of Bernice, a socialite shown smiling in a double strand of pearls and
dangling pearl earrings. Thin face, lips, pale skin, dark hair frizzed out
like a space helmet.

The image galvanized Wulfmeyer's attention. He lifted the pic-
ture and studied it. It twitched in his hand like a bird, pulsing with his
own pounding heart. At last he reached for the phone and dialed
Mulgrove.

"Jack, hey listen, it's Wolf. Glad I caught you. Hey, you happen to
have a number for that security guy? Henrietta's guy, Doyle Horgan?"

17

Sometimes, like deaths of the famous, a manager's crises also came in threes. It was karma at work—fate thumbing its nose at mortal man—and it was happening again. First Kane's injury, followed by another incident with Castillo: He'd reacted poorly to another benching, in spite of a two-for-twenty-six skid, and busted up the clubhouse before going AWOL again. No telling where the little bastard was or when he'd be back. Look out, Disneyland.

Now came the third part of the triple whammy: Bernice on the phone, saying she wanted out. The marriage was over.

"Can't we talk about it?" Sharkey said with alarm. "We should sit down—when I get home. Discuss what you want."

"That's part of the problem, you're never home!" she said bitterly. "No, this is it, I'm not changing my mind again. You want your baseball? Play your little boy's games? Fine, you do that! Take the whole rest of your life and do that!" She hung up. He held the receiver a long time before dropping it onto the base. So much venom, but beneath it was a hard nodule of truth that Sharkey had to

accept: They were different, and the gulf between them was widening steadily. It was hard because a part of him still loved her, always would. And yet—should he fight to hold her? Maybe not. Maybe this was best.

Sharkey turned back to the papers spread before him. He had just received, by FedEx from Howlett, the board secretary, the Ravinovich personnel file, dredged up from archives. This quiet morning in the hotel room was the ideal time to peruse it, though now Sharkey wasn't sure he could even concentrate.

Sighing heavily, he let the *vita turpis* of Kenton Randall Ravinovich fill his mind like scenes of black comedy: 7/21/71—Questioned by police on suspicion of cutting the antennas off parked cars. 5/3/76—Arrested along with Sawyer and Dietrich for pushing a bouncer through the front window of the Alligator. 2/16/79—Questioned by authorities on allegations that he was stalking Rita Kataya. No charges filed.

Sharkey stopped. He knew that name. Rita Kataya. Oh, yes, yes, the game-show hostess. *Dialing for Love.* Quite a popular show in its time—lovely lady—but, oh, gosh—hadn't Rita been killed? Murdered in '86 or '87?

The phone rang. It was Wulfmeyer.

"Listen, Fish, we've got to make some moves. This race is just too close for comfort."

For a single, blood-chilling instant, Sharkey was sure he meant a managerial change. Goossell coming in. An irrational thought, with the Sox in first, but it vanished only when Wolf announced, "I'm reassigning Benito. Sending him down to Pawtucket. He's not hitting his fucking weight, he's ruining morale, and, Jesus, if he's our, you know, bad actor, it'll wreck everything if they arrest him and he's on the big club. All the disruption, the publicity—I'd rather have him at Triple-A."

"I would, too."

"Break the news. Tell him to fly back today."

"I can't. He just went AWOL again. Last night."

"What!" Wulfmeyer's voice rose sharply. "Good Christ Almighty, Fish! What the hell is going on out there?"

Wulfmeyer went into a rant, triggering a trace memory in Sharkey's mind. Had Wolf phoned last night, screaming? Or had he only dreamed it? Not that it made any difference. Sharkey thought about raising another subject—the possibility of taking an emergency leave, flying home to save his marriage—until Wulfmeyer demanded, "That it?" His tone all but closed the door to further dialogue.

Sharkey hesitated. "I guess that's it." He couldn't abandon the team during the race.

"Keep me posted, then. Soon as you hear from him, I want to know, so I can give Gamboa the what-for!"

Ravinovich joined him at breakfast. They arrived the same instant, each alone, and Sharkey immediately saw there was no polite alternative but to eat with the arrogant son of a bitch. It was the last thing he wanted this morning: to stare into that mangled mouth while the Raven stuffed it with eggs and bacon and struggled to try to seem the nice guy—meaning he might or might not drop in some barb about how Fish had cost him a chance for the Hall of Fame.

Ravinovich was unusually garrulous because Wulfmeyer had just called him. Wolf wanted him to return right away to Fenway to begin planning his big year-end tribute, "The Day of the Raven." He could hardly talk about anything else.

"Fish, let me ask you, you think it's too much a gamble if we try to plunk down this little extravaganza in the middle of the World Series?"

"The Series?" Sharkey nearly choked on his link sausage. What a horrible prospect that was: finally get to the World Series and have it marred by the colossal distraction that such a ceremony would cause. "It's—yeah—quite a gamble. Why not the regular season? Maybe the last week? That way you know there's going to *be* a tribute."

"Yeah, yeah. True. You're right." Ravinovich sipped his coffee with a noisy slurp, his fiery blue eyes betraying the fact that it was World Series or bust. "Only thing is, I never got to play in the Series, you know. Sure would have loved that experience."

Ravinovich went on at stupefying length about his unsated dreams, and whether he should arrange to have his body frozen when he was gone à la Ted Williams, perhaps the greatest hitter ever, who'd been virtually whisked away under cover of night and stuck in a cryonics tank amid some of the worst family feuding in club history. It was a regrettable episode that had caused no end of embarassment in newspapers and on talk shows and newscasts nationwide, but it had inspired Ravinovich to think that he, too, could salt away his body for a time when he might live again—or, at the very least, when his precious DNA might be mined to create a new, younger, hard-slugging and hard-loving replica of himself.

The topic plainly fascinated him. Sharkey could not remember him in quite such a loquacious mood. In fact, it was difficult to imagine that this was really a dying man.

Finally, Ravinovich excused himself to pack for the airport, neglecting, as usual, to leave even a nickel toward the tab. Sharkey paid it and tried to fill the time in a bleak afternoon. He pulled the card from his wallet—ANNIE OCCASION GIFTS—and called Annie Tusch, the woman he'd met at the fund-raiser. She seemed delighted to hear from him. They talked about Kane's injury, about the fickle nature of momentum in baseball, and then made plans to have lunch once Sharkey was back in Boston.

That lifted his spirits slightly. He visited a bookstore outside the Sheraton and picked up a copy of *Sensuality Cut Short: The Rita Kataya Story.*

The cover showed a seductive Rita in net stockings, recumbent on the roof of a red Rolls-Royce. Sharkey thumbed through it for references to Ravinovich.

The biography was chock-full of scandalous stories, love and betrayal involving half of Hollywood's leading men. About a hundred pages into it came the first meeting between the Raven and Rita, at a drug-filled party in October of 1983 hosted by Ned Duchesne, the movie producer. At the time Rita was seeing Duchesne and three other men, including the head of a record label and a Costa Rican diplomat, but she nonetheless took up with Ravinovich on the sly. They enjoyed weekend excursions to Cancún, Puerto Vallarta and the Virgin Islands, and continued to meet in various cities after the 1984 Red Sox season began.

It was a tempestuous romance, apparently. After being cracked on the nose by a Coke bottle at a New York disco just before Christmas of that year, Rita tried to break off the relationship; however, the possessive Ravinovich was unable to let go. He began showing up on the *Dialing for Love* set, at her home, even at her health club, prompting a complaint and a restraining order, big news in the tabloids. Her death came seven years later, January of 1991, when her lime green Jaguar plunged over the southern lip of the Grand Canyon, Rita strapped to the passenger seat, her head covered by a paper grocery bag. One of America's great unsolved crimes.

Sharkey found himself thoroughly absorbed in the account. He remembered her death only vaguely; he had been completely unaware of her connection to Ravinovich before seeing the startling mention of her name in the personnel file. The book made it sound as if a jealous heavy-metal star had been responsible for the murder, but Sharkey had to wonder.

The final game of the series with the Angels was a marathon: a seventeen-inning, 6–5 defeat, dropping the Sox back into a tie atop the East. The Yankees had pummeled Oakland. Sharkey got a drink in the hotel bar with Uziak and dragged himself up to bed. He slept only long enough to have a jarring dream about free-falling down a bottomless mine shaft. The phone woke him up.

"Augie Sharkey?" The voice was deep and bearlike, half muffled.

"Yeah. Who's this?"

"We've got your wife!"

"Bernice? You got Bernice?" His heart began pounding; he sat up, fumbling for the light switch.

"It's me, Augie!" Her voice came through, hysterical. "Oh, Augie, Augie, help me, Jesus help me—oh God, please, pleeeeaaaase, *pleeeeeeeeeeeeeeeeeaaassee!*"

"Bernice! Bernice, try to be calm! Stay calm!" he shouted, and then, "You! What the hell do you want? Where is she?"

The caller spoke with no inflection at all. "Follow our instructions exactly, or she'll die. No cops, no tricks." He told Sharkey to return immediately to Boston and take a room at the Seaport Roadway Inn in Quincy. Further instructions would be forthcoming.

"Aaauuu-gggiieeeeeeeeeeeee!" Bernice's voice came through again, and the line went dead.

Sharkey felt a balloon explode in his gut, a powerful internal jolt followed by a horrifying emptiness. His hands trembled. His whole body was shaking. What a nightmare! Poor Bernice, a woman who freaked when she lost an earring; he'd seen her cry once after spilling Chianti on a lilac dress. Oh, the stain, the stain!

Such a princess would not react well to an abduction. She'd moan and shriek and cycle in and out of hysterics for days.

Money. These guys probably wanted gobs of money. Damn it, there went Augie Jr.'s college fund. Why in the hell would these

bastards decide to kidnap a *manager*'s wife? Why not Langley's? Or Frolicky's? They could probably get themselves millions.

He called Wulfmeyer. The shock in Wolf's voice nearly equaled Sharkey's own.

"No, no, of course you can't go to the cops!" Wulfmeyer said. "Jesus Christ on acid, Fish, this guy—these people—they might go ahead and kill her! And don't forget, excuse me for saying, but that task force was poking around you. Marzoli, that murder in Texas. My God, they might think you've got some *involvement* in this!"

"Involvement? How could I have any—"

"Who knows? Like you're trying to get money out of the club. We'll help with this, of course—"

"You will?"

"Maybe half. Eighty percent. Who knows? Find out what they want. You're going to have to go there, follow their instructions, and see. Just do what they say."

18

The nightmare now seemed prophetic, that god-awful plunge down a black mine shaft. Sharkey was now in full flight, falling headlong into an abyss of despair. No past hurt, no crisis during all the previous years of losing, the hard years of marriage, had prepared him for the current fiasco: Bernice kidnapped. The Sox, battling for a pennant, on the road without him. Kane injured because of a clubhouse fight. The *Herald* speculating again that Sharkey would be cut loose at the end of his current contract—that Greg Goossell would take over, or Ted Uziak.

Surely that talk would sweep the majors now with Uzi in charge and Sharkey inexplicably back in Boston. Critics seemed to think a chimpanzee could have piloted the Sox into a tie so far atop the East Division, given the talent on the roster, and Sharkey was not about to fool himself. He fully realized his job was hanging by only the thinnest of threads—the IV tube attached to the arm of a ninety-four-year-old man.

Bad as all that was, things were likely to get worse. Unbeknownst to anyone—yet—the task force was out there, secretly combing for

clues and physical evidence to connect the club to the rash of murders. God forbid, it might soon come to light that one of Sharkey's millionaire athletes was sneaking out at night to hack off people's heads.

The desk clerk had recognized him, a minor humiliation that Sharkey had almost expected. "Oh, Augie Sharkey!" A voice rough with cigarettes and beer, a wizened diehard who no doubt remembered every near miss of the past thirty years. "Hey, glad to have you! How come you're not with the club? I saw that thing on ESPN—"

A *SportsCenter* report tacitly suggested some sort of mental breakdown—a scenario that was close to truth, actually. Officially, the club was invoking that vaguest of nonexplanatory explanations for Sharkey's unplanned leave: "personal reasons." He didn't care. Let them guess, let them say he'd been locked up for fondling barnyard animals. Sharkey had bigger problems than the media. He told the clerk he was undergoing medical tests—probably nothing serious—and went inside, dropped his bag, took a couple big spoonfuls of the pink stuff, and sat alone in the dark without turning on the TV.

Just waiting.

The call came at eleven that night. The same low voice.

"A smart man, Augie Sharkey, doing exactly what you were told. That kind of behavior, you might actually see her again. Keep in mind we're watching you. Saw you arrive—looks like you're losing some weight."

"Where is she?" he shouted. "What in God's name do you want?"

"Aaauugg-GIIEEEEEEEEEE!" Her voice filled his ear, a shriek of numbing terror.

"Ber-NICE!" he shouted back.

"Shut up! Get a grip on yourself!" the kidnapper said. "You see she's still alive—"

"Tell me what you want!"

"We're working on that. Still formulating our demands."

"What? Formulating your . . . ?" Sharkey thought he might have a stroke. "I think you can have the decency—the goddamn human decency—to tell me! You kidnap my wife and you don't even know what you want? Jesus, that's about the—"

"We *will* know, don't you worry about that. We're thinking pretty damn hard about it. Soon as we figure it out, we'll clue you in, you'd better fuckin' believe it."

"What, and I'm supposed to just wait? Wait here in the meantime for you to figure out something?"

"You won't mind being patient, I hope."

"Patient? Christ! How long's it going to take?"

There was a pause. "Would you care to make an offer?"

"No! I don't—of course not! Just give her back! Let her go!"

"Nobody's lettin' her go till we settle this thing, till we establish a price."

"You can go straight to hell, that's what!" The sweat began running down Sharkey's cheeks. "I can't just—goddamn it!—would you say, maybe ten thousand?"

"Ten thousand? Come on, Augie, you cheap fuckin' bastard. This is your *wife* here!"

"She's divorcing me!"

"Yeah, right. Don't try jacking me around."

"She is! Ask her!"

"Well, a screamer like that, you'll be better off. But I don't think you want her dead."

"Twenty thousand."

"Look, it's going to take some time. We've got some differences of opinion here—my partners and I. Things we'll have to hash out." He advised Sharkey to settle in, try to relax. "Leave if you want—get yourself a steak up the street—but don't stray too far. That hotel there, that's where we'll contact you. Remember, no tricks, we're

watching, and we'll phone you with our price in the not-too-distant future, you'd better fuckin' believe it."

Two days dragged by in a sleepless, numb hell. Fear or instinct prevented him from calling the authorities. He sensed that Bernice might really be killed. He'd been part of so much concern over serial murders that he easily imagined the bastards slitting her throat. Sharkey knew he'd never forgive himself. He also feared the cops. He'd been a target of suspicion himself after the Marzoli murder and the slaying in Texas. If he popped up now in connection with another big felony, his wife's kidnapping, he might be in the radar again. The cops might think he was part of his own wife's abduction, like in that movie *Fargo*. And if she was killed anyway . . .

No, he couldn't risk bringing in the authorities yet. He'd have to wait. At least hear what the bastards wanted.

The second afternoon, sick of TV, sick of worrying, Sharkey tried to pass the time by visiting the public library at lunch. Thumbing through the periodical index, he decided to do some bird-watching. Look deeper into the life of the Raven.

Much of the material was on microfilm, old profiles from Ravinovich's heyday. Sharkey made copies and brought them back to the room. It was difficult see an entire picture from these brief glimpses, but, like bright pinpoints of light, the long-buried words and phrases offered a sharp insight into the Raven's character.

The New Yorker: ". . . and in his pique, Ravinovich confronted Yastrzemski in the Red Sox's crowded clubhouse, demanding that Yaz cancel his appearance on the popular network program if producers did not agree to feature the Raven, as well." *Esquire:* "He'd rather die, it seems, than share the spotlight, an attitude that forced Boston to trade away its highly touted number one draft choice. . . ." *Time:* ". . . perhaps the game's most exciting player, but a troubled star. He taunts, swaggers and

generally behaves as though no creature on earth is quite so important or gifted as that long-maned, aquiline fellow he sees in the mirror." *Sports Illustrated:* ". . . and then, only three weeks after the 'Farrah fiasco,' as the papers dubbed it, Ravinovich sallied forth into the Topless Kitty nightclub and, according to witnesses, attempted to grab the leg of a young woman. . . . Club officials began to circle the wagons. . . ."

Sharkey's eyes hung on that last phrase. *Circle the wagons.* That was well before Wulfmeyer's time, and before Sharkey's, but clearly the Sox had found themselves in a dilemma: either cover for Ravinovich—minimize his antisocial tendencies—or bow to public outcry and get rid of him, trade away a monster talent who had clubbed fifty-five home runs in 1972. It had been so easy to be seduced by the idea that he might mature, change his ways. But. . . .

He was the first of a breed, part of a vanguard of athletes—along with Hawk Harrelson, Joe Pepitone, and others—who became media darlings as the free-spirited antiheroes of post-Camelot America. Except that Ravinovich truly possessed a dark side. He crossed the line into recklessly immoral conduct, overt criminality. His transgressions were never enough to demand prison time, yet he was one of the first Red Sox players to see the inside of a jail cell—and he had done so more than once.

Sharkey picked up the phone. It was time to tell Wulfmeyer, damn the consequences. This asshole might be a killer, and he had to let Wulfmeyer know.

Wolf sounded harried. "Fish! You okay? You'll get her back, don't worry. I talked to Henrietta, and we'll go halfsies on the ransom."

"You mean . . . ?"

"Up to a point. Sure. Up to a max of, say, fifty or sixty thousand dollars."

Sharkey grunted a thank-you and said there was another matter, the issue of Ravinovich. He explained his concerns. Wulfmeyer cut him off.

"Fish, he's a dying man!"

"Who says? You believe that? We've got only one source on that, and it's Ravinovich!"

"Like he needs a note from his doctor? Look at him!"

"He wants sympathy, Wolf! Wants a reason for this big tribute so he can build up his own legacy. So he can whip up some sort of fervor with the writers and get himself voted into the Hall of Fame!"

"It's not him, Fish. Believe me."

"How do you know?"

"You're going to have to trust me. But look, okay, I'll check it out. I'll have Mulgrove do some background, follow him, whatever will ease your mind. All right?"

Sharkey hung up feeling more desperate than ever. Wolf just didn't get it. Wolf would pay lip service to the idea, but nothing more. He was so high in his ivory tower he could not truly comprehend the terrible dangers involved. Wolf saw no personal risk in allowing this killer to travel with the club, hang out, sleep in the same hotel.

It was time that attitude changed. Sharkey decided to help change it. He slipped out for dinner and swung by a stationer's and a Barnes & Noble, bought scissors, marking pens, a couple magazines and a children's picture book *Little Red Riding Hood*.

Toiling into the night, feeling a sick therapeutic satisfaction from it, Sharkey cut out an irregular pattern of letters and pieced together a note: "Hey, you fuckin Wulfmeyer. Watch yr back and yr head 2, cause eye'M cummin at ya." Above it he glued a picture of a headless Big Bad Wolf, the head on the ground, red pools of blood all around it.

It went out the next morning in the mail.

Seventy-two voice messages had piled up by the end of a week. Half were the usual drek—people wanting him fired, blaming him for years of collapse. One was from Castillo, a vicious, pseudo-English

piece of yammering about Fish being a "peeese a shit flushin' rye down the fuckin' Kornblume sewer cock into hell!" Nonsense, not even intelligible.

A surprising number of calls were supportive. One was from Annie. Sharkey called her and they met for dinner, an Italian place she picked out. Candlelight and wine. Sharkey was used to an occasional dinner with a lady friend; it was inevitable on the road, and he was well aware Bernice made the rounds with the dapper theater men and downtown artists, guys dressed all in black. Still, the vibes he got sitting with Annie caused him some guilt. Her dark eyes fixed on him. She seemed to regard him as some sort of celebrity. It was more intoxicating than the merlot.

Sharkey told her what he could of his ordeal—the kidnapping. She squeezed his arm. They talked a long while. To meet such a woman, to make her smile over his stupid manager's stories, anecdotes about Stu and Langley and Ravinovich, was a slice of heaven. A thin slice, because it was wedged between megaliths of misery, but it was a lifesaver to him. She kissed him good night as she left, and he allowed himself the daring thought that he might see her again.

There was other good news: Stu phoned with an update on Kane. The arm was coming along. Some soreness above the elbow, but he might start throwing—light workouts—in a few days. What a relief. With Kane back, the Sox might still have a chance down the stretch. It was enough to give Sharkey hope.

At least once a day the kidnapper called. The freak was almost sociable, but he continued the veiled threats and remained elusive about a price.

"We're thinking at least a hundred grand," he said on day nine. "But it might be more."

"What about one fifty?" Sharkey said desperately.

"Maybe. Or two hundred. One of my guys, a greedy son 'va bitch, he's talkin' half a mil."

"Half a mil? I'm only a goddamn manager!" Sharkey realized he might have to liquidate his e-trade account. If these guys really pressed, he might have to mortgage his house.

"We'll talk. We'll get back to you."

It was torture to follow the club's fortunes on the road trip. Watching on TV, Sharkey was helpless to control even the tiniest aspect of the game. He'd watch, turn it off, and invariably turn it back on, a nervous wreck. The Sox, without Kane, were reeling; they lost two out of three in Oakland and three out of four in Seattle.

The Yanks were suddenly in front by three games. The Sox crashed and burned again in Minnesota, blowing a four-run lead in the opener. Sharkey sat stunned, cradling a glass of Stoli. A news report flashed on: A body had been found in a bakery kitchen in Weymouth, the latest victim of an apparent serial killer.

His mouth went dry. A newscaster stood near the colorful bakery window. The victim had been a night chef. His severed head was discovered in one of the huge ovens—in with a batch of sticky buns. A member of the morning crew had seen it upon arriving at work. She was being questioned by police at Queen of Angels Hospital following treatment for an irregular heartbeat.

The investigation was continuing.

Henrietta's cigarette smoke floated across the table like a tule fog. She was as sullen as Wolf had ever seen her, her face hard with unspoken fears. The bakery murder had eliminated just about every member of the club as a suspect; for exactly that reason it was anything but a cause to rejoice.

"I don't know why—I can't imagine why, after all this *fucking* trouble—they say this organization is cursed!" The sarcasm blew out of her like sulfur from a cinder cone. "That just *fries* my *ass!*"

Wulfmeyer felt the total breakdown of his underarm deodorant. He was seated across from her in the upstairs office, overlooking the garden, though it was dark now and the clustering maples created an ambience straight out of Transylvania. He had just explained, as per Mulgrove's late-afternoon phone call, that Kane had not been home for even a moment on the night of the Weymouth slaying. Wolf had finally taken the bold step of having Mulgrove run surveillance on Kane, and immediately the news was bad. The way his luck was running, he'd step off the curb in an hour and be hit by a Greyhound.

"You know," Henrietta said, watching the smoke, "I've got half a

mind to end this farce and give Kane to the cops, I really do. Maybe you along with him! One more of these charming decapitations, Neville, and I swear to God it could happen!"

"This guy in Weymouth," Wulfmeyer said, in as even a tone as he could manage, "he was sixty-eight years old. How many good years did he have left?"

"That's not the point!"

"You want to ignore that? He might've died of cancer before long. Heart attack, kidney failure. At that age, Christ, and working nights at a bakery, he was probably diabetic. His arteries were probably hard as buggy whips."

"Look, Neville, you may feel very comfortable with the course we've chosen, this particular brand of *population control,* but I was raised differently." Henrietta's eyes looked red, savage. "I'm not very proud of myself, not proud at all. I was out at the country club, and I ran into the Khalids—Abdul and Celeste, you might remember they endowed the Basque Center—and it was hard looking them in the eye. Decent people. I very seriously doubt, if they were in my position—"

"If I may—"

"Say it! Speak up—my God, you've never been short of opinions."

"Number one, we've got a damn good chance to win it all this year, once Kane gets back. He saw the trainer today—Jesus, those young, strong tissues, they're healing up like crazy."

" 'Crazy'—that's a choice of words."

"And the Yankees lost Willoughby last night." Ben Willoughby, New York's third starter, had piled up fourteen wins against seven losses, with an earned-run average under 2.80. Wulfmeyer leaned through the smoke. "Blew out his rotator cuff. He'll be lucky to be back by next July."

"Hallelujah."

"So there's a golden opportunity here, a chance we may not see again in our lifetimes—certainly not in Gordon's lifetime." Wolf

hated that he could not read her expressions, that stolid face frozen under its chemical enhancements. "And, you know, we're not dead yet, so far as the cops. We lucked out on the Weymouth location—not far at all from Quincy."

She knew immediately what he meant: that Sharkey, at the Seaport Roadway Inn, remained a viable Plan B or C or X, whatever option you assigned to the very desperate scenario in which they might need to frame him—it was still possible. A sore subject with Henrietta, though, and one Wolf was delicate in bringing up. She'd been more than appalled, aghast beyond any definition of the word, to learn about the kidnapping.

Her stony gaze was not the acknowledgment Wulfmeyer wanted, but he'd been right, it had worked, and he knew that she knew it.

"This idea with Fish," Wulfmeyer persisted, "you know it may free us of having to consider other avenues. In terms of my tapes."

Henrietta crushed out her cigarette. "Have we heard anything yet from Benito Castillo? His whereabouts?"

"Not a damn thing. So—chances are—anyway, let's assume he's still a likely."

"Good." She exhaled.

"Don't misconstrue my intentions, but if we didn't have, you know, this option of nailing Fish, we might be in real trouble. I mean, Castillo? Maybe. But who else? Fish himself mentioned he's seen some provocative background on Kenton. Things the cops would probably—"

"Neville, you stop right there!" Henrietta thrust an angry finger. "I told you already, made it *very clear* to you, that nothing should happen to that poor man! Nothing!"

"That's why I say—having Fish—"

"Did you destroy that tape?"

"Not yet, but I—"

"You destroy it, burn it! Get rid of it! You try anything with that

tape and so help me I'll ruin you for life. You hear me? You're in enough trouble without that."

"Yes—believe me—he's totally, absolutely safe. Nothing in the world is going to happen to Kent Ravinovich." Wulfmeyer tried to smile; his lips seemed stiffened with epoxy. He made a mental note to get rid of the Ravinovich tape.

"Are we through here?"

"Yes, just about." He wanted to leave her with good news. He reminded her the club would be flying back to Boston in two days. Sharkey's wife could go free. It was looking as if Kane would be ready to rejoin the team for the next trip, and Sharkey could return to managing. So the kidnapping scheme, one of the season's truly nerve-racking events, was about over.

Not only that, but Mulgrove, who'd been working the task force, had picked up a rumor of a new police development, a potentially wonderful turn of events. If true, it might carry the club into the playoffs. "Some Booster, an ex-judge, flew back early from Seattle. The cops are looking at him hard. He may have known the first victim—Marzoli."

"What's his name?" Henrietta demanded. "What do you know about him?"

"Nothing yet." Wulfmeyer glanced at his watch. "Actually, I'm due to meet him in a few minutes. Meet Mulgrove, I mean. He's supposed to have some more."

"All right. Get going. You keep me up-to-date every goddamn second, you hear?"

Wulfmeyer slunk away like a scolded pup. He sat for a moment in the Eldorado, trying to collect his wits, before heading west toward Lord Jake's.

Mulgrove had picked the spot, a highbrow joint renowned for its martinis and prime rib. He was already there, tilted back in a plush leather bar chair. Gold watch, neck chain, dark sport coat. Half-empty

Bacardi in easy reach. Mulgrove seemed to maintain an easy separation between the proliferating duties the Red Sox were assigning him: tracking extortionists, monitoring Kane's curfew violations, and poking into the murder task-force investigation. If he inferred any connection among those disparate activities, he kept it to himself. He seemed to buy the notion that the Sox were at risk from some crazed fan.

Wulfmeyer grabbed a seat and ordered up a Jack Daniel's. He wanted to know all about the judge, and Mulgrove had the goods: He was Rudy Thomlinson, sixty-two, two years into his early retirement, a lifelong Red Sox fan who'd attended every game the past two seasons until the recent road trip. He'd flown home early from Seattle, ostensibly to attend his mother's funeral.

"Interesting thing, here: He didn't get along with that other fan, Angelo Marzoli, victim number one," Mulgrove said. "You probably know Marzoli was a real Sox baiter. This guy and Marzoli, they got into it in a parking lot in Chicago last year. Thomlinson bloodied his lip."

"Really? That's fantastic news," Wolf said. "I mean, it sounds like there's a chance the judge is our perpetrator."

"There are no charges yet."

"His mother—" Wolf said. "She really dead?"

"Oh, yeah. Fell down the stairs in her basement. It took two or three days before her sister found her down there, her neck broke."

"Too bad. I guess that's an alibi."

"The point is, he was here in town during the bakery murder. That fact can't be ignored."

Wulfmeyer wished there were more than that. He wondered if there was time to collect photos, have the lab produce another video. It was a risky proposition to decide when to play that ace, because it was a big one, and he could play it only once.

" 'Nother thing, we got some politics here," Mulgrove went on.

"All his years on the bench, Thomlinson's been perceived, certainly by Hardeway, as soft on crime. Easy on the pushers, burglars, child pornographers—you name it." Hardeway had hated the man for years, Mulgrove said. Not only that, but the chief, facing reelection, was under immense pressure to put an end to the serial attacks. "I wouldn't be surprised at all if they pop this guy."

Wulfmeyer felt his heart leap. Oh, God, how he hoped. It was too much to expect, but, Jesus H. Christ, what a boon it would be to the ever-loving Red Sox. He quickly turned to another matter, removing from his jacket pocket an envelope containing a tiny square of paper.

"Here's that thumbprint I got—the one you said you could run for me." Wolf had noticed it on the lower left corner of the threat he'd received. A gluey print that might be Kane's or might not. He had clipped it from the note so Mulgrove could have one of his buddies run the print without seeing that gruesome beheaded Wolf.

If it was Kane's . . . well, Wulfmeyer had to take that into account, but the postmark was Quincy.

Mulgrove held it up in the light and slipped it back in the envelope.

"No problem. Have it for you tomorrow."

The key item was section XVII, subparagraphs 14, 15, and 16. Sharkey was due bonuses totaling $450,000 if the Sox could somehow reverse eighty years of ignominy and advance through the playoffs to a championship.

Wulfmeyer pondered it—a good chunk of change, though a lot rode on that little word "if." What Fish actually got might be far less, should the Sox suffer the usual season-ending collapse. It made working the figures hard, because Wolf wanted to be fair. He wanted to recover no more in the ransom than the club was likely to shell out in extra remuneration for what was really only Sharkey's job.

He number-crunched a few scenarios, figured the Sox to advance at least beyond the first round, and deducted the necessary expenses: paying the kidnappers, the hotel bill, and the club's supposed share of the ransom. At last, grabbing the phone, he dialed Horgan.

"Doyle? Hey, it's Wolf, how are you? Just thinking, you know, regarding that lady we've got—let's let her go for two hundred grand. Yeah, that's enough. I think that'll work just fine."

He went over the logistics of the release—Bernice would have to be blindfolded and brought to a new location, where Fish could pick her up once he had left the cash. It sounded easy, but anything could go wrong. They still had to worry about the possibility of police intervention and about Bernice, the socialite, making a big stink.

Horgan was helpful; his suggestions, and his impressive network of contacts, made Wulfmeyer feel more at ease. Wolf hung up and felt reasonably good about himself. He'd engineered an extremely touchy gambit without any screw-ups or any real damage to Fish. Two hundred grand, and the club kicking in $60,000, that would mean $140,000 out of Sharkey's pocket. He'd make it up the first week of the postseason as long as the Sox could win a few games. This wasn't like that extortionist bastard, $5 million for a fucking videotape.

Wulfmeyer decided to call Stu, got him on the cellular, just to reassure himself. Yes, Kane was healing fine, Stu said. Throwing in the low nineties, getting his arm strength back, and hitting some ropes in BP.

"He'll be ready to bat in a week or two, I'm pretty sure of it," Domato said. "Minkowitz is looking at him again tomorrow. Might be a little longer before he can actually pitch a game."

"Will he make the road trip?"

"Oh, no doubt. He's still popping the ball up, you know, got that hitch, but the power—Jesus. Be worth trying to get that bat back into the lineup, 'specially now with Tynes going down again."

Wulfmeyer agreed. Jimmy Tynes, in his first week back from injury, had torn a shoulder ligament diving into second base. Wolf

told Stu to have a good talk with Sharkey, once he was back, and Uziak. Fish might return any day now, he added, and hung up.

Ten seconds later his phone rang. Oscar Gamboa.

"Oscar, you fucking asshole, how the hell are you?" Wulfmeyer tried to make it sound affable. Let him guess how much he meant it.

Gamboa shot back, "Fine, you fucking prick. When you buying me that lunch at Les Deux?"

"When hell freezes over. What's on your mind, Oscar?"

"My misunderstood client, the greatest glove on the eastern seaboard. He wants to play some baseball."

Benito Castillo. Wulfmeyer tilted forward. "Where is the little bastard?"

"Miami. He wants certain assurances in terms of playing time. He can't hit unless he's got time to get in a groove."

"He can't hit, period. How long's he been in Miami?"

"A while. This thing's in your lap, Wolf. You want to win in the playoffs, it's all about pitching and defense. Defense, Wolf, defense."

Wulfmeyer pressed the question. "Clarify for me, when exactly did he fly to Miami?"

"Hell, I don't— I guess when he left the club. His brother's down there. Two of them, actually."

"Tell him he's got two days to get back here or he'll be riding the pine in Pawtucket." Wulfmeyer adopted the hard line; going AWOL was not about to win any concessions on playing time, that was for damn sure. The little prick had a contract and he had better live up to it. Gamboa had been around the block enough to know the situation.

Hanging up, Wulfmeyer immediately brooded on the new information. If it was true, if Castillo had flown directly to Miami, which he probably had, there would be airline records; he was no longer a viable suspect.

"Son of a bitch!" Wolf slammed his fist on the desk. What rotten luck, the guy going AWOL just when they needed to fly him to

Boston. Fucked up one of the most promising options. Wolf felt a sudden wave of fatigue; he wasn't sure he had the emotional strength to pull himself through these final weeks. Like a prisoner in one of those medieval torture chambers, he could feel the walls closing in, spiked walls coming for him.

"You all right?" Samantha said.

"Just hassles! Christ!"

"Jack Mulgrove's holding for you. On three."

Wolf picked it up. Mulgrove said he had run the thumbprint.

"Take a guess," he said.

"Edward Kennedy."

"August Nicholson Sharkey."

"I knew it!" Wulfmeyer felt a huge block of fear inside him suddenly transmogrify into anger. He thanked Mulgrove for the info and hung up, seething. He'd hardly been able to sleep since getting that horrifying note with the severed wolf head, and it was nothing, just a stupid-ass prank from his own manager. Just Fish making some point. The bastard. Hell, he wanted to resort to dirty tricks—all right, two could play that game. He wanted to jerk someone around, hell yes, he'd get a taste of his own medicine.

Wolf thought a moment. Picked up the phone and dialed.

"Doyle? Hey, Wolf here again. Listen, on that thing, let's make it three hundred grand."

20

Rolling toward the airport, watching the familiar stream of lights out the window, Sharkey felt oddly detached from his own life, as if nothing were real except the hypnotic swaying of the bus. He was back, heading into the stretch run. He couldn't quite define the wash of emotions he felt at rejoining the team—the joy, the anxiety over the pennant race, the ever constant fear of a killer on the loose. The whole last week was already a blur, consumed with obtaining Bernice's freedom. Now he felt it moving behind him; the road motion was calming, the bus a protective capsule whisking him further and further from the unspeakable ordeal.

He'd had to scramble, pulling from stocks, borrowing on his platinum cards, taking cash from his 401(k), to cough up the ransom. The kidnappers had left Bernice bound and gagged in a room at the U-Stow-It lot in South Boston. A phone call directed Sharkey to the hidden key, and he found and untied her. She whimpered, hugged him and cried a lot. She was insistent that they report the crime, and Sharkey had to assent despite his concerns about dealing with the cops. They stopped at Boston PD headquarters even before they

drove home. No one brought up the Marzoli murder, or any other beheading, and Henrietta cried out her statement. He felt better afterward. Maybe they'd catch those assholes, get back some of his money.

The anger came later: Tears, lashing words. Accusations that stung like whips on the pink underbelly of Sharkey's mind. "If you weren't gone all the time, these things wouldn't happen! . . . It's your fault, can't you see? . . . Mr. High-Profile—your name in the papers—of course we'd be targets for this type of—this horrible rape!"

"They raped you?" he had said.

"Not literally, you idiot, emotional rape! Tying me up! Holding me hostage! You think that's not rape? You just have no idea—no idea!—of what I've had to go through!"

She still wanted out. The marriage was finis.

Sharkey didn't blame her. He wasn't bitter. They had become different people. He was starting over, a man alone, moving toward his destiny, rolling into East Boston on his way to Logan. A significantly poorer man who, in spite of all the troubles, in spite of turmoil sufficient to shrivel the gonads of a lowland gorilla, embraced the chance to be back in charge of his team, the glimmering opportunity to erase eighty years of Red Sox ineptitude. Yet haunted by all his own failures. Haunted by his freak rotten luck.

"Fish, it's Wolf." Domato fell into the seat beside him, offering his ubiquitous cell phone. Sharkey grabbed it.

"Yeah, Wolf. What's up?"

"Don't ask. This goddamn season, worst of my life. Anyway, Castillo should be meeting you in Detroit. Just got confirmation he made his flight in Miami. He's been down there, I guess, visiting his brothers, the stupid fuck."

"Detroit? I thought you were sending him to Pawtucket!"

"Can't do it with Tynes out again." Wulfmeyer voiced the opinion that none of the Triple-A infielders would hit much better than Benito, and his glove might come in handy. It was one more blow that

Sharkey had no choice but to take, like some old fighter, like Jerry Quarry getting one in the kisser. He hung up and stared out the window, sat sullenly during the flight.

The Red Sox got into Detroit well past two in the morning. Traveling after a night game invariably sapped the reserves of everyone on the club, particularly in the wake of a tough defeat. The last game of the home stand had gone down the tubes by a score of 2–1, Frolicky's twelfth loss of the season, and Boston was now four games behind New York. The club was tied with Cleveland for the wild-card spot and in danger of missing the playoffs altogether.

Sharkey got to his room, stripped off his shirt and shoes, and fell across the bed, still in his slacks. In no time at all he was deep in a dream about being disembowled by jungle cats.

Room service brought coffee, a Spanish omelette and a copy of the *Free Press*. Sharkey switched on the TV and immediately caught a news report: A retired judge, Rudolph N. Thomlinson, who had been crisscrossing the country as a member of the Boston Red Sox Booster Club, had been arrested in connection with the nationwide series of ritualistic murders.

Sharkey stood and turned up the sound. The former judge had been taken into custody the previous night, after a search of his home in Wellesley. Authorities had confiscated a quarter pound of cocaine and an undisclosed amount of marijuana but declined to comment on evidence linking the sixty-two-year-old jurist to the skein of ten murders. The spree included attacks in Texas, Chicago, Cleveland, Anaheim and, of course, Boston. The dates and places of the incidents, the news anchor intoned dramatically, exactly followed the travels of the team.

Anaheim? Sharkey had not been aware of a murder in Anaheim. It must have occurred during the last trip. He was losing track of

them all. An inner valve seemed to spring open: Sharkey became filled with a dizzying sense of unease. The arrest was good news, certainly. Fantastic news, if they had busted the right guy. The Sox now had an unimpeded chance to win. They could play out the season and, with any luck, advance through the playoffs and World Series without the specter of the unthinkable—a star being arrested for murder.

If. If it were true. The fly in the ointment, a big, ugly horsefly, was that searing doubt. Sharkey had traveled the country with Castillo, Davenport, Kane and the Raven. The odds that a retired judge would be more off-center than those screwballs seemed disturbingly remote. And now, good gracious God, it was public knowledge that the pattern of murders followed the travels of the club. That new disclosure was the most troubling of all. Now the whole world knew the broader picture.

The television report had not been precisely accurate, Sharkey realized. The last attack in Weymouth had happened while the club was out of town. He wondered how the judge's travels correlated with that particular event. Maybe the media—NBC, at least—had not probed to that level of detail. In any case, the Sox would get some coverage now. Every laughing hyena at every newspaper and network in the country would be sniffing around for some sensational angle.

He was right. The clubhouse before the series opener was pandemonium: scores of them when Sharkey arrived, three hours prior to game time. Five networks, including CNN and ESPN. Most of the questions centered on whether the team had been in any danger. Had Thomlinson been stalking any players? Had anyone seen him? Had anyone been aware of the attacks? The investigation?

Mad Dog and Reeling were outspoken; they'd had no idea and were pissed. Langley made asinine observations about the pressures of serving on the federal bench. Sharkey waded through with "no comments" and finally ran the reporters out. He had a pennant race to worry about. He decided to hold Kane out of the lineup during a

riotous, 9–8 victory, and again the next night in a 3–1 win. There was no sense risking re-injury, rushing him back. A few at-bats as the designated hitter tomorrow night, against the left-hander, and some throwing every day on the sidelines, and he'd be full throttle in no time.

The Sox were dark horses to catch the Yanks, but they had a solid chance to make the postseason as a wild-card team, especially now with Kane returning. The easier schedule belonged to Boston. Sharkey, allowing himself to believe that the killer was really in custody, felt a swell of elation. He sat in his clubhouse office listening to radio updates of New York's battle with the Twins. The Yankees were trailing, 9–2, in the eighth.

Suddenly Kane entered the cramped office and slammed the door closed.

"Ron, hey, come in, sit down."

"Why didn't you use me today?" Kane made no move toward having a seat; instead he took a menacing step in the direction of Sharkey's swivel chair.

"Just a precaution. Give that wing of yours an extra day to heal. Can't hurt." Sharkey forced a tense smile, showing all his square, white teeth. "These next few weeks, Ron, you're going to have to carry us. Not only pitching, of course, but—Christ, Tynes out, Claxton hurt, I'll probably play you some in right field. Take advantage of those athletic gifts. Let you DH some nights and play some right field."

Kane showed no change in expression. His stolid freckled face seemed illuminated by its own incandescence, a fierce orange heat like the filaments of an electric heater. He had maintained his average at .292 before being injured; he was proud of his hitting and zealous about getting the chance. Kane looked at Sharkey's long jaw, his deep-set eyes, and saw a cheat, a man who had cheated him out of the opportunity to perform. Any homers Kane might have hit, any great

plays he might have made, were wiped out even before the fact by this smiling retard cheating bastard, this sorry, fish-lipped, dick-headed ignoramus. Kane moved toward him, the contempt and rage driving him forward, and with lightning quickness he reached and grabbed Sharkey's shirt collar, grabbed it and lifted him straight up off the chair. Kane hoisted him like a forklift, the same power and leverage, and spun him, slamming Sharkey's back against the wall.

"Ron!" Sharkey's eyes widened; he struggled to grab Kane's wrists.

"Listen to me, Fish, I come to play. Get it?"

"Yes. Put me down! We want you to play."

"Fuckin' put me in the game."

"Stop this! Right now! I'm *going* to put you in the game!" Sharkey fell to his feet as Kane let go. "God-*damn!* Don't you see I'm here to put you in the game? Jesus!"

Kane did not answer. He gave Sharkey a visual stab and turned, cursing again before disappearing out the door. Sharkey exhaled, trying to catch his breath, hoping to hell he wouldn't keel over with a heart attack. He sat down and tried to regain his composure, make sense of the harrowing absurdity he had just experienced. Sitting, his mind whirling, he became aware in a moment that his tobacco tin was gone. His lucky Honus Wagner tin was no longer on his desk. It had been there, he thought, just a second ago.

Sharkey moved to the door and leaned out toward Kane's locker.

"Ron! You take that tin? That thing with my sunflower seeds?"

Kane glared back. "I'm not fucking Castillo! I'm here to fucking play!"

"I'm talking about my tin! My tobacco tin!"

Castillo shouted, "Shut up, you fuck-eeeng sheeethead!" A retort directed at Kane, or at Sharkey, no way to tell. Other voices quickly joined in, cursing, wise-assing. Some of it a joke, some of it so caustic he cringed.

There were clearly still problems with clubhouse chemistry.

Sharkey slammed the office door shut. Christ, that tin was a valuable artifact—worth more than his car. Had it been on his desk? Or not? Sharkey's mind was so cluttered he couldn't be entirely sure. He might have left it somewhere else—his locker, the team bus. But if Kane had filched it . . . well, it'd be fruitless to go out and confront him now. Kane would never admit to having taken it and would never allow himself the surrender of handing it over. He'd make a keep-away game out of it. Have Sharkey poking around, going apeshit, just for yuks. Try to make him a laughingstock.

The answer was to search later, when the guys weren't around. Search Kane's locker and his own. And Castillo's. That little twerp, Christ, blowing up strongboxes, going AWOL, putting Ex-Lax in Sharkey's beer. He wasn't above stealing anything. He'd rip off anything he damn well could.

A chilling thought entered Sharkey's mind. Castillo's last disappearance had occurred just before the kidnapping. He lifted a pen and jotted on the corner of an envelope: *"Castillo . . . Bernice???"* He stared at it. He grabbed the phone, dialed Boston PD, and left the tip on the voice mail of the case investigator.

Now the other question: what to do about Kane's tantrum? Sharkey had not been so physically manhandled by a player since big Crawdaddy Crenshaw had tried to stuff him into a supply closet in the Baltimore clubhouse seventeen seasons ago. Big, bad Crawdaddy—six foot four and ugly as a new-hatched turkey. He'd had an excuse, though: a brain lesion, discovered two months later, after he'd raced his Trans Am through Grace Heart Cemetery, knocking down sixty-some headstones.

Kane was different—presumably. Sharkey would have to fine him. Clearly. That was the recommended remedy: force the player to pay through the nose. Except Kane was making so damn much loot—and he seemed to react so very poorly to disciplinary action. In the

case of his curfew violations, it often made things worse. He seemed to go out of his way to show he could not be reined in.

Jesus. Sharkey stewed over it. He realized he might have to keep the incident quiet, let it pass. It was not the kind of heart-to-heart he normally liked to encourage with his players, but managing modern athletes required a certain measure of flexibility: They were individuals, they all had their own ways. And, looking at it another way, Sharkey had just seen a powerful demonstration of Kane's desire to play. That was good. He could work with a star who wanted to play.

Kane batted sixth and patrolled right field in the Sunday finale against the left-hander Norm Lejune. The prodigy's return—even as an outfielder—was news enough for another media swarm. Kane had not played a nonpitching position since a year ago in the Dominican Republic, but he handled five chances without an error and made a strong play on a drive into the corner. Kane also doubled in three at-bats as the Sox squeezed out a victory in eleven.

The short trip continued in New York, where the Sox went head-to-head with the Yankees in the biggest series of the year. The media onslaught was stunning. Bryan Hazzard, relying almost exclusively on a belt-high, hanging curveball, got shelled in the opener, but the Sox won the following night on a squeeze bunt in the eighth, after Kane belted his third home run, a titanic blast into the upper deck.

Kane made his return as a starter in game three, going six innings and reaching 102 mph as the Sox triumphed again. Castillo rapped the winning single and strutted around like a horse's ass for what seemed like hours.

Boston returned home only two games out. It was exhilarating to be in such a race. Pointing his Olds toward Fenway on a brilliant, clear Friday afternoon, Sharkey took time to notice the glorious colors of the changing leaves—maple, oak, others he'd seen his whole life,

never knowing what the hell they were. Bright RED SOX banners hung from downtown lampposts, the largesse of a New England financier. They gave him butterflies, but he was happy. In spite of all the frustrations of managerial life, and the fact that he still had not found his treasured tobacco tin, he was reasonably upbeat. He was due to have dinner again with Annie.

Then he stepped into the clubhouse and saw Uziak's face. Uzi looked as if Kornblume had died.

"What's up?" Sharkey said.

"Dunno. Wolf's looking for you. Just called, and boy is he pissed."

His heart pounding, Sharkey hurried up to Wulfmeyer's office. He walked in and Domato was there. Wolf pointed to an empty chair.

"Sit down. There was another one in Detroit."

Sharkey looked at the faces. "Another what?" His first reflexive thought was another manager fired. Poor Hauser, just when they'd started winning.

"Another fucking space alien, what do you think?" Wolf's bitter sarcasm caused Domato's fat face to roll Sharkey's way.

"The Barnacle's here," Stu said soberly, nodding in the direction of the head.

An instant later the detective reentered the room. Sharkey understood very clearly. He felt his colon begin writhing, like a python on hot asphalt. Schachter's expression was grave. He nodded to Sharkey and sat, crossing his legs, repeating for Sharkey the particulars of the new murder, an attack that had occurred in a hair salon. The shop had been closed, but the proprietor evidently lived in a unit upstairs. No signs of forced entry indicated that the killer had obtained a key or talked his way inside, possibly for a trim. It was, tragically, the barber himself who'd had too much taken off the top.

"Now, what we don't know—"

"Wait, wait," Wulfmeyer interrupted. "You were about to respond

to my theory—about a copycat killer." Evidently that had been under discussion when Sharkey walked in.

"It's not a copycat," Schachter said firmly. "These bodies are marked, the heads marked in a very particular way that's not public knowledge."

"Yeah, I know—gash lines. Parallel gash lines across the scalp," Wulfmeyer said. "That's not public knowledge?"

"No, it's definitely not." Schachter's gaze became a laser.

"*I* knew it," Wolf said, flashing a crazy-me grin. It was a detail Mulgrove had picked up. "Christ, man, if *I* knew it—"

"We should probably check on *your* whereabouts that night," Schachter interjected. "Or your manager's." He swung his gaze to Sharkey, who came within a hair's breadth of urinating in his chair. "The fact is," Schachter went on, "these markings are a signature of the killer every bit as reliable as fingerprints."

"Of which there are none," Wulfmeyer said pointedly. "Now, I want to mention another possibility, which I'm sure you've thought about—which I hope to hell you've thought about."

"Which is?"

Sharkey couldn't wait to hear what he'd say.

"Some other fan, and I think it's an obvious possibility." Wolf's face took on a sheen of intensity. "Someone like Thomlinson, except he's not a Booster. A secret traveler, or even an *accomplice* of the first killer. Using the same rituals, you know. You'll scoff at this, but if there's a satanic sect—anything like that. I know damn well that stranger things have happened."

"We're figuring there's only one killer," Schachter said evenly. He noted that authorities were still examining the astronomical number of flight records, and he invited Wulfmeyer to pass along any information that might be useful. The request seemed to whiten Wolf's lips, they were clamped so tight. Sharkey realized he was not about to volunteer anything concerning Castillo, the Raven, or anyone else.

His own impulse to come forward was somehow bottled up in his throat.

Schachter stood, preparing to leave, and said Thomlinson would almost certainly be released in the morning.

"Thanks for your time. Sorry about this little courtesy call."

"Courtesy?" Wulfmeyer made a sudden, irascible wave of his arms. "If this is courtesy, Jesus God, you might as well go piss in my sink!"

"Another time." Schachter gave them all an unhappy glance and let himself out.

Sharkey felt embarrassed for Wulfmeyer, but also numb, overcome with dread. Domato seemed to bloat up to twice his usual size, inflated with stress.

"You needed me here for that?" Sharkey muttered.

"He mentioned you. Something about that murder in Texas." Wulfmeyer looked around without seeing anybody.

"What about it?"

"I don't know. I thought he'd come back to it. Something about where your room was, the alley. He's just fishing, just poking wherever he can poke. Goddamn cops."

"We'll have the press on us now," Domato said. "After that judge gets free—"

"Oh Jesus." Wulfmeyer stared at a point on his desktop. He looked up, thrashed his head around, and said they should all refuse comment. "Send 'em to me. Fish, try to keep those players quiet. They don't know a fuckin' thing anyway. I might have to hold a press conference." He paused a moment. "Shit, those cops. I should threaten a lawsuit. They disrupt this club in the playoffs, the World Series—my God, the millions at stake! What if they arrest the wrong guy again? One of our players?"

Sharkey suddenly felt angry. He reiterated his concerns about Castillo and Ravinovich—points that Wulfmeyer should have known

by heart—but Wolf shined him on with the usual blast of nonsensical rhetoric.

"You're talking about one of the most beloved athletes in the history of Boston," Wolf said of Ravinovich.

"Oh, I guess that means he can't possibly kill anybody!"

"Look, Fish, if the Raven's a serial killer—and I don't think so— the police will find out. And I'll help them, I swear to God I will."

"I dare you! I don't think you have the guts!"

Sharkey turned and stormed out. He could hear Wolf yelling from the doorway—"Fish! Fish!"—but he kept going, skipping down the stairs to the clubhouse. He was boiling. So livid he was ready to quit. Give Wulfmeyer what he deserved—quit and finger all those guys, not just Castillo. Tell them about the Raven lurking around, Kane slamming his manager up against the wall. Tell the cops what those fuckin' fruitcakes were really like.

It would mean destroying his own lifelong dream—that was the rub. Just when he was so close. Just when it seemed the Sox were gaining the momentum to go all the way.

Sharkey locked himself in his office. He needed time to think. He closed his eyes, took several long breaths, and let his gaze fall idly on one of his stacks of mail. The letters had been pouring in since his forced vacation.

The envelope on top caught his eye. No address, nothing but *FISH* in scrawled black ink, like a child's handwriting. He tore it open and pulled out the note, typed all in capital letters:

"FISH, I'M FIXING TO RIP YOUR HEAD OFF AND THROW IT DOWN A SEWER."

Wolf felt strangely exhilarated, so involved in the moment that the rush was almost sexual. He gazed over the throng of reporters, stared into the dark, seductive eyes of the big Sony TV cameras, and summoned just the right amalgam of reasoned intelligence and righteous indignity.

"That's so absurd it's laughable!" Wulfmeyer said, not quite laughing. "You know yourself, Mitch, these guys have busted their tails for years—their *whole lives*!—to get to this position. The notion that one of them might be committing these crimes—when we're, what, only *weeks* from the chance to play in the World Series? You can't even *think* that's a serious question!"

He went on—faith in the cops, desire to see justice, et cetera et cetera, yakety-yak-yak. Harkwood had broached the possibility that, if the killer was traveling the circuit, maybe it could actually be one of the ballplayers. Wulfmeyer had anticipated that type of inanity; he'd given it, he thought, an appropriate response—a vehement counterargument based almost entirely on the type of sound logic a serial killer

would never use. There was an art to shooting down a dead-on thesis.

Several more questions were shouted; Wulfmeyer ripped through answers, glancing a few times at his watch, and wrapped up the press conference with a thank-you for coming. He slipped away to the Eldorado and gunned it for Henrietta's.

Every damn radio station was carrying reports about the release of the ex-judge Rudy Thomlinson and the thwarted serial-murder investigation. That these grisly beheadings seemed to correlate with the travels of a top major-league club seemed to catapult the story into the rarefied media air known only by the likes of Lizzie Borden and O. J. Simpson.

Henrietta met him in her office overlooking the garden. She had restyled her hair—coils of it hung down the sides of her cheeks—but her face was so drawn her eyes seemed to tilt in a new direction, as if some emergency plastic surgery had gone terribly wrong. She was sucking hard on a Kool.

"Just saw you on television," she said as Wulfmeyer sat down. "You are really a piece of work."

"I hope that's a compliment."

"Take it any way you want. We'll probably both burn in hell."

Wolf was struck by the contrast in their moods. He was still feeling hyper, jacked up, ready for the challenge, but she was plainly distraught. He realized he had to rally her, do whatever he could to keep her eyes on the prize, now more than ever.

"You know," he said, "I been doing some reading. It really gives you perspective, the sheer fucking number of people that have died on this planet. Dying in vain, dying for lost causes, the puniest little rewards. Pyrrhic victories. Nothing like a World Series, let me tell you."

"Neville, I'm tired. Is this relevant?"

"Damn right it's relevant."

"I'm sure it relates to our murdering superstar in some oblique way, but frankly, I don't know what the hell you're talking about—"

"The Panama Canal. All right? I read this thing on the Panama Canal. The death roll—take a guess—twenty-five thousand people! Just to dig a fucking ditch from one ocean to the other. And get this: yellow fever. Most of them died of yellow fever. Can you imagine?"

"Died with their heads on, I bet."

"Like that's a consolation? Seriously, twenty-five thousand people, Henrietta. They don't draw that in Oakland. That kind of suffering—Christ, reminds me of our fans. And Iwo Jima—"

"You think that justifies—"

"Let me finish! The horrors of Iwo Jima, my God, I forget how many marines bit it. For what? Read about the place and it was nothing—a godforsaken rock in the ocean! Barren, worthless. Thousands of guys—young people!—getting murdered with machine guns! Blown up! Under the full sponsorship of the United States government! Oh, I tell you. So we could hoist up Old Glory, let some guy take a pretty picture? It's sick! I can't even—Christ Almighty, you see that shit, I almost laugh. That we're feeling guilty over eleven or twelve fatalities—when we've got a championship on the line."

"I'm not sure I share your views entirely."

"Oh, you do, I know you do." Wulfmeyer gritted his teeth. "You're on the same page, Henrietta. Not condoning murder—we don't want that. We wish to God these crimes weren't happening! But the importance of this season—"

"Neville!" Her eyes flashed angrily. "Let's not go over this again. Let's figure out what to do."

Wulfmeyer watched her stand and move to the window, looking down on her fine water lilies, rhododendrons, whatever the hell grew down there. Her mind was overloaded. Her ability to handle the severe realities of this particular crisis seemed to fade in and out like a weak FM signal.

"All right," Wolf said gently. "Let's think." He kept watching her. "How's Gordon?"

She glanced at her watch. Actually, the doctor wanted to see her. "I'm worried he might need more surgery. At his age . . ."

"Poor devil. I mean angel." He regretted his automatic choice of words. "The man's an angel. Too good, really. Sure like to see him win this year."

"I've got to go. Let me say— This theory, your secret traveler. I met Hardeway last night. He came over. They're actually checking that."

"Good. Did he stay long?" Wolf hoped she had tried to seduce him; that she would instinctively consider that tack as the one sure way to develop an information pipeline. "Not that it's my business—"

"No, it isn't." She swung around to look at him. "We should be damn thankful. The cops could identify us right now as the target of this investigation. Can you imagine how that would look? What I'm wondering . . . this traveler theory, how long you think that'll hold them?"

"They've got to run flight records. Who knows? The point is, a traveler like that, a murderer traveling secretly, he could fly under phony names. The fact he doesn't surface, that doesn't prove a damn thing about our guys. You should tell him that. You really should try to sleep with him."

"Neville!"

"Sorry, just trying to—oh God—suggest something constructive. Be better than other options."

"I can't believe— Like what? What other options?"

"Well, like using those tapes."

"Look, get out of here. I've got a bad feeling about this mess. I'm just not up to this today, and I've got to go see Gordon."

Wulfmeyer left. Her negativity was beginning to infect him. She was right: The secret traveler would not hold the cops through the

postseason. The attention this case was getting now, Kane could get himself arrested popping the top off a Budweiser.

Domato was in the outer office with Samantha. Wulfmeyer cringed, realizing they were scheduled to discuss preparations for the Ravinovich tribute. He barged past, told Stu to come in, and plopped down behind his desk, reaching in the drawer for a couple Tylenols. He downed them with cold coffee while Domato fell into the facing chair. A grin played across his thick lips.

"Want to hear something funny?"

"Funny? *Funny?!*" His voice rose to a shout, the pressures in his head scaling up to the brink of apoplexy. "Hah!" Wolf swallowed; he tried to bring down the internal gauges. "Sorry, Stu, I just—just got back from—I just saw Henrietta." He took a breath. "Nothing—*nothing!*—is funny."

"Just that—oh God, the Raven." Domato laughed anyway. He launched into a story about Ravinovich and his rehearsals for the tribute. He had been trying different speeches, various deliveries. The last tape, newly arrived in the morning mail, included a number of bastardized lines from Poe's "The Raven," rewritten to reflect the highlights of the Raven's own career, his heroics on the field and in the bedroom, and the terrible illness that had struck him down.

"He's got this line in there: 'Will I live? Tell me, tell me, I implore! Quoth the doctor, "Nevermore!"'"

"Oh, sweet Jesus. Look, we need to talk about the curfew."

"And Henrietta's saying, 'Let him do whatever he wants.' You said you just talked to her."

"Not about that, for crying out loud. Midnight. Just move it to midnight. Fuck the players' association. We can say it's for their own protection."

"Fish already done it. Two nights ago—one A.M."

"He did?"

"But they're ignoring it. Mulgrove says Moses and Uggams got back at three-thirty the very next night. And five or six guys came in after that." Domato raised a question about hiring more private detectives, and Wolf had to explain it to him again: Mulgrove and his guys—there were four agents working for him now—were damn reliable people, but if you started adding more you couldn't know for sure what you'd get. You'd be bound to eventually run across some guy with real scruples, the type who, if he saw something—saw a murder in a back alley, for example—would feel obligated to report it.

"Mulgrove can't keep up with those guys," Domato said. "He told me himself."

"That's why I'm talking about the curfew," Wulfmeyer said. "You tell Fish: midnight. And tell the Raven, he wants a tribute, he's got to can the Poe crap."

"Right. He wants to tape it, though. Play a tape and lip-sync it, 'cause he's afraid he'll be nervous."

"Fuck. Just handle it. And tell Fish I want Mad Dog in the eighth spot."

"Right-o." Domato half smiled and left. Right-o. Right-o. What a fuckin' loser. Dipshit smile of his, he could run for village idiot.

Wulfmeyer tried to force Ravinovich out of his thoughts and dive into other matters, represented by twenty-eight message slips. One was from Gene Morrissey at Tank Ball. Wolf had forgotten today was the deadline for the company's counter, that's how bad it was. A counter when he'd issued the so-called last and best offer four days ago.

To hell with them. They could sweat it a while. Wulfmeyer tied himself up, busy beaver, until four o'clock, then finally got Morrissey on the horn.

"Gene, hey, Wulfmeyer here. Sorry I'm just getting back. Listen, you know, thinking about this . . . let 'em walk. Close the whole

fucking factory. That's right . . . we gave 'em our offer. I don't care if they're the Teamsters. Listen . . . yeah, this ain't rocket science; Christ, they're making flotation tanks for goddamn toilets. I could train a band of monkeys . . . yeah, you tell Lozello I've got a shipment of macaques coming in from Malaysia. . . . They can sell pencils on the street corner."

Wulfmeyer hung up. His other line was already ringing. Why wouldn't they just leave him alone? He grabbed a couple more Tylenols. Thomlinson free, every goddamn newspaper and network in the nation now wondering what was up with the Red Sox, Tank Ball about to close down, Old Gordo facing the possibility of another surgery. What the hell else could go wrong?

Samantha called out, "Neville!"

"Yes!"

"Line two."

He saw the blinking button. "Who is it, for chrissakes?"

"The White House."

Sharkey was in the Olds rolling toward Fenway when he heard the radio report of Thomlinson's release. The news was almost anticlimactic, yet it caused a tightening of Sharkey's chest, a gasp for air. His body seemed to begin a slow adrenaline drip to prepare itself for a battle with no set time or place.

Traffic moved on, a disjointed flow through the helter-skelter Boston streets. Sharkey scanned the cars, the sidewalks, unsure what he hoped to find, except possibly some seam in the fabric of space, an invisible portal that he could slip through, be whisked thousands of miles away. Seeing nothing like that, no escape at all, he proceeded on to Fenway, into the teeth of the media frenzy.

The clubhouse and the exterior tunnels were jammed with reporters and TV goons, their lights casting long shadows. Sharkey

ducked most of the questions, just said he hoped they'd find the killer, hoped he and his guys could concentrate on baseball. No, he didn't think the Sox were a target of the madman. Anything else, talk to Wulfmeyer.

Whether the Sox were distracted by the latest alarming twist in the case was impossible to know for sure, but the initial signs were discouraging. Bryan Hazzard, the club's number-three starter, pitched as if someone had tossed a lug wrench into the delicate springs and flywheels of his delivery. He gave up four walks and three home runs in two innings as the team came apart like a box kite in a Gulf hurricane. The following night the story wasn't much better as the Orioles won once more, vaulting the Yankees three games in front again in the East. Cleveland was a half game behind Boston in the wild-card race.

Sharkey drove home to the cramped one-bedroom apartment he had taken near Tufts Park. Annie came by, and they had a late dinner, but not even that and a couple Stolis could lift the tension enough to sleep. He lay locked up rigid as an ironing board, brooding on the possibility that the Red Sox could lose *and* the fact emerge that there was a psychotic killer on the roster. That double-barreled disaster would certainly be the end of Sharkey's career; he'd be run out of town like a child molester.

He finally drifted into another falling nightmare: being thrown out a window and plummeting at incredible speeds, down, down, down a wall of painted numbers—the East standings—and, forty games out, landing with pile-driver force right on top of Kane, breaking off Kane's head. In a frenzy he kept trying to pick up the head and put it back on, but a killer whale leaped out of nowhere and sank its teeth into Sharkey's midsection, shaking him furiously while it roared and snarled like an Indy car.

Jerking awake, eyes pulsating, Sharkey trudged to the bathroom, poured himself some Pepto, and studied the deepening purple vein on

his nose. He wondered how long he could hold out. He seemed headed for a breakdown. He understood what Domato had been saying about Wolf; Sharkey was fighting the same battle, a secret inner war that was really the greatest contest in sports.

The struggle for sanity.

"Listen, you asshole!" Wulfmeyer said, his whole arm shaking with the phone. "Ten million is a *hell* of a lot of money! I've talked to my people and we can't get it that fast. No, we just cannot! We need at least a week—at least!"

He listened. His throat had gone dry as the Gobi Desert.

"Fine," he told the extortionist. "That's what I'm asking—a week. Next Thursday night. Of course we won't try anything!"

Wulfmeyer slammed down the receiver. He thought he might black out.

"Shit!"

22

Few bands of men in recorded history had become such a focal point of international attention. For sheer news-making power, the Sox were right there with a short list of legends: the Beatles, Jesus Christ and his twelve disciples, Genghis Kahn's marauding Mongols, Hitler's army, Michael Jordan and his Chicago Bulls teams, the Apollo 11 moon crew.

Kane's arrival had elevated the club to one level; now the mysterious connection to America's bloodiest crime spree had vaulted the Red Sox over the top, into some freakish outer stratosphere.

Sharkey could not even estimate the size of the crowd that engulfed the team bus as it pulled up at Kauffman Stadium in Kansas City. There were at least a thousand people, maybe more. Reporters and TV crews stood six deep along the short route to the visitors' clubhouse, aiming their Sonys, jousting at the darkening sky with their foam-wrapped microphone booms. Sharkey ignored their shouted questions and knifed through them in grim silence. Still, he couldn't help but wonder if the bedlam was as strange to them as it

was for him. He wanted to grab someone at random—a writer for the
Star, a commentator for some podunk radio station in Topeka or Jefferson City—and find out which of the angles really mattered to the
faceless masses of the heartland.

Was it Kane and a brilliance never before seen on a baseball diamond? Was it the murders? Did people find it hard to believe that two
such unlikely phenomena could be associated with the same ball club?
Did they imagine wild scenarios to link those things together? And
did anybody care about the one issue of greatest importance to the
men at the center of the storm: the pennant race?

Kansas City was the last stop of the regular season. The Sox still
trailed the Yankees by two games and stood a game in front of the
Indians. A strong finish would nail down at least a wild-card berth in
the playoffs. However, the Royals, after playing sub-.500 ball much of
the season, were hot in September; they had won nine of their last
twelve.

Lumbering into the visiting manager's office, Sharkey sat down
and pondered the never-ending puzzle known as the lineup. Carl
Caruby was back—he had finally returned from drug rehab—giving
Boston two of the best outfielders in the game when he was out there
with Davenport. But otherwise the defense was thin. Doug Maynard,
in center, was bothered by tendinitis in his right knee and was slumping at the plate after a sizzling August. Two newcomers—Tito Robles
and Alan Abramowitz, just up from Pawtucket—were already sidelined with injuries. Sharkey decided on a bold move: shifting Caruby
to center when Kane wasn't pitching and installing Kane in right.
Kane had raised his average to .306 and would finish the year with
more home runs—nine so far—than any other pitcher in baseball,
quite a feat even considering his DH duties. He had also collected
thirteen doubles and a pair of triples. Maynard would play center only
when Kane was on the mound and otherwise ride the bench along

with Moses, whose batting woes continued. He was hitting under .210 and hadn't driven in a run in nine games.

The new combination proved productive. The Sox pounded out seventeen hits, including homers by Bauer and Villalobos, and defeated Kansas City in the opener, 9–1, behind the strong pitching of Claudewell Diller.

Victories by the Yanks and Indians kept the pressure on Boston, however. The Red Sox showed signs of nerves the following night in a game they led, 5–3, in the ninth. Two walks, a bunt single and two wild pitches by Hazzard allowed the Royals to tie the score and put the winning run on third. Sharkey called time-out and made the unusual move of bringing in a position player—Kane—to work out of the jam.

Kane struck out the next batter, the dangerous Mike Sweeney, on a hard curve, then allowed a chopper to Langley that brought the runner charging home. Langley's throw to Ray Tarver appeared to be well in time—a play that Mr. Magoo could have called—but the runner was inexplicably ruled safe, giving Kansas City the win, and Sharkey burst out of the dugout, throwing his hands and kicking dirt. All he got for it—as he later learned, in a call from the league office— was a whopping five-thousand-dollar fine. He clattered down the clubhouse tunnel with a white froth marking the corners of his mouth. He sat heavily, threw down his cap and stomped on it. Took a swig of the pink stuff and stared disconsolately at his shoes. Looked up and caught sight of Ravinovich.

The Raven was chitchatting with Kane; his Sox cap, pulled low over his can opener of a nose, fluttered with laughter. The Sox had just blown a game that had probably cost them any chance of catching the Yankees and earning home-field advantage throughout the playoffs, and the Raven was clowning around like Rodney Dangerfield. Good God Almighty, what a loser, an asshole loser thoroughly

oblivious to the concerns of the ball club. A classic loser who would spread his losing ways like smallpox. And a killer, maybe, a dark, twisted man who would drag this club down just as he dragged down all the Red Sox teams he ever played for.

Fragments came back from the magazines: "Ravinovich confronted Yastrzemski in the crowded clubhouse. . . ." *The New Yorker.* "Rather die, it seems, than share the spotlight. . . ." *Esquire?* Or *Time?* Didn't matter. Only now mattered, and Sharkey saw with alarm that the Raven had shifted into an imaginary batting stance, showing something to Kane. Instructing Kane, who was batting for a higher average than six of the regulars. No doubt advocating his own ferocious uppercut, an approach that would never in a million years work for a batter with a hitch like Kane's. He might go into a tailspin like Mad Dog, not get another hit the rest of the fall.

The idea touched a torch to some cerebral gasket, blowing gasoline into Sharkey's boiler. He bounded up and across the room to end the ill-advised clinic. He stuck his nose right up in the Raven's face.

"No! You are not to give this man batting instructions!"

The Raven's fierce blue eyes showed only the quickest flash of surprise. Then came the anger that always lay just beneath the surface, a temper of such hair-trigger volatility that he once punched out a maître d' for trying to take his suit jacket. He came right back at Sharkey with a sputtering blast from his half-amputated mouth.

"Fuck you, Fish! You forgettin' who I am? Four hundred and ninety-eight fuckin' home runs! You don't think I'm qualified to give the man a tip?"

"I don't care who you are! I don't care what Wolf says, or who you know on the board—I don't want you bothering these guys!"

"You're history, you mess with me!" Ravinovich stabbed a finger into Sharkey's chest, a long, thin digit that was like a knife where it hit. "You think you're hot shit, but I know a thing or two about this

game! I ain't bothering anybody! Ask him, ask him yourself—was I bothering you, Ron? Interfering in some way?"

"It was pure wisdom to me, man; you're the fuckin' Oracle of Delphi far as the curveball." Kane grinned, enjoying the conflict. He liked to see people clash, their rough edges grinding like stripped gears. It was so much more real than the phony-baloney civility you saw almost all the time, people hiding their resentments and hatreds, their pain. Shed that veneer and rip into each other, that was the only way to see what people were really like, who was dominant, who was submissive and weak; it was the thing that shaped the whole world, put some men and nations in power, turned the rest into nothing but pissant followers. "You show me how you swing," Kane said to Ravinovich, "and I'll know what not to do."

"This ain't a joke," Sharkey said. "You, get out! Players only in here!" He looked Ravinovich straight in the eyes.

"Since when?"

"Since right now! Go, or I'll have the cops throw you out of here." Sharkey swung his face to Kane. "Ron, I want to see you in my office."

Sharkey led the way and turned to make sure the Raven was leaving—he lingered at the door and finally disappeared through it. The whole club was watching: Mad Dog, Castillo, Frolicky, Cool Daddy—everyone; the clash had turned into quite a little drama. Kane straggled into the office, dropping into the chair opposite Sharkey's desk. His hair was still wet from the shower, hanging in commas on his forehead.

"That old geek ain't nothing to worry about," Kane said.

"I disagree with you." Sharkey reminded Kane that a homicidal maniac might well be tracking the team—and the Sox were fighting to secure a playoff spot. "I'm not saying Ravinovich is a killer, nothing of the sort—I just don't trust him. He's a spoiled, self-centered

jerk, and always has been. A distraction. He'd love nothing more than everyone paying attention to him when they should be paying attention to baseball."

"A legend. What the papers say."

"Forget the goddamn papers. I'm warning you, Ron, like I'm going to warn everybody: Stay away from him."

"Right." Kane sat slouched, unconcerned.

"I'm dead serious. Now I want to ask a question: You have my tobacco tin? I think you—"

" 'Nito had it."

"Benito? How the hell did he get it?"

"Or Langley. Somebody had it."

"I know *somebody* had it. I want *you* to see about getting it back!" Sharkey clenched his jaw. The blood rose in his long face, anger forcing it up through faulty pressure lines. Sharkey fought to control it, knowing Kane's temperament, knowing how badly Kane could respond to rigid authority. "If you find it, I want the damn thing. And stay away from that asshole Ravinovich. He's a bad influence. Now, go on."

Kane got up and left. Sharkey squeezed his eyes shut, wondering if he should call Wulfmeyer, warn him about the clash with Ravinovich. Surely the Raven would go bitching to Henrietta. Hell, Wolf wasn't even returning his phone calls. Incommunicado. What could that mean? Domato had said he wasn't doing well: pale, agitated, throwing tantrums, sometimes when there was nobody in the room.

Luckily, Old Gordo was hanging on; he'd sat up again yesterday, according to Stu. He was overjoyed to learn that his club was still in the race. Poor bastard, waiting his whole life to win.

Sharkey saw Castillo about to leave and moved to confront him at the door. He minced no words: Where was the tobacco tin?

"You get loss, no speaka me," Castillo said.

"I want that thing—hand it over!"

"You play me. No bench."

"Give me the tin and we'll talk!"

"No, no have. *No lo tengo.* Look in locker. Look." Castillo gestured toward his cubicle. Sharkey took a cursory glance, but he knew it was hopeless. It wasn't here. Castillo had put it somewhere, or Kane still had it; maybe they had lost the damn thing. Honus Wagner had scratched his name right into the metal. These jokers, they'd probably throw it under a steamroller. Sharkey cursed and moved away. Damn.

The stress of the game hadn't been as intense as this series of knuckleheaded conversations here in the clubhouse: Ravinovich, Kane, Castillo—boom, boom, boom. Like dealing with Curly, Moe and Larry, one after the other. Could anyone imagine it, seeing him amble out to the mound, seeing Sharkey's face on TV as he met before the game with the umpires? Could anyone even guess what his life was really like?

A thunderstorm had come in. Lightning flashes and rolling, crackling thunder kept Sharkey awake much of the night. Twice between 3:10 and 3:20 A.M. the phone rang. Nobody there. By morning the storm had eased to a drizzle, and he got up, head pounding, toes numb, his sinuses so jammed up it felt like somebody had stuffed a couple of pecans up his nostrils.

He peeked out, thinking he might walk to Starbucks, and saw a cardboard box on the hallway floor, about the size of a hatbox. Written across the top was his name—SHARKEY—in black marking pen. The box was wrapped tight with duct tape.

Sharkey picked it up, wondering what the heck it was. He brought it inside, set it on the lacquered wooden desk. He hadn't ordered anything. He pulled at the tape. A gift? Well, Lohaus, the

Royals' manager, was an old friend, one of baseball's truly decent people. Lohaus, maybe—a smoked ham, something like that, to wish the Sox luck the rest of the way. A hell of a guy, Lohaus.

Stripping off more of the tape, Sharkey noticed leakage—blood? Could it be blood, dripping out? Christ, not another dead fish. A catfish? It was heavy as a chicken. His hands moved quickly, yanking the last strip of tape, pulling it open.

A head. A human head.

Oh GOD! A goddamned human head! Like some movie prop, severed at the neck, a thin, wizened head, duct tape wrapped crudely a couple times around the mouth. The skin was pale white and just beginning to become mottled with blue. He wasn't long dead. The face looked about seventy. Whoever he was, he was bald except for a gray fringe of hair. A long, curving gash traced the arc of the hairline, and two short, parallel cuts were centered in the middle of the skull, a couple inches above the forehead.

The marks of the ritual killer.

The head wore wire-frame glasses, one lens badly scratched.

Sharkey was not so fortunate as to pass out; instead he nearly gagged up the masticated vestiges of last night's Chinese chicken salad and popped out in a glistening cold sweat. Leaving the box on the desk, he staggered to the bed. He fell into the pillow and lay sweating a long time before the awareness crystallized that he had to collect himself, do something.

Do what? Rolling over, staring at the ceiling, Sharkey began to consider the ramifications of this royal mind-fuck. What he should do—what any rational, responsible person would do—was to call the cops. But the cops were just waiting for one more scrap of evidence against him. If there was any certainty here, it was this: A human head in Sharkey's possession would require a lot of explaining, most of it before a jury.

Sharkey sat up. Get rid of it. That was the only answer. Get rid of the goddamn thing.

How? He had to think. Think it through. He liked to imagine he was quick-witted under fire, that when the pressure was on, when it was late in the game and his pitcher was tiring, or when he was trailing in the ninth with a runner aboard, he could make clear-minded decisions. Now he had this severed head—a real jam. A human head. He couldn't just throw it away, couldn't leave it in a field, toss it in a Dumpster. He owed it to society—owed it to this man's family, his relatives—to get the head into the proper hands.

All right. That made sense. He could never live with himself if he did anything else. Still, it had to be anonymous. He couldn't mail a severed head, couldn't take it to the post office. Unthinkable.

All right. All right. One step at a time. Rewrap it. No matter what, he had to rewrap it. He'd need some tape—the old stuff on the box was ruined.

Sharkey got up, wiped the blood off the table, and put the box in the bathtub. Let it drip there. Hung out the DO NOT DISTURB sign and took a cab to the hardware store. Found what he needed, returned and got back to work. Wrapped the package right in the tub, pulling the tape tight, sealing the corners first.

When he was halfway finished, the phone rang. Loud as an air-raid siren. It was Domato, a floor up.

"Fish, hey, what's happening?"

"What do you mean?" Sharkey froze.

"Just asking. Finally spoke to Wolf a minute ago. Man, I'm telling you—lay low."

"Why? What's up?"

"He got wind of your fight with Ravinovich. He's really freaking out. Raven went straight to Henrietta and made a stink."

"Surprise, surprise."

"Anyway, I'm thinking about lunch and a matinee up the street. That new Richard Dreyfuss movie is out."

"Not today, Stu. Just going to hang around and, ah, take it easy."

"Cameron Diaz is in it. Uzi says it's great." Domato lobbied a minute and gave up.

Sharkey returned to the box. Oh, God, how he would like to hang around and take it easy. Or see a movie. He finished retaping the box, the top and all the corners, and wiped it off, checking carefully against leaks. Washed out the tub, got everything cleaned up. Tucked the box under his arm and hustled out to the car.

The trunk seemed the only place to put it. He wedged it where it wouldn't bounce around and took off toward the nearest police station.

A very tricky matter now, to leave it where the box would be found and yet Sharkey himself would not be noticed. Extreme caution. That was the watchword. He crossed some railroad tracks, drove through a busy, tattered commercial strip and found a low, glass-fronted substation next door to a Staples office supply. Sharkey parked and got out, casually as his mushy knees could manage, and took a stroll in the rain past the substation. There were surveillance cameras scoping the entire perimeter. Not good. Time for Plan B.

There was no Plan B.

Cold sweat began to ooze out again. He would have to do it at night. Think, damn it. A bag. He might need a bag. He walked into the Staples, bought a marking pen and a bunch of odds and ends, and drove back to the hotel. He carried the head back upstairs in the Staples bag, cleared room in the mini-refrigerator, stacking the little bottles of liquor and snacks on the counter, and stored the head inside. Keep it cool. Keep it from decomposing.

Sharkey dead-bolted the door and tried to sleep. He rolled around like a pig on a spit, thinking about the head, about who might have

left it for him. Ravinovich was one obvious answer. After the clash in the clubhouse, the Raven was certainly of a mind to retaliate in some hostile way, and what was more hostile, more symbolic of hostility, than a decapitated head? If Ravinovich was indeed the killer, he had also left that priceless little note in Boston, the threat about ripping Sharkey's head off and throwing it down a sewer. The hatred ran deep. It preceded the tiff over batting instructions, that was for sure.

Still, other possibilities festered in Sharkey's mind: Castillo, Kane, Davenport . . . a lot of them. Tortuous strands of thought run through a manager's mind in the middle of the night, when he is skittering toward madness, and Sharkey played with those strands like a frolicking cat, spooling them out, seeing where they'd go, chasing them to all sorts of wild ends. He could invent ridiculous leaps of logic to connect the murders to Domato, or to the club's play-by-play announcers, or the equipment man. The dark fantasies flickered for hours, until Sharkey finally got up bug-eyed, feverish with exhaustion, and rode the team bus to Kauffman Stadium like a man headed to the gallows.

The media throng outside the clubhouse looked like Huns assaulting a French castle. Another body had been found, only a body, the head having been altogether removed, and of course they wanted to know if there was a connection to "the Red Sox murders," as some headline writer had dubbed them. Sharkey kept them out of the locker room; that was his policy now, until the whole friggin' year was over. Keep the bastards out, cut down on the distractions.

Intermittent rain continued to fall. After three fitful innings, consuming four interminable hours, the contest was postponed. Sharkey returned to the hotel, got out the head, and wrote on the box, using his left hand to disguise his writing:

TO: KANSAS CITY POLICE DEPT.

He frowned, studied the childlike block letters, and wrote RETURN in front of it—RETURN TO: KANSAS CITY POLICE DEPT. Imply it was theirs. Better idea.

Finished, satisfied with the lettering, he wrapped the box in a sheet and stuck it in the Staples bag. He waited until 2:00 A.M. and set out on his ghastly mission. For half an hour he drove around before seeing Yancy's Doughnuts, a large, octagonal kiosk out on the commercial strip. He parked along a side wall.

Yellow neon tubes gave the place otherworldly illumination, rising vertically at every fold in the wall. There was a single patrol car in the lot, two officers standing at the walk-up window.

Sharkey kept his engine running. He waited until the cops had driven off. The lone employee disappeared from the window and Sharkey made his move, carrying the package quickly to the counter, extracting the box and leaving it right there, next to the napkin dispenser.

Then he hurried back to the car and vanished into the night.

The following evening, under a wondrous full moon, the Red Sox stranded nine base runners in a 3–1 defeat. The season's final record, 97–65, placed them three behind New York and one up on Cleveland.

23

Wulfmeyer peered through the cigarette smoke, thinking what a sight it must have been—Henrietta in bed with the chief of police. It was a disturbing image, like some sort of bestiality, though the real kicker, what he dared not tell her, was that her hard-won intelligence was actually no better than Mulgrove's.

She offered it with uninflected fatalism: Members of the task force had questioned Kane prior to game one of the first-round play-offs in Chicago. The Sox had opened on the road, where Kane, despite the meddling cops, had fired a brilliant one-hitter. His overall record now stood at seventeen wins and two defeats, with an earned-run average of 0.63, staggering figures for any hurler, never mind one burdened by the pressures of hiding a long string of heinous murders.

"But we don't know what he told them, if anything," Wolf pointed out. "We don't even know what the hell they were trying to find out."

"You can bet they weren't asking for autographs," Henrietta said.

"I wouldn't be so sure about that. You seen the figures on eBay?"

Henrietta stubbed out her Kool. She ignored the comment and

said Hardeway was exasperated. The bottom line, so far—thankfully for the Red Sox—was a remarkable shortage of physical evidence. Nothing at all to link Kane to any headless corpses. That might soon change, however. Crime Scene in Detroit had turned up a number of human hairs that did not match the victim there.

"They're going to want samples—hair samples—from everybody on the roster," Henrietta said.

"Correct me if I'm wrong," Wulfmeyer said, "but didn't that one happen in a hair salon?"

"I think it did."

"That makes me—I mean, could that affect . . . ? I wonder how often they swept the floor?"

"I should know that?" Henrietta's voice crackled like a downed power line. She was especially on edge, not only because of the growing police interest in Kane, but because tomorrow night was the next money drop.

Only an illegal transfer from the Amalgamated pension pool and some creative chicanery involving the Sox's discretionary funds had enabled her to finally pull together the $10 million.

"It's just—" Wolf couldn't drop the subject. "How can they rely on hair samples?"

"I don't know!" Henrietta snapped. "Do you know, Mr. Rhetorical Bullshit?"

"No, I don't know! If I knew, I wouldn't have asked!" Wolf cursed and looked away. He wished he could get out. He had begun to envy people he saw on the street: delivery drivers, hardware clerks, even that filthy wino living in the refrigerator box on James Avenue. No front teeth, but he'd grin for a buck, and his problems surely paled compared to the magnitude of this predicament.

He watched her a moment, eyes cast to the Neiman, then darting to her cigarette case. She lit up another smoke. Wolf wasn't sure how much to lay on her. She wasn't coping well. Neither was he, actually.

"I spoke to Mulgrove," he said cautiously.

"Yes?"

Wolf told her the detective had scored on the ID. It was good news/bad news. They now knew the extortionist's true name: Dennis Vincent Tortolano, a fifty-two-year-old Indianapolis businessman who owned warehouses in Kansas City, Chicago and St. Louis. Unfortunately, he was a brother-in-law of Carlo "The Load" LoFrancesco, head of the powerful Chicago crime family, and believed to be active in the organization.

"Oh, that's just *fan-tas-tic,*" Henrietta said, agitated again. "So where's that leave us with Doyle's friends? Or don't they even know?" A cadre of Doyle Horgan's friends, themselves reputed gangsters in one of Boston's notorious Irish mobs, had been enlisted to try to intercept the extortionist or his emissary. They were planning to employ one of the Teamsters' tried-and-true means of persuasion to make sure the bastard understood that he'd collected quite enough money.

"They don't know yet," Wulfmeyer admitted. "I wonder if it would screw things up."

"Neville, I'm *sure* they'll want to know if they're pinching some other crime family."

"These guys are Teamsters, right? This can't be the first time they've—"

"Don't assume anything! I mean, right, okay, they're Teamsters, but we're talking about a world of unwritten rules, codes, et cetera, et cetera, we know nothing about. There's a pretty damn good chance they might, you know, object."

"Object to what?"

"To pinching these Chicago guys!"

"Oh, God, listen to you!" Wulfmeyer's voice rose in exasperation. "We're not pinching *them!* They're pinching *us,* for crying out loud!"

"Yeah, whatever. Neville, I just really think we should tell Doyle's

people up front. This ball-cock business has been in my family sixty years, and take my word for it, these people react very poorly to being jerked around."

"You let me worry about that," Wulfmeyer said decisively. He thought there was one other matter he should bring up—a possible solution to the Kane problem. The idea had been rolling around in his mind like a burning ingot, a painful idea, an idea he hated—and certainly *she* would hate it—but it was there, scalding his brain everywhere it hit. He couldn't ignore it.

He broached it by reminding her that they'd gleaned vital inside information on the nature of the serial murders—to wit, the mysterious parallel gashes found on the heads of the victims.

"So? We should do a quiz? Something on the Web site?"

"This is deadly serious, Henrietta."

"You're scaring me, Neville, you really are."

"You want to hear this?"

She nodded without speaking.

"All right, what they've got against Kane—one vital fact—is he's been in every city where there's been a murder. What if, and I ask this hypothetically, what if there were a murder—the same parallel gashes, the same decapitation, everything exactly the same—in another place, somewhere Kane wasn't?"

"How in the hell's *that* going to happen?" She braced herself.

Wolf plunged ahead, lowering his voice. "I'm thinking, again hypothetically, if some of Doyle's friends—"

"Oh, no! That's just about the most *asinine*—!"

"—were to find some guy—some bald guy, like in the other—"

"No way! Neville, you're crossing a line here—"

"—and, you know, *replicate* what Kane—"

"*Ab-so-lute-ly* not! We are not replicating any such thing!"

"Like what's so ridiculous?" Wolf's voice boomed back to full

volume. "Don't you understand what we've gone through getting to this point? What's at stake here? Jesus Christ on a Shetland pony, we're a few wins away from the motherfucking World Series! Think of the revenues, the title. Gordon's lifelong dream. You heard anything I've been saying these past few weeks? Iwo Jima? The Panama Canal? Twenty-five thousand fucking lives! Yellow fucking fever!"

"Calm down, Neville!"

"Maybe you still want to give him up? Turn him over to your lover boy?"

"Neville!"

"The man threw a one-hitter last night. Don't forget that little fact."

"Shut up! Shut up! I don't care if he hit five grand slams—we are *not* going to go out and *replicate* some atrocity. I have *got* to draw the line!"

He turned away, fuming, and surrendered in a mocking nanner-nanner tone: "I have *got* to draw the line!"

The White Sox turned home plate into a revolving door: seventeen runs in the worst slaughter in Red Sox playoff history.

Sharkey flew home in a state of almost catatonic numbness. His left ear had begun a high-pitched ringing that occasionally broke up into Morse code. Every time he closed his eyes he saw that wizened head, the little mustache. The horror of discovering the atrocity was rivaled only by the guilt he felt at passing it along. Some other poor sucker, probably some desk sergeant, now shared with him the unenviable knowledge of what it is like to open a box and find a severed head. It was not an experience that faded soon after impact.

His futility in reaching Wulfmeyer only added to Sharkey's anguish. He arrived at Fenway early, before game three, and marched

upstairs to confront him. Overpowering Samantha's rebuff, he barged into Wolf's inner sanctum. Wolf was on the phone; he covered the receiver and bared his teeth.

"Fish, get out of here!"

Sharkey held his ground. He said no way, he'd left four messages, and they were going to talk now or he was quitting and going to the cops.

"Jack, let me call you back," Wulfmeyer said, hanging up, forcing a quick laugh. "Sorry, Fish—fuck it, sit down. Sit! Let's talk, get that last notion out of your head. You're frustrated, and I don't blame you."

"It can't go on like this," Sharkey said. "Specifically, I—me—" He tapped his chest. "*I* can't go on like this!"

"Me neither! We're in the same goddamn boat!" Wulfmeyer lifted a stack of message slips, cursed the crisis at Tank Ball, and moved abruptly to his miniature wet bar. "You're a Stoli man, right? Let's have one. A drink to relax us. The kind of stress we've been under—"

"I'm ready to crack, Wolf. I swear to you!"

"Me too!" Another laugh, high and quick. "It's a fucking nightmare, isn't it? Don't think you're alone in this—oh, no. To reach for greatness—that's what we're really doing here—you pay a price. The stress, Jesus Christ, it's probably like Normandy, Omaha Beach." Wolf poured the vodkas and mentioned, as if in passing, that the task force wanted hair samples; they'd be down in the clubhouse before game time.

"Oh, that's no distraction," Sharkey said, taking the drink. He wasn't sure if Wolf caught the sarcasm.

"Won't take long. Fucking cops."

Sharkey sipped the vodka without tasting it. "Wolf, you heard about my clash with Ravinovich?"

"Yes, yes I did—and I'm none too happy about it. You should have heard Henrietta. Can't you just humor the asshole? Henrietta wants

him to experience this thing—a championship, if we get it. We're going to let the guy have access, period. He's dying, for chrissakes."

"Well, I doubt that. The guy's a fraud, and very possibly a serial killer. He's no more dying than you are. He's faking it to justify a big tribute, to drum up Hall of Fame votes." Sharkey's anger welled again. "Listen to what happened after the argument—the gift box I got."

"A gift box?" Wulfmeyer took a second to realize it was nothing from Macy's. "Don't tell me you got another barracuda? A sword-fish?"

"A head!"

"Head of what?"

"A *human* head!" Sharkey hissed. "A goddamned human head, Wolf! It was in a box, marked to me, outside my room in Kansas City!"

"You're kidding—was it real?"

"Of course it was real! Bled all over the place!"

"Holy God of mercy, shit! Hope you got rid of it."

"That's another— Never mind that. Never mind that fucking—" He couldn't even finish the sentence. "Point is, I think it came from Ravinovich. Ravinovich or Castillo, the little bastard; he might have my tobacco tin. But I've got a gut feeling it's the Raven." Sharkey noted the Raven's many prior scrapes with the law, the mysterious death of Rita Kataya.

"Keep an eye on the bastard," Wolf said finally. "Anything he does, you let me know—anything. But remember, we've got people watching him, our PI's, and you're going to have to try to relax. The White Sox, they're—"

"What if he comes after me? When I'm sleeping? Not that I sleep."

"Fish, listen, we're right in the thick of it now. We can't let these threats, all these problems, distract us. I was reading a quote, a great quote from Robert Oppenheimer: 'Sometimes the answer does not

lie in explaining away fear; sometimes it lies in courage.' Something like that. Oppenheimer, he built the bomb, you know. A goddamn genius. Blew up a hell of a lot of innocent people with that thing, but we did it for a reason, a legitimate reason, and we won. Won that war just like we're going to win this championship. It's a big thing to win, I'm telling you. Sometimes you just gotta grit it out, be strong—and really kick some ass."

The unprecedented security in the clubhouse should have eased Sharkey's mind, assuaging his fears about being attacked by the psychopath. Instead he fixated on the possibility of being arrested. The fear that they would link him with that severed head—through a loose hair, perhaps, or a fingerprint—blew through him like an arctic wind.

He found it difficult to concentrate on the pregame routine. Wolf was right, sometimes courage was what mattered. It took all he could muster to assemble his players prior to game time and address them as a group. The Sox had been flat in game two in Chicago; Sharkey now felt the need to light into them, give them a blast of the old Knute Rockne rah-rah-rah.

"This is it, men! A game as important as any so far this season, and when we go out there, out there in front of these great fans of ours, we'd better show what we're made of! Show them some fight! Show them some killer instinct!" He thundered it and tried to gauge them, alert for some tic or change in posture that might betray the madman's identity.

Castillo's head had been turned, following the path of a fly up the wall. Kane clenched and unclenched his fists, tensing and relaxing, a slow pulse. Davenport's dark eyes swept the room. He and a few others—Mad Dog, too—had caught the relevance of it.

Ravinovich sat in front of the clubhouse TV, tuned low to a dog-food commercial.

"If we can beat this team—" Sharkey went on, "and we can!—and go on and take the next round, which I know we can!—then we're in the World Series!" He scanned the room. "You all know how important that is, what a dream it is. We've come a long way, gentlemen, and there's still a long way to go. We all want to play hard, think clearly, and look our best out there. Look like we belong at the top! That's why we're all getting haircuts."

"Haircuts?" The cry went up in unison. The expressions on their faces couldn't have betrayed more shock if he had pulled out a gun and shot himself. An option that was still in the back of Sharkey's mind.

"Yes, I know it's irregular; hell, I questioned it, too," Sharkey said, keeping the hard edge of authority in his voice. "But it's coming down from on high. Let's just bite the bullet this time, eh? Bite the bullet and do it. The guy there in the back, Jason, he's going to make us all look like Tom Cruise. Won't cost you a dime, 'cause Old Gordo's picking up the tab."

Sharkey couldn't believe what he was saying. A great salvo of bitches and moans rattled around, and then the guys began dragging themselves to the back of the clubhouse and falling into the swivel chair Stu had brought down from Advanced Sales. The barber, an FBI man, was practiced and quick, but he was no Cristophe. He seemed to be into flat tops and severe angles. Moses came away angry, and Johnny Uggams was so upset Sharkey had to come out of the office to calm him down. Then Sharkey sat down for a humiliating above-the-ear job that made his jaw look as long as a Buick.

Still, the feds were satisfied, and after the barber left with all his carefully labeled plastic bags, the Sox went out and reclaimed the advantage in the series, winning a defensive thriller, 3–1.

24

What should have been a joyride, guiding a team to the brink of the World Series, was instead, for Sharkey, only a grim endurance test for his ravaged nerves.

Kane's two-hitter, a nineteen-strikeout tour de force wrought by fastballs of 108 mph, dispatched the White Sox and moved Boston into a showdown with the Oakland A's, upset winners over the New York Yankees, for the American League title. The Red Sox traveled west, into another media firestorm, to meet an Oakland team with solid starting pitching and a lineup capable of scoring runs in clusters.

The opener played to form. Home runs by Kane, Larry Langley and Ray Tarver gave Boston a 4–1 lead through five, but Bryan Hazzard, who got the start, faltered and gave up a bases-loaded triple in the sixth. The A's added single runs in the seventh and eighth and held on to win, 6–4.

Claudewell Diller took the mound in game two and kept Oakland off balance with a dazzling display of control and changing speeds. He struck out nine and yielded only two unearned runs before

giving way to Rick Reeling in the ninth. Kelvin Briscoe's two-run double started the scoring for Boston, a play marred by injury: Briscoe retore the ligaments in his bad left knee on a hard slide into second, and had to be carried off the field. He would be out for the rest of the playoffs, depriving the Sox of much of their left-handed power. Still, with Bauer and Maynard contributing RBI singles, the Red Sox claimed a 5–2 victory and leveled the series.

Kane made his next start in game three in Boston. He was brilliant and erratic, hitting speeds of 111 mph but walking the leadoff batters in three of the first seven innings. The A's capitalized twice, scoring in the third on a bloop double and in the sixth on a fielder's choice and a rare error by Villalobos. The Boston attack was anemic. Langley scored while Moses was trapped in a rundown, but otherwise only three runners advanced past first base. The Red Sox squandered the great opportunity that Kane's start gave them and fell, 2–1.

In the restroom afterward, as Sharkey stepped to the urinal, he caught sight of a familiar stooped, white-haired figure exiting a toilet stall.

The Barnacle.

"Hey, Augie, how ya doin' there?" Schachter said in his avuncular way. "Tough one today."

"Any tougher and I throw myself in the Charles."

"You won't mind a few questions, I hope. Specific points."

"I'm sure it'll lift my spirits. If it's about those hair samples—"

"No, naaah, something else—if you got a minute."

Sharkey tried to finish up. The only thing worse than being interrogated by the cops was being interrogated while pissing. Because the clubhouse was packed, and an Iraqi army of reporters was camped outside, he led Schachter out a side entrance and down a narrow service tunnel that snaked through the bowels of the park. They found a cramped storage room stocked with brooms, snail pellets, resin bags and gallon bottles of cleaning solution.

"The A's, they got moxie," Schachter said. "Surprised you had Davenport running in the sixth."

"That wasn't illegal, was it?" Sharkey's edgy sarcasm masked the fact he was a hairbreadth away from losing it, just screaming out loud. Surely the papers would be second-guessing the same move—the right play, percentage-wise, though the failed stolen-base attempt had killed a possible rally. "You're wanting to know about what, exactly?"

"About Kansas City. Just a couple things."

Kansas City. The words hit like a cattle prod. Sharkey tried to affect a look of blank-faced innocence.

"That one, you know, was quite a thing," Schachter went on, "because the head turned up later. It's our only case, so far, where the head was actually removed from the crime scene—eleven miles, I believe—and still ended up being recovered by the authorities."

Sharkey lifted his eyebrows in a deliberate attempt at surprise. He didn't trust himself to speak.

"So I'm just wondering: See anything strange?"

"Strange?" His mind seemed to undergo a meltdown, his left cheek suddenly twitching like the haunches of a Clydesdale. "Nothing I remember offhand. In terms of actual strangeness."

"Hotel security guard says he spotted you leaving one night around two in the morning. Carrying a bag."

"I was meeting a woman. A woman in—ah—she was in Kansas City, of course. A woman I met last season, and, you know, I had something for her." He was taking her a gift, Sharkey went on. A vase he'd picked up. He felt compelled to elaborate, touching on her love of roses, and in a panic, certain his lies were transparent as window glass, he decided to add something else. To hell with Wolf; he told Schachter flat out it might be Benito Castillo. Castillo, who had actually spoken about slitting Sharkey's throat.

"He's been ruled out," Schachter said flatly.

"Ruled out? How can that—?"

"We're sure. It ain't him."

Stunned, Sharkey voiced his suspicions about Ravinovich, the fact that the Raven had lost his cool in the clubhouse in KC, the second night there. Schachter pressed for details. Sharkey gave him everything he knew about the Raven's checkered background—Rita Kataya, all of it. He sensed that the hard facts were not impressing Schachter to the degree he had hoped. He wondered if Schachter might be one of those inveterate Ravinovich fans.

"Anything else?" Schachter looked up from his notebook.

"Well, that night, you know, on my way to this woman's, I thought I actually saw him out on the road." Sharkey hoped to make doubly damn sure the cops looked into Ravinovich. "Surprised me. It was hard to tell—so dark."

"Where do you think you saw him?"

Sharkey scowled a moment. "Think it was—ah, oh Christ, is there a Yancy's Doughnuts?"

Her self-righteous bullshit was driving Wulfmeyer crazy. There was no dealing with her, no way of appeasing her, after the latest money drop—an unmitigated disaster. The desire to work an ill-advised sting on the extortionists had resulted in a shoot-out between the LoFrancesco crime family of Chicago and the Gallivan men of South Boston. The hail of gunfire caused the deaths of PI Jack Mulgrove and six others. Amid the wail of police sirens, a man in a rented red Taurus sped away with the $10 million.

Henrietta's whole attitude seemed to suggest that the fiasco had been Wulfmeyer's express vision, that he hoped to trump himself by escalating the death toll.

He rolled his eyes; that got her right back up on her high horse.

"I am dead serious! You think this is some kind of *joke?* I am so *ashamed* of what this season's come down to, I can hardly look at myself in the mirror!"

He smirked. "Imagine that."

"You better imagine it!" She crushed out her cigarette. "You'd better *damn well* imagine it! Now: Chief Hardeway was over last night. Here's something else we've got to worry about—"

"You're pregnant?"

"Shut up! Shut up right now, Neville Wulfmeyer!"

"Why? To listen to you? No thanks." There was no point trying to treat her with respect, not anymore. Respect was a two-way street. She had veered down some one-way alley because she could not handle her own part of the blame for losing the $10 million and getting the PI killed.

"Let me remind you, you strutting ass, I'm trying to keep us informed," Henrietta said. "You want to hear what Hardeway says?"

"It isn't encouraging, is it?"

"No, it's not. Not in the least. The police have learned, apparently, and I don't know from where, that there are certain records we failed to turn over. Crap, mostly, but one of the missing items is Kane's personnel file—and since I haven't seen it, since you're in charge of those things, I'm wondering what exactly is in there."

Wulfmeyer exhaled sharply. He had made a particular point of keeping Kane's file in the security of his office safe, and he began a mental inventory of the file from the standpoint of what might interest the police. It contained dozens of progress reports, mostly written by Stu, chronicling Kane's stints at Raleigh and Sarasota in the Sox's minor-league system and his subsequent lengthy apprenticeship in the Dominican Republic. Some were disturbing: fights, drunkenness, vandalism. At Raleigh he had knocked the head off a statue of a Civil War general—an act that only in retrospect took on its deepest significance.

The behavioral problems were such that Kane spent less than a month in each minor-league town. The club invested a small fortune in organizing the special instructional league in the Dominican so Kane could develop as a pitcher away from the pressures of public scrutiny. Hiding him offered the hope of curbing his antisocial tendencies before they derailed him completely, the way they'd done the young pro-football quarterback, Ryan Leaf. A kid that age had to be handled with the utmost care.

Kane's grooming had included two sessions a week with the renowned French psychotherapist Dr. Jean-Luc Matthieu, a man specially enlisted by the club. Matthieu's voluminous report was also in the file. The doctor had detailed all the essential facts of Kane's background—the beatings he suffered from his father, the drug abuse and manic-depressive rages that destroyed his mother. The family's poverty and rootlessness. The two years Ron spent, as a young teen, working in a Mexican slaughterhouse, and finally, the futile attempts of Catholic social workers and teachers in Odessa to straighten him out.

Wulfmeyer remembered a crinkled file photo of Kane's dad, the late Richard Dalton Kane, an "American Gothic" shot taken outside a Texas roadhouse. Richard had been in his mid-sixties, a severe man, bald, his eyes filled with the fire of a Baptist preacher, though he was no man of God. A truck driver, a mechanic, a service-station attendant, Richard was a hard man who had passed along the genetic makeup of a superathlete and psychological scars that defied full understanding. Wulfmeyer could recall only a single verbatim phrase from Matthieu's pedantic assessment—Ron Kane was "a troubled, troubled young man"—but the gist of the findings was clear.

What wasn't spelled out was that Ron was not so different, really, from a lot of other young athletes. The Sox had taken a chance on him just as they had taken chances on Davenport, Caruby, Castillo—and even, going way back, on Jimmy Piersall and Kent Ravinovich.

What separated them from Kane was really only a matter of degree. Those others were just as incapable of controlling their dark impulses; theirs were simply more benign.

Wolf did his best to summarize the troubling material for Henrietta and concluded, "Those things are headed straight for the shredder."

"I wouldn't waste any time. We'll have to say, I guess, there isn't any such file. Or it was stolen."

"Right. Let them try to prove we're lying." Wulfmeyer regarded her a moment, a woman so rent by inner conflict it was a wonder she could see straight. It occurred to him that he needed to defuse the acrimony; they'd have to make a diligent effort to work together, no matter how difficult it was, over the final few weeks. "We're just about there," he assured her. "Pretty soon you'll be saying, 'Thank you, Neville Wulfmeyer.' You'll be damn glad I was your point man on this thing, you mark my words."

Sharkey tweaked one of his pregame rituals, cocking his cap ninety degrees sideways to fill out the lineup card, and it seemed to help. The bats came alive and the Sox won three straight, including a 9–1 victory by Kane, to vanquish Oakland and advance to their first World Series since 1986.

They would meet another wild-card team, the Dodgers, who had come on strong in the playoffs, winning seven out of eight. It would be the biggest event of Sharkey's life, his chance at redemption after all the years of losing. A chance that might not come again for years, if at all, considering the problems surrounding the club.

Two off days were scheduled before Saturday's first game at Fenway, giving a brief rest to the overworked pitching staff. Sharkey decided he would go with Frank Frolicky in the opener and Kane in

game two. Travel days would enable Kane to start game five and probably even pitch game seven, if the Series went that far.

Sharkey tried in vain to will himself into a relaxed, positive state of preparedness. His nerves were bound up like springs. He feared picking up the papers or turning on the news; any moment might bring the discovery of another victim or a corroborated report that the players themselves were suspects in the murder spree. That the task force had managed to keep that angle out of the headlines represented a resolve on the part of authorities that was truly impressive. They were determined to keep the circus from exploding into a full-blown Barnum & Bailey extravaganza, issuing nothing but no-comments and denials. Still, the rumors were swirling. The idea was out there. Sharkey saw the evidence of it on Saturday morning as Annie drove him to the ball park.

On Commonwealth Avenue and Beacon Street, sidewalk hucksters offered T-shirts and bumper stickers, some with a serial-killer theme: RED SOX: MURDER AT THE PLATE, and, BOSTON: BE-HEADING TOWARD A CHAMPIONSHIP! The day was cool and blustery, animating thousands of GO RED SOX! banners hanging from lampposts and shop windows. Annie kissed him and presented Sharkey with a good-luck charm—a silver leprechaun pin—before he stepped from the car and entered the media crush.

Sharkey had to fight through the crowd to the clubhouse. The hours before game time disappeared in a blur of images: Kane releasing tension with a succession of loud whoops, Ravinovich laughing and wearing Langley's jockstrap like a nose helmet, the team assembling in the dugout for player introductions.

Hairy white clouds frosted the sky. The atmosphere was surreal, electric.

Frolicky was masterful for eight innings, but he walked two batters in the ninth, and Kane, playing right, mishandled a shot into the

gap, allowing both runners to score. The Sox rallied with successive hits by Caruby, Davenport and Maynard, and the game was tied until the twelfth, when the Dodgers roughed up reliever Rick Reeling for five runs to win going away.

The loss weighed heavily on Sharkey as he entered the sullen clubhouse. The Sox had just forked over home-field advantage to a club as hot as a broiler oven. His own frustration was also apparent on the faces of his players. A shouting match erupted in front of Castillo's locker—Castillo and Ravinovich. Sharkey bounded across the room to break it up, chewing them both out. Castillo shouted back and moved toward the showers, but the Raven, grabbing center stage, made a joke of Sharkey's authority.

"Right you are, Skipper," he said mockingly, leering at Kane. "Man sure knows baseball. Had more than a measly cup of coffee in the big time, that's for sure. A cup of coffee and a doughnut."

"Just drop it!" Sharkey ordered.

"Lit up the Appalachian League. Hoooo-boy." The Raven wasn't letting it die. "The crowds down there, the women—"

Kane laughed. His eyes had that electric glow of intensity, but he had performed poorly: the error in right and three strikeouts.

Sharkey glared hard at Ravinovich and said, "Speaking of women, let me ask you about one: Rita Kataya."

The Raven's expression changed, his chinless jaw dropping slightly, and he demanded to know why Sharkey would bring up Rita Kataya. Sharkey confronted him with details of the late sexpot's death and the Raven's apparent fixation with her. Ravinovich was visibly shaken. He tried to dismiss Sharkey's suspicions out of hand, laughing again in Kane's direction, but when Sharkey firmly suggested he leave, the Raven accepted the chance to back off.

"I'm going to do that. Got to rehearse my speech." He gestured toward Kane. "Don't forget, Ron."

"I might. But I've got that party."

"Come after, have one for the road. Remember, I'm not just a Raven, I'm a night owl." Ravinovich cracked another grin, not so carefree this time, and reeled off his address, thumbs up, before finally moving away, a slow amble, making it a point to betray no outward change of demeanor. But Sharkey knew he would be furious; he'd hold a grudge.

As soon as Ravinovich left the clubhouse, Sharkey turned to Kane. "Follow me. Let's talk a minute."

"Let me grab a shower first."

"Now. This instant." The terse power of the command was enough to move Kane, whose circuits were programmed to respond to a challenge. Kane threw his wadded uniform shirt into his locker and set off toward Sharkey's office, bare-chested, loose, pores still flowing.

The chair opposite the desk was skewed at an angle. Kane knocked it straight with his knee and dropped himself into it, running his hands through sweaty coils of hair.

"What's up?" Expecting his wrath.

Sharkey studied him a moment: the sinewy chest, strewn with faint freckles, wide and strong like a doryman's; the copper hair, wet and plastered against the skin; the thick blue veins of his neck.

"I don't trust that guy, and if you're smart, if you're thinking about your own well-being, I don't think you should either." Sharkey tried to tread carefully. He could see, almost smell, the volatility in Kane, and he wanted to be firm and still defuse it.

"Ain't a threat to me," Kane said.

"He might be and you don't know it. What's he talking about? Later on?"

Kane fixed on him. He shrugged.

"Wants to have a few beers. He asked me to come by, but I'm going to a party."

"You know you're pitching tomorrow?"

"Yeah. And we got his tribute."

"You should get some rest."

"Fuck that." Kane got up and moved to the door. He looked back with a strange indifference. "You and your goddamn orders. It's just baseball. Who the hell cares?"

"I care!" Sharkey said hotly. "This whole city cares—all these fans! It'd be nice to win this thing. It woulda been nice to get ahead in this series."

Kane smirked. He let the words tumble out recklessly: "I thought you got a head in Kansas City."

And he laughed and walked out.

25

Sharkey sat in the dark of the apartment, his Stoli propped at his elbow, thinking it over one more time. There seemed only two real possibilities: Kane had left him that head in KC, or Ravinovich had done it and been so brash as to brag about it. Maybe the Raven really was dying. Maybe he was so sick and twisted up, so angry, that he was killing and yakking to his friend with no heed of the repercussions.

One or the other. The only other scenarios—that Wolf had told someone, or the cops had let it slip—seemed too unlikely. For a moment Sharkey imagined that the head had become some macabre in-house joke among his players, but he dismissed the idea and lifted the receiver. He dreaded the sound of his voice.

" 'Lo. Raven."

"Kent? Hey, listen, it's Fish. Got a second?"

"Yeah, a couple seconds. What's the deal?" Coolness, but he was willing to hear the apology. He assumed that Fish was calling to apologize.

Sharkey edged his way in, mentioning the tribute, how much he was looking forward to it. Then he voiced his fears, the serial-killer madness. "You know, Kent, how much that weighs on my mind. Been going on since June."

"I did *not* kill Rita Kataya!"

"You know what? I believe you. I think I believe you because it's probably Kane."

"He killed Rita?"

"No, no, those other guys. Killing those people all over the country. Unless it's you, somehow, it's Kane. I'm almost sure of it. Watch out, stay away from him. I'm warning you."

"You're warning me?" Ravinovich sounded incredulous. "Let's cut to the chase, Fish. What are you saying?"

Sharkey couldn't imagine being any more clear. "I am saying Kane may be the serial killer." He said it one word at a time, like speaking to a five-year-old. "Don't have him by for a few beers, if that's still your plan. Call and cancel. *Stay away* from him—he's *dangerous.*"

"Right. Like I'll believe that?" The Raven's voice became accusatory. "You're not going to shut me out with some stupid-ass story like that. Like it or not, I'm a Red Sox—always was, always will be. No shit-faced, fucking, has-been manager is going to tell me who to hang out with! You can take that advice and shove it right up your blowhole, mister, because it's not going to work!"

Ravinovich hung up. Sharkey sighed heavily, wondering what was next. It was almost eleven. He polished off the rest of the Stoli in the dark. Tried another call to Wolf, left another message, and finally gave up and went to bed.

Morning was dreary—heavy clouds and wind. Sleepless and unshaven, Sharkey got to Fenway early and marched straight up to Wolf's office, barging past Samantha. He found Wulfmeyer tilted

back, tossing a rubbery Koosh ball toward the ceiling. He sat up spastically and glared.

"Why the hell don't you knock?"

"Look, we need to talk. I know who it is!"

"Talk? Don't you have a game coming up? But, hey, it's only the motherfucking World Series." Wulfmeyer's quick rat-a-tat laugh was filled with ridicule. He quaffed from a tumbler of Chivas while Sharkey repeated his assertion. "I'm very impressed—you got the answers and the entire federal task force hasn't been able to make that determination."

Sharkey recounted the conversation with Kane. Wolf immediately debunked his reasoning.

"You told me that same thing—the same head, right? Kansas City? I told . . . well, I pretty much had to tell Henrietta. That's probably how Kane found out—or from one of her people."

"Henrietta knows?" Sharkey swallowed hard.

"She's got, you know, influence. Jesus, what if you don't tell her and she hears it elsewhere? Anyway, who the hell knows how many *she* told? That loose tongue of hers . . ."

"Oh . . . my . . . God!"

"Fish, listen! We're all under a lot of stress. You've got to forget about this and focus! We're in the middle of the goddamn World Series!"

"Wolf!"

"We blew a big chance yesterday. Still can't figure out why you took Frolicky out."

"He'd thrown a hundred and thirty-eight pitches!"

"Yeah, but our bullpen— All right, never mind, just focus. Focus! We got Kane throwing today, we'll even it up. Now, you've got to get going—I'm up to my eyeballs in this Ravinovich monstrosity. We're trying to get the sailboat airlifted in. And I don't think it's either one, frankly. This head thing, it's probably all over the ball club."

Wulfmeyer made a shooing motion and Sharkey reluctantly got up to leave. He turned around at the door.

"I may talk to Schachter."

"Yeah, right, you go ahead and do that—right when we're on the brink of a championship." He knew precisely what button to push. "Just go ahead and torpedo the big ship! The very moment it's coming in! That's exactly—*exactly!*—the type of thing Ravinovich would do!"

Henrietta was all gussied up, wearing pearls the size of goose eggs, a billowy saffron gown and enough makeup to whitewash a barn—all in preparation for the Raven's big day. Her mood, however, was icy as ever; she scarcely made eye contact as Wulfmeyer slipped into the office and sat down.

"Just about everything's set," he told her breezily, trying to avoid the blow-ups of recent meetings. "They're airlifting the sailboat. Should be arriving any minute."

"Cutting it close." She was terse, checking her watch.

"Plenty of time. Anyway, fuck, I'm just a little concerned. Fish thinks it's Kane. He threatened to go to the Barnacle."

"Is he?"

"I don't know. He thinks it's Kane or Ravinovich. I tried to convince him otherwise."

Henrietta opened her cigarette case and lit up. She said the task force had found disturbing evidence in its analysis of the hair samples. Hardeway had just told her last night.

"There was a match with Kane. The only player who matched."

"Isn't that the case—" Wulfmeyer shifted in his chair. "Didn't that occur in a hair salon?"

"Yes. Fortunately. It gave me quite a jolt, at first, when he told me. But it was a hair salon, like you say, and the evidence was not

exactly— Well, let's just say they were looking for a needle in a haystack in some respects."

"A lot of hair."

"Exactly. Kane's being in there, too. Luckily, he had a receipt. He'd gotten a trim."

Wulfmeyer stared, thinking about that.

"Makes sense, I guess," Henrietta said. "That he came earlier to check out the place."

"Probably got an awful cut." Wulfmeyer sighed heavily. For a moment he'd feared he might have to employ the forbidden Ravinovich videotape. But no. He was relieved. Relieved and beginning to sense they might yet make it to the wire. "We're down the home stretch," he said. "Some good baseball, a few hits out of these guys, and we'll do it. Faith. Faith. Nothing bad's going to happen."

"God forbid."

"God forbid."

A foot propped on the dugout step, Sharkey gazed out at the grandstands, filled with people and strangely dark, like the skies. Dark with heavy coats and rain gear, flecked with bright parkas, yellow slickers.

The gifts stood waiting on the infield under bright tarpaulins made to look like gift wrap: a forty-foot sailboat, the *RavenSea;* a combine, for the Raven's older brother, Karl, a Kansas farmer wiped out in the past summer's wheat blight; and, most spectacular of all, a cabernet Rolls-Royce limousine trimmed with inlaid zirconia. Etched on each side was a breathtaking blackbird, shown in profile, with calligraphy below it: THE RAVEN—NO AUTOGRAPHS PLEASE.

Without warning, Wulfmeyer appeared in the dugout.

"Have you seen him?" he demanded.

Sharkey wheeled around. "Raven? No, no I haven't."

"Where the hell is he? Damn it!"

The presentation was running late. Wulfmeyer stared at his watch: sixteen minutes late. He groused about the snafu; the network was on his ass, the commissioner's office had flunkies running around upstairs saying let's go, let's go, let's go.

Sharkey frowned and turned back to face the field. After Wulfmeyer's callous reprimand a few hours ago, he was in no mood to be solicitous. Wulfmeyer snapped open a cell phone and desperately punched some numbers.

"Stu," he hollered, "no dice. Fish hasn't seen him either. Keep calling! Try him again at home. Find him and get your fanny down here!" Wolf switched off the cellular and jammed it into his coat pocket. "Shit!" He glowered at the field and then turned to look at Sharkey. "Three hours. Three hours I've been trying to reach that asshole!"

"He's never been very reliable."

"We're going to have to get started. Any minute."

Sharkey stared at the field. He recognized that big-haired Vegas singer, what's-his-name, who had flown in to emcee, standing out near the Rolls. A mini-Jumbotron screen had been wheeled into place in short center field to show highlights of the Raven's illustrious career.

Domato burst in. "Wolf, trouble," he said, his face white and anguished.

"What is it? Where is he?"

"The killer—last night he got—he got the Barnacle, got Barney Schachter, and—" Domato broke off, his eyes welling up. Wulfmeyer's expression showed great alarm. He was moved to put an arm on Domato's sob-racked shoulder.

"It's okay, Stu, it's all right. Shit, that's shocking news, God, and I feel as bad as you do, I really do, but right now we can't worry about that. Right now we've *got* to find Ravinovich!"

"We can't," Domato blubbered, "because the killer got the Raven, too."

The words made time slow down. Sharkey tried to comprehend them, antiwords, impossible to grasp, even while he watched Wulfmeyer and Domato. They moved in ultraslow motion. Wolf appeared to be swallowing his tongue. Domato's eyes, glassy with tears, lifted to the level of the playing field, reflecting the Bermuda grass, and he struggled to speak.

"He was—they told me—hacked to death. They found his—his head—found his head in his basement bar—burned up in—oh God!—in the fireplace. Police just told me—"

Wolf was frozen.

"What should—what should we do?" Domato looked out to the field, all the gifts out there.

Sharkey could tell what Wolf was thinking. Surveying the stands, seeing the signs up there—WE LOVE YOU, RAVEN . . . YOU'RE THE WORD, BIG BIRD—Wolf was aware that the fans were expecting a tribute. Henrietta was counting on a tribute. Christ, the whole board was up in the owner's box, looking forward to it. None of them knew yet. There would have to be a tribute—or an explanation as to why not.

"We could say he will appear—on videotape—by his own request." Domato's distress appeared to ease slightly at his own suggestion. He reminded Wulfmeyer of the rehearsal tapes.

"Yes. Right." Wolf thought about it, thought about it for a long moment. "We wouldn't have to say anything yet, insofar as the murder." He glanced again at his watch. "Christ Almighty! Fucking problems!" Hesitated again. "Okay, we're in this up to our goddamn eyebrows. Let's do it. You go out there, tell the emcee. Explain the fix we're in. Have him make an appropriate announcement to the crowd as far as Ravinovich, you know, not being able to make it today."

"Gotcha." Domato nodded and hurried out toward the mound, his backside jiggling as he ran. Sharkey stood next to Wulfmeyer, both stiff as statues, thinking. Sharkey turned and studied his players, waiting on the bench for the ceremony to begin. It seemed all the more

certain now that Kane was the killer, a man about to pitch to even the Series. Or if not Kane, one of them, one of these athletes. Probably Kane. Kane, who was down near the far end of the dugout, laughing with Langley, showing no nerves at all before one of the biggest games of his brief career. Davenport was slouched between Mad Dog and Uggams, hat off, looking bored, inscrutable. Castillo was—

Where was Castillo? Sharkey's eyes moved up and down the bench; he looked down the clubhouse tunnel.

"Benito! Ben-*EEE-TO!*"

While he was looking in the tunnel, the emcee gave a signal and the Red Sox players bolted onto the field, lining up near home plate, alongside their counterparts from the Dodgers. Domato returned, breathing hard, and Sharkey said, "Castillo's missing! He's not out there!"

Wulfmeyer's first response was outrage. "Missing? Again? God-*damn*! That son of a bitch Gamboa, he promised me."

"Maybe it's him," Domato said.

"If it is, he'll come after me next. You watch." Sharkey thought about Castillo's alibi, that he was in Miami during the bakery murder. That had come from Gamboa. Who in the hell believed Gamboa? Of course, supposedly the police had checked it out. Supposedly.

Rain began to fall, splattering the dugout steps, as the emcee at last moved to the microphone. The crowd grew hushed; the emcee spoke: "Ladies and gentlemen, late last night our beloved Raven—the great Kenton Randall Ravinovich—was attacked and killed in his own home—"

Mr. Coif Job mentioned the fireplace, and the crowd's initial gasps turned to groans, then to boos and screams and hysterical shrieks. Sharkey could see Wolf's hands trembling.

"*Oh, my God!* Stu! STU!"

"I told him *not* to say that!" The anguish on Domato's face seemed to sum up the whole season.

The emcee spoke of the Raven's many heroics and began announcing the gifts—hastily, since there was no one to receive them. A crew of teenagers in Red Sox colors scrambled to pull the tarpaulins off each one in turn. The Jumbotron then flashed to life, and Ravinovich's face dominated the screen. The huge image, bald and chinless, only magnified the shock that still sizzled through the capacity crowd.

The Raven's haunting eyes stared a moment before he began reciting his foolish bit of poetry, his clumsy takeoff on Poe.

The rain worsened, turning to hail. Ravinovich segued into a maudlin, rambling diatribe, his voice cracking, even during the taped rehearsal, and finally he drew toward a close: "Some people say I've been given a bad break—"

Sharkey watched the fans scurrying for cover, some popping umbrellas, some trying to pull coats over their heads.

"—but today I consider myself . . . the luckiest man . . . on the face of the earth."

Half the grandstand stood empty now, exposing the drab military green that seemed so emblematic of Fenway. With a crazy flicker, the Jumbotron went out. The groundskeepers raced to pull tarp over the infield while hailstones bounced off the roof of the limousine.

During the two-hour rain delay that followed, a miserable, lonely eternity in the cold clubhouse, all but about nine thousand spectators went home. Fenway was eerily deserted when at last the teams took the field, and in the dreary, damp late afternoon, on the most dreadful day that anyone on the club could ever remember, the Red Sox somehow managed to come out and play magnificently inspired baseball.

Kane lasted for eight innings, hitting top speeds of 108 and 110 mph, and then his arm tightened. Doug Albright took over in the ninth, the first of four Red Sox relief pitchers as the Dodgers rallied for six runs to snatch a 7–5 victory and move ahead in the Series, two games to none.

26

Wulfmeyer stared at Tara's tit in silhouette against the window. Its lovely contours were outlined by the luminous clouds. Strange how the afternoon's dark nimbus now looked so whitish in the night sky.

The deep silence was broken by the chirp of his cellular. He twisted laboriously and lifted it from her nightstand.

"Wolf here," he whispered.

"It's Henrietta." Black grief seemed to waft like oil smoke right out of the phone. Wulfmeyer hunched on his elbow; he could now see the city lights below. "Just got some news," Henrietta said in a ragged voice. "Apparently the task force found some evidence—" She began to choke up. "Found some evidence on Kenton's—they recovered a—"

"What is it?" he urged.

"A tin. Some sort of tin thing. It was—"

He waited. A tin thing?

"—jammed down, ah—" She was bawling miserably.

He waited. Had to be. Oh God, it just had to be.

"—down his throat."

He struggled to comprehend it. Yes, it was probably—almost certainly—Sharkey's tobacco tin. The Honus Wagner tin. Was it?

"A tobacco tin?"

"Burnt some, but—yes!"

Oh God. The tobacco tin. That it would end up in the Raven's yapper . . . well, that was a shocker, another sordid twist in this ever-worsening farce, but it didn't take a genius to see the intent. Kane was trying to frame him. Trying to frame Sharkey. Wolf remembered the phone call, how Fish had complained about Kane stealing the blasted thing.

"It's not Kane's," Wolf said quickly. "I don't recall him having a tin like that." He couldn't remember if she knew that Sharkey owned it. He wasn't going to mention it now. He had to think. "Look, let's talk in the morning. All right? Let's see where this is going. Again, I'm sorry—I'm sorry beyond words—about poor Kenton, what a tragedy. Would have been an incredible tribute—except for the rain."

"There's going to be—" She broke off again.

Wulfmeyer waited. He could hear her racking sobs, until, with considerable effort, she managed to collect herself.

"—hell to pay."

Click. She was gone.

Wulfmeyer sat all the way up, inhaling sharply. He glanced at Tara, still fast asleep, her curled red hair like dark flames against the pillow. He thought a moment. Grabbed her arm and shook just hard enough to wake her.

"Baby. Tara!"

"Whaa-*aaaat*?" She rolled her face into the pillow.

"Gotta go. Back later if I can." He got up and dressed and headed for Fenway.

Wolf knew exactly what Sharkey would do. He'd tell those cops about Kane stealing the tin. Hell, he'd been ready to finger him any-

way, over nothing more substantial than that stupid "got a head in Kansas City" remark. Ready to finger the greatest ballplayer ever born right at the moment when they needed him most.

Clearly, it was time for a preemptive strike. Time to drop the napalm.

Game three, in Los Angeles, was scoreless and nearly hitless through seven innings, with Diller turning in another masterful performance and Kazuhisa Ishii, the Dodgers' left-hander, nearly as dominant. Kane, who was batting only .230 in the Series, pulled a change-up into the bullpen in the top of the eighth, giving the Sox a 1–0 lead, but the Dodgers scored three times in the bottom of the inning and hung on to move within a game of the title.

Sharkey sat a long time afterward in the clubhouse, feeling as ravaged as a Dresden survivor. His lifelong dream appeared to be vanishing at light speed. The Raven's horrific death filled him with overwhelming guilt and sadness. Guilt because Sharkey had been wrong, and because, in the ill-fated tango they had danced over the years, they had never been in sync. Ravinovich had been a gifted, rebellious child that Sharkey had wanted desperately to reach. Nothing had worked. There had been failures due to timing and circumstance and failures due to their own roles and attitudes.

Surely Ravinovich had been one of the most conceited, selfish, irascible and unmanageable stars in the long history of the game, especially in that austere final season when he played for Sharkey, but he had illuminated locker rooms with his charisma, and he had flashed across the outfield with a flair you could see from the upper deck. It was beyond Sharkey's comprehension that all of it was over and there would never come another chance to reconcile.

Crossing the lot to the team bus, Sharkey walked with his head

down, watching the tops of his shoes. He looked up only when he heard the shout.

"Freeze!" Ten men ran at him, uniformed officers of the Los Angeles Police Department.

"Drop it!" one yelled, and Sharkey could not imagine what to drop. His mind was glazed over, ticking far too slowly for the hair-trigger commandos of the LAPD. One grabbed his bag and another grabbed his arm, dumping him facedown on the asphalt. In the next disjointed instant he was frisked, handcuffed, hauled back up, and manhandled in the direction of a waiting van. His last awareness, before the door slammed closed, was of the sounds from the team bus—cries of outrage, antipolice curses and a scattering of less sup-portive noises: wild hoots and giddy cackling.

His attorney, Andrew Wong, discovered that there were three new pieces of evidence that would prevent Sharkey from ever in a million years receiving bail. One was the tobacco tin found in Ravinovich's throat. Another was Sharkey's apparent knowledge that the head in Kansas City was abandoned at Yancy's Doughnuts. Item three was an anonymous videotape whose exact contents the police refused to divulge.

"Videotape? How in the name of Jehovah can they have a video-tape?" Sharkey demanded over the phone. He was seated in a green plywood cubicle where inmates could exercise their rights to speak with counsel.

"Listen, they got a tape, and they tell me it's a smoking gun," Wong insisted. "Think about a plea. You plead to this, cooperate, and I can line up some psychological testimony. I'm sure you've been under stress. There's a half-decent chance we can avoid the worst-case scenario."

"What's the worst-case scenario?"

"With all these murders, the state of the bodies, I'm sure you can—"

"Just tell me."

"Clearly they'll want the death penalty."

"Death penalty? Oh, Jesus God! *Jeeee-sus Gaaaaaawwwd!*"

Wong implored him to calm down. Sharkey saw mental pictures of himself choking in a gas chamber. Or would they fry him? He could feel himself in a wiry skullcap, the numbing blast of voltage. He had zapped himself as a kid on a pitching-machine motor. It would be like that, only they'd never turn off the juice. He imagined his teeth chattering, his whole body shaking like a man on a jackhammer. His flesh would burn. The charring skin, fat, hair, dental caps—he might reek like burning rubber.

Wong digressed into legal esoterica—the McNaughton insanity test, *U.S.* v. *Hinckley,* things Sharkey had never heard of—and asked a barrage of questions. Sharkey told him that the tobacco tin had been stolen. He said he could prove it, or nearly prove it. He'd written it down, made a note of it in his journal. Wong sounded heartened; he said he'd speak to Wulfmeyer and promised to do what he could to learn more about the tape.

The horror of the moment sent Sharkey into mental catacombs too deep for him to retain contact with the outside world. Hours went by in motionless, unspeaking contemplation of how he'd come to be there and how it all might end. The worst-case scenario: the inside of a coffin. That's what Wong meant. It didn't get any bleaker than that. Shit, man, it was all pretty hopeless at that point.

A guard came the following afternoon and removed Sharkey from his isolation cell. He was led through a windowless gray corridor to a long row of visitation booths. Through the bulletproof glass, looking stiff as cardboard in a charcoal three-piece suit, was Wulfmeyer himself.

"Look at the bright side," Wolf said into the phone connecting them. "You're the most famous baseball manager that ever fucking lived." He sounded none too pleased to say it. Apparently the media were according Sharkey's arrest the sort of gang-bang coverage reserved for urban riots and declarations of war. Wulfmeyer went into a long spiel about how sorry he was, how awful this was. "Fish, I assure you, we're behind you a thousand percent, in spite of, you know, things I've said. Out of anger."

Sharkey thanked him; he appreciated the support. Wolf flashed a tight smile.

"Hang loose, huh? Once this Series is over, we're going to pull out all the stops in getting you out of there. Every stop you can imagine."

"Once it's over? Wolf, *do something*! It's the World Series, and they're charging me with *murder*!"

"Yeah, we're there, Fish, we made it! You helped to make it happen, don't forget it—and *we* won't forget it. We're all grateful, the whole club. We've got our backs up against the wall, but let's see if the guys can turn it around. And we'll get you out of this joint, don't you worry. Don't think for one minute we're going to let you rot in this place."

"There's some evidence in Boston," Sharkey said. "A journal in my office. I've got to get it to my lawyer, Andrew—"

"Hold on, let me get it down." Wulfmeyer grabbed for a pen and pocket notebook. "This journal—it's about Ravinovich?"

"It's about that tobacco tin. The tin that Kane stole from me. They found it in the Raven's throat."

"Horrible. Just horrible." Wolf made a face. He asked Sharkey for the name and took down Wong's e-mail address and phone number. "Now, let's think a minute. Let's stand back a second and look at this whole thing very clearly. A question I should ask you, in terms of timing—can't it wait? Another week?"

"Wait? For godsakes, Wolf!"

"This evidence, if it fingers Kane—he's got two starts left, if we can stay alive—and isn't it worth . . . ? I mean, without him out there, without his bat, all that he gives us—"

"You can't be serious!"

"Fish, I'm begging you: Can't you just take one for the team for a couple of days? Put aside your own selfish concerns?"

"Murder, Wolf! They're talking the death penalty!" Sharkey told him to have someone find the journal. It would be in the cabinet in his office. It was the one marked July–September.

Wolf raised up slightly. He said okay, don't worry, he would do what he could. He understood. He understood completely. He'd get on it right away. Wolf gave Sharkey his word of honor and flashed another smile and left.

Hearing Sharkey's desperation—his humiliation—had crystallized the issue in Wulfmeyer's mind, lit him up inside with a clarity that was almost frightening. He couldn't take the wrong stance. He had to be strong enough to do what he truly believed was right. History might well judge him by his actions this very moment.

Out in the jail lobby, beyond Sharkey's earshot, Wulfmeyer reached for his cell phone and got Samantha on the line.

"Sam, listen, I need you to do me a favor. ASAP." He instructed her to go down to Sharkey's office and collect all his recent journals, the ones in the cabinet. "Check the desk, too, get 'em all. Look in his locker, his file drawers—make sure you've got every last journal that's floating around down there."

"All right," she said. "Shall I send them to you?"

"No, no, just take them home," Wolf said. "Find a good safe place—someplace where nobody's going to bother you—and burn those motherfuckers."

27

Jail was not as bad as Sharkey might have imagined. It was incalculably worse. A damp cell that stank of urine. Food of a consistency that balled up and hardened in his colon like plaster of paris. Nights were the worst: interminable black tunnels filled with the screams of some jackass in a distant cellblock. Sharkey slept a few hours at a time, thrashing like a baboon caught in an electric fence.

A guard with a radio tuned it loud enough to hear the Series Sharkey was missing. The Sox, with Ted Uziak again filling in as manager, won game four on a home run by Villalobos. Kane made his second start of the series in game five, struggling with his control, giving up three walks and a two-run single in the third, before finding his rhythm and shutting down the Dodgers in the final four innings. Kane, Langley and Caruby all doubled in the eighth as the Sox rallied for a 4–3 win, moving the series back to Boston with L.A. ahead, three games to two.

Once again the club would be forced to try to stave off elimination, but this time at home, before nearly forty thousand screaming Red Sox fans. The game-six starter would be Claudewell Diller, an

erratic arm with twelve wins and seven losses during the regular sea-
son. Diller had been hot, however, winning three of his last four.

And if the Sox could squeeze one more victory out of him,
they'd again be able to put Kane on the mound. He'd have only two
days' rest, but he was young and bullishly strong and for a chance to
win a single ball game—a game that might mean more to Boston and
its fans than any game in eighty-some years—there was no one better.

No one even close.

"Andrew, I told you I checked twice," Wulfmeyer barked into the
phone. "Yeah, I checked twice, and now I told you twice. It's not
there. . . . I don't know if he's lying or not. Well, I *thought* he kept a
journal, but how the hell do I know? . . . Right, if it was there, I'd
certainly have found it. . . . Fine, you let me know. You, too."

Wulfmeyer hung up. Sharkey's pesky attorney, the man didn't
understand the meaning of "no." Asshole claimed to be a Red Sox
fan, but he'd sink the whole ship now just to get his client out of the
hoosegow.

Aggravations. A million things to worry about. Henrietta was out
of touch, no word from her since her sob-racked call on the night of
the Raven's murder. Now the prodigious funeral was imminent—the
biggest send-off since Mother Teresa's—but where was she to help?
All the goddamn lilies and birds of paradise, the hymns and testimoni-
als, were of course falling into Wolf's lap. On top of which, miracle
of miracles, Old Gordo was feeling so well he was planning to attend
game seven, provided there *was* a game seven—another logistical
nightmare. You could squeeze the Celtics into the owner's box more
easily than you could Gordo and all his nurses and bodyguards and
oxygen bottles.

A glance at the watch. Game six was an evening start, mere hours
away. He lifted the phone just as the other line rang.

Samantha called out, "For you. Says it's urgent."

"Wong? Or that asshole Gamboa?" The little cretin Castillo still hadn't surfaced.

"No." A pause. "It's the White House."

Wolf's whole body grew rigid. "I can't—no, I can't talk to him!"

There was a long pause. "It's the Oval Office."

"Fuck!" He slammed his fists on the desk. "Fuck, fuck, *FUCK!*"

"He says he'll talk to you or the police . . ."

"Oh, God, I'll take it! I'll take the goddamn fucking call!" Wolf lifted the phone. "You motherfucking son of a bitch, what the hell do you want now!"

Tortolano spoke evenly. He needed another $10 million by tomorrow noon. Failure to deliver would mean Kane's arrest on the eve of game seven. Not only would the Sox lose the services of the game's greatest pitcher, but the sheer magnitude of the media circus would render the Sox incapable of tying their own shoes, let alone playing the most important game anyone could remember.

"You're bluffing!" Wolf said desperately. "It couldn't happen that fast!"

"Try me."

Wulfmeyer swallowed hard. Game seven would be another night game. The task force, if it got that tape, the real tape, would have quite a few hours to authenticate it, serve warrants, ruin everything.

"All right, all right! You'll get your fucking money!"

Wulfmeyer hung up. Henrietta. He had to get hold of Henrietta. He dialed her at home, got the machine again.

"Pick up the phone, you stupid bitch!" He left a ranting message about the new extortion demand, hung up, and felt the stomach acid climbing like mercury in his throat. There were occasions when the word "catastrophe" began to seem like an understatement. This was catastrophe in supersized proportions, catastrophe as clear as fork lightning on a New Mexico night.

Time raced and dragged all at once, the normal flow of life so thoroughly discombobulated that he couldn't think straight. He spent the afternoon making futile attempts to reach her and blowing off every other phone call, every obligation, just hitting redial and brooding. Could the Sox even get to game seven? They'd have to win tonight's battle first, score some runs and hope Diller could hold himself together. Boston's chances were scarcely fifty-fifty, even with the game at Fenway.

Henrietta's silence was ominous. Her devotion to that knucklehead Ravinovich was such that she might be having a very hard time dealing with his death. Had she withdrawn into a cocoon of grief? If so, Christ, she'd never round up the $10 million in time. Or had she veered into some other mind state? Denial? Anger? Clearly the woman was inflated with enough anger to supply the entire Middle East. She might lash out—might lose her head, so to speak—and try to retaliate against any convenient target, Wulfmeyer being the most likely. He could not even imagine what she might do, but he could hear the echo of her cryptic comments: "There's going to be"—cry, cry, wail, moan, bawl—"hell to pay." *Sheeesh!* It was enough to make a man shiver.

Wulfmeyer reached the owner's box forty minutes before game time. Six or seven board members mixed in a crowd of a few dozen; they avoided him as if he were carrying a killer virus, Ebola maybe. Holding him responsible, no doubt, for the disastrous handling of the tribute. No litany of apologies would ever make that right. He tried to ignore them, forcing those thoughts from his mind, as he cradled a Löwenbräu and settled into a seat at the rail.

The Red Sox and Dodgers battled into the fourth inning tied at 2–2. Stu appeared, balancing a cardboard tray of hot dogs.

"There you are," Domato said. "You get Sam's note on the funeral? They're a thousand lilies short and want to know if you'd mind extra geraniums instead?"

"Tell them they can use dandelions. Or plastic sunflowers. Who the hell cares?"

Domato offered a relish dog and Wulfmeyer unwrapped it, realizing hazily that the complaints were right—the things were cold as leftovers. He asked if Domato had heard from Henrietta. Yeah, she had called around four-thirty, Stu said. Her mental outlook didn't seem too good. She was very, very unhappy about the new extortion demand.

"Like we're not?" Wulfmeyer grew shrill. "Oh, I'm grinning ear to ear, I'll tell you. We should throw a party. Rent some clowns, get an elephant. *Whooo-pee!*"

Domato looked at him with deep concern. "She's feeling the heat. The cops are still grilling her about Mulgrove, the circumstances surrounding that shoot-out. Chief Hardeway himself, I guess he called her, and she got a call from Harkwood. She's afraid he's about to land some piece in the *Herald*."

"Saying what?" Wulfmeyer had ignored three messages from the Brillo-haired twerp.

"I dunno. Maybe that we're the suspects, one of our players. It'll look pretty bad if it hits the papers first, before we say something."

"Well, what's she going to do?" Wulfmeyer demanded. "Let that little jackass scare her? The cops? She'd better collect her wits and start scraping together some cash."

"She doesn't know if there's enough time—given the deadline. She sounds tired."

"Tired? Jesus H. Christ on a flying camel, she'll have all winter to sleep! We're under some pressure here! We're in a little bit of a crisis! You'd think that might be enough to get some adrenaline flowing. You'd think, if she needed some help, she might finally get around to calling me. I'm sitting here—" Wolf gestured to his cell phone. "Good God, I'm about to have an embolism!"

Domato promised to send someone to her house and also to the

Embassy Club, in case she'd gone there. "I'll check back, see if we can't reach her again," he said. "Let me try a couple of things. Come get me up here if you need me." He gestured and started climbing the aisle, and Wolf realized Stu had been watching the game inside, at the bar, with the VIP guests. The owner's box contained a short bar where celebrities and Kornblume's friends could get shit-faced and watch the game through view windows or on closed circuit. A lot of the board liked to watch in there, out of the chill, gossiping and killing brain cells.

The Sox had taken a 3–2 lead in the sixth when Domato again hurried down.

"Wolf, hey, we found her: Henrietta's in there on TV. Doing a press conference."

Spinning to look, Wulfmeyer saw a minor commotion inside, people moving around, and Henrietta's gaunt face dominating the television at one end of the bar; the one at the other was still showing the game. All eyes seemed to be fixed in her direction.

Wolf stood and hurried in to catch the news. It was as bad as he could have imagined.

"—regret this decision, but I'm ashamed of what this franchise has become, and it's time to issue a deep and very heartfelt public apology for this extremely sad state of affairs," she said bitterly, the first comment he picked up. "It is more than bad judgment that we have allowed this succession of unfortunate, grisly murders; it is a slap in the face to the fans, an insult to humanity, and completely—I mean *completely*—out of character with the very excellent traditions of the Boston Red Sox.

"I will be cooperating with the authorities," she continued. "In coming days, as the evidence is compiled and evaluated, I'm afraid to say it will become clear that one of our own athletes—yes, a man that many idolize—is the dreaded serial killer, responsible for so many

gruesome murders, including the death of our own beloved Kent Ravinovich—"

Wolf's larynx went into full arrest, but Stu, at his elbow, expressed it all with two muttered words.

"Oh, shit."

Henrietta kept going. "It's come to my attention that there's a videotape out there, a film of a body being dumped. Whoever has this tape, I implore you to send it to the task force. Do the right thing."

Wolf swallowed hard. He pictured someone seated on a bundle of dynamite, pushing the plunger.

"I also have reason to believe," she went on, "that our general manager, Neville Wulfmeyer, planned and carried out an elaborate cover-up, and the result of this cover-up has been the unfortunate arrest of Augie Sharkey. I beg the authorities to investigate these matters as quickly as possible in hopes that justice may be swiftly carried out."

Wulfmeyer felt compelled to respond. Hard stares locked on him, accusing eyes.

"She's lost her fucking mind!" he bellowed. He bolted out, breaching the door and catching the elevator, riding it down to the Eldorado. The fuse had been lit. Time to skedaddle. He had shepherded the team as far as he could, to the threshold of a championship, and now he had to leave it and hope. Pull the ripcord and pray to sweet Jesus that they could go the last mile on their own.

His passport. It was probably at home in his desk. He hoped. He wondered if he could make it to Belize. He'd read there was no extradition treaty with Belize. Not that he knew anything about Belize, really, but it had to be better than prison. Hide out a few years, change his identity—start a new life. Sure was going to be different now. If you aimed for greatness, if you had the guts to reach for the top, you took these chances.

Wulfmeyer swung into his driveway. An unfamiliar car awaited him there—a black Thunderbird. A Dodge minivan stood in the street. The instant he stepped from the Caddie, a half dozen men emerged from the hedges and around the side of the house to surround him.

"Good evening, Mr. Wulfmeyer," one said cordially, sounding like the maître d' at Mulrooney's. "Please come with us."

"Look, I'm kind of in a rush—" His heart pounded in his throat.

"No need to rush. Slow down. We ain't in no rush."

Wulfmeyer looked them over. "You guys—I guess you're all friends of Doyle's—"

"That's right, we're all friends. Let's go talk about it."

They ushered him into the T-bird. They set out through the night across the Harvard Bridge, east past Fenway, and down into South Boston. No one spoke, no one turned on the game. The landscape turned to freight yards and warehouses.

"You guys eaten yet?" Wulfmeyer said finally, voice quavering. "Let's splurge, have dinner somewhere. My treat. You tried La Brasserie? Best goddamned chateaubriand you ever tasted, melts right in—"

"We had a steak at Mick's," the driver said tersely.

Another excruciating silence. They turned down an alley and stopped at a graffiti-marred loading dock, got out just as the minivan pulled up, carrying the rest of the entourage. Ten or twelve beefy men, all bar-bouncer types, leading Wulfmeyer up the concrete steps and into a dim room cluttered with wood crates and rat droppings.

The tallest, a goon at least six-four, with a nose bent thirty degrees starboard, stepped forward and brandished a knife that he seemed to pull from midair.

Wolf spoke frenetically. "Gentlemen, let's try to be mature about—you know—whatever differences we might have. This is—hell, it's great to meet Doyle's friends. I've worked with Doyle—"

"Shut up," the goon said implacably.

"Yes, sir. I'm not looking for trouble."

"I got a question for you, Wulfmeyer."

"Sure. Anything. You'll find I'm very open."

"Wonderin' how many testicles you got."

"What?"

"How many testicles you got?"

"Two," he said weakly.

"They're comin' off."

28

Moving past the gray interrogation room, where he'd been grilled like a flank steak only days before, Sharkey entered a larger room, dominated by a scarred oak table, and saw smiles. One of the highest-ranking officers of the Los Angeles Police Department, Commander Pete N. McWilliams, a bespectacled man in a white shirt and tie, invited him to sit and offered the hope that he'd been sleeping well.

"Like a baby," Sharkey groused. "Crying all night."

"Not the best place to catch up on your forty winks," the commander allowed, "but this ordeal may be over soon. Spare you the details, but your board prez, Henrietta Prichard, just conducted a press conference, and our people are with her this very minute. She has some theories we're going to check out, posthaste. Remarkable disclosures."

Sharkey was stunned; he wanted to ask a dozen questions, but McWilliams kept talking. He said a technical analysis of the video-tape in evidence showed it to be as phony as a flying moose. "And we've also turned up a revealing bit of electronic surveillance. Play it, Rick."

A member of the task force switched on a tape recorder. In a moment Sharkey heard Wulfmeyer's voice, tinny and agitated:

"Your colitis attacks are not my problem, frankly. Just keep him happy. Stop the antisocial high jinks, but keep him happy."

"He's a terrible influence," Sharkey heard himself answer. "He's just like Davenport—won't listen to me at all."

"He's the greatest talent that ever lived."

"Yeah, but what about discipline? Half the guys hate him. I think he stole my tobacco tin—that thing, it's a keepsake; it's valuable. He was in my office, and it disappeared, and he still won't give it back. Says he gave it to Castillo."

"Maybe he did."

"I think he's still got it."

"This missing— You say it's a tobacco tin? Give me a break, Fish. Who the hell cares about your fucking tobacco tin?"

The conversation went another minute and the cop switched off the recorder. McWilliams arched an eyebrow. "In answer to his question, *we* care."

Sharkey took a deep breath. He almost dared to smile. "I remember that conversation. We lost ten to nothing that night."

"So you *think* Kane took the tin? Or did Castillo end up with it?"

Sharkey explained the whole incident. McWilliams said the task force was now concentrating its efforts on Kane, with Ms. Prichard fully cooperating, but as yet no conclusive evidence tied Kane to any of the murders. It was unclear if and when he would be arrested. Twice already authorities had nabbed the wrong man—that judge, and now Sharkey—and there was deep resolve to keep it from happening again. At the same time, the president himself was leaning on the FBI to end the atrocities.

"It's blowtorch heat, and it's frying our asses to a crisp," McWilliams said, scanning the room for agreement. He asked if Sharkey would be willing to examine some photos.

"Of the bodies?"

"Bodies, heads, you name it. We've got it all on film, and if there's anything you can contribute, no matter how small, we'd welcome it."

Although he would have preferred to have his blood sucked out by leeches, Sharkey nodded with dogged stoicism.

A folder slid across the table.

"Brace yourself," someone said. "They're not pretty."

No, they certainly weren't—hideous, full-color glossies featuring more-or-less identical ritualistic markings. Each bald scalp defiled with a long, curved cut running just above the ears and around the back of the head, and two parallel gashes centered above the forehead. The mouths of many victims were sealed with gray duct tape; a few others were not.

"Those cuts, they signify something," a young task-force sergeant said. "We're groping, got a hundred different ideas, speculations."

"The curvy line, the long one over the ears—it's shaped a lot like the seams of a baseball," Sharkey said.

The officers regarded one another, unsure whether they had just heard a brilliant insight or one of the stupidest observations in the annals of crime.

"Oh Christ," Sharkey said. "Those gash lines, I think—ahhh, it's a weird idea."

"What? Spit it out."

He could hardly speak. His tongue seemed to inflate to the size of a Polish sausage.

"I think it's his number. Kane's uniform number. Number eleven."

Sharkey fought his way through three armies of reporters and news cameras: the first outside Central Jail in downtown Los Angeles,

another at Los Angeles International Airport, and the last at Logan. Swollen by banner-waving fans, the crowd in Boston numbered at least two thousand, even though Sharkey had taken the red-eye and arrived just as dawn crept into the sky.

Annie met him at the gate. She gave him a long kiss. Her arms around him, the feel of her breath on his face, her smiling lips rising to meet his lips, they were a jolt of life, like mainlining endorphins. He did not imagine he would live so long as to feel that good again.

He'd heard the news while being processed out of jail: The Sox had pushed over a run in the ninth, on back-to-back hits by Langley and Davenport, to take game six. Now Annie gave him a full account of all the action, including Henrietta's press conference, the shocking accusations that had galvanized the city. Henrietta had stopped short of naming names, except for Wolf's, but she was telling the task force everything she knew.

"Know who it is?" Annie said. "Who it might be?"

"It's Kane," he told her.

"Kane? Oh, my *Gawd*!"

"Has to be. I keep looking for ways that it isn't, but I can't see it. Sucks, you know, because I've got to decide—unless he's arrested in the meantime—"

"Awful. So incredibly unbelievable." Annie seemed unwilling to accept such a stunning possibility. Her face, as she guided her red Lexus onto the East Boston Expressway, surely was a glimpse into the future of every Red Sox fan, once the terrible truth was out. They would all look so stricken, devastated. The worst part of the horror was, after all this, all the carnage and upheaval, the club might well be doomed to lose again. On top of pain, more pain. "Decide what?" she asked suddenly. "Whether to play him, that sort of—"

"Right. Because this is our— My God, we'll never have another

chance like this, and he's scheduled to start. If they don't find the evidence right away—"

"Augie, you can't *play* him!"

"I could, that's the problem. People will *expect* him to be out there! He's the best shot we'll ever have—"

"But a serial killer? Oh, I don't know about that. I don't know if that's the best thing, Augie."

Sharkey watched the oncoming cars. He was too tired, too freighted with stress, to argue it with her. Too consumed by events to decide it now. There would be time later to pass that managerial kidney stone.

"You're coming home with me," Annie said. "Hot bath, a few hours of sleep—that's what you need."

It sounded good. He soaked an hour and fell into her bed, a cloud scented with lilac. Game seven, and all that madness, was scarcely twelve hours away. He dreaded it. Oh God, he'd be hung in effigy—maybe even lynched—if Kane were available and he sat him. And if they lost, Christ. The agony was too much to comprehend. He let it go, let the waves of fatigue slosh inside him, washing his mind over a dizzying cliff.

He tumbled and floated, moving in and out of ethereal spaces, drifting into one of the strangest dreams of his life: alighting on a pedestal, miles above the roof of Fenway, in the brilliant glow of a figure in red and gold. A question booming across the sky, Sharkey's question, but from the heavens: "Should I put Kane in the lineup?" The blinding figure shaking its head: No. Then another booming question: "Can the Red Sox win without him?" This time the figure staring down from the pedestal, down toward the green roof of Fenway, and the words booming out with resounding slowness: "No . . . way . . . in . . ." And the last word taking a very long time to arrive, long enough for Sharkey to wonder who was speaking. The word finally rumbling up from some great depth: ". . . *hell.*"

Hell. Hell followed by the low, guttural sound of laughter.

Annie's hand landed on his shoulder. Her breath was soft in his ear. "Augie, better get up. Big game tonight."

He felt no better prepared to manage a major-league club than to conduct the Boston Philharmonic. Jet-lagged, dazed, grieving, distracted, stressed—and fearing further disaster.

Some of the Sox were already out on the field, getting early BP. A lot of them were going through the simple rituals of dressing, preparing, a few—like Mad Dog—shouting occasional cries of encouragement. Sharkey called the team into the clubhouse immediately after his arrival, four hours before game time. Most of the guys—Dog, Langley, Maynard, Cool Daddy, Reeling—welcomed him back with handshakes and backslaps. Sharkey was touched. He felt proud to be their manager, despite everything. But he knew that his final speech of the year would fall short of creating the optimum frame of mind. He might as well try to hypnotize a roomful of kangaroos, that's how hard it would be to brush aside the hard facts of the moment.

By now the players understood that they were the sole focus of the investigation. They had seen the tape of Henrietta's press conference, had watched the TV news, had read the reports in the papers. They were keenly aware that the killer was probably among them.

"Whatever you do out there tonight," Sharkey said, summing up, "it'll be remembered for the rest of recorded history." He clapped his hands and told them to get ready, get loose, see if they could surprise some people.

The room erupted in cries and whoops, then a flurry of motion. Kane remained hunched over, elbows on his knees, inscrutable. Did he know of the closing trap? Did he care? Sharkey watched him stand

suddenly, snap up his glove, and disappear into the tunnel to the field. He still expected to start. Sharkey had yet to talk to him.

Ducking into his office, Sharkey took a swig of Pepto and checked the cabinet, wondering how in the hell those journals had vanished. He took a while to polish his spikes and study his notes on the Dodgers. The phone rang and he picked it up. Stu, sounding as though he had run up a flight of stairs.

"Castillo show up?" Domato said.

"No." Nor had Sharkey expected him.

"Shit. Shit, shit, double shit! He was supposed to be there, except Gamboa wanted a fax from Wolf, and Wolf's in the hospital."

"The hospital?"

"You wouldn't believe—anyway, I guess he didn't get it. The fax. That asshole."

"Is he all right?"

"Gamboa?"

"No, Wolf. What's wrong?"

"He's living. He'll be okay. I'm swinging by there on my way in. I'll tell him you said hey." Domato hung up. Sharkey exhaled sharply. He stood and slipped on his cap and the leprechaun pin and finally entered the tunnel. Ominously, two dozen Boston cops were stationed there, awaiting a signal from afar. One carried a radio tuned to the pregame show.

"Not much of a view from here," Sharkey said in a tone he managed to keep casual.

The lead officer, a Sergeant Todd Talcott, extended a hand. "Good luck tonight, Augie. Sure be great if you guys can do it." They were all Sox fans, he said, sorry to be clouding the moment with official business. Orders being orders.

"What's it look like?" Sharkey said.

"No word yet." Talcott's expression darkened. "We should tell you, though, the word comes down, they want us to go get him. No

matter what. They've told us to go grab him right off the field—not what you want, I know, but it's not us, it's the FBI. They don't want any chance he'll flee."

Sharkey's mind filled with the image of all these cops chasing Kane across Fenway's velvety lawn, fans screaming. They'd be loath to shoot him, and Kane would exploit that; it'd look like the Keystone Kops.

Talcott went on to say the task force was in the process of serving warrants and negotiating to obtain a videotape. A resolution could come at any moment.

Sharkey moved numbly to the dugout. He sensed that this would be his final game. Tynes, Uggams and Briscoe were still hurt. Castillo might be in Havana, for all he knew. If Kane didn't pitch, the only fresh starter was Frolicky, a man with a career mark of four wins and seventeen defeats in must-win ball games.

Alone as he reached the bench, Sharkey gazed for a moment at the players out warming up. Kane was beyond view in the distant bullpen, beginning to throw. The stands were filling under a black autumn sky. Sharkey thought about Annie. He searched the field and saw Frolicky walking with Reeling, not far from the dugout. Both men were in their Sox windbreakers.

"Fro!" he called out.

Frolicky turned.

"Get out to the pen," Sharkey ordered. "Start getting loose. Send Ron in here to see me."

Frolicky looked puzzled. "Now?" He was expecting to be used in relief, if at all.

"Now! You're starting. Tell Ron to come on in."

Kane reached the dugout just as infield practice was ending. The regulars clattered down the steps behind him. Kane's voice was tight with anger.

"What the hell's going on?" he demanded.

"Ron," Sharkey said gravely, "I'm sitting you down today."

"Sittin' me down?"

"You've had a busy year. Take a day off."

"A day off? The fucking seventh game of the World Series?" Kane's face scorched up hot as blast-furnace steel. "You've got to be joking! This is jus— Tell me what this is about! What the hell is this about?"

Sharkey exhaled hard. "Ask that head in Kansas City."

"You can't sit me down!" Kane took a menacing step forward, his fists balled up like rusted anvils, things that could kill all by themselves. Sharkey stood and thrust himself into Kane's chest; he knew he couldn't give that machinery the space to get moving. The two men collided like robots, bumping chests and shouting, and the nearest guys jumped in—Moses, Villalobos, Langley, even Davenport, six or seven others. They seemed to grasp the implications of the fight and grabbed hold of Kane and held on. His muscles were like rope cords, his eyes fixed on Sharkey.

"You fucking loser! LOSER! You've lost your fucking mind!"

"I still got this head!" Sharkey shouted back, gesturing.

"You *f-f-fu-fuu-fucker!*" Kane threatened to leave, go home if he couldn't play, but Sharkey assured him there was no way out. The tunnel was blocked. There was a whole pack of security guards—he decided not to call them cops—waiting to make sure Kane stayed put.

Kane's rage took a while to neutralize; his teammates had to restrain him for most of the first inning before he could resign himself to sitting in place. The crowd, in a frenzy, well aware now of the unfolding police drama, reacted to Kane's benching with a clash of groans, boos and cheers. A charge was flowing, ions sweeping through the air like a fast-moving aurora, a feeling that nothing tonight would be ordinary, nothing tonight would bend to the normal arcs and planes of mere baseball.

The game was an old-fashioned barn burner. Frolicky walked the first batter on five pitches, then yielded a triple and a home run. The Sox fought back. It went into the seventh with the Dodgers up, 7–5. The pressures, mounting all year, now reached deep-ocean atmospheres, as if all of Fenway were sinking to the bottom of the Mariana Trench.

Sharkey stood frozen, his foot hiked on the dugout step, as precious outs slipped away. With two gone in the ninth, the Dodgers were on the threshold of winning it. Carl Caruby walked. Mad Dog was due up. Suddenly the Sox's final chance.

Down the bench sat Kane. Sharkey looked for an instant, and their eyes met. Now would be the time to use him. Sharkey thought about his troubling dream, thought about the screaming fans and Old Gordo and that head in Kansas City. He clenched his jaw and turned away.

Mad Dog fouled off two fastballs and connected on a high, twisting drive that found the screen atop the Green Monster in left for a wild, improbable, game-tying home run.

Teammates mobbed him at the plate. Deafening cheers cascaded from the grandstands.

Into extra innings it went. The Dodgers scored in the twelfth, and the Sox tied it. The Dodgers got two more in the fifteenth, a rally that ended when Maynard hauled down a drive in deep right and crashed heavily into the wall. He had to be helped off the field.

Trailing by two, the Sox were again three outs from defeat. A grounder to short and a pop-up moved them to the brink. Then Villalobos rapped a single. Jeremy Davenport was due next. Pulling him aside, Sharkey urged him to do the same, just rap a little single, keep it going.

"Let him hit you if you can."

"He hits me, I'll break his neck."

"Just get on base."

Davenport swung twice at low curves and then, facing a pitch that could end the season, blooped a single into right.

Now Maynard. He'd made a great play in the field and now the team needed him to come through at the plate. But his right cleat was off, his ankle nearly double its normal size. The trainer was working on it. Sharkey bent and put a hand on Maynard's shoulder.

"Can you go, Doug? Help us, Mayn man?"

Two officers entered a narrow garage in Somerville that Kane had rented in July. They had found the address on a key ring in his bedroom.

The garage contained a lamp and a beanbag chair, a stack of forty-seven *Playboy* magazines, several black latex masks scattered on the concrete floor, and a freezer. Opening the freezer, the taller of the two officers, from the FBI, peered in and turned to his partner.

"Looks like evidence."

"Jesus Christ!" the other said. "Is that actually what we think it is?"

In a white metal pan, canted on one ear, was a thin, liver-spotted head, marked up with gashes. Duct tape covered the mouth.

"We'd better phone this one in."

"Can't put weight on it," Maynard said, trying to stand.

Sharkey watched. His nervous system edged toward a shutdown, his fingers going numb, the numbness creeping down into his toes. He glanced toward the base runners, the scoreboard. The field began to look gauzy and indistinct, as if he were seeing it from farther away, through a dusty window.

He inhaled, looked down the bench. There was no one else left, no one still eligible except the sullen young man at the far end, the

angular redhead. Sharkey stared a very long time, his strong, thick, leathery face hiding all the tumult inside, the arcing wires, the leaky membranes, the acrid soot billowing up and coating the insides of his eyes. He stared at Kane hunched over, looking at the tops of his shoes; stared for over an hour, it seemed like, but it was really only seconds before the umpire wandered over, clutching his mask, barking into the shadows of the dugout.

"Hey, Fish. Let's go! Get a batter up here!"

Sharkey answered by raising a hand, but he said nothing, only stared down the bench until Kane felt the pressure of his gaze and looked up. Sharkey jerked a thumb at him, a let's-go gesture, the summons of fate.

Even at that moment Sharkey was aware that his thumb was not entirely his own; it was part of a larger apparatus, that unseen machinery of the universe. It had lurched into motion again, the vast array of pulleys and levers, trapdoors, cranks and gears. It had all been moving for some time, its various wheels and wires yanking players this way and that, moving them into the game and out again, depleting the roster, slamming Maynard into the wall, spraying hits to the outfield grass—the timing of it all flawless, bringing about this one incomparable moment.

There had been a time when Sharkey believed that these orchestrations meant that all of life was predestined, but baseball had taught him otherwise; the machinery was really there like the pin-setting devices of a bowling alley, putting pieces into place so the gods could play their own game. They were locked in battle now, great powers whose motives were always dubious and unclear. Powers that might even be evil, for all anyone could tell.

Kane rose slowly. He stood and twisted side to side, moving his shoulders to loosen the cold muscles, edging his way to the bat rack, silent, looking at no one. His eyes were dark, staring straight ahead, seeing only what was in front of him—the rack, the battered black

plywood, the narrow cylindrical bays loaded with Adirondacks and Louisville Sluggers.

He took his time and selected one, hefted it, and skipped up the steps onto the field, into the thunderous roar of the faithful. The fans were not yet aware—even if circumstances made them suspect it—that Kane was a killer. They saw him only for what they knew him to be, a ballplayer, the ballplayer of all ballplayers. The announcement cracked the night like thunder:

"Batting for Maynard, number *eeeeee*-levv-ennn, Roonnnnnnnn Kaaaa-aaaa-aaaa-aaaanne!"

Out into the halo of home plate he moved, swinging the black bat, the ropes in his chest and back stretching out, growing limber. He sucked in several deep breaths, his blood charging up with oxygen.

Sharkey watched him dig in, wag the bat, those long arcs, smooth, metronomic, lines and angles that were his and his alone. For all of the season's travails, all the death and horror, the fighting and conflicts, the sleepless nights, the failed attempts to communicate with his mercurial star, Sharkey found himself rooting for him now harder than he had ever rooted for any man in his life.

Len Arbogast, the Dodgers' game-five starter, had come on now in relief. He was one of the National League's premier fireballers, a big right-hander who had struck out 336 batters while winning nineteen games and losing ten. Arbogast stared in for the sign. He swung into motion, unleashing a ninety-nine-mile-per-hour laser beam that flashed over the outside corner.

Strike one.

The videotape rolled in the task-force office at Boston PD headquarters. A dozen tired men who had coordinated the months of investigation watched it together, Kane removing the body from the trunk, dumping it, taking that one quick glance in the direction of the cam-

era. Going back in for the head, turning, tossing it underhanded into the trash can.

No one spoke. The phone broke the silence.

"Granville here."

"Hey, Jarrad, it's McCauley. We're out in Somerville. Found a head in a freezer."

"Damn. We'd better call Fenway."

Strike two was another dart inside at the letters.

Sergeant Talcott, in the tunnel, answered his cellular. The crowd noise surged like surf pounding through a narrow fjord. He struggled to hear.

What at first sounded like "Ho bekkum" turned out to be, on clarification, a simple directive: "Go get him." He motioned to his officers and they started toward the field, tiny inching steps, like elderly men crossing a marble floor in socks.

Arbogast's next pitch snaked toward the outside corner and Kane flicked at it, lining it foul into the seats. Sharkey could feel his coronary arteries trying to shut off blood flow to the brain. He could scarcely force himself to watch as another fastball came in. Kane ripped at this one and fouled it to the screen.

A two-strike slider was low, inches out of the strike zone. Talcott and his men flooded the dugout. The cop nudged Sharkey's arm.

"Sorry, Augie, got to do it."

Wheeling around, Sharkey knew, and the words spewed out before he knew he was saying them: "No, no. Not now, *please, oh my dear God, you can't—not now. Pleeeeeaase!*" Deep in the deepest part of Sharkey's soul, a heart that had been so badly broken so terribly often that it seemed impossible it could ever break again—it broke again.

"Sorry. So very sorry."

Sharkey turned around. The next pitch was on its way. Kane took a vicious swing and ripped another foul down the left-field line. The police quickly climbed the dugout steps. They had reached the on-deck circle when Sharkey frantically caught them. "Sergeant! Sergeant, wait! You got a warrant?"

"A what?" Talcott turned back.

"Paperwork. Authorization."

"I've got *orders*!" Talcott had to shout to be heard above the din of the crowd. "They found a head!"

"A *what*?"

"A *head*? Up in Somerville!" He turned away, resuming his march toward the plate, but Arbogast had already begun his windup; he let fly.

Kane swung.

From where he was standing, Sharkey could now hear the play-by-play over a portable radio, the one officer's radio, even as the ball shot skyward like a mortar shot: "He pops it up! A pop-up! Way up there! Left field!" It was carrying; Sharkey could tell it was carrying. Kane, with his hitch swing, the slight uppercut, had got good wood on this one. "Washburn started in; now he's drifting back . . . back! To the track! Up against the Monster. . . .

"It's gone! Gone! Home run! And the Boston Red Sox—the Cinderella Red Sox!—are the world champions of all of baseball!"

Sharkey leaped and bounded toward home, Talcott and his men trailing him. He flung his arms wide, and his mouth flew open as if it were spring-loaded. All the pain and frustration welled up from way down deep in his gut, bubbled up through Sharkey's chest and his heart and his windpipe, and reached his throat, producing a sound that was like the sound of a fish: no noise at all, just that mouth wide open and gaping.

Kane came down hard on home plate with both feet, and he was immediately engulfed by teammates, slapping him, embracing him, shouting to the sky, a team of men that had struggled together, hated one another at times, hated Kane in particular, and yet emerged triumphant, able now to forget the jealousy and acrimony and death.

They were winners at last. Kane raised both hands, his fingers showing number one. He was surrounded not only by teammates but also by the phalanx of officers. In the pandemonium the two groups merged, together hoisting Kane on their arms and shoulders—a scene that would simultaneously grace the covers of *Time, Newsweek,* and *Sports Illustrated*—and carrying him slowly out through the hordes of delirious fans who had poured down from the grandstands, a slow, inexorable journey, like the procession of a king or a dead war hero, out through the tunnel, out the players' gate to a waiting police wagon.

As soon as Sharkey saw Kane go up, illuminated by the stadium lights, the gauze came off his eyes and he could see everything just as razor sharp as if he were eighteen years old, see the freckles on Kane's wildly grinning face, see eyes flashing in exhilaration, Langley and Moses and Davenport and all of them, the sweat beading and running on their faces, the dust and grass stains on their uniforms, the distant banners and streamers and Sox caps in the crowd.

Looking up into the stands behind first base, he saw Annie waving, blowing kisses, and to her right, up above in the owner's box, his eyes like telescopes, Sharkey could see Old Gordo, flanked by Stu and Henrietta. They held him by the arms and Kornblume was standing, the first time Sharkey had seen him stand in months. Domato was laughing, and Henrietta raised her free arm in the air. Old Gordo only gazed in wonder, peering over the asymmetrical beauty of Fenway as if to memorize it, and then, in the jostling, Sharkey thought he saw Gordo's hand go to his fly. It looked for all the world as though he

forgot himself, or just figured to hell with it, and was unzipping to urinate down into the lower grandstand.

There was no way to be sure. The surging crowd on the field swept Sharkey in the direction of the clubhouse, a frenzied march that became its own battle. He was slapped and pushed and shoved every bit as much as Kane was, manhandled violently, lovingly. It was a pinnacle that towered above the rest of his long career, the end of the curse, the end of his bitterness, the end of all his woeful days as a loser.

Epilogue

Three days after the Series ended, a victory parade wound its way through the heart of downtown Boston, an outpouring of unabashed adulation that was well in keeping with the tradition of such rousing spectacles. Four hundred thousand fans lined the streets, and by nightfall two people were dead and one hundred and twelve were injured as a result of violent revelry and gunfire.

The parade was Sharkey's last official function as manager of the Red Sox; he announced his retirement the following afternoon, a tearful farewell. He was glad to be able to quit at the top. He saw that it was the right time to go, even with a season left on his contract—while he still had his health, his mind, good years ahead.

For a while Sharkey allowed himself to decompress. He spent most of a week just sitting in an easy chair, no TV, no radio, just a deep silence during which the anxieties could discharge into the still air. He could feel them moving through him, quivering up and down in sporadic tremors, static electricity, but gradually the poles adjusted and the tremors stopped. A strange and blissful serenity began to settle into him, a feeling he had never known.

He was a happy man. He had time, a fat pension and a hefty World Series share, and he used those resources to fashion a new life. He bought a vintage, cherry red Triumph TR7, and he started seeing Annie just about every night. They were soon talking of marriage. They traveled together throughout Italy and France; fans recognized Sharkey in Vatican City and at the Louvre. He had become exactly what Wulfmeyer said he was: the most famous baseball manager on the planet. Upon his return he moved onto the banquet circuit, commanding five-figure fees as a motivational speaker.

Gordon Malcolm Kornblume continued a slow recovery, suffered a setback, endured a liver transplant and a delicate drilling procedure to relieve the pressures of a blood-flow problem in his brain, and managed somehow to rally again. He celebrated his ninety-fifth birthday in late February in an intensive-care unit but was home by late July and talking excitedly about the Sox's prospects of another pennant drive; they were just four games behind the Yanks.

Stu Domato returned to scouting; within a year he had found, in a remote corner of Arkansas, a rail-thin young slugger with a swing like Ted Williams and the foot speed of Mantle. He kept wearing the fine suits and delighted in showing off his gaudy World Series ring in a seemingly endless procession of podunk towns.

Henrietta remained on the board and strongly influenced the revamping of the club for the following season. The biggest of several trades sent Moses, Castillo and Reeling to the Giants for a good young left-hander and a promising minor-league shortstop. Henrietta was granted federal immunity and testified at length in the criminal trials of Neville Wulfmeyer and Ron Kane, separate legal proceedings that enthralled the nation. Her unwavering candor provided some of the most compelling moments ever seen in a courtroom.

Wulfmeyer's lawyers sought sympathy from jurors by introducing the grisly account of his castration, but no connection could be established to Henrietta or her employees, and the testimony was stricken

as irrelevant. An unpenitent Wulfmeyer was convicted on a sufficient number of counts to sentence him to prison for 147 years.

Kane's trial was beamed live across the globe. It lasted six unforgettable weeks and ended in guilty verdicts in twelve of the fourteen beheadings. A vigorous insanity defense spared him the death penalty; he was given a dozen consecutive life sentences without the possibility of parole.

Due to his enormous celebrity, federal officials kept secret the site of Kane's incarceration, and so it seemed that the earth had just swallowed him up—the one-season wonder, the mythic talent so stunningly flawed, the flash out of nowhere who became for a fleeting instant the single greatest player in the history of baseball.

Special Thanks

A number of individuals played a role in keeping this project alive. They include Noel Greenwood, whose insights made the story work; Steve Wilson, who rescued the original draft from the scrap heap; and my agent, Philip Spitzer, who believed in the project when others did not.

Several friends read all or parts of the manuscript and gave me their suggestions and encouragement. My appreciation to Orman Day, Scott Harris, Anne McAndrews, Martin Miller, Peter Schmuck and, of course, the freethinking members of the Allegores, Southern California's only cold-blooded writers group.

Finally, thanks to my editor, Mauro DiPreta, for making me look smarter than I really am.